DAUGHTER OF STRANGERS

Charlotte Le Jeune was a child of twelve when Nicholas Gaillard came to claim her. She was an extraordinary child, uncommonly beautiful and well educated. Only her pale, haunted eyes suggested the strange isolation in which she had been reared. During the ride to his plantation in South Carolina, Gaillard hadn't the heart to tell the exquisite young creature, chattering excitedly beside him, that she would never see New Orleans or her dear black nurse, Poulette, again. How to tell a gray-eyed, fair-skinned child of twelve that she was, by birth and law, his slave?

Elizabeth Boatwright Coker's
breathtaking novel of plantation life—
and a love affair that transcended time
and shattered tradition!

DAUGHTER
OF
STRANGERS

Elizabeth Boatwright Coker

for my husband
JAMES LIDE COKER

*This low-priced Bantam Book
has been completely reset in a type face
designed for easy reading, and was printed
from new plates. It contains the complete
text of the original hard-cover edition.*
NOT ONE WORD HAS BEEN OMITTED.

DAUGHTER OF STRANGERS

*A Bantam Book | published by arrangement with
Mockingbird Books*

*PRINTING HISTORY
E. P. Dutton edition published 1950
Bantam edition | July 1977*

ISBN 0-553-10508-6

Published simultaneously in the United States and Canada

---

*Bantam Books are published by Bantam Books, Inc. Its trade-
mark, consisting of the words "Bantam Books" and the por-
trayal of a bantam, is registered in the United States Patent
Office and in other countries. Marca Registrada, Bantam
Books, Inc., 666 Fifth Avenue, New York, New York 10019.*

PRINTED IN THE UNITED STATES OF AMERICA

Contents

PROLOGUE

New Orleans
February, 1830

The tall, very blond young man leaned his sunburned face wearily against the ornately carved post of the huge mahogany bed. There was a mouse in the armoire by the fireplace, and the scritch-scratch of its gnawing sounded loud and ugly. The room was dimly lit by a candle on the table by the bed, and he could barely see the figure, face bound with a death cloth, lying under the pink silk coverlet.

"How dark she looks." The young man, whose name was Auguste Le Jeune, spoke without thinking, and the large Negress, watching him closely from the other side of the bed, nodded.

"Yes, *Maître*, the fever of childbed burned her up."

"Did the baby die also?"

"No, *Maître*, the little one lives easily. The priest gave her the name of Charlotte Le Jeune. I hope that pleases you."

He leaned over the bed, searching the dead girl's face carefully.

"I did not remember that Céleste was so dark!"

"The night you first met her at the Quadroon Ball she was not so dark."

No, she had been the color of a May peach and she had worn a white egret feather in her shining black hair. Together they had danced a pavan and their hands had trembled at each other's touch.

He covered his eyes with his fingers to shut out the sight of Céleste now lying so still, so still; burned brown as ash by their shared passion. He had loved Céleste; truly he had loved her. At first, knowing that she was

3

virginal, he had been gentle; later they had rushed, to the most pointed mountaintops of desire. But this unlovely thing on the bed—was this *that* Céleste?

A delicate Dresden clock on the mantel tinkled the hour of six.

"Was she alone these past five months I have been in the West?" he asked the woman.

"But for me, *Maître*. Vignie allowed me to stay, from the money you sent Céleste. Did you find gold in that Godforsaken desert?"

"Some; the search has taken me like a disease. I will return there within the month. I only came back this time to see Céleste and the child."

Poulette, the woman, came nearer the bed into the range of the candlelight. The orange-tawny skin of her bosom that bulged at the low-cut neckline shaded up to a burnt-sugar color in her broad intelligent face. Clad in a bright merino dress of crimson and blue with a kerchief of blood-colored silk around her head, and in each ear a long golden hoop, she looked like a gaudy tiger lily in the dismal room. Her fruity lips muttered brokenly as she bent over the bed.

"What a beauty she was!" Poulette wept, patting the slender young body outlined under the satin. "When she was small I tried to make her play with the little Negro children who lived near my hat shop, but she refused to accept them. No, she turned up her aristocratic nose at their dark faces. She would run from the courtyard when the first customer arrived to busy me in the morning, and return at dusk, her pointed little face striped from pressing against the closed iron gate of the park, watching the little porcelain white ones, with their pink cheeks and yellow curls, dancing and singing in the sunshine.

"Céleste would describe this one and that one to me in the evening and I would watch the crimson of her cheeks ebb and flow with the excitement of her heart, like a fast-running tide—"

"*Sang de crépuscule,*" Auguste whispered dreamily, hypnotized by Poulette's lament.

"At sixteen Céleste was as beautiful as a princess from the *Arabian Nights*. Her strange, wild quality

4

made me tremble; but it made Vignie assume his most counting manner.

" 'Show her at the Ball,' he said. He gave me money. 'We will find for her a rich patron. We will line our pockets.' " Poulette's eyes ceased to trickle tears and blazed, full of hate, at the sad young man. She went on in a hard hoarse voice. "One look at your yellow hair curling so crisply at your temples and pht-t-t!—out of the window flew the rich patron! 'Poulette, give me this one for a lover,' Céleste cried. So, weak fat woman that I am, I took Vignie's wrath and gave her to you instead. *You*—with your great gray eyes and white face! A god, she called you. Well, she is with God now. She no longer struggles to affirm or to deny her *sang de crépuscule.*"

The wind which had been blowing since sunset with a far-off keening, now rose to a mighty moaning, and rumbled in the chimney. Clouds of soot and ashes blown from the fireplace whirled in dark drifts around the floor. The mouse scurried away with a sharp, frightened squeak. Over the roofs of old New Orleans could be heard the running of the rain; the draft from the window swelled out the white gauze curtain and floated it like a tortured ghost halfway across the room, straining and whipping at its pole; outside, the black magnolias bent and rose.

Poulette gave a little shriek and hastily crossed her bosom. "Come with me to see the child." She opened the door and the young man went with relief into another room.

The other bedchamber was small and gay with many candles. Poulette handed him a taper and he took it over to the dark old cradle carved in the shape of a swan.

"Can you see?" Poulette asked.

"God—yes! But you joke with me, Poulette! This cannot be the child. This is a white child!"

"It is very close, *Maître*." Poulette watched Auguste brush a finger over the infant's ivory cheeks, little almond-blossom cheeks on which black lashes quivered like tiny feathers.

"Her hair is almost red!" His voice shook with

5

emotion. "My mother had the most gorgeous bronze hair you ever saw."

"She is very white, *Maître*. It sometimes happens with an octoroon." Poulette looked craftily at the serious, intensely moved young man.

As he continued to stare, Poulette purred on. "Only Vignie would have to know."

"Why Vignie?" Auguste knew all about Vignie. Everybody in New Orleans knew all about Vignie. Vignie was the most famous *encanteur* in the whole slave trade. His marble desk in the rotunda of the St. Louis Hotel, which held the slave exchange, was the busiest of them all. Last year alone, it was whispered, he cleared over fifty thousand in light-skinned girls!

"You know that I belong to Vignie," Poulette said impatiently; this young man was so dense—so used to the solitudes of the desert that he forgot the exigencies of the city. "Because I became famous for designing hats, he set me up in a hat shop. I have done other work for him, also. He hires me out on occasion. You must bargain with him so that I will be allowed to nurse the child for you, in your house, while you are away. She must be most carefully reared and sheltered."

Strangely the old story of Miriam popped into Auguste's head. Miriam hiring herself as a nurse to the infant found in the bulrushes by the Pharaoh's daughter; Miriam assuring her son's future by having the little Jew raised as a gentile.

"Were you Céleste's mother?" He wanted very much to hold his baby but he did not dare ask the woman because he was a little bit afraid of her.

An expression of bland innocence spread over the round orange face.

"Who, I? Fat Poulette the mother of the most beautiful Quadroon Queen who ever danced a pavan with an egret feather blowing so proudly in her smooth black hair? Ha! Ha! It is now *you* who joke, *Maître*."

Outside a heavy cart rumbled to a stop and a bell rang mournfully, muffled by the roaring wind. Tears again crowded Poulette's eyes. She gave Auguste a push.

6

"You will find Vignie at the St. Louis Hotel. To-night there is a big auction. If he agrees, I will bring the baby to your home on Toulouse Street tomorrow."

Auguste took one last look at his daughter and, almost as if she knew, the baby opened her eyes and stared, unblinking, at the lighted candle in his hand.

"My eyes!" he breathed reverently. That settled it for him.

"She must never suspect that she is not entirely white," he spoke quite loudly to Poulette who, now that she had turned the trick, held her head low in a most ingratiating manner.

Auguste blew the candle and hurried down the steep stairs in search of Vignie.

What an ending, he tried to tell himself, as he made to cross Chartres onto Royal, but he was so intent on not looking at the ominous vehicle waiting for its passenger, that he stumbled in a slop pail left lying in the gutter and knocked his hipbone most painfully on the iron wheel of the death cart.

The rest of the way he moved carefully, limping badly. The lights along Royal Street had been lit and they showed him the handsome entrance to the St. Louis Hotel where a thick, well-dressed man was lolling by the yellow doorman, under a canvas canopy lifted against the rain.

The lamps shone in Auguste's eyes and he noticed a brilliantly lighted shop window next to the entrance. As he passed it, the thick man approached him and held out his gloved hand.

"*Bonsoir, Monsieur* Le Jeune. And how did you leave California?"

"*Bonsoir, Monsieur* Vignie. I am on my way to discuss a matter with you. I left California precisely as I found it. No richer, no poorer for my sojourn there."

Vignie was short and rather squat. He had a common face, the cheeks heavy under the small sharp eyes, the eyes shaded by heavy brows, long black mustaches turned up efficiently, and large ears, themselves bristling with hair.

"How do you like my display?" Vignie was cheerful and his eyes were most friendly.

7

I don't like them when they are friendly, Auguste thought. *Slave dealers should be coarse and crude and very ill-mannered. Then one could know how to meet them.*

"Your display?" Auguste followed the stubby finger Vignie pointed proudly at the shop window, lined with candles and lanterns. In the window a stunningly beautiful quadroon was sitting on a French gilt sofa. She was dressed in crimson velvet and a scarf of gauze sprinkled with sequins glittered over her smooth bare shoulders. Her hair was done in long curls and little knots of velvet ribbon caught it back from her narrow pouting face. Seeing Auguste staring at her, she simpered the scarlet thread of her lips into a smile and held up a big placard for him to read. *For Sale—This Beauty! Fully guaranteed. Also a fast pacing sorrel thoroughbred mare and two cows, one fresh—all for Five Thousand Dollars! Any or all may be purchased separately. The mare must bring three thousand—the wench two thousand; the cows are free to the lucky buyer.*

Auguste tried to speak, but his mouth was stiff and tasted of acid; for a moment, instead of the simpering quadroon, he seemed to see in the space of light the little white face of his baby Charlotte grown to womanhood, a cloud of bronze hair flowing over her shoulders—a sad smile on her full red lips—a deep loneliness in her gray eyes—holding a placard. *For Sale!* it read. *For Sale!*

"It is about Poulette that I have come, *Monsieur* Vignie," he finally said with difficulty.

"Ah, yes, Poulette, my nice fat hen of a Poulette!" Vignie laughed, a dry unpleasant laugh, and slapped his gloves three times against his thigh. "So you want to hire my Poulette! Well, my dear young gentleman, you may—you may!" Again the dry dusty laughter racked discordantly on Auguste's ears.

"Can we go in out of the rain?" Auguste was shivering from many causes.

"Yes, yes, let us go into the bar and drink a brandy." Vignie signaled the erect, yellow doorman who opened the door wide and bowed coldly as the two men went into the hotel. The carpet was thick and the hall long and Auguste blinked with surprise as they entered the sparkling rotunda. Here he had never been before. The hugeness of the room, floored in mingled marble with a domed ceiling supported by marble columns, completely bewildered him. He felt Vignie's hand steering him over to the marble bar, but he, Auguste, seemed to have gone somewhere else entirely.

The bar which surrounded the room was supposedly the finest in the world, and this night it was crowded with *encanteurs* and planters and odd gentlemen from many lands and ports. There was noise, noise, noise from the dozens of small platforms opposite the bar; for on each platform was a marble desk holding an *encanteur,* gesticulating, turning quickly from side to side, shouting merrily and eloquently, first in French and then in English, the qualities of the human wares which he was auctioneering off to any who paid the price.

Vignie ordered a rare old brandy. Auguste did not observe the proper amenity of warming his nicely in his hand before sampling it appreciatively, but poured it thirstily down his tense throat, calling for another as Vignie continued the one-sided conversation.

"Yes indeed, you may hire Poulette. Her taste in hats grows more atrocious and gaudy with each year, and the business has dwindled accordingly. But, I warn you, I charge very highly for her services. She is a money-maker, that one, in more ways than in her fantastic hats. I bought her long ago, and not so long either; in fact, just in time for Céleste to be born in my ownership. Before that, Poulette belonged to a wicked, impoverished aristocrat who objected to her when she changed, in the course of nature, from a slip of a tawny girl into a thick, fat-bellied woman complaining of her back. But Poulette has ever been a clever one; getting her way sometimes even with me, Vignie, who has no heart at all—at all—"

"How much will you charge?" Auguste signaled desperately for another pony of brandy.

Vignie vaguely waved a glove and sipped thought-

9

fully on his cognac, now that he had made it the proper temperature. "That, my worried young man, we will settle another time. Now I must make haste and sell my beauty from the window. She is probably freezing out there in the weather and I don't want her to look too pale to seem vigorous and capable of much movement. Will you remain?"

Auguste shook his head and limped painfully through the chiaroscuro of faces ranging from whitest white to brownest brown which blended harmoniously with the murals depicting various celebrations of American liberty.

An elderly gentleman who had been watching Auguste so recklessly gulping his liquor accosted Vignie.

"Who was that most distraught young man?"

"Oh, a young hothead about town. The last of a good line, with a little money and a severe case of gold fever, among other foolish fancies."

The white-haired gentleman clucked disapprovingly and invited Vignie to drink a brandy with him, but Vignie refused politely and made his way over to his marble desk, laughing a little, then sighing, whispered to himself. "The children of a slave mother and a free father, whatever his color, are themselves slaves, since they follow the condition of the mother. Young fool! Doesn't even realize that the damn baby belongs to me!"

BOOK ONE

Normandy
1842

Chapter 1

***

It was not difficult in the New Orleans of 1830 for such a man as the reckless Auguste Le Jeune suddenly to install in his artistic small house on Toulouse Street a large competent Negress and a tiny white "ward." There were the usual distant cousins who sniffed and gossiped, but after one or two rather uninteresting visits they found other wickednesses to investigate.

When Charlotte was six months old and beginning to notice, crowing delightedly, the gay birds and flowers in the old flagged courtyard, Auguste made arrangements with the Abbé to come once a week and give money for the house to wizened black Shisi Zana, the cook, and also to hand a sum to Vignie each month for the services of Poulette. The wanderlust had hold of Auguste again; he joined a party of other gentlemen and returned happily to his exciting, feverish life.

So while more or less fortunate little girls were squabbling with their brothers and sisters, being young princesses over slave children on plantations, playing tag and hide-and-seek in fashionable city parks, sitting through long dull sermons in the family pew, or going on picnics by the river, Charlotte amused herself in the pretty courtyard, outgrowing an easy instinct for group play and developing in her eyes an aloneness which never quite left them.

There was only Potee, Shisi Zana's sharp black son, who occasionally was allowed to catch a ball with her or to sit with Poulette, as an adoring audience,

13

while Charlotte danced for them in the courtyard, around the two gnarled old fig trees casting green-leaved shadows on the duck pool's marble bowl, itself stained green from the copper tenons which tied the stones together.

Charlotte was a delicate, willowy child with the enormous gray eyes inherited from her father, along with his mother's high cheekbones and the proud carriage of a shapely head covered with bronze hair. But it was from Céleste that Charlotte had the ivory tinge of strangeness which made her beauty unusually provocative; from Céleste, too, came the indefinable quality that lingered on the pointed face as it changed from babyhood to girlhood to recall to Auguste a wild, sweet irrevocable passion.

When Charlotte was six years old, Auguste Le Jeune returned for a visit and found her a delightful companion. He attempted to ease her loneliness by arranging for Roman Sisters to come and train her in a culture rich in art and tradition; he engaged dancing masters and music teachers, and persuaded the Abbé himself to sit at table once a week, so that Charlotte might become versed in the graces of conversation.

"Until she is twelve," Auguste told Poulette, "this will suffice. At twelve, the Sisters will take her into the convent for four years and you can return to your wonderful hats. When she is sixteen, I will have a mansion in California built for her to grace, and no shadow will ever darken one short day of Charlotte's life."

Auguste was careful in his ideas and after buying a playful little poodle puppy for the child, he again left New Orleans, retracing his restless journey to the West.

"Charlotte."

"Yes, Poulette."

"Let us not go into the park today. Fifi will amuse you here. I have thought of a very old tune to match the new steps you learned yesterday from the dancing master. Fifi will dance with you. It can be gay."

"No—no—I insist on going to the park today.

14

The little boy who laughs so much, rolled his hoop quite near me day before yesterday. Today I am sure he will ask me and Fifi to roll the hoop also. I *will* have a friend besides Potee!"

"Ayee—Poulette is ill today, my pet." Poulette sighed purposely, her fat face a crinkled orange of appeal, her rich voice pleading low. "The back is aching like a worn-out tooth. The little boy will tie a stick to Fifi's tail. Boys are like that. Tomorrow surely I will take you out. We will seek another park where the boys with hoops roll them another way."

Charlotte stormed and cried for a long time and Poulette was cleverly patient, though Charlotte kicked and slapped her. Poulette knew that the temper would soon pass, for Charlotte was as ardent and volatile as summer rain which gives its all in a rush and spilling of the whole cloud. Her anger was quick and hot, her good humor sudden and gay; as easy both to come and to go as thunder and sunshine.

By late afternoon Charlotte was gay again. To the full-throated singing of Poulette, watched by thin Potee and curly Fifi, she danced many dances on the worn old stones. A saraband, deliberately slow to follow the windless clouds; a *canzone* whose pathos, matching the expression in her soft sweet eyes, was spoiled by a sudden untimed mad pirouette; at the last, a pavan with swift glissades, in and out among the old trees, snatching poppies and lilies as she passed their beds and pausing above her reflection in the pool to fasten the brilliant flowers in her hair. Thinking, as she watched her face glimmering in the dim green water, *Someday I will deceive Poulette and find myself a boy and a girl to play with me; this is what comes of being an orphan, with no mother, only dark Poulette who keeps me prisoner in this tiny space. It is like being the Sleeping Beauty, only not asleep. It is always waiting, waiting, waiting for the small door in the court to open wide. Why does my guardian stay so long away? If he were here he would see that Fifi is no longer enough to interest me and keep me happy.*

15

Charlotte and Poulette went each week to the opera. Afterward they would walk home along Royal Street, peering in the shop windows. As Charlotte dreamed her way through the gay New Orleans crowds, she gradually came to wonder why none spoke to her. How could all these people fail to notice that she was a girl marked for some great adventure some day? Why did no one ever come and knock upon her door?

Always afterward, she would lie in her carved gilt bed, her high arched feet patting time to the aria sung that night, and listen to the voices—indefinite, fading, magical—which floated up to her window from the street; a young Creole lover strumming a guitar, en route to serenade his beloved, who would surely throw him a red rose from a filigreed iron balcony; a candy man calling his sweets pleadingly; a flock of pigeons cooing as they rested.

Once—one autumn night when she was twelve —she heard Poulette's deep voice talking from her window to a man on the street.

Charlotte slipped out of her bed, pulling a peignoir over her long flannel nightgown, and tipped on her cream-colored toes to the window, opened a bit to let in the fresh night air.

"No—not a penny for many months now; no word, either."

"Perhaps he is dead. It has been six years since he was here."

"No, *Maître* Vignie, news of that comes quickly."

"I intend to find out. If he is dead, I will not make the same error as the affair of Céleste. This time I will take the money when it is offered. I want no more moonstruck Célestes eating up my pocketbook."

"No, no, *Maître!* Give us two months at the latest!" Charlotte shivered in the October starlight that spilled into her room, hearing Poulette's voice take on a whining, snuffling tone. "Dear *Maître,* you with your kind heart—do not hurt your fat old Poulette."

"You have always your hats." The man laughed in a dusty manner. "And just think what fantastic atrocities will be possible for you to pour your heartache into. Poppies, larger than moons, can festoon the tiniest bonnets of straw—ribbons of red and orange and pink you can pile on chenille creations like meringue on a party pie. Ah—those hats can compensate much, my fat one. And the money for the young biddy! Of that you will have a share also."

"Oh, *Maître!* Oh, *Maître!* No—no—no, *Maître!*"

Charlotte was frightened. She pulled and jerked the petit-point cord by her bed.

Potee, who was now sixteen years, appeared with a torch in answer to the ringing. He was very black with sharp straight features and a most beautiful head. He seemed tonight, in the darkness of the room, to be completely bodiless. To be only a face; a persecuted face in his terror at being summoned to the small *Maîtress's* bedroom at this late hour; a face fastened hopelessly above the taper's flame, his sad eyes glinting thin sparks in the wavering circle of light.

"Hurry—hurry," Charlotte whispered. "Light first the candles and then the fire. Poulette is weeping in her window. I must quickly comfort her."

Potee's arm shook as he touched the fire to the wax candles. Charlotte felt a deep urge to go and steady his arm. He looked lost and sad in the dainty room. Once she had confessed to Poulette that she thought Potee handsome, but Poulette had been very stern and threatened to tell her kind guardian when he came from the West. The idea! Poulette had been scornful. A black one handsome! The idea!

"Hurry—hurry," Charlotte repeated crossly, as Potee knelt to light the fire. "Now, you are finished —tell Poulette to come to me immediately." Outside a lone bell chimed midnight. Poulette came at once and to Charlotte's amazement the round orange face was composed—the voice its usual rich fruity self.

"I heard you—I heard you! What is wrong? What was that man saying to you to make you cry?" Charlotte flung her arms around the soft thick waist.

"Ah—ah, little excited one!" Poulette laughed gently, and sitting on a *bergère* by the warm fire, she took Charlotte on her lap and began teasing her about

17

the ears which had grown so long that they reached clear from the window to the street, hearing another, but definitely not Poulette, arguing and weeping in the starlight.

Two months passed and Christmastime with its bells and singing took the picturesque city. On the day after Christmas, a note came for Poulette concerning a precious hat. She struggled into a warm cloak and after giving Charlotte and Shisi Zana close instructions to go out nowhere, left the house.

Around five o'clock in the afternoon a ring came at the door. Shisi Zana opened, and let two men into the tiny hall. Shisi Zana knew well the squat, hairy man who laughed so peculiarly. The other man was unknown, and she shook in her worn-out shoes at such a tremendous piece of a male. He was six feet three at least and filled out in all the places that count the most in a man, though he was old. But with men you could never be sure, perhaps he was not that old. Shisi Zana was frightened. Poulette had told her about the past, and she realized that the message carrying Poulette away this afternoon must have been sent by *Maître* Vignie, now explaining so pleasantly to the giant the merits of the manner in which the little Charlotte had grown up within this house.

As the giant asked a question, Charlotte came darting from the sitting-room into the hall, hiding a ball in the folds of her green wool dress, followed by Fifi who yapped excitedly. Charlotte stopped short on seeing the two strangers. Behind her in the doorway appeared Potee, tall and narrow in a tight gray jacket.

"Ah, here is Charlotte Le Jeune herself," the squat man announced with pride to the giant. "Charlotte, curtsy to Mr. Gaillard of South Carolina."

The gray-eyed, full-lipped girl, so pretty but so startled, shoulders heaving from her chase with the poodle, tossed her bronze curls proudly back from her face and bent one leg in its lace-frilled drawers. No longer a child, not yet a woman, she did not know what words to say to these strangers in her house.

She did not like the hairy man's knowledge of her

18

name and when suddenly he laughed a dry, racking laugh, she knew clearly that Poulette had lied to her that night in October; this was the man who had made Poulette weep.

"Yes, she will serve perfectly," the large man said, staring too hard at her.

Charlotte, ill at ease for the first time in her life, turned away and glanced at the black boy who had picked up Fifi in his spindly arms. Then, unable to bear the rude scrutiny any longer, she rushed from the hall as fast as her quick little feet would carry her.

"You are sure of the legality of the sale?" Mr. Gaillard did not like the expression on Vignie's face. It was too pleased, too smug.

"When five thousand dollars hang in the air, *Monsieur* Gaillard," Vignie gave the French pronounciation to the name, which further irritated the large gentleman from South Carolina, "I am always sure of myself. I am too old a hand at this business to be caught in a mousetrap." Then he added quietly to himself, "Once caught in the mousetrap by the fat Poulette —but not twice."

"Can the girl be ready for me to pick her up at dawn?"

"Yes, yes, surely. I have it all planned. She need not be told tonight. Poulette will be away until tomorrow. I have sent her to another parish, to make an old harridan a batch of the most outrageous hats ever to be worn in Lousiana. Poulette will be so intoxicated with her mission that she will forget her biddy for a night. Thus there will be no tears at the separation."

"You are convinced of the father's death?"

"The Abbé himself brought me the news only this morning. Auguste Le Jeune was killed in a gun fight protecting a nigger cook. He! He! How he did get his come-uppance!"

The black boy stood as if frozen, clutching the poodle. Vignie chuckled more and more at the horror in the dark eyes. He reached out a glove and slapped the narrow face smartly. "Mind you keep your mouth shut. Go away with that animal. Zana—a word with you."

"Boy!" the large man called and Potee turned sullenly to face him. "Tell her that she can bring the dog if it will please her. But not until the morning. I do not want to fret her this last night."

Shisi Zana pulled Charlotte from her warm bed and dressed her, still half asleep, though complaining.

"Make no sound. Be ver' quiet," Shisi Zana whispered, and Charlotte, bewildered and confused, obeyed, following Shisi Zana down the stairs as a loud ringing shattered the chilly silence of the house.

"Where is Poulette? Has something happened to her?" Charlotte was coming awake now and her nervous system was ringing alarm bells louder than the doorbell, all over her cold little body.

"Come—*vite*—*vite*—" Shisi Zana pulled Charlotte roughly down into the hall—pulled, then pushed her straight at the huge man whom Charlotte had seen there yesterday afternoon.

"Are you quite ready to go?" the man asked gently.

"Go—go?" Charlotte cried. "Oh, Poulette! Poulette! Where are you?" Her eyes darted back and forth like those of a deer pursued on all sides. Potee's hands were shaking but he held out Fifi and made Charlotte take the sleepy little dog into her arms.

"Well, little girl—come on—come on."

"*Adieu*, Charlotte." Shisi Zana closed the front door quickly. Charlotte's feet felt like wood as the strange man pulled her out into the dawning. The cold struck sharply on her cheeks and her hand fumbled with the curls on Fifi's neck. A carriage waited at the gate and the horses' breath blew out like ghosts from their nostrils. *I am afraid of horses,* was all Charlotte could think; *they are waiting to take me to something too terrible. I know it. I can feel it. Oh—Poulette—where are you?*

Potee ran up to the gentleman and shook his arm. "She not know nothing, *Maître*," he gasped. "She think she is a white girl—please, *Maître*—be kind to her—she is such a white little girl."

20

Chapter 2

━━━━━━━━━━━━━━━━━━━━━━━━━━━━━━━━━━━━━━

"Are you taking me to Poulette?" Charlotte asked desperately as the horses' hoofs struck sparks from the brick street and the coach began to bump and sway along.

"Poulette?" Nicholas Gaillard reached over and took one of the icy little hands in his. "Didn't they tell you, child? We're on our way to South Carolina."

Charlotte shook her head in disbelief. "Poulette will be very cross that I have gone away to visit you without her consent. I am sure my guardian will be angry, also. I think you had better take me straight back to Toulouse Street. I will visit you another time."

"Eh? Eh? Visit?" Nicholas cleared his throat, which had been hurting since midnight, and coughed a few times to relieve a tightness which persisted in his chest. He was becoming progressively uncomfortable over this whole affair. He knew that the child was most certainly better off with him than she would have been with Vignie. Vignie would have displayed her in his lighted window and sold her to any old roué who fancied such a delicate morsel.

The worst worry was his wife, Tafra. Now she was going to be in one of her finest rages. She had always questioned his judgment in the purchase of slaves, buying Whydahs who inevitably pined away and died of homesickness, when they needed Pow Pows, industrious and sturdy of body, for the cotton fields; experimenting with Congoes, Gaboons, and Eboes

21

because he liked their yellow color and believed that it made them immune to malaria, though all these were apt to commit suicide in odd ways before they even learned the language; bidding in whole groups of easy, gay Gullahs, because they smiled and sang melodiously, when a dozen or two would have been sufficient.

And today, this girl! this Charlotte who had no idea that she had been sold into slavery; no suspicion that she was not a cherished member of the white race.

He'd been hoodwinked yesterday morning at the cotton exchange by that scoundrel of a Vignie, purring in his ears, "Niggers and cotton; niggers and cotton; what dry, dusty subjects! Let us have a very old cognac, *Monsieur* Gaillard, while I tell you about the rarest bargain that has ever come my way in the slave trade; a gift for your charming wife; one in all the thousands who have slipped through my fingers; a beauty, educated as a lady, clean and healthy. Today —this very day she is to be sold. She will be snapped up at once. I will let you see her the first."

When he allowed himself to be persuaded by Vignie to go and inspect the girl, it had seemed ideal. His only son, Inigo, was tragically unhappy in his marriage. Yesterday this one had looked to be the perfect answer to that problem.

But not this morning! Looking down into the pure little face with the great lonely gray eyes, at the shining hair, heavy in its snood, a guilty lump grew in his increasingly sore throat. *I'll just have to let Tafra handle it,* he decided suddenly. So, having made up his mind that it was his wife's job to tell Charlotte about herself, he reached over and patted Fifi and began to try and make the sadness go away for the frightened child.

"You will like Normandy," he told Charlotte.

"Are there children there for me to play with?"

"A little boy of eleven who is very bad. He is my oldest grandson and if he teases you or your little dog, I will thrash him."

Charlotte nodded gravely.

"Then there is a baby. The baby is a darling. He is only two months old and he can hold his head up already."

"Oh—I will love a baby." Charlotte felt the sickness of her stomach begin to ease. "Will the mother of the baby let me hold him?"

"Yes," Nicholas answered her softly, "the mother of the baby will let you hold him as much as you like."

"But I will only be able to visit a week with you in your house. Poulette would miss me if I stayed too long."

Chapter 3

It was the custom for Inigo Gaillard to inspect all the horses each morning before he rode across the fields to watch the slaves at work. Today he was even more careful in his routine than usual for this was the day his father had named for his return from a business trip to the cotton exchange in New Orleans.

"I'll go and look at the yearlings, first," Inigo decided, crossing the west field and coming first to the jumping lane where the yearling Eclipse colt, Edisto, was kept alone. Edisto had kicked his mother the day he was foaled and, thereafter, every two- or four-legged beast coming within the range of his hoofs. The big, bony black colt was standing quietly in the drizzling rain. He pricked up his soft little hairy ears as Inigo opened the gate and fastened it again with a click. "Here, baby—here, baby!" Inigo called, taking a bright red apple from his pocket and holding it out. "Here, boy—it's time for you to learn some civilized ways!"

Some quality of Inigo's voice seemed to irritate

the leggy yearling; the small ears flattened, and before
Inigo realized what was happening, Edisto reared and
came bucking and slashing out with his sharp front
feet. But Inigo was quick. His powerful fist cracked
the side of the black thoroughbred head. The colt
screamed, more in rage than in pain, though the blow
had been hard enough to have stopped a grown horse;
he wheeled and plunged back to attack again.

"Damn you!" Inigo shouted, and he met Edisto,
running. Grabbing the arched neck, he fastened his
arms around it and forced the black head back—
back—until the big colt lost his balance and fell heavily in the soft, sandy dirt. Twisting easily, Inigo sat his
tremendous bulk right squarely on top of the colt's
head.

"I'll sit here as long as there's a kick left in your
mean black skin," Inigo said. Pulling a flint from his
waistcoat, he lit a long Spanish cigar which he calmly
proceeded to smoke.

*I didn't know anybody but my wife was that
mean,* Inigo said to himself, flicking a cone of ash down
into a baleful red eye rolling wildly as the overgrown
colt heaved beneath him.

The colt's vicious hate of him made him think of
Emily as a girl. He and Emily had been children—he
sixteen and she fourteen—when they had romantically
eloped on the night of the Tournament Ball over elev-
en years ago and been married by an ignorant minister
of a country church in his dingy parlor.

It was still as vivid in his mind as though each detail had been exposed on a daguerreotype plate. The
Tournament was held in Pineville early in March in
the year 1831. At sixteen, Inigo was already six feet
three, carrying his two hundred and twenty pounds as
rhythmically and powerfully as a mature man. His
mother had cut his thick black curls in a cap shape,
like a painting of Tristan she had once seen. And his
white satin costume shone and glittered in the sunshine.
Color blazed everywhere. The woods were yellow with
tender new oak leaves and scarlet with redbuds and
Judas trees; lit with alabaster dogwood blossoms; car-
peted with wild plum petals sifting like a new snow

24

onto the pine-needle-strewn lanes; perfumed by yellow jasmine and purple wistaria spilling like colored waterfalls from the tall singing pines.

The thirty knights were the best horsemen in the Low Country. Richly mounted and costumed, each bore the name of a member of King Arthur's Round Table. Their company headed by heralds, the King-at-Arms, the King's pages and the Master of the Horse, they filed into the arena amid the applause of the brightly dressed Low Country folk, sitting proud as royalty in the gay pavilion. As the knights lowered their lances and saluted the gallery, lined in a curved formation, Inigo caught sight of Emily Allston sitting in a front box, looking like a porcelain princess, a garland of arbutus in her flowing corn-silk hair. He had seen her and not noticed her at picnics and dances, but today, out of all the days, she was beautiful.

When he rode up and asked for her favor she gave him the ribbon she had brought, tying the crimson length of silk tightly about his muscular arm. And her high girlish voice urging him on— "Sir Tristan! Sir Tristan!"—excited him so that he dug his spurs deep into Phenomenon's sides, galloping full speed down the course with outstretched lance. Six times he caught all the rings from the three racks suspended above the course, and rode proudly with them up to the judges' stand.

The whole pavilion of gentry went wild. They threw flowers like confetti each time the great young Gaillard thundered by, until finally he was called out as the winner—The Perfect Knight of the Tournament!

For a minute he sat uneasily on Phenomenon, pondering which head would wear his crown. But the scent of fragrant arbutus had been strong on the March wind, and lowering his lance, he rode up and placed the crown on Emily's pretty head, making her for the day his Queen of Love and Beauty.

That night he and she led the Tournament Ball and were bewitched by the mood and splendor of the medieval Court of Love, reproduced in luxurious pageantry. So strong was the punch, and so enchanting the spell of themselves as the ideal knight and lady, that neither ever knew which suggested that they elope and continue the romance in which they were caught. The everyday world was gone. Emily was enraptured at the idea of riding pillion with her knight through the forest to Normandy while their parents danced and bowed at the ball.

He remembered the way Emily giggled as he ran up the curving stairs with her in his arms. He remembered throwing her on his bed and tearing off his satin costume. But to Emily the clock struck midnight when the young knight emerged from his shining white costume and stood before her in his awful nakedness. She took one terrified look at him and shrieked, "Oh, how dark and ugly you are!"

But midnight had struck for him, too. He was beginning to be afraid of what he had done. Now he became angry and his temper, always hot, mingled with his passion and flared cruelly against this fourteen-year-old girl who lay clutching the cover about her, daring to despise him.

He expected her to kick and bite and scream. All maiden mares did the first time; he had helped too much in the breeding field not to take this for granted. He had never lain with a woman before, so he thought that that was the way it was supposed to be with them, too.

Her continued refusal of him only added to his determination to possess her, and he took her several times before he began to realize that this was not the way it was supposed to be between a lover and his sweetheart. She never left off fighting. He had never dreamed so much strength could dwell in a small girl's body, and when finally he lay back exhausted and tried to pull her tenderly over and tell her how sorry he was that he had hurt her—she raised herself on her elbow and he gazed with bewilderment at the hatred in her distorted, tear-streaked face.

"I'm sorry—" he began, but she gathered herself and spat full in his mouth, cursing him—reviling him —loathing him.

He leaped out of bed, tremblingly pulled the torn remnants of his soiled satin garments about him and fled to the stable, where he saddled a horse. He remembered galloping away into the dense pinelands to Mad Willie's hut.

Thank God, Cuffee had been in the stable and had followed him, or he might have killed himself, he was so confused and ashamed. Cuffee stayed with him and soothed him and tended him. And though he returned to Normandy a few days later, the shame which was on him had cast a blight on his exuberant maleness that even the years themselves had never removed. He sometimes thought that if he could just have fought a clean duel with himself, everything would have come all right.

From that night he and Emily had been enemies. Nicholas made an effort to get the marriage annulled. He hated Emily with her sharp shrewish ways from the first. But the night had resulted in Robert and since divorce was against South Carolina law, Emily remained at Normandy.

Occasionally through the years Inigo forced himself on her after a ball or picnic they attended together, when he had drunk too much punch or claret cup, trying to pretend they were like other married couples. Nick had followed the last St. Cecilia. She must have forgotten to lock her door that night, for he woke up in her bed—hating himself—hating her. He had slipped quietly out of her room, leaving her snoring in her wine-heavy slumber, and going to his room had washed until he was raw and sore, resolved never to touch her bed again. Priests lived without women and managed to survive and get old. The hell with women, anyhow.

But that afternoon Emily had faced him in his office, waiting until his father left with Big Jake for the gin house.

"Sit down," he invited her, ashamed to meet her eyes, fumbling with his quill pen.

"No," she said coldly, "I won't sit down. I can talk better standing up. I will hate you until you die for taking advantage of me last night when I was asleep. And if a child comes of it—I will hate him, too."

27

He was unable to answer her, had only doodled on a piece of foolscap fecklessly. When he did not defend himself, she said what she had really come to say —what she had meant since the first day she had smiled on him with arbutus sweetening her hair.

"And don't let that wily mother of yours persuade you to attempt to divorce me. I know how she has brightened up since that Spartanburg man almost succeeded in divorcing his wife last summer. But I know the woman kept him from getting it by not mincing words about the bestial way he treated her in bed. I read it all in the paper. Even the part where it said that the judge was so embarrassed by her testimony that he cleared the courtroom.

"I'll do more. I'll tell every detail of our wedding night to the whole Low Country, right out loud in the Charleston court, if you ever try to divorce me. It pleases me to be the rich Mrs. Gaillard. Yes, the Gaillard fortune pleases me very much. But I warn you that someday I am going to get even with you. I'll stoop to anything to hurt your pride as you've hurt my body."

He still hadn't answered her and she went away.

That was his wife!

She held the dagger. She could always turn it.

Yet they must continue to kneel and pray side by side in the parish church on Sundays, attend balls and races together, entertain as Nicholas and Tafra did. A deep line cut between his eyes—a hardness came about his broad red mouth.

His mother teased him about his devotion to his conception of what honor meant in a man's life. But it had only been his rigid adherence to the public code that had kept him tall in his own eyes, despite the constant undermining innuendoes of Emily, both in private and public. The whole Low Country looked on him as the perfect essence of a gentleman. He was still Sir Tristan to them. It would kill him if anybody knew that he had only had his wife by raping her.

Honor! Inigo said to himself. *It is a great security. But oh, how tired I get of it sometimes. Of it and all the endless round of days spent doing all those things*

28

which I ought to do, and leaving most of those things undone which I ought not to do. Yet I must concern myself with honor, and the honor of the others who make up my kind and class. It is like a uniform a soldier wears. It demonstrates the rank and privilege of a gentleman. It proves that such a man lives properly.

Now that Inigo's rage was dissipated in his weary thoughts, he changed from thinking into being excited over his father's return this afternoon. In the rain he was coming; in the winter rain. Nicholas would find his horses snug and warm and safe, his Negroes happy, the fields prepared for the coming of the spring. There had always been a sense of excitement for him when his big, kind father came from off a trip. It was like the excitement of a carnival; Nicholas always arrived with so much enthusiasm for whatever part of the country he had just been in, unlike himself, who was completely satisfied to be an exponent of the Low Country, which was more a way of life, a state of mind, than a geographical location.

At last the cigar was smoked and Edisto lay still. Inigo got up and looked down at the little horse. "Get up." He prodded his toe into the black flank. Edisto sat up dizzily on his haunches, his front legs spraddled out stiffly, and shook his head to be sure that the great weight had lifted. He gave Inigo an ugly look before placing his back feet unsteadily under him. His legs held up and, turning away, he put his sore head high, lifted his ears and tail disdainfully, and trotted weakly over to the fence.

Laughing and exhilarated by the struggle, Inigo brushed off his trousers and was starting to the gate when a voice startled him. "Run, Mass Inigo—fuh Gawd's sake, run!"

Inigo ran. Edisto came plunging after him, but a short black man slipped through the bars and caught hold of the colt's mane, dragging him back just in time for Inigo to roll under the fence.

"Whiskers!" Inigo lay on the ground and tilted his left eyebrow in wonder. "He'd have killed me that time. I wasn't looking for him. He's a man all right."

29

"Now, baby—shame, baby—come wid Cuffee, baby." The young Negro was speaking softly to the colt and Inigo smiled ruefully as he watched Edisto nuzzle Cuffee's head and whistle friendly in answer to a bit of loaf sugar.

"I'm going in, Cuffee. My clothes are a sight."

"Sho-sho; git purty fuh Mass Nicholas. Hagar say she kin smell dat he bringing a new kind ob present dis time."

Inigo trudged through the dampness to the house.

Normandy was a Palladian type of villa built by Inigo's great-grandfather in 1740. The exterior was of hard, baked pinkish brick, but the design of the house was so perfectly proportioned that it offset the ugliness of the material. The front that faced the avenue had an upper and lower piazza with delicate wrought-iron railings suspended between white columns. The other side, facing the river, did not have piazzas, but an arch of steps curved up to and across a fanlighted doorway, then flowed on down to the velvety terraced lawn sloping gently to the swift tidal river.

The front entrance gave onto a paneled baronial hall that was thirty feet wide by forty-five feet long. At the far end of the hall was a fireplace as wide as a church door and as deep as a stall, with an elegantly carved crest on the overmantel, worked after a design of Inigo Jones. On this floor were a dark library, an airy spacious dining-room, and Emily's drawing-room, known as the "small" drawing-room. This room was richly paneled and fancily furnished but nobody ever dropped in or out of it. The pillows remained stiff and smooth, the chairs at proper angles, the windows closed against the heat and the cold, Emily unpleasant and critical of the noise penetrating her immaculate walls from other parts of the big house.

A symmetrical, double stairway lifted itself to the second floor where, in addition to eight large bed-chambers, was the great room itself—Tafra's drawing-room. Here the Adam mantel was carved as exquisitely as precious jade and the oak-lined avenue of the proud Gaillards was painted by the famous miniaturist,

Fraser, on the overmantel in rich vital colors. Fluted columns and pilasters adorned the white-painted, paneled side walls and the pink plaster ceiling, artistically molded in ornate designs, shadowed the shining crystal chandeliers.

This room was the heart of the house. What tales of joy, love, and cruelty it could have told! Of kisses and christenings; of heartbreak and the violent face of death. All the important milestones of the Gaillards had been passed in here. It was a room of happenings; of beginnings and endings. This room *was* Normandy. It was waiting now to warm Inigo when his clothes should be changed. It was waiting for Nicholas and the perilous present he was bringing from far away.

Chapter 4

Nicholas and Charlotte reached Normandy in midafternoon. A thick moisture needled through the dark, drooping live oaks lining the mile-long avenue, and the clouds lay low and somber. The hoofs of the horses sank dully into the sodden sand and the branches above the coach sagged, as though from a sadness too great to be endured by such lofty ones as they.

A presentiment of disaster came over Charlotte; nature herself seemed to have shrouded her head in damp grief.

The rough trip had seemed endless; the inns had been chilly and uncomfortable; Shisi Zana had packed all the wrong clothes; her hair had not been properly brushed since she left home; she was quite determined to go right back to New Orleans just as soon as it could be arranged. As the house came into view, her head began to ache with apprehension. Why had Mr. Nicholas been so quiet all this day? The other days he had talked much. Why did he stare at her so peculiarly? Why had he inspected her fingernails for moons?

The house looked enormous. It was so different from the delicate French city houses that she had known; this dark closed-in avenue so unlike the busy streets; this silence, both in the coach and all around, so oppressive. She could sense that Nicholas, too, was nervous. He kept clearing his throat and the minute the carriage stopped, he jumped out and ran quickly into the house, leaving her alone with Fifi in the coach.

Well—at least she had Fifi. But Fifi hopped out of the opened door, and though Charlotte called and whistled, the poodle was too glad to be free and ran barking and yapping in circles, getting himself wet and full of sand.

The footman helped Charlotte down and she dragged her feet along, trying not to reach the house, not to walk up the steps. When she came to the piazza, a middle-aged Negro, with the dignity of a duke, opened the front door and greeted her.

"Afternoon! Yunnuh is sho' wetted clean through. Make haste and git in out of de weather. Here come yo' dawg. I'll jest pick um up and tote um to de kitchen and feed um good fuh yunnuh. He cute. Hit's a misery day, enty? I is Hercules, Missy. Now what might be yo' name?"

"Mistress Charlotte." The words were hard to get out. She was very tired. She had no business being in this formidable hall. This place could never suit her, no matter how many children she might have to play with. It was too big; she was too small.

And then she saw him. He was huge and his head was covered in close-cut black curls; he was very like Nicholas, only quite young. She smiled at him and he said, "Hello. What a nice surprise Pa has brought to Normandy." He knelt down to her and began to unbutton her sopping cloak, managing the

32

swollen buttons with ease. She noticed his handsome brown hands; she felt how gently he touched her. Now he looked her full in the face and she saw the corners of his mouth turned up in a smile. His teeth were large and white in his broad, ruddy face. He had a fine nose, sad black eyes, and a broad mouth with full red lips. He kept smiling, his face close to hers, kneeling as he was, and she felt suddenly merry and not exhausted, and quite welcome in this long cold hall.

"How nice that you've come," he said. "I hope you laugh a lot. We need a little girl who laughs here at Normandy."

How beautiful he is, she thought; *what strength he must have. It quite takes away all tiredness.*

"I do laugh a lot." Laughter would come easy to her with such a one as he. "And I can dance many kinds of dances, also. I will show you before I return to my home in New Orleans."

He now stood opposite her and she tilted back her head to look up into his face. They smiled at each other, staring strangely the while, each wondering who this other could be. And more and more she felt how easy all would be with this one.

"Perhaps you can teach me some of your dances," he said as a door opened and a childlike blond woman stood in the opening, sniffing disagreeably at the man handing Charlotte's wet cloak to Hercules.

"You will probably enjoy them. They will certainly be most savage dances," the woman said, with a pinching sound in her voice.

She is cruel, Charlotte thought; *she will not like me to be here; she makes me want to leave even more than this man, who causes me to feel so good inside, makes me want to stay.*

They all stood there staring at each other, not speaking.

Meanwhile, upstairs in the drawing-room, Nicholas was having a rough time of it.

"But why did you do it?" Tafra kept asking him. "Why?" Nicholas tried to explain the unexplainable. To tell her that no man could live the celibate life which Inigo was condemned to endure. That the child

33

was educated and beautiful and he had not thought it was his place to tell her and to spoil her first trip in a coach; children got such a thrill out of trips. That— He gave up and humbly bent and kissed his wife. "I love you so, my Tafra," he said, and she held him fiercely to her and he knew that he was forgiven.

"You're feverish. Lie down for a while," Tafra told him, running her bony fingers over his broad, burning brow. So, hoarsely whistling a new tune picked up in a New Orleans music hall, he went into his bedroom and closed the door. He did not want to hear Charlotte cry when she learned that she had not come to visit him, but to belong body and soul to Normandy.

Tafra rose from her carved chair, moaning a little, because the pain low in her back gnawed like an animal. She went to the stair well and called down to where Charlotte and Inigo and Emily were standing. "Inigo, please, dear, send the little Charlotte up."

And as Charlotte went up the curving stairs Inigo looked searchingly at his wife, who returned his stare with such insolent, daring superiority that his face flushed red. Then they turned from each other, he slamming the door into the library, she slipping into the sitting-room.

Tafra, leaning on her cane, met Charlotte at the head of the stair. "We are so glad that you are here with us," she said simply and Charlotte's breath came easier. She had been afraid that this one might be like the other downstairs. But this one was kind—and how beautiful her face was, even though she must be very old—sixty or more. Perhaps, now, she would stay a week. But just one; no longer.

Poor Nicholas was defeated in his reason for bringing Charlotte to Normandy at the moment that Tafra came close to her. For Nicholas had reckoned without the effect of the girl's candid, intelligent eyes on Tafra's heart. Tafra immediately loved Charlotte. She saw in her first glance a small, thin girl of twelve whose bright cream-colored face brushed with youth's pretty coloring delighted her eye. It was easy to see why her father had thought so highly of her and had educated her well; her wide brow and gray, wistful

34

eyes told a taste for learning. But after speaking to Charlotte a little while, the thought came to Tafra that the girl's pale spirit eyes told of something more than a taste for her lessons, and she noticed that Charlotte's full red mouth did not seem to match her eyes. It was a sensual mouth, shaped for love. The lips had a lush softness that was made for delight. And her voice, as she answered Tafra's questions, had a ringing quality that Tafra had never heard before. Her thick hair fell like a cloud upon her shoulders, a thin strand of gold ribbon outlined to advantage the line of her shapely head. She had on a dress of pale gray silk with a soft saffron apron draped up in back and outlined with delicate gilt fringe.

"Will you fetch me that book, child?" Tafra asked gently. With alert, light steps Charlotte gracefully crossed the room.

"You have a lovely room." Charlotte smiled shyly as she brought the copy of Rousseau.

Now is the time to tell her, Tafra thought. With not an extra word, using no maudlin note of sympathy to break down the rigid horror of the child who stood in front of her, Tafra told Charlotte that she had come into this house as a slave, not a visitor. That she had been sold in New Orleans for five thousand dollars as a bondmaiden for Normandy—that Africa was responsible for the strange ivory tone of her complexion.

For a minute after Tafra ceased talking the only sounds to be heard in the room were the loud ticking of the gilt clock on a near-by table, the pop and hiss of the fire as stray drops of rain came down the chimney.

Charlotte was hypnotized. Her brain could not absorb the meaning of the horrible words. She felt herself begin to shiver with anger, to tremble with cold fear.

She shrank back as Tafra came nearer to her, and her voice rasped loudly from her tightened throat.

"No—I am not a Negro. You lie. You are a wicked old woman!"

Charlotte slapped away the skeletal hand that Tafra reached out sympathetically to her. She darted over to the gold-leaf mirror that hung across the room and stared and stared at her face, touching her cheeks, her chin, her eyes. *She lies,* Charlotte thought triumphantly, as the mirror gave her back the same pointed face, as pallid as ever; the same gray eyes, only sad; the same bright bronze hair.

"You see!" she cried, shrill in her excitement. "You see! I am *not* a Negro. I am *not* black. This is like an ugly fairy tale. That large wicked man has stolen me away. I knew it. I knew it."

Suddenly Charlotte dropped down on a chair. And a sense of pity such as she had never before known, overflowed Tafra's heart.

"How I hate to be the one to tell you, child, but I will tell you everything once more."

"No—don't. Don't!" Charlotte hid her head in her arms and began to cry, very softly, as a deer cries when wounded, or a small animal when trapped.

A still greater sense of pity, tenderness, and love welled up in Tafra.

"We will never speak of it again, Charlotte. And I will let you be my very own little girl. Like my daughter—I always wanted a beautiful daughter. I will take Poulette's place in your heart," Tafra said, tapping her cane thinly on the floor, wanting to take Charlotte in her arms; not daring to be too kind, lest that be crueler.

The gentle, cordial tone of the woman seemed very far away and cold to Charlotte.

"You have your whole life before you," Tafra said. "You would have been worse off in New Orleans, now that your father is dead and no longer able to protect you from the world."

"My life before me!" Charlotte raised her tear-swollen, rebellious face and looked angrily at Tafra. "No! Everything is over for me. I can't suddenly be somebody else. I won't be a Negro. I won't. You can't make me, either."

"All over?" Tafra made a great effort and lifted herself to limp painfully over and pull Charlotte to her feet, taking the youthful but half-womanly body in her thin old arms, forcing the love and pity she was feeling to penetrate the grief she had caused.

Charlotte stood stiffly, keeping her face hidden

in her arms; her whole body racked with noiseless, convulsive sobs which choked her. *I wish I would choke to death,* she thought hopelessly; *then they would be sorry.*

Tafra put a hand under Charlotte's face and lifted it from her wet sleeves. She was amazed at the adult expression of bitterness in Charlotte's eyes.

"Leave me alone! What do I care for your lies? I know that the large old man stole me away. My father isn't dead. I never had a father. And I shall die unless you send me back to Poulette!" Charlotte said vehemently, wrenching herself from Tafra's arms with a vicious effort and sinking down again onto the chair.

"Charlotte, I wish for your good. Listen to me." There was a power about Tafra and for a moment the weeping stilled; the bronze head took on a vestige of its former proud carriage. "Sit there, if that is what you want to do. I won't touch you. But listen carefully to me. You do have your life before you and you must accept it. You must accept the fact that you are a Negro. You will be wasted if you don't."

At this Charlotte burst into fresh sobs with the despairing violence with which people bewail utter disaster. Tafra was about to speak again, but Charlotte cried out.

"Go away! Go away! You are all against me. Even the handsome one in the hall. Now he will hate and despise me as you do."

Tafra tried to admonish her, insisting that they would all love her and comfort her, if only Charlotte herself would try to control herself, to be calm.

Charlotte did not reply but again the sobs lessened. Finally they ceased and Charlotte sat on in the chair, with pale face and fixed wide-open eyes looking straight in front of her until a knock came at the door and a man's voice called.

"Mother!"

"Come in, Inigo."

Charlotte jumped from the chair and ran wildly over to a French door on the far side of the room.

"Come back to the fire, child," Tafra called as Inigo came in.

But Charlotte's frantic fingers had found the knob and she slipped out onto the upper balcony, closing the door behind her. If it had been a window she would have gone out of it as surely. She seemed not to notice the floor under her feet. It was like hanging in the air.

She looked down upon the seemingly limitless expanse of open wet fields, brown and desolate though newly furrowed, that spread out from the environs of the house. She contrasted it with the familiar view from the iron-grille balcony of the house in New Orleans. She had come to know that wide vista of the city in every detail, yet she had sensed that the life that went on under those well-known roofs and chimneys and steeples was of a complexity that eluded her understanding. On the city streets, aristocrats brushed elbows with near-savages, Creoles with Kentuckians, Catholics with devotees of Voodoo, modest ladies with painted women from certain unsavory quarters. How different was this view—a rhythmic unity of plowed ground, tender new rye, heavy borders of overhanging trees, silence and the singing sound of the tidal river flowing harmoniously into that silence. The uncluttered spaciousness, the freedom of this view suddenly seemed to hold out some distant hope. "Someday," the wind whispered, blowing rain into a fillet of diamond tears for Charlotte's hair. "Someday!"

She touched her skin and felt her lustrous hair that had a ripple in it. Surely these said she was white. Standing there on the balcony, worn-out with crying, she mused upon the problem of her identity, on the mother who was a name and a vision of her imagination and the father who survived in her memory as little more than a warm, tender voice and a figure moving through a few short scenes in recollection.

A flock of wild geese seeking the marsh's edge winged loudly overhead as two figures appeared around the side of the house. Charlotte stepped up to the rail and looked down on them. The first was a tiny old Negro woman with keen, black features outlined by a white turban mitered like a bishop's hat; the second was a young Negro man. For a moment she almost cried out to him—he looked so much like Potee, with his fine head and sensitive aquiline face; but as he walked forward she saw that he was very short and that though his shoulders were powerful and broad, his legs were so bent that they caused him to walk with a queer rocking gait. Withal he carried himself proudly and as the two passed in front of the house she called weakly down to them, "Good afternoon."

They looked up and the woman spoke. "Who is yunnuh?"

"I am Charlotte."

"Well, yunnuh is sho de whitest nigger chile Hagar ever seen."

How did the woman know? Charlotte shuddered back from the rail. Was she already changing color as she had feared? The other woman downstairs had known, too. She could feel it now.

Then the young man spoke and his voice was like music and the roll of his words was like the rhythmic cadences of the Song of Solomon.

"Yunnuh is lak de young spring moon up dere so high—lak de soft white feathers from de white goose breast. Dis Cuffee and he am glad yunnuh has come here."

The soothing, singing greeting of the black man comforted Charlotte. *Perhaps he will be my friend, like Potee was,* she thought. *Perhaps he will look after me.*

The door on the balcony opened. "Come back in where it is warm and dry, child. I have just told Mr. Inigo about you and he has fetched the baby for you to play with. He thought Nick might make you laugh. He is such a funny baby," Tafra said to her, and Charlotte dazedly followed her mistress into what would henceforth be her home.

Inigo peeped in, a little later. Charlotte had pulled a low chair close to the fire and was cradling his infant son in her slender arms, singing a small song to him. *What a damned shame about her,* he thought, *for she's going to grow into a beautiful woman.*

Chapter 5

Charlotte's heartbreaking arrival at Normandy was immediately overshadowed by the death of Nicholas himself. The uncomfortable cold developed into the grippe; the grippe became lobar pneumonia, and a week after his return from Louisiana, Nicholas was laid in a heavy iron coffin and borne by twelve powerful bucks to the Gaillard burying-ground on the oak-crowned hummock beyond the avenue.

Charlotte watched the confusion and grieving, feeling nothing herself, not caring what happened to these people to whom she now belonged as Fifi belonged to her. The afternoon of the funeral she heard the plantation bell tolling, but she made no move to leave her bedroom. She was not interested. She did not care.

She sat by the window uneasily watching the richly dressed men and women and children who streamed past to line themselves up for the procession. She was startled when Hercules came to summon her to march also, beside her mistress. She listened to the old man whose lips were puffed from much weeping, and looked at him coldly with dry, fixed eyes.

"What ail yunnuh?" the mourning Hercules asked, snuffling a little. "Yunnuh ain't been know um well enough to look dat sad—is yunnuh been hagrode?"

Charlotte's face took on a colder, malevolent expression and she did not answer.

"I says—is yunnuh been rode by uh hag? Yuh sho pears to been, wid dat snarled hair and dat dreened white face."

After a moment's silence Charlotte answered, "Yes, hag-ridden."

"Wal, hag-rid or no, yunnuh git up and come wid me. Effen Miss Tafra wants de people to see yunnuh, yunnuh gwine git seen."

Charlotte was agitated and unhappy, but she went with Hercules to the drawing-room, where two sturdy bucks were slipping a board under the fragile cane chair in which Tafra sat in frigid, controlled dignity. Tafra nodded at her and Charlotte followed close to the makeshift palanquin which took its place at the head of the long procession, trailing the iron box down the avenue.

Inigo and the blond woman and their son, Robert, walked behind Charlotte and Tafra. The blond woman cried noisily, in proper fashion. Charlotte shut her eyes so she would not look back at Inigo. She held onto a leg of the cane chair, letting it guide her, pretending that she was blind and deaf.

But she was amazed whenever she peeped through her lashes to see people staring at her rudely. And her ears burned at the rippling remarks: She really does look white! She would have fooled even me! What a strange thing for Nicholas to have done! Not so strange —circumstances, you know—Inigo and Emily—

She was even more bewildered and horrified by the hordes of Negro slaves who swarmed among the gentry like flies, screaming and beating their hands together, shouting,

"*Ahoooooo, ahooooo, yeddy ole Egyp' duh yowlin'*
Ahoooooo, ahooooo, yeddy ole Egyp' duh yowlin'
Ahoooooo, ahooooo, yeddy ole Egyp' duh yowlin'
Way down yonduh een dat lonesome grabeyaa'd.

"*Mmmmmm, mmmmmm, yeddy ole Egyp' duh yowlin'*

41

*Mmmmmm, mmmmmm, yeddy ole Egyp' duh
     yowlin'
Mmmmmm, mmmmmm, yeddy ole Egyp' duh
     yowlin'
Way down yonduh een dat lonesome grabeyaa'd."*

Charlotte looked from the black ones to the white
ones as a hunted animal looks at the approaching dogs
and hunters. Which of these were her people?

I will not *be a Negro like those savages,* she told
herself, holding harder onto the swaying chair; plod-
ding along in mournful time, like the others. *It is not
true that I have Negro blood.*

But it must be true. The house on Toulouse Street
was unnaturally isolated from everybody. *That must
have been the reason Poulette never let me make any
friends. Never let me go to the same park often enough
for people to remember me.*

Tafra spoke to her. "You look so pale, Charlotte.
Are you ill?"

"Yes, ill," Charlotte whispered. Then unable to
speak further without bursting into sobs, she made a
sign with her hands to Tafra to leave her alone.

Tafra patted the bright head at her knee, glaring
defiantly at the city and parish folk, Nicholas's friends,
who were exchanging hostile whispers about her unveiled face and dry eyes.

I am a pariah to these people, Tafra thought.
*As much so as poor little black-white Charlotte here.
It was only through Nicholas's fingers that we ever
touched hands.*

Her mother's death had loosed her from her background long ago. Augusta Gordon had died of cholera
when Tafra was nine. After his wife's death, John Gordon, a hawk-beaked aristocrat who had always dwelt
restlessly on his ancestral rice plantation, was unwilling
to remain on the miasmic acres, abounding in fevers.
He pulled some strings and secured a diplomatic ap-
pointment to the court of France. Gathering up his
trunks and his small girl child, he quitted his native
land without regret for a land where gay good health
and cosmopolitan society awaited him.

The alert French children had delighted the little, sharp-faced American girl, and one subtly lovely creature, Natalie, who oddly enough was of the essence of the strange Charlotte, had become Tafra's most devoted friend. Tafra soon spoke French smoothly. "We will share with each other our secrets," Natalie said. Tafra twirled happily on her thin, agile legs and set about having long talks with her father's important colleagues so that her secrets would be as fascinating to Natalie as Natalie's tales of counts and princesses and Madame La Guillotine were to her.

From Paris, John Gordon had served in Budapest and London and Moscow in successively important posts, and when Tafra was seventeen he had landed the plum of places—Vienna! Vienna! Where she had met Nicholas! The one love of her life, the one man of them all for her. From there she had come here to live with him. But the years she had spent enjoying the flavor of European capitals, sharpening her keen wits, as her father's hostess, with some of the most brilliant men in the world, had rendered her talk uncongenial to the Sendeniahs and the Bessy Grays and the Talullahs of the parish. Yet now that she was old and ill the remainder of her days would be spent here among these people who disapproved of her and her queer ideas, even at her husband's burial. She could feel them condemning her for not weeping loudly as that stupid Emily was doing. But she was determined to hide her sorrow from the curious; to keep it inside herself, as she had done her love for the large, wonderful man who now lay dead.

Chapter 6

The next evening, Tafra sent for Inigo to join her in the great drawing-room, though funeral guests still thronged the downstairs rooms, bringing condolence and advice to the new master of one of the most extensive cotton empires.

The huge crystal chandelier was bright with dozens of lighted candles which made shadows on the far side of the wall and, as he entered, Inigo lifted his left eyebrow at the forlorn little figure crouched there in a chair, holding the poodle on her lap.

"You look too sad," Tafra said to her son.

"I'm going to miss Pa so much." Tears rolled over Inigo's cheeks and he made no movement to brush them away.

"Come here." Tafra pulled him down and wiped the tears off with her sheer cambric handkerchief, sighing, "You are such a sentimental one, Inigo. Your feelings are too obvious. I am sad also, but no one has seen me weep a single tear."

A tight sob from Charlotte made them turn and look at her perched so miserably on the small gilt chair.

"Oh, please don't cry, Mr. Inigo," she wailed, hiding her face in the crook of her elbow, unmindful of the poodle's pink tongue desperately seeking to comfort her.

"You are too far from the fire," Inigo said. "Come

over here and let me look at you. I'm afraid I had forgotten that you had even come to Normandy."

Charlotte came, the dog trotting along beside her feet, and Inigo frowned at her rumpled frock and her hair rough and tumbling on her shoulders. Her shoe ribbons were untied and she looked unkempt and ill at ease.

"You have changed," he said unkindly. "You are not the same little girl who came in from the rain and told me how she loved to dance. Not the same little girl whose coat I unbuttoned because of the swollen buttons."

"Hush, Inigo."

"No, Mother—let her understand her position. The sooner she accepts it and gives in to the inevitable, the better for us all. My wife and Horst Adams are downstairs now telling everybody how I welcomed Charlotte here as though she were a princess. The whole Low Country is joking about how taken in I was."

Charlotte said nothing, and gave no sign of having heard Inigo, only looked queerly into his flushed face. Suddenly he smiled, reached over and playfully ruffled his hand across her unbrushed hair. "Little gay girl," he said softly, "can't you laugh a little?"

"Did you go for a walk this afternoon?" Tafra said, not liking the sight of the handsome brown hand ruffling Charlotte's hair so gently.

Charlotte kept her eyes on Inigo's face, thinking, *His hand feels good upon my head; it is big enough for my whole head to nestle in.* Saying, "Robert and the Singleton children chased Fifi to tie a brick onto his tail. Cuffee saw them and came and picked me up, though I am quite as tall as he, and took me and Fifi into his house. But not before I kicked the dark-haired boy and also scratched his arm and made it bleed."

Inigo and Tafra gasped. "I hope Mildred Singleton will not hear of it and come demanding punishment," they said.

"I like Cuffee. He talks like some of the old songs

Poulette sings to me. He says that someday he will find a way to get me free from belonging to anybody."

"Ha!" Inigo was unaccountably angry. He made a wry face, and pushed the poodle with his shiny shoe.

"Did you go to the Street as I suggested, and look for some girls your age to play with?" Tafra asked.

Charlotte began to breathe in an agitated manner. "I hated it! I hated it! I will never go there again. Cuffee says I don't have to and I won't. The girls sang ugly songs and lay down on the ground and made horrid gestures at me. I was glad I couldn't understand the things they said."

"What are you looking at?" Tafra tapped Inigo smartly on the arm with her restless cane.

"Her."

"Do you see anything different from what you saw when you came into this room?"

"No," said Inigo oddly. "I would like some coffee." Thinking, *I didn't realize Charlotte was so spirited, so impetuous.*

"Yes, so would I. Charlotte."

Charlotte came over to Tafra. "Mr. Inigo and I would like some coffee. Will you please go down to the kitchen? It's on the bottom floor. The stairway goes down from the back of the hall. Ask Sweet to fix us a tray and you can fetch it up to us."

"I can't carry a heavy tray. I'd drop it surely. Then Miss Emily would run from her drawing-room and scream at me. Oh, don't make me, Miss Tafra —please! please!"

"Tell Sweet just a little tray. Tell her to let you select the cups and that you want to bring it yourself."

Charlotte went out of the door slowly and sullenly.

"Gracious!" Inigo lifted a thick black brow. "She's really on the wrong foot. What's ailing her?"

"How would you feel if you had turned into a Negro all of a sudden?" Tafra asked him testily.

"I guess I wouldn't care about combing my hair or lacing my shoes, either. What in the world possessed Pa to buy her, anyway?"

46

"Don't you even suspect?" Tafra said under her breath. Aloud she said, "I wish I could free her. With her background she'll hate being a slave more than she minds being a Negro when she grows up."

"Did you ask Lawyer Ball this afternoon when he came about the will?"

"Yes and he gave me quite a stern lecture, repeating over and over how it is not only illegal but punishable with imprisonment to free a slave in the state of South Carolina. I don't want to go to jail."

"No—and neither do I. It's a good law though, Mother. It was the Free Negroes who instigated the Vesey Insurrection in 1822."

"Poor Denmark Vesey and Gullah Jack! Both hung high muttering Bantu curses and clutching charred crab claws. Twenty years ago—and not a Negro has been freed since! I'm glad Cuffee and Hercules were freed before that. Cuffee would never have survived the stigma of knowing he was the son of a Corramantee king and yet a slave."

"Cuffee is different. Everybody knows he's the best horse breeder in the state, and he never gets beyond himself."

"He would if he cared," Tafra said. "But he doesn't live in this world at all. Hagar has kept him pure African ever since Nicholas brought him here in his baby basket. Charlotte is just the opposite. She has no experience or conception of the Negro race; they're as foreign to her as the Chinese people would be to you if somebody suddenly set you down in Canton."

"I'm afraid it won't be much easier for her to fit into Normandy," Inigo said.

Tafra studied her son's face. "Your father had his ideas and plans for her, but his outlook was not yours. I'm fully aware of that. I shall take the responsibility of Charlotte. I can have a most interesting time keeping her from being wasted. I can help her gradually accept the fact that she is a Negro. You see yourself how impossible it would be to send her to live on the Street. She would either go mad or run away. I can train her so that when she is grown, she can face her

47

position as a Negro and not hate it so much as she does just now, while the shock is still so raw and new to her."

"Then I hope she'll prove helpful to you, Mother."

"People won't expect me to go out into society any more, now that I am a widow. Charlotte will help fill my days. She and I will live up here in a veritable ivory tower. I don't want to be in the way of you and Emily running Normandy. I want Normandy to be all yours and Emily's. I intend to hand the household keys over to Emily in the morning."

"Emily!" Inigo laughed sourly. "Charlotte could run the house better. You needn't make plans for Emily, for she has already decided to make the town house her official residence. She is taking Robert into Charleston and enrolling him in Carroll's Academy tomorrow."

"And baby Nick?" Tafra leaned forward as though she would devour both Emily and Inigo.

"He can dwell with you in your ivory tower. Emily says she's too delicate to have the burden of such a big, dark, ugly baby. She wants to leave him here."

"Has she ever unlocked her door to you since—" Tafra's curiosity made her grief-laden eyes suddenly bright and icy blue.

Inigo turned scarlet. Why would his mother harp on things that no lady was supposed to mention?

"Don't let's talk about my lawful wedded wife tonight. It suits me perfectly to leave her in her role of precious invalid; it keeps her out of my life."

"No! She can't be out of your life unless you get up the courage to brave a lawsuit." Tafra glanced hopefully at him, but he shook his head, so she continued spinning out her plan. "I had an idea that if I turned everything over to her and let her play the great lady she might gradually come to be a great lady and accept the duties that go with such a position—even the physical ones."

"Not Emily. She exists in her own selfish world, and that sarcastic Horst Adams encourages her in all her superficialities. They even make fun of the Code

48

Duello and all the Low Country privilege of being a gentleman."

Tafra was not interested in hearing her conventional son cant his dull feudal beliefs. On those beliefs she blamed his subservient acceptance of an impossible marriage through snobbish dread of scandal. She rubbed her hands wearily over the smooth ebony of the cane.

"Then I'll keep the keys, and I shall train Charlotte to manage the house and to keep your books and accounts straight, as I did for Nicholas. You're going to have a grand time running Normandy. Nicholas was smart to convert to cotton while the majority of the planters still clung to rice and indigo. You are well on the way to becoming one of the richest men in the United States. What have you decided to do about an overseer?"

"I have decided against hiring a white overseer. Big Jake and I can manage. Harry Singleton almost burst a blood vessel when I told him I could manage the place more efficiently by handling my Negroes personally."

"Harry is lazy, and Mildred is a fool."

"Pa always said he never saw an overseer who wasn't, at some time, cruel to the slaves. Handling my people is going to be one of the least of my worries."

"What are you going to do when the necessity for emancipation faces you?" Tafra's eyes blazed with excited interest. She dearly loved to get Inigo worked up.

"You're a trouble-thinker." Inigo stretched his powerful legs comfortably, determined *not* to let his mother force him into an argument. "Our Southern bubble is nowhere near ready to burst, our Negro substratum is the finest foundation for a state in the world."

"Humph." Tafra began tapping her cane on the floor. "You talk like a hotheaded gentleman of twenty-seven is supposed to talk. Don't you ever think for yourself? Your scalp is so full of Southern moonshine that you don't even see the big black cloud hovering. Substratum indeed! Loaded overhead you'll find it someday."

"Pa was a Union man, I know." Inigo smiled indulgently at his mother who was facing him like a hard icicle.

"Yes, your father believed we Southerners should act first and free the slaves gradually, so we'd never be forced to give up too much of our invested wealth at one time. One thing I believe hastened his death was his fury at John Calhoun because of the way he fought the railroad that would have linked the South with the free West."

"Pa was always furious with some orator."

"Yes, but Calhoun, with his wonderful power over words and his blazing hypnotic eyes, has made it almost impossible now to foresee any way to emancipate our slaves in an orderly fashion. Where would they go? How can white immigrants come into our state to balance our Negro laborers?"

"You can't honestly disapprove of slavery?" Inigo asked.

"Yes; I think, and Nicholas did, too, that it has been one of the main reasons Southern gentlemen use the word *honor* instead of the word *law*."

"Well, at least you must admit that though our group might split on local politics, when the honor and pride of the community is involved we are all on the same side."

Tafra smiled, and recited mockingly:

> *"We vex our own with word and tone,*
> *But love our own the best."*

"Well, you can't deny that our early training as rulers makes us brave men." Inigo was determined not to get serious, but Tafra kept the attack going.

"It's this institution of slavery that's so largely responsible for your acute sensitiveness to criticism, your feeling of personal injury whenever you're opposed, contradicted, or interfered with—and for all this exaggerated worry over your 'honorable obligations.' "

"Don't you approve of the Duello? I've heard it told that your father was a marked success in the field."

"No! Dueling is a literal sword of Damocles hanging over the head of the Southern gentleman."

"But if any gentleman fails in his inherent chivalry, the Code Duello most assuredly brings him to his right mind. Why should we bother with law? Honor is much cheaper."

Tafra sniffed impatiently, out of words.

"Men are supposed by nature to be the power, women the ornament." Inigo had to laugh at the look of ire in his mother's eyes.

"Well, I'll train Charlotte to be both."

Inigo yawned, hearing the departing carriages of the funeral guests with relief. He was tired of talking —even with his mother. She was too intense, too mathematical in her thinking.

"I'm going into town tomorrow. Can I do anything for you?"

"Nicholas left a silver cup to J. H. Holloway for the Brown Fellowship. Will you take it to him?" Inigo nodded sleepily. "And he was planning to geld the Edisto colt tomorrow. The almanac says the moon is right for the genitals. Geld him before you leave."

"I've decided not to geld Edisto. Cuffee was in about it this afternoon and I told him to turn the colt loose in the big pasture and let him grow as big and strong as possible. He's much too fine to give up for breeding purposes."

Tafra tapped her cane irritably. She hoped Inigo was not going to prove troublesome; Nicholas had been so easy to manage.

"But I insist on Nicholas's wishes being carried out. He said the colt is vicious and there's no point in taking any chances with a stallion which will probably prove too dangerous to cover."

Inigo reached over and stroked Tafra's wrist, stilling the restless tapping.

"I'm master now," he said gently. "I'm not going to geld Edisto. He's too male to spoil. Someday I'll buy a filly which will be as swift and powerful as he to stand to him and then Normandy will have the finest blood line in the country."

"Even Cuffee advises gelding him." Tafra was untrained in the art of losing an argument. Inigo flattened his lips stubbornly. "Someday you'll be sorry,"

Tafra said, determined at least to speak the last word.

Mother and son looked at each other with hostility and both welcomed the gentle knocking on the door. Charlotte, all smiles, walked proudly and lightly in with the coffee tray.

"Sweet let me use the best cups," she said, "and I could carry it—it wasn't even hard."

"Thank you, Charlotte. I love these cups. It always makes me happy to use them. Mr. Gaillard and I bought them in Dresden on our honeymoon. Go over there now and turn on the music box. It will make us all gay."

A fast Viennese tune tinkled out complete with bells and dancing figures. Charlotte clasped her hands in delight. The day was ending better than it had begun. With Inigo here it was like a family, almost.

"I am going to keep Charlotte close in my ivory tower with me," Tafra repeated, pouring thick golden cream into her cup. The cream was the color of Charlotte's throat where it disappeared into her pale green dress. "She and I can solve much for each other and I shall find her a fascinating experiment."

Inigo and Charlotte looked at each other and a smile slowly touched Charlotte's full lips. Inigo felt a pleasant stir in his heart and he said kindly, "Did you walk to the kitchen with those trailing ribbons? Come here and I'll show you how to tie your shoes—if a little girl tripped on her shoe ribbons she might fall all the way downstairs."

So, while he wound the black velvet closely around the delicate ankle, Tafra told him that she was planning to continue Charlotte's education.

"The child is practically ready for a university, and I shall find it most interesting to see if, as a human being, her Negro blood will make her any different as she matures from me or you—or Emily."

At the mention of Emily's name all three of them smiled together as though they shared a secret which bound them in a tight circle.

"Why do you want to make a bluestocking out of Charlotte?" Inigo asked, keeping his fingers closed around her tiny ankle. "Women don't need to be too educated."

"Don't you like me educated, or do you prefer minds of Emily's type?"

"Now, Mother—"

"I'm also planning to train Charlotte to understand the complete management of the plantation so that when I am gone you and Nick will have somebody you can depend on to help you."

"Would you like that, Charlotte?" He put down the shapely foot and Charlotte answered him breathlessly.

"Oh, yes, Mr. Inigo. And I will work so very hard. It will make me so happy for you to need me."

"Won't people disapprove if they know about your educating a Negro? It's against the law." Inigo's brow creased with worry.

"Oh pooh! Inigo, aren't you ever going to throw off your provincial turn of mind? I intend to show the Low Country ladies a new type of soul."

Inigo stirred his coffee uneasily and felt very lonely. His father had been such a bulwark between him and life. The hearty strength of him had been there to lean on when his days with Emily seemed to stretch out too tragically into a never-ending future of sterility.

"Why don't you try to woo Emily's attention away from Horst Adams?" Tafra, sensing his disapproval, was all at once purposefully tactless. He put down his cup and kissed her coldly.

"Good night, Charlotte," he said to the gray-eyed girl who smiled warmly as he left. Closing the door he heard Tafra say, "Run and rinse out this cup, Charlotte. There's enough coffee left for you to have a cup with me."

Inigo went slowly down the steps, thinking. He liked to be conventional, he wasn't like his mother, so secure within herself, so right that she could thumb her nose at society and take up the silly idea of educating a Negro slave to see if she would react like a white person! He almost snorted with disgust and angrily tore the pale-faced Charlotte out of his heart.

Nearing the bottom step, he noticed a thick cord stretched across it.

"Who the devil put this damned thing here?" he bellowed.

Robert stood out from the screen by the steps.

"It's to trip Charlotte when she comes back down. I've got to punish her for not letting me and Hal Singleton cut off her hair to make a wig for Nancy's doll. It's far too pretty a color for a nigger to have, anyway."

"Why, you whippersnapper! I'll thrash you within an inch of your life if you ever hurt one little finger of her hand. I'll—"

Emily and Horst Adams, hearing Robert cry out as Inigo smacked his face, came from the small drawing-room. Robert ran and clutched Emily around the waist, hiding his face in her dress. "He hit me," he howled. "Make him go away."

Horst Adams licked his lips delightedly. A scene. He'd lay his money on Emily. She always won.

"Up to your old tricks, Mr. Gaillard?" She never called him Inigo. Inigo tried to glare at her but the sight of her tight sneering mouth was too much for him. He walked out of the front door and slammed it hard behind him.

Emily and Horst exchanged glances. Then Emily pushed Robert roughly away. "Stop staining my new dress, you naughty boy. Go right away and tell Rena to put you to bed."

As they went back into the room Charlotte came downstairs with the tray. Horst Adams adjusted his glass and looked at her.

"And where did this strangeling drop from?"

"Old Mr. Gaillard brought her here from New Orleans just before he died. Nobody's paid any attention to her what with the funeral and all—for a maid, I suppose."

"So? Don't tell me, innocent one, you don't know why the elder Mr. Gaillard thought fit to bring such beauty into this staid old house where a frustrated man might look on her and be tortured as the old monk was with the vision of Thaïs?"

"No, Horst—I really hadn't given it a thought. Negroes don't interest me in the way they do these Gaillards."

"Then let the little joke play itself out. Far be it from me to snatch a juicy bone from under the poor dog's nose. Come here, wench," he ordered Charlotte.

She looked unbelieving at him. Then she clutched the tray and ran toward the dining-room, calling back over her shoulder, "No—No—I can't—not now."

As Inigo walked up and down the piazza in the starry night he heard his people singing. A great sense of contentment replaced the bad feelings of the past hour. His mother was wrong—there would be no necessity for emancipation. These people were far better off where he could look after them. They didn't need book learning. He looked after them when they were well and when they were sick and old. They didn't have to think—they weren't supposed to. They sang:

> "I am dreaming
>   On a pillar—pillar
> I am dreaming
>   On a pillar—pillar.
>
> "I am climbing
>   Jacob's ladder—ladder
> I am climbing
>   Jacob's ladder—ladder.
>
> "Every round goes
>   Higher—higher
> Every round goes
>   Higher—higher.
>
> "I'm a soldier
>   Of the Cross!"

Chapter 7

After seeing Charlotte, Horst Adams didn't linger talking with Emily. He complained of a headache and made his way to the tiny pink Greek temple which served as a guest house for bachelors visiting Normandy. God, that little Negro girl was really beautiful! What a time she was going to have if Emily took a notion to dig her claws into her. You could tell at a glance that the girl was sensitive.

Horst Adams was a disillusioned dilettante, viciously witty, with a keen nose for scandal and an infallible sense for spreading ugly tales where they would cause the most stir. He was the youngest son of Bishop Adams, who took great pains to explain to his parishioners that Horst had inherited all his traits of character from his mother's side of the family.

In appearance Horst resembled the Bishop, being erect and slender, with a beautiful head covered in soft, silky black hair, and such fine, slanting eyes that it was hard not to believe that a soul lurked within. Unfortunately, when Horst was young and tender he had indulged in a pagan affair with a gay, laughing brown girl for whose kisses he was quite willing (at that age) to brave the gossips. The girl's father discovered this distasteful romance and reported it to the Bishop, who immediately hustled Horst off to Oxford, where eventually and philosophically he renounced love, both in general and particular.

On his return to Charleston he attached himself

to no particular social group, being acutely conscious of their laughing whispers about his youthful misdoings; and devoted his brilliant mind to achieving a life of indolent ease at his father's expense. In one of his more bored intervals he took up with Emily Gaillard at a ball, entirely because he was a little bit weary, a little bit sad, and Inigo had looked so self-satisfied and honorably correct.

He and Emily had drifted out into the moonlit garden and her soft hair had blown like a mist in the wind.

"You look like a young witch with your ash-blond hair and white face. Are you as wicked as I am?" Looking down on her thin lips and her tiny, feral hands, holding a scented lace fan, he felt no desire to touch her at all.

"Aren't we awful to come out here by ourselves?" she had simpered, slipping cold, tight fingers into his hand.

Instant revulsion had seized him, disgust, dislike for the whole social order she represented as Inigo Gaillard's wife. Then, immediately, he had determined to use her stupidity, and before she knew it he was always around, pouring his vitriolic impressions into her transparent ears and applauding as they leaped spitefully from her cruel tongue.

Yet he didn't want Emily to hurt this little one. Suddenly he felt a wave of fear for the viciousness he had helped come to flower in Emily. Dear God. He hoped she would never let it loose on him!

Chapter 8

━━━━━━━━━━━━━━━━━━━━━━━━━━━━━━━━━━━

Charlotte slept very little that night. Repeatedly she asked herself the same question. *How can I be a Negro when I don't look or feel like a Negro?* But now she remembered more distinctly, from the days with Poulette, things that had seemed unimportant then.

"Poulette, who was my mother?"

"A beautiful woman with the skin of a peach and a tender heart; a woman with dove's eyes; a woman who could dance like the moonbeams themselves on a full summer's night."

"Poulette, who is my guardian?"

"A wild young white gentleman, but kind in his way, and very generous to take you into his home."

Always Poulette had named a "white gentleman" when speaking of her guardian who, she realized now, had been her father. She had often spoken of the color of gold in describing her mother. She had described her as beautiful and swift and sensitive.

I must have got my Negro blood from her. Else how could all this have happened to me?

But what can I do? I refuse to go on the Street any more. And I'm afraid of the white children who chased me. I'm going to be very lonely and sad for the rest of my life.

There's only Fifi and the funny little baby, Nick, whose mother doesn't love him. I'll be his mother. I'll ask Miss Tafra to let him sleep in my room with me. Then I'll be less lonely.

But what will I do when I'm grown? Who will I marry? She found no answer to these terrible questions.

Morning came with its usual bustle. First the guineas ran potracking shrilly past her window, then the big plantation bell tolled for the slaves to come to the cook pots for their morning meal. The sun struck through the white-and-gold canopy of her big bed. Hercules came bringing a tray with soft-boiled eggs and hominy and tea upon it. He fussed about where she was to eat. With the niggers in the servants' hall? With Miss Tafra in her drawing-room? He did think they ought to decide something. To affirm positively that she was black or white.

He was so querulous that Charlotte laughed with relief when she noticed the care with which he cracked the eggs and spooned them out for her.

"Will you comb my hair, also?" She smiled, suddenly in a better humor for the first time since she had come here.

"Comb dem hag stirrups? I tole Hagar yunnuh bin hag-rid, and hyar de evident. Gimme dat bresh. I ain't never seen sich heading hair in all my life. Des de same," his thick old fingers trembled on the coppery lengths of curl, "hit's de purtiest hair I ever had muh hands on."

Hercules brushed and combed and fussed some more while Charlotte ate her breakfast. Then he made her put on her shoes for him to tie; and he shut his eyes while she struggled into her best dress, so that he could button it for her.

When he was gone Charlotte tiptoed into the upstairs hall. Passing Inigo's door, she could hear voices inside. She listened shamelessly.

"There's just one more thing," Tafra was saying.

"Still confident that you can make black out of white?" Inigo made a hitting noise against his shaving-stand.

"I couldn't sleep last night. There a horrid suspicion in my mind that Nicholas did not sift the facts about Charlotte. That he might have been fooled about the child. I insist on being positive that she definitely has a strain of Negro blood before I shut her away from

59

the world with an old woman and an infant boy."

"What do you want me to do about it?"

"Take her to town with you today and have Ptolemy Ball question her further about her life on Toulouse Street. She can't do anything for herself at all. I'm going to have to cut the snarls out of her hair, and I know she's never buttoned a button before in her life. I watched her the day of the funeral and compared her color with Nancy Singleton's. Anybody would pick Nancy out as the African instead of Charlotte."

"Everybody knows the Singletons have Indian blood."

"Perhaps Charlotte is a Creole. Anyway I *must* be sure. That sly Frenchman, Vignie, must have poured double portions of brandy and fuddled poor Nicholas when he passed this child off onto him."

Charlotte crept closer to the door and pressed her ear against the keyhole. Ah, this was fascinating talk. She had liked Tafra from the first, even when Tafra had told the lies about her Negro blood. Now they were beginning to see! They would find out and send her back to sweet Poulette, who was probably crying her eyes out this very minute.

Inigo's deep voice came impatiently. "I'll be leaving as soon as I eat breakfast. Can she be ready to go with me? Of course, I want to do everything that is honorably possible for the child, but I think you're just stirring up false hopes for her."

"She's dressed now. Hercules took her breakfast a good while ago. I've had Cuffee send the new phaeton to the front instead of your horse. Emily and Robert have decided to go up to town by boat, so they won't be taking the trotters. You can make good time with them—Nicholas said they were the fastest we've ever bred. Oh—and Horst left an hour ago. He was determined to get away before Emily fastened her claws on him and made him spend all day in the boat looking after her and Robert. He came up to my room and amused me greatly with his description of Nanny Myers and Emily arguing last night about the proper method of raising boy children."

"You're quite a manager!" Inigo said, so crossly that Charlotte ran from the door and went to get her cloak.

She was waiting out in the hall, buttoned nicely, when Inigo and Tafra came out.

"Look at her!" Inigo's eyebrow tilted almost up to his hairline at the spectacle of glittering bronze hair, combed not into curls but spread like a living fiery shawl about her shoulders.

"Hercules combed it, but I buttoned the buttons!"

"Get your breakfast, Inigo," Tafra said sharply. "Charlotte, come into my room and I will put your hair neatly into a net."

"No," Inigo said, "I like it that way. Leave it loose."

"Absurd, absurd! Do you want her to ride down the Battery with her hair streaming like a savage? Ridiculous! Remember the cup; it's in the phaeton, wrapped in a flannel bag. Give J. H. my message about the pox."

When Charlotte was safely in the phaeton, a tiny black velvet Scotch cap placed at the proper angle on her close-bound hair, she was too excited to keep her feet still.

I'm dancing in time to my heart, she thought, patting her soft kid slippers rhythmically under the furry robe, as the messenger horses lifted their knees high and reached far out in their fast, ground-covering trot.

She chattered gaily to Inigo about Mardi Gras, about the French Market where they drank early coffee after mass in the Cathedral, about Potee and Poulette and the closed courtyard; she mimicked the candy man's call; she sang snatches of a hearty French song she'd heard. After a while, however, she stopped chattering and just enjoyed thinking about what a wonderful, wonderful man Inigo was. And so handsome to look at! If she were his wife she would never travel by boat when she could ride in a phaeton with her knees close to his under the rug. Ah, she had seen the cold, formal way the young master and Emily had with each other. She would never be cold if she should ever be lucky enough to marry such a husband!

But such thoughts as these were bad for her, for

61

they brought with them the fear that she was no longer, after all, the same Charlotte she had been in New Orleans, to whom all doors of romance and delight were built to swing wide at a touch. A Negro girl must never dream such dreams. She became very still and stiff and shyly stole a glance at Inigo.

He must have been thinking the same thoughts for his mouth had lost its good humor and his eyes had narrowed oddly.

They were self-conscious with one another. *He looks over-large and too white,* Charlotte thought. *Do I suddenly look smaller and darker to him, by our very thinking of this thing? Can it be that all our lovely good time is over? The horses are still trotting handsomely; how can this change have happened so quickly? One minute he was laughing at a story I was telling; the next he has clamped his lips together and his eyes are hard and black.*

Charlotte turned from Inigo and looked out over the forlorn winter landscape. It was such a flat, gray country. There were no hills or turnings anywhere; only rivers and fields, rivers and fields—

She clung to Inigo's hand while he led her into Lawyer Ball's office. And as she answered Ptolemy Ball's many sharp questions with a gentle, intelligent honesty, she surprised a proud appraisal of herself back in Inigo's eyes. That made it easier for her to hold her head at the proper angle.

"You seem older than twelve years," Lawyer Ball told her.

"That is because I have never played with children."

"Where did you go to church?"

"The Cathedral St. Louis."

"Where did you sit?"

"In my guardian's family pew."

"At table?"

"Alone, except the night each week the Abbé came for dinner."

"Never with your nurse?"

"Oh, no. You see, they were all Negroes in the house except—"

"Yes, yes, go on!" The lawyer's interest now was fully roused.

"You know it all," she told him wearily. "I was just a child who lived alone with the servants. I was well treated and very happy, though lonesome. I can't tell you any more because I do not know myself. I never thought much about it until I came here with Mr. Nicholas."

"I will have to go to New Orleans myself to learn the truth, Inigo." The lawyer sighed laboriously. He had a bad digestion and hemorrhoids; long coach trips always left him in a very weakened state. "It will be an expensive trip. I shall stay at the best places. Is it that important?"

Inigo saw with pity that Charlotte had begun to hope—to pray. Her cheeks had red spots and her lips were parted with her hasty breathing. Her little hands fluttered out to him, pleading with him that he help her —that he make her white again.

"Yes, Mr. Ball. It's that important. But she's a Negro—Hagar says so." Inigo spoke very quietly, not looking at Charlotte.

"Then you're a fool to waste your money and my stomach. Any court of law would take that old witch's word on the subject. Hagar couldn't be fooled."

"Go anyway. Mr. Jessup, my factor, will give you your necessaries." Inigo brushed a fly off his brown beaver with a soft yellow chamois glove. Taking Charlotte's hand in his, he led her back to the phaeton.

"Don't feel too badly." He tucked her in gently, but she drooped dully against the seat, lowering her eyelids that he might not see the bleak disappointment his last remark about Hagar's sure knowing had caused in her.

The phaeton bumped along over the cobblestone and brick streets. *I hate the sound of horses' hoofs,* Charlotte thought bitterly; *I always learn terrible things whenever I come near horses.* She sneezed twice, and then she sneezed three times. *It's these horses,* she told herself; *the smell of them is burning in my nostrils. I hate it here in this flat, sandy state. I want Poulette. I want to go home.*

She covered her ears so that she would not hear

the palmettos rasping or the gulls which flew screaming overhead into the salty sea breeze blowing in on the tide.

Inigo sought to lighten her mood. "This is the section of Charleston where the free Negroes live. It is most respectable."

Charlotte opened her eyes. They had left behind the delicate wrought-iron fences and immense gracious town houses, elegantly gardened. The houses here were built of brick or clapboard and were mostly rather small two-story affairs. Neat tidy matrons soberly clad in merino and linsey-woolsey walked along the streets and she noticed several churches and a big school, its yard filled with free Negro children.

"Is this right in the city?" She was curious despite her disillusionment.

"Yes, but remote from the body politic," Inigo answered as though she were a woman. The lot of the free Negro had always worried him and Nicholas. "Here the dark-skinned Ishmaels make a good living in all sorts of trades and crafts, in spite of discrimination shown them by their own people who are slaves as well as by the white people—not the gentry!—who compete with them as artisans, shopkeepers, jockeys, and apprentices."

"Are we going to see one of these people?"

"Yes, we're going to see J. H. Holloway."

Chapter 9

At that moment sixteen-year-old Leon Cavallo was in his grandfather's shop hard at work on a pair of thin leather reins. Leon was a boy hot and hasty, unsure of himself, impulsively bold but ashamed of his dusky face. His wavy black hair, as silky and soft as a young seal's, fell into his eyes as he rubbed oil into the fine English leather.

"Why won't you be vaccinated, Grandfather?"

"Why should I be vaccinated? I've never had the pox."

"That's why—so you won't have the pox. There are several cases down the street and a scratch with a needle won't do anything to you. All of us in my class at school went together up to Doctor Hugenin's and he vaccinated us in twenty minutes. See my scar—it's healing nicely."

"I'd rather have the pox than have something out of a cow put in my arm with a needle. Besides, it's a sin."

"Oh, Grandfather—not a sin! If vaccinating people is a sin there's no use for me to go away and study to be a doctor. If my own family won't take my medicine I don't stand a chance to make any money."

"Yes—a sin. If the good God wants J. H. Holloway to have the pox—who am I to dispute him? We've got along all right in this town for a long time and nobody has made me do anything I didn't want to do yet. I'm no slave. My body is mine—my arm is mine."

"You're just being stubborn. Please be vaccinated."

"That's not the point any more," the elderly coffee-colored man continued in his gentle unobtrusive voice. "I have also decided to refuse to pay the small fine which has been imposed on me for not being vaccinated, and shall probably have to go to jail."

Leon dropped the oily rag on the floor in consternation. He knew that it would be useless to argue further. He knew the implacable pride of free will and racial purity that dominated his grandfather, who seemed the mildest of men but who had cast his own daughter out of his house because she had presumed to mix his blood with an alien strain; who was so proud that the white citizens of the city granted him the dignified respect reserved for a priest of a dying cult; whose worship of his race was almost fanatical in its fervor.

J. H. Holloway's father and grandfather and great-grandfather had all been free men. They had accumulated considerable wealth that they had carefully kept and that now made J. H.'s life comfortable and pleasant. Among his own people he held the chief office in the "Brown" or "Century" Fellowship, a society founded in 1790 on the principles of charity, benevolence, and racial purity. He was an aristocrat and proud of his ancestors, whether they had pointed their dark toes in the quadrille or beaten their heels to a tom-tom.

So when Leon retrieved the rag all he said was, "Won't your going to jail hurt Grandmother and Aunt Julie?"

"Not particularly. They have the same values I do and they'd much rather see me exercise my rights as a free man than knuckle under to a law I heartily disapprove of. You'll have to run the shop and bring me work to do while I'm in jail, so the business can go on as usual until you leave for Scotland."

"But won't they beat you in jail, Grandfather?"

"You and Jonas can come along to court with me tomorrow to the hearing. You'll see how our family is regarded by the people who count in this town. I want you to come with me, for you are the last man in direct line in our family. I'm sorry that because of your mixed blood you can't bear our name, but"—he smiled with deep affection on the sensitive mulatto boy— "you can make Cavallo a good name. You're lucky— you don't have any apologies to make for others of that name. It's all yours—a clean piece of paper for you and your children to write on."

The bell at the front door tinkled violently and a loud voice called, "J. H.! Oh, J. H.!"

Leon followed his grandfather to the front of the shop. He gasped when he saw the girl and the man standing there hand in hand. This must be the girl the drums had told of when she came to the Low Country! This must be the little white girl who hadn't known she was a Negro slave. Oh, she was worse off than he was; much, much worse! He wanted to run up and snatch her hand out of the big gentleman's grasp. There was too much hurt around her mouth, too much sadness deep in her gray eyes. But being naturally shy around white people, he merely hung his head while his grandfather greeted the gentleman.

"You have my deepest sympathy, Mr. Inigo. You and I have both lost our best friend."

"Thank you, J. H." Tears gathered in Inigo's eyes. "I brought you a cup he left your Fellowship in his will."

J. H. bowed low as he reverently took the heavy tankard of chased silver.

Leon inched out from behind his grandfather and tried to smile at Charlotte.

"Hello," she said surprisingly. He was a Negro, but she felt that she wouldn't mind playing with him. Maybe he was the kind of person she'd have to marry. But she'd much rather marry Inigo.

"Don't tell me this is Sarah's son?" Inigo dropped Charlotte's hand.

J. H. nodded, looking sorrowfully at the youth who stood with all the grace of a forest panther, though civilized eyes slanted widely in his intelligent, high-browed face.

"He is the image of—"

"His name is Leon Cavallo," J. H. interrupted positively, "and his father is sending him to Edinburgh next month to study medicine. Doctor Hugenin has made all the necessary contacts. He went there himself, you know."

"I didn't think his father had that much gumption. Is my bridle ready?"

"Leon!" J. H. spoke more sharply than he intended. He had seen Leon staring at the girl. He knew all about this strangely appealing little person. All the Negroes—free and slave—had mourned over her, when the drums from Normandy tapped out her secret on the very first night she arrived. But she was a slave; she would never do for Leon. Leon was free. His children must be free. "Leon—did you finish rubbing Mr. Inigo's reins?"

"Yes, sir." Leon ran hastily to the rear. How dare that man know who he was? How dare his grandfather speak in such a tone to him in front of that pretty girl? His blood pounded heavily in his ears. He wanted to keep right on running. Right on out of this life where he had been born all twisted up. Away from luminous gray eyes and big noisy men who had authority over them.

"If you don't stop breaking bridles, Mr. Inigo, your fortune is going to belong to me."

Inigo glanced up at the framed statement hanging above the door: *Let your moderation be known to all men—in charges.*

J. H. went up to the frame and turned it over. Inigo read:

> *Know old Charleston? Hope you do.*
> *Born there? Don't say so! I was too.*
> *Born in a house with a shingle roof*
> *Standing still, if you must have proof,*
> *And has stood for a century.*

"Say, that's good, J. H.," Inigo approved, while the frame was turned back to its former message.

"Can't let many customers see it. It makes them uncomfortable. I don't know what's keeping Leon. He's been upset all day because I insist on going to jail."

Charlotte had watched the boy run to the back of the shop. What had ailed him? She would have played with him if he had asked her. He was much nicer than Robert. However, she didn't interrupt the two men who, oddly enough, were laughing about the jail sentence.

"I lose fifty dollars on you, J. H. Mother said she'd be willing to wager her music box that you wouldn't be vaccinated if you didn't want to."

"I can hear her saying— 'Let the old fool have the pox if his mind is set on it!' "

"That's exactly what she did say. I thought maybe you'd like to have me go along to court with you."

"Thank you, Mr. Inigo, but Leon and young Jonas Bethune will be with me. Young Jonas is going to Edinburgh along with Leon, to study law. The judge is

68

a friend of mine. He'll have to give me the minimum sentence, but the whole procedure will be dignified and genial. I want those boys to see how easy it is to get along even if they are Negroes, if they make themselves a place as I have done."

"Does he know that I'm his guardian, now that Pa has passed away?"

J. H. shook his head. "I'll tell him tomorrow. He knows his father is in town today because his boat fare and a lovely rug were delivered here a few minutes ago. The man has been most generous to the boy, but neither he nor I want Leon ever to discover who he is. Leon's so torn up by knowing his father's white that I'm having a hard time trying to weld him to my heritage—so that when emancipation comes he can help his less fortunate brown brothers get started."

"I can help, too." Charlotte spoke for the first time. "Can't I, Mr. Inigo?"

"Yes, little girl!" J. H. smiled at Charlotte sympathetically. "You can help, too."

"Does Leon want to be white very badly?" she asked the kind brown man.

Inigo reached for her hand. "We'd better go now. Say 'good afternoon' to Mr. Holloway."

"Good afternoon, Mr. Holloway." She curtsied low with trained grace.

"Good-by child; and I'll answer your question. Yes—he wants to be white more than anything else in the whole world. But when he grows up and becomes a fine doctor, he won't care at all."

"Oh yes, he will care; and so will I! I'll hate it worse and worse!"

Charlotte stood facing the two men, her fingers squeezing hard on Inigo's big thumb, her full mouth pouting with repressed emotion. She stamped angrily on the floor. Inigo and J. H. laughed. This made her even more furious.

"She's a termagant all right." Inigo chuckled. She snatched her hand free and marched, head high, in front of him, out of the shop onto the street, winking back the tears that smarted in her eyes.

Chapter 10

Leon ran up one street and down another. Evening found him standing behind one of the fat, round columns of the Hibernian Hall. He searched the faces of the elegantly caped and hatted gentlemen who were each, for a moment, spotted by the lanterns as they made their way convivially into the hall to doze through a string ensemble. The ladies' faces did not interest him, and the gaudy feathers and flowers that decorated their evening hairdos were mere shadows to his eyes.

He was trying desperately to find a white face with the same high-bridged nose as his own, the same slanting black eyes, the same chiseled brow and fine long fingers as the brown ones that he was now clutching together in excitement.

Perhaps it will be tonight that I'll recognize him, he thought nervously; *what will I do if I'm sure that it's he? Will I stand before him and say— See, here is your Son? Shall I thank him for the clothes and gifts he leaves at Grandfather's for me? Shall I tell him when I'm sailing? Or shall I strike him in the face for deserting Mother—for causing her own father to turn her into the street—for having lit the crimson lamp that's in her window tonight? For forcing me night after night to sneak into the little room kept for me at Grandfather's because fancy carriages come to her house by dark and leave before dawn?*

"Hey, Leon!" A boy's black face—blacker than

the night itself—protruded into the panel of light cast by the lamps of the hall.

"What are you doing here, Jonas? Why must you always follow me?" Leon whispered as he stepped away from the light close to his playmate.

"Come away—there's been trouble near here and the streets are swarming with patrolers and police. Let's get back home where we won't run any risk of getting mixed up in anything."

Leon looked longingly at the white faces moving in their glittering procession toward light and sweet music. Even though he was a free Negro, his first lesson of all had been, "Keep out of white folks' way. Be unobtrusive and you will be safe. Merge with your background. Retreat!"

"What kind of trouble?" he asked, catching step with Jonas and cutting back through an alley.

"I don't know. Your grandfather sent me. How did he know where you'd be?"

He always knows, Leon thought bitterly. "Let's go by Mother's house." The two boys scurried lightly through familiar streets and alleys, but when they came to the house where his mother lived he looked up to see if the lamp was lit. Yes—it was. Its red trail spilled evil onto the upstairs balcony.

Jonas tried to put his thin arm around Leon's shoulders, but with a cry Leon wrenched himself free and ran swiftly to Beaufain Street to his grandfather's two-story brick house. He slipped in quietly so that no one would hear him. His own small room was cold, but clean and comfortable. He undressed in the chilly dark and slipped between the icy homespun sheets, grateful that not even a small candle was aflame to flicker on the sickness that knotted his heart and stomach.

Chapter 11

Ptolemy Ball returned from his trip to New Orleans in such a rancid humor that he minced no words in describing the folly of his useless voyage. He had been so mercilessly pounded on the hard coach seat as the horses trotted roughly along the rutted roads leading to Louisiana and back again, that he was ready to risk a duel with Inigo by presuming to criticize that honorable gentleman's sanity in pursuing this matter.

Vignie was perfectly and justly within his rights, Charlotte being the daughter of a slave of his, by name Céleste. Auguste Le Jeune had died a wealthy man. His blood cousins, though distant, now lived in luxury in the house on Toulouse Street. Shisi Zana and Potee had vanished. The Abbé was very shocked and sad; he would have bought Charlotte for the Church, if he had been informed. There, no danger of dark children would have arisen, and she could have lived out her life in quietness and peace.

Then there was Poulette—fat Poulette! Her he had seen, also. She was the one bright spot of humor in all the whole drab business. She occupied a stall in the French Market, selling hats of such atrocity, such crude and ugly obscenity, that people flocked to buy, hiding them away for carnival.

"Charlotte Le Jeune?" Poulette's tawny face had sullened at first, then her round cheeks had quivered with her strained laugh. "You speak of black moonbeams, *Maître*," she had said. "You speak of things that never happened; that never could have happened."

BOOK TWO

The Master
1848

Chapter 12

The six years that followed 1842 in South Carolina were years of destiny. In these years the Utopian life of the Southern planter, which had seemed an eternal verity, began to tarnish and tremble. The Negro substratum was no longer the firm foundation of a society, but a seething maelstrom, churned this way and that by opposing forces. There were the vindictive attacks of Abolitionists in the North. Southern cotton planters were agitating for the reopening of the slave trade. The fanatical hymn of murder was sung hysterically by John Brown in Kansas. Fear grew among the white minority population of the South in the face of the rising tide of bitter emotion against slavery, of hatred fierce enough to fetch the ghosts of Denmark Vesey and Gullah Jack from their shallow graves. Brilliant orators like Calhoun and Webster selfishly sowed discord and disharmony of mind and heart among lesser souls in both sections of the country. The wrath felt by conservative Northerners mounted at the spectacle of runaway slaves, many of them almost white of skin, being captured and returned to slavery. In the South resentment hardened against the interference which could mean political vassalage and economic disaster, for slaves constituted more than half of the region's invested wealth. From plantation to lonely plantation, the restless throbbing of slave drums bore the dream of emancipation that would soon come galloping to them on the thundering hoofs of hate.

Though thousands of thinking people in the South were sick to death of slavery and its whole stench, and earnestly trying to work out a practical scheme for gradual, orderly emancipation, a greater number, incited to rage and fear, passed more stringent laws against Negroes than had ever existed in the state before.

The ban against freeing any slave, for any reason, was continued in South Carolina, and enforced relentlessly; travel with slaves, excepting body servants, was prohibited; teaching a slave to read or write became a crime, punishable by flogging, plus a prison sentence; free Negroes were no longer accorded justice in the courts; curfews tolled loudly at nine for free and slaves alike. Stones were thrown in J. H. Holloway's window and ugly words were written upon walls. Jonas Bethune, armed with a law degree from Edinburgh University, was forbidden to appear in a court which would have welcomed him a short decade before.

The times were bad. Suspicion walked the land. Brother began to look askance at brother and wise ones foresaw and mourned the settlement which could only be upon a field of blood.

But of this tension in the Carolinas, this fiery political picture so far removed from his former placid existence, Leon Cavallo, M.D., was unaware as he leaned on the rail of the plunging ship and watched the phosphorescent seas fling themselves wildly upward in the moonlight. A May night but a grim one, with seas breaking over the weather bulwarks to flood the main deck with charging tons of water as the gale blew itself out, herding the seas and the torn wrack of clouds under the glory of the moon. The fury of the sight suited Leon's raging mood. For the first time in six years he had been made conscious of his dusky cheeks, had fumbled aimlessly with his finely trained surgeon's hands.

That morning a woman had been confined, thanks to the heavy weather, before her time, and he had been hastily summoned to her cabin. One glance at her blue mouth and cyanosed color told him that things were going badly. He quickly took off his coat and began to roll up his sleeves.

"Fetch me some boiling water at once. I'll make a brief examination and then I'll hurry to my cabin and bring my instruments." The captain gratefully rushed off; then the door opened and the husband came in.

"What are you doing in my wife's room?" the cultured, Bostonian voice demanded.

"I am the doctor. I am preparing to deliver the baby."

"God—do you think I'd let you lay your black hand on my wife?" A disgusting oath came from the man's mouth. Leon thought he was going to vomit, but the nausea passed and in a moment he controlled himself enough to say, "Her death and your baby's death be on your own head, sir. I have just completed my training in the most modern hospital in Scotland and I must ask you to leave your personal feelings aside at a time like this."

The captain and two maids came running into the room sloshing scalding water from big iron pots.

"Get this nigger out of here," the husband shouted. From the bed came a low moaning that rose in a shrieking crescendo of animal pain and anguish.

Leon picked up his coat as the captain tried to reason with the man, but there was no reason in him. The captain took off his coat and rolled up his sleeves. Leon—the most skilled surgeon in his class at Edinburgh—stood on deck, hearing the screams come closer and closer together until finally they ceased. No tiny wailing followed the silence. He knew she had died even before the captain, a Britisher, found him and told him.

"For God's sake, why don't you go back to Europe?" he asked Leon.

"I promised my grandfather to come home."

"How can you bear it?"

"They aren't all as bad as that man back there, and my people need me quite as much as any other people need a doctor."

"I wouldn't have expected a Yankee to feel like

that," the shipmaster said, "not as ready as they are to go to war and die to free the slaves."

"They don't like Negroes in the North as much as they do in the South." Leon's tone was very dull and flat. "Haven't you ever read Carlyle's summing up of the situation?"

The captain shook his head.

"The North says to the Negro, 'God damn you! —and be free.' The South says to the Negro, 'God bless you!—and be a slave.' "

"Have a drink with me," the captain urged uncomfortably. He had seen many people die before. This young woman and her baby had been killed by prejudice. He took no blame to himself; he had done all that he knew to do, and he had got a doctor for her. He hoped the young man from Massachusetts roasted in hell for all the lifetimes to come.

"No, thank you, Captain, I'm going to turn in. We ought to sight land tomorrow, oughtn't we?"

The captain bade him good night and made his weary way below.

A blast of wind reached down and whisked Leon's cap into the sea. His silky hair blew wildly and for a little while longer he stood there staring at the lonely expanse of the night, his heart choked at the tragedy below decks that had served only to make him the more conscious of his own deeply rooted sense of race.

He had of late spent most of his time wondering just how he was going to fit in with his people back in Charleston. Now with this ugly incident such a storm arose in him that he clenched his fists and groaned, pacing restlessly back and forth across the poop. He seemed to see his mother, her glittering eyes burning, with bare brown shoulders and a languid, lustful look on her face; and then immediately he saw beside her the handsome faceless one, the insolent, hard and mocking one who was responsible for her and for himself.

Someday I will kill him. The day that I recognize him, I will kill him, he told himself. *He is to blame for all the divided, warring loyalty that upsets my soul.*

78

And he vividly recalled that moment in his grandfather's shop when he had seen Charlotte holding Inigo's huge hand, and knew that she was one even more unequally divided than himself.

That afternoon he had run from the sight of her, but he had stopped at the side of the building to watch her go away. He had seen that she was crying when she started to enter the phaeton. One of the horses had stamped a steel-shod hoof against the cobblestones and she had jumped back against Inigo, sneezing. Inigo had laughed and picking her up had hoisted her, high in the air, safely into the seat. Then, jumping in over the wheels, beside her, he had carefully tucked the robe over her knees and she had looked up into the virile, handsome face, her own lighting up even with the tears still wet upon it.

As he had done so many times during the years away from home, and particularly since Jonas had contracted tuberculosis in the Scotch climate and returned to Charleston, he conjured up Charlotte's face and held it before his soul as though his soul were a reflector holding the luminous quality of her eyes, the warm ivory of her coloring, the lush scarlet of her lips, the poignancy of her smile. Should he seek her out when he landed? Was she still Inigo Gaillard's slave?

He felt the blood rush to his heart and he beat the smooth rail with his clenched hands. He was suffering physically at that moment; there was a weight on his chest and he could not breathe. He knew that he must learn not to suffer so deeply, either when he was cried out against because he was a Negro, or when he saw Charlotte's eyes glow for another than himself. But what he wanted to do was some terrible thing. Something like tearing off a piece of the rail and rushing down below and beating the husband until he was dead as his wife and child. He felt a momentary delight in thinking how good it would feel to hurt somebody instead of help them.

Then, sighing, he reached up and smoothed his soft, wind-whipped hair. *I have too much of Grandfather Holloway's good, quiet blood,* he thought, *ever to do anything unconventional. At least, I have had six good, quiet years to grow up in, six years of respect and good fellowship.*

Chapter 13

~~~~~~

Six-year-old Nick Gaillard found Charlotte sitting on the steps on the river side of the house, eating a June peach, leaning over so that the dripping juice would not stain the thin yellow lawn dress that fell gracefully over her slim, curving thighs. There was a basket of the small pink and white fruit beside her and when she had finished eating she wiped her lips with a wisp of a cambric handkerchief. There was no way for Nick to slip up and scare her without being seen, so he came and sat down on the grass by her feet.

Nick was like Inigo, big and dark, his cheeks richly colored like a true Breton. He had not yet grown up to his joints and his knees and arms were always in his way. But someday he promised to be as huge as Gaillard men were meant to be.

"I've been looking for you everywhere," he complained, measuring her tiny ankle with two grubby hands.

"I was on my way to the house with these peaches; then I'm going into the swamp by the tea house on the river to gather some wild woods lilies and bay blossoms. I heard the Dwarf Rumpelstiltskin out there last week. Come with me and see if we can find him."

"I can't; Cuffee is going to tell me a story about Platt Eye and the Ghost Dog finding a treasure. Cuffee and Pa were gone five whole months and I'm tired of just hearing fairy stories. You never tell me bloody stories like Cuffee does. Whiskers, but I'm glad he's back. Even gladder than that Pa is home. 'Course, if Ma and Robert weren't here, Pa would be nicer. You come with me to the stables; Cuffee would be glad for you to hear, too."

"No; I wouldn't risk a sneezing spell for anything this afternoon."

"Why?"

Why? Confess to yourself, Charlotte; confess that it is because Inigo came home yesterday, and, while he rode in to Charleston this morning, he will ride back this afternoon. And, though he has not paid you any attention since the day Lawyer Ball brought the fatal proof of your Negro blood six years ago, someday he will notice you again. It might even be this afternoon! Is that why you put on your new dress and brushed your hair two hundred strokes? Is that why you don't want to be red-eyed and streamy-nosed from sneezing?

She remembered the time the sneezing had come on her the worst of all. She was fourteen and taking Fifi for a walk. A brown rabbit had hopped from under a camellia bush and Fifi had chased it, deliriously yapping in his high shrill way, through the shrubbery, across the lawn, over to the field where Edisto was grazing. The rabbit had sprinted under the fence with Fifi close behind, still with his screaky barking. Edisto had answered the bark with a neigh which had ended in a cruel quavering sound as he thundered toward the dog and before her very eyes savaged the little creature into a bundle of dirty lifeless fur. She had tried to call Fifi—to warn him. But the minute she had heard the horse's neigh she began to sneeze. Even Cuffee had been afraid to go in while the stallion murdered darling Fifi, the last link with her father. Cuffee had gently led her to the house, and she had continued to sneeze until Tafra sent for Dr. Hugenin, who came and held handkerchiefs soaked in chloroform under her nose.

"You don't sneeze nearly as much as you used to around the horses," Nick said, picking up an end of her trailing black velvet ribbon sash, and winding it around his sweaty neck. "You didn't sneeze a single time in the carriage yesterday."

"You and your Gran and I were too happy. I didn't even feel a tickle of a sneeze. I loved driving down the sandy beach along the ocean. I loved getting barefoot and wading in the foam while you rolled over and over in the waves."

"Pooh, that couldn't keep you from sneezing. Cuffee says it ain't horses, anyway. It's 'cause you don't have a crab claw like you're supposed to have."

"Oh, Nicky, Nicky, I don't need a crab claw. The good Virgin looks after me better than a bit of dead fish shell can."

"Cuffee says you need it, and so does Hagar."

"When did Hagar say that I needed a crab claw?"

"This morning. She said you had just enough Negro blood to need it to protect you from white man's magic."

Charlotte tried not to blush at Nick's mention of her blood, but she could feel her face throb crimson.

"Will I have white magic when I'm a man?" Nick did not notice her agitation.

"Yes; you have it now," Charlotte whispered. Her throat had tightened with unhappiness; she could not trust herself to speak aloud.

"Does Pa?"

This time she could only nod her head.

"Maybe Hagar thinks you need a crab claw to protect you from Pa. Ha! ha! That's funny. Pa wouldn't do anything to you. He might whip me or Robert, but not you."

"No, not me. He doesn't even know that I exist."

Nick looked at her curiously. She was acting very odd. He didn't like her much this afternoon. He scrambled up and took her hand, pulling her to her feet.

"Come and listen to Cuffee's story. It will be full of blood, and shivery."

"Maybe—after I get the lilies. But I don't like scary stories."

"Can I have some of these peaches?"

"Take them all. You and Cuffee eat them. I'll

pick some more for the epergne in the drawing-room tomorrow morning."

Nick ran off swinging the basket. But Charlotte stood for a long time at the foot of the steps looking down over the wide terraces that led to the swamp by the sweep of river. On her left was a serpentine walk a thousand feet long, bordered with flaming nasturtiums and low roses and phlox, behind which grew a shrubbery background of figs and pomegranates, sweet tea olive, fringe trees, holly, and camellias. Beyond this dark-green wooded screen was a boxwood maze which led to an artificial mound crowned with forest trees and ferns, as high as the second story of the house, which afforded a panoramic view of the river and the cotton fields. On the left of the boxwood maze was the bowling-green, sunk a little below the level of the rest of the garden with a walk-around edged with catalpa trees.

It is all so quiet and empty, Charlotte thought. *My life here these past six years has been like a life spent in a nunnery, minus the spirituality. For though Miss Tafra has taught me much, religion is not one of her main interests.*

Today I keep wondering, where am I going? Will the rest of my life be spent in this cultivated garden, watching the bowlers laughing, I hidden in a thick tree? Or will it be like walking through the maze? Walking—walking—walking alone, coming out at the same place where I went in? Or will it be like standing on the mound looking out for miles and seeing all the possibilities that lie along the horizon?

And while I don't believe in luck, seeing Inigo again today has broken the pattern of these past six years, and many things seem possible that yesterday looked very dull and lonely. I am glad to be getting something back that has been missing inside me for a long time. I even feel like twirling in a dance, the way I used to for Poulette in our courtyard. I must really be getting to be like myself again. I will pick both my arms full of sweet flowers and mass them everywhere so that the whole drawing-room will be fragrant and full of beauty.

Chapter 14

All this time Tafra rocked on the front upper balcony watching the afternoon shadows lengthen from the massive oaks across the sandy road. She loved this hour of the day always and now she watched it, feeling summer warm within her bones, as though she were a very part of the slow shadow that comes with the sinking sun. The oak trunks below her were hard and permanent.

She could not keep from thinking of the next generation. So she thought, *I have a malignant disease and soon I will follow Nicholas to the burying-ground beyond these very trees. It is imperative that I seek to insure the future of this Normandy, which has become my world. My own years are as nothing to these trees. When this house, in which I have dwelt and worshiped, is three hundred years old, these trees will still be standing here. A Gaillard might still be living in this house, to guard these trees as jealously as Nicholas and I together did. We put our hearts into our life here, in this place which was handed down to us and which I desire to hand down to Inigo and Inigo's son (but Nick, not Robert) and to his son's son. And in the face of Inigo's tragic marriage, I must take steps to be very sure that the acorns that fall under the Gaillard family tree will be as pure in strain as those oak seedlings blowing in the summer breeze.*

If only Inigo would brave a divorce! There are

plenty of fine girls who would jump at the chance to be the second Mrs. Gaillard.

Inigo came thundering up the avenue, waving his gauntlet as he galloped toward the stables, calling, "I'll be out and chat with you when I get bathed. I've got a lot of good news to tell you."

She nodded and rocked on, wondering, *What do I really think of Inigo? I heard him prowl last night under these very trees like a restless stallion, after watching Charlotte (who thank God is unmindful of her peculiar splendor) check in the Negro women from the fields.*

I know he is a thoroughbred and brave, a true Carolinian of his era, the epitome of chivalry, holding true to his faith in his own kind, his God, his politics. But unfortunately, he stuffs his mind with Walter Scott and poohs at the vitriol thrown by American writers like Emerson and Longfellow into the very face of this portion of the land, where knighthood is still in flower.

I also know he isn't the man his father was. Nicholas never would have kept cold Emily; he needed a woman as much as he needed sleep. And in the bed he wanted it, his own bed—in his own home. Nicholas would have stood like an oak in any court, and the devil take his honor. Inigo expends himself in synthetic excitement with his swift running horses, drinking brandy to lull his body's crying, shutting his eyes to the solution Nicholas bought for him. Not that I'd let him touch her for the world. His mere looking at her last evening has worried me enough already.

Tafra looked at the watch pinned on her breast and thought, *I wonder what really goes on behind Charlotte's spiritual face? If I must face the problem of deciding what to do with her, I would like to know just how she feels about herself. Whether she has completely absorbed the fact that she has Negro blood— whether she will be willing to go and live among them on the Street. Could she stand it? And if she couldn't, would she be wasted as a person?*

Suppose I am wrong and Inigo was not thinking of her when he was walking unhappily last night in

*the moonlight. Suppose he is not as restless as I fear
he is? Then things can go along as they stand now. And
I can live out my life in peace of mind and soul. But
after I am gone what will happen to Charlotte?*

*Will she fall in love and want to marry? How odd
I never thought of that before. But gracious God—
there is no one for her to fall in love with!*

The door from the drawing-room made a whispering sound and Hercules came onto the balcony, in-
terrupting her reverie.

"Sweet say will she fix Marse Inigo some rum
punch or some blackberry shrub when he get bathe?
Hit's powerful hot—I think de rum punch."

"Rum punch, then, and ask her to send me some
peach sherbet. Isn't it nice and quiet this afternoon?
Where's Nick?"

"Lyin' out in a manger listening to Cuffee talk
'bout Platt Eye. But, Miss Tafra, I gots to ask yunnuh
a favor."

"What is it, Hercules?" He had been Nicholas's
friend—she would do anything for him. He and Cuffee
were her favorite people on the whole plantation. She
was always happy that they had been freed before the
terrible law of 1822 had prohibited the freeing of any
Negro.

"De kitchen am in a uproar. Murriah down dere
crying 'caze Miss Emily th'owed out de flour fuh de
drudging of de rice birds fuh Mass Inigo' supper. Murriah done skunt um 'caze he specially ast fuh dem
roast wid a pastry crush an' Miss Emily say he ain't
gwine git um."

"Humph! I'm not dead yet! Here's tke key to the
little pantry. Measure Murriah all the flour she needs."

"An'," Hercules was having a fine time, "Miss
Emily done wrop up de grapevine silber teapot an' de
fiddle-thread teaspoons to carry up to Newport nex'
week we'n she tek Mist' Robert up dere wid dem common Yankees."

"Where is Miss Emily now?" Tafra was furious.

"Visiting wid Mist' Robert to Heronfield'."

"Then I'll have the teapot put back tonight."

"An'," now it was coming, all the other had been

86

merely preliminary, "Mass Inigo ain't sleep a wink las' night. Cuffee say he ain't sleep none fuh a long time."

Tafra wanted to tap Hercules with her cane, but instead she struck it on the balcony rail.

"You old rascal—why didn't you tell me sooner?"

He grinned broadly. His talk was taking root. If anybody could make Miss Emily behave, old Miss could. She could do anything. She'd even ruled Mass Nicholas, and Mass Nicholas had been one man of a man.

"Yunnuh ain't been ready to listen to nobody no sooner. I'll hurry down and git de rum punch. Mass Inigo am on he way up here now."

Inigo's black curls were damp and they clustered thickly about his temples. His eyes shone and a vibrancy emanated from him that at once made Tafra feel many years younger and set at naught all the coldly reasoned facts that had been buzzing around in her head about this beautiful man-child of hers.

"Isn't it nice that Emily is not here?" she asked wickedly.

"It's nice to have you all to myself."

"You and Cuffee have certainly been bringing honors to our stable lately. Was Cuffee pleased at winning the Stake in Philadelphia with Edisto?"

"He was like a wild man. He's certainly justified Pa's faith in him. Pa knew what he was doing when he trained him to run the Normandy stable, but the way he takes on over his horses is ridiculous. I've tried to make him work up some interest in a woman and diversify his attentions, but not even Finger Ring's snake dance moves him. Sometimes I think he's a little bit crazy—he lives in a world of complete make-believe. He's a king and the horses are his subjects."

"I want him to fall in love with Charlotte." A scheme suddenly popped into Tafra's head.

"What a revolting idea, if she's anything like she was as a child! I've meant to ask you for a long time —how *has* your experiment with the poor girl turned out?"

"Poor girl nothing!" Tafra's eyes flashed. "She's got twice as much education as any girl in the Low

Country. She could run Normandy today quite efficiently without you or me here."

Inigo guffawed loudly. His mother was a rare one with her peppery nature and her odd humor! Taking Charlotte to New York and Boston and White Sulphur, before the laws clamped down; having her sit by her side at the Dock Street Theatre instead of in the wings with the other ladies' attendants, letting her stand by her chair at the concerts in St. Andrew's Hall, dressing her in silk and lace! And now she talked as though a Negro girl could wear the shoes of the mistress of Normandy.

"Laugh—laugh." Tafra was piqued. "Someday you will be glad she knows and, heaven help her, she needs a field for her tremendous ability."

"I stopped by J. H. Holloway's when I was in town this morning, and his grandson is back from Scotland. He has grown into a fine-looking chap. I asked him to come and set Jupiter's leg tomorrow. Why don't you let Charlotte go back with him for a visit with J.H.? Charlotte can't continue to be your toy forever. And while I've watched you enjoy your ivory tower existence—has she? I'll have to ask her. You know, I don't believe I've talked with her in over two years."

Tafra shook her head. "No need for you to talk with her. Charlotte can't be spared during cotton chopping. Too many slaves are working beyond their task and she has to keep their time. Were the Hamptons in Maryland and Philadelphia?"

"Yes, they were running Fanny. They are planning to stay East until after New Year's. Wade doesn't want to. He's crazy to go back West before them. He says their Mississippi plantation is a marvelous piece of property." Inigo's eyes took on a wistful quality.

"Why don't you ride West with them when they go next winter?"

Tafra's voice held the thrill of new horizons.

"Oh, things are too prosperous here. Cotton went up five points today and from the looks of things I'll make more money this year than all of us can spend. Still—lately I have been dreaming over and over about a big river, and the sound of its flowing makes me feel that if I could get in it, I'd just float wonderfully along, without making any effort to swim."

"Don't you ever get in it?"

"No. Once I let go and jumped, but instead of landing in the water, I kept on swinging in the air— back and forth, back and forth!"

"It might be one of those dreams that is going to happen to you someday." Tafra realized the sadness and frustration that caused her son to dream thus—and she again became heavy with the dull ache that engulfed her when she allowed herself to contemplate his life with Emily.

"No—I'll never get in the river," he answered, and his usually overloud voice was soft.

Hercules came quietly out with a silver tray. The tall pitcher of rum punch was frosted and damp mint bristled from its mouth. He set the tray on a table and with great ceremony unwrapped a frosted silver goblet from its linen napkin and filled it, placing the bunch of mint in the top.

"Dis will ease your heart and mind." He bowed ceremoniously as he handed it to his master. Then he uncovered a silver bowl and ladled out a mound of peach sherbet in a deep Limoges saucer.

"And dis will cool your parched tongue," he said to Tafra.

She knew he could not have overheard. The sherbet would have melted if he had stood even five minutes in the heat. He was warning her to be careful in talking to Inigo. She searched his bland brown face, but not by a flicker did he betray himself. Yet as he went quietly away through her drawing-room she heard him chuckling softly to himself.

The two looked down from where they sat on acres of rank, green, bushy cotton. Field hands dotted the green carpet, chopping under Big Jake's supervision as he rode up and down the rows on Prince, resplendent in his bright-blue overseer's coat and hat. The gaudy reds and purples and yellows of the slaves' clothes and turbans swayed like full-blown tropical flowers in the hot, late afternoon sun, and their work song kept the hoes rising and falling as one.

89

"What you gwine to do fo' June month?
                    Jerusalem, Jerusalem.
Pull off yo' coat and go to work
                    Jerusalem, Jerusalem.
Jerusalem in de mornin'
                    Jerusalem, Jerusalem.
You mus' pray hard
                    June a hard month.
June a month a choppin'
                    Jerusalem, Jerusalem.
What you do fo' June month?
                    Jerusalem, Jerusalem.
You pull off yo' coat and go to work
                    Jerusalem, Jerusalem.

The somnolent, too sweet smells of summer and the lazy hum of bees, drunk in the honeysuckle vine that climbed up the pillars, relaxed Inigo and he looked almost boyish and full of an unusual contentment.

Suddenly the door from the drawing-room opened and Charlotte came out. Her cheeks were the color of deep moss roses and her arms were full of wild lilies and fragrant swamp bay blossoms of a pearly whiteness. She smiled slowly and her mouth held all the rich, sweet provocativeness of woman unawakened. Inigo put down the goblet of punch and stared as though he had never seen her before. He reached out his strong brown hand saying, "A flower for me, Charlotte?"

"Of course, Mr. Inigo," she answered in her throaty lovely voice, handing him a satiny bloom, redolent of the dark secret swamps and full of cool perfume.

Their eyes met and held and the salt river in the distance made a rushing sound as the tide began to flow into it. The bees hummed louder and the bay and the honeysuckle were overpowering in their sweetness.

Tafra saw Inigo's quick fascination. She saw the conventional young businessman, a starveling at the altar of love which he was so richly endowed by nature to have made into a shrine of joy and beauty. She saw Charlotte, as innocent as a girl reared in a convent, a novice with prayer beads still warm from childhood devotions, become aware of Inigo's passion.

She saw her precious experiment, which she had

started to show people that Charlotte was every bit as white one minute as she had been the minute before, boomerang with a shattering force back onto her own house.

"Shall I put these in water for you?" Charlotte asked, her eyes full on Inigo, and Tafra shuddered at Inigo's hungry expression, watching the swing of Charlotte's round girlish hips as she walked back into the drawing-room.

Inigo lifted his goblet for a moment toward the door through which she had passed. He raised it high and then, holding it to his lips, drained the whole contents at one gulp. He reached for the pitcher and splashed more punch into it.

"Your experiment really worked," he told his mother.

Chapter 15

That night Charlotte was too excited to sleep. Inigo's face, as he had looked at her when she came onto the balcony, was of such dream essence that she could not tell whether she was sleeping or waking; whether it was her heart jumping in wild anticipation or whether it was she, Charlotte, skipping like some druidical spirit around an altar of fire.

Once near midnight she heard a night bird startled in its singing, and going to her window, which overlooked the formal garden, she saw Inigo, illuminated by the late moon, limned in heroic proportions against the flowering olives, his face whiter than the flowers.

She knelt down watching until he suddenly looked away from her windows toward his mother's and raised a clenched fist in the air.

And when he came into the house he walked up the stairs with reckless, noisy abandon.

Later, just before the dawn came, she rose once more to quiet Nick crying in nightmare that Cuffee's Platt Eye was by his bed watching him. When she took the little boy into her bed he lay comforted in her arms, and she thought with a thrill, *He is really mine and Inigo's child!*

Tafra, too, spent a sleepless night and was unable to get up the next morning, but her instincts were sharp. She sensed Charlotte's restlessness and carefully kept her busy in the bedroom on one pretext and another until they heard Inigo calling for Hero. But after Inigo had gone to the city Charlotte settled back into her accustomed quiet gentle way, and Tafra thought perhaps she had been imagining it all and that Charlotte was really unaware of Inigo's aroused interest. So in the afternoon, burdened with pain, she slept.

Charlotte sat in the drawing-room to be near if her mistress should wake and need anything. The house was very still. Robert had gone courting Nancy Singleton. Nick was again ensconced in the stable, open-mouthed with fascination at Cuffee's marvelous tales of primitive beliefs and magic; and Emily, locked in her room, querulously sorted clothes for Rena to begin the packing of trunks, boxes, and bags that must accompany her to Newport.

Only one person came to the drawing-room. Hercules announced the arrival of the young Negro doctor from Charleston to set Jupiter's leg.

"Come long wid me and meet um. He a nice boy."

"I've met him. But I don't want to talk with anybody this afternoon."

"Ki, Charlotte—hit's time fuh yunnuh to quit being wase up here in dis big lonely room. Come meet de doctor."

"No; Hagar is in the sick house."

Shaking his head, Hercules left her alone and for a

minute she was sorry that she hadn't gone to see what Leon Cavallo looked like, grown up. But her throat was too tight from whispering another name over and over to herself and saying, *He did* look *at me again, and he will again and again and again. I know it; all of me knows it.*

And when she heard him call for Quash to take his horse, when he ran boldly up the curving stairs and burst into the room, she was standing by the open window waiting for him, looking like a part of the golden sunset, a dream full of the past day's loveliness and foretelling the darkness of tragedy.

"Where's my mother?"

"She is asleep."

"Then I will give you a present I bought for you in town today. I saw it in a jeweler's window and it was meant to be worn by someone with your skin." He threw open a velvet box which he had almost crushed in his hand, and a topaz necklace set in intricate filigree gold gleamed like flame in its satin depths.

"Oh, lovely—lovely!" she cried, quickening with eager animation as she had so often done when she was an excitable child. "Can you fasten the catch? Oh! I'm so glad the neck of this dress is low!" Inigo fastened the catch with trembling clumsy hands. Then he laughed at the way she whirled delightedly around to show him his gift before running over to look at herself in the mirror. And the face which looked back at her was a face that Poulette had once seen—the face of one born to rush headlong, with outstretched arms, not reckoning the consequences, into the embrace of the one lover out of all the world who could set her golden candle aburn.

Then Charlotte saw, in the mirror, the pupils of her eyes dilate with passionate anticipation as Inigo came up behind her and buried his fingers in her hair —pushing it back from her neck. But after that there was no such thing as sight; only sensation, happiness flowing into every cell of her body from his full mouth pressed hungrily, greedily on hers. When he loosed her a little she buried her face in his chest and heard him murmur as his arms bruised her with their

93

strength, "I will be so tender with you, little Charlotte—I hope I will not hurt you." She was too moved to speak, so she lifted her face willingly, as he cupped her heart-shaped chin in his hand, and gave him her mouth and they clung to each other, voluptuously possessed of love of one another.

Suddenly a third face showed itself in the mirror, breaking the enchantment, extinguishing the moment.

"Take that necklace off!" Tafra beat her cane harshly on the floor, tormented and harrowed, as Charlotte and Inigo stood for a moment, heart to heart, looking at Tafra as though she were some repellent stranger whom they had never known. Then Inigo loosed his arms and fumbled awkwardly with the tiny gold catch of the necklace. But Charlotte snatched the necklace off, breaking the slender chain in half, and dropping it on the floor, rushed from the room.

Down the curving stairs she ran, down the piazza steps she fled, from the ecstasy of Inigo. All the way to the garden she held in her heart the knowledge that he had kissed her—that he was back there in the house. And what that look in his eyes meant—oh yes—she knew! She came to a pomegranate tree whose branches wept like green rain to the ground and she hid herself there.

The scarlet fruit hung within easy reach, the leaves folded her in. Faint color washed fitfully across her cheeks; her eyes roamed restlessly through the garden but found no solace though the warm boxwood smelled sweet, almost as sweet as the passion that still held her. Oh, this was a wonderful thing to happen to her. This was the way she had imagined love would be. She had been thrilled by the wondrous feel of him, intoxicated by his hard splendor, and she wanted to be all white just once more! Please God—just once more!

The years spent with Tafra during which she was supposed to have effortlessly and painlessly absorbed the fact that she was a Negro had not been enough, for now all she could think of was the desire to turn back in her journey—to be Inigo's sweetheart—to be as white as he had thought her when he had knelt down to her on the day she had come here.

She began to pray in a small moaning voice. And as she did so another terrible thought struck her— *Holy Mary, Mother of God, he is already married! I had forgotten—I have sinned to desire another woman's husband. The Abbé would be displeased with me— Forgive me—*

As she crouched there in sorrow, brooding on her inexplicable problem, she became aware of a shadow on her green curtain. A brown hand parted the leafy veil and a bright-skinned man with large wondering eyes stared in at her in puzzled admiration.

Half hidden by the screen of pomegranate leaves, catching the glow of the fruit, her beauty startled Leon, it was so much more vivid than he remembered, and for a moment he silently drank in her loveliness as he leaned through the branches.

Charlotte recognized him at once and turned her back hoping that he had forgotten her and would go away.

But he had waited and dreamed of her too long. He, too, was lonely.

"Aren't you Charlotte?" he asked softly. "Hagar told me to see you before I left. Come—let's walk down to the river."

His voice was pleasing and being too overwrought to trust herself to speak, she put out her hand and he took it, pulling her out from the protection of the tree.

In the still flaring sunset he noticed the tremor of her chin, the state of excitement she was in. Something had upset her terribly and she was far too docile, with those fiery cheeks, as he led her into the coolness of a little swamp by the river's edge.

Here it was damp and dim and the heat of Inigo's kissess eased as Leon, trying to avert her near-hysteria, told her how different the ferns in the Low Country were from those in Scotland. He picked handfuls of the delicate green fronds and explained how they uncurled from ugly brown balls into graceful green-skirted dancers circling in the wind.

Trying to divert her he showed her a patch of jack-in-the-pulpits and dug up a matted clump of pitcher plants, pointing out the odd red roots. Finally, seeing her becoming weary and wretched as her distraction wore off, he broke a curving branch of sweet bay blossom and handed it to her, saying simply, "These flowers are like you, Charlotte. The blooms are cool and white but the roots must go far down into good black mud or the tree will have no blooming." His nostrils began to quiver and his fine slanting eyes to burn with the wonder and appeal of Charlotte.

Charlotte clutched the flowers tight, shielding herself, and the satiny petals became brown and bruised even while a sweeter fragrance spilled from them.

He wants to kiss me, too, she thought miserably; *but I won't let him. I'll scratch his face if he comes close at all.*

"You must have been hurt very much by someone to have run from the house like you did," Leon said, wanting yet not daring to take her in his arms.

"Let's go back." Charlotte was in no mood to discuss herself or to accept sympathy. She needed to be alone to think this thing through. To understand the Tafra who had condemned her—the Inigo who had desired her. And thank goodness Leon *didn't* want to kiss her.

"Perhaps I am too dark-skinned for you?" Leon's sensitive feelings were hurt at her unfriendliness.

This caught her attention and for the first time since Inigo had come in to her, her everyday mind began to function and she could think with some degree of normalcy.

"Oh, no—no!" she told him. "It was Miss Tafra who upset me. I haven't meant to be rude to you. I like you very much. I would enjoy having you for a friend. I don't have any friends and I'm afraid I've been very lonely. More so than I realized."

Why should his skin matter? His clean bright skin? What gain would she have from her magnolia cheeks? He was free—a doctor; she was but a slave who loved her master. Leon would despise her if he knew, not look at her with his very soul in his eyes.

96

She gave him her hand and they walked slowly back to the house talking about Jupiter's leg and would he come back to tend it? And if he did she would come out and help him.

Back at the house Inigo was having a poor time of it.

"Sit down, Inigo."

Inigo angrily stooped and picked up the broken chain, stuffing it into his pocket. Then taking up the heavy poker, he gave the unlit logs such a jab that they fell clattering down and rolled out onto the marble hearth.

"If you're quite through—I'd like for you to sit in that chair and talk to me."

He sat heavily in the chair. His face was red and his mouth ugly. Tafra knew she had him at a disadvantage as long as he remained sitting; he hadn't been born to sit still and he could think better moving about. But now he was so incoherent with bewilderment and distress at his mother's finding him kissing Charlotte that once seated he was grateful for the support of the chair. Sweat was pouring down his back and he could feel his knees actually shaking.

"Aren't you ashamed of yourself?"

"For God's sake, Mother, don't talk to me like I was sixteen! After all, you've had precious little to criticize in me since Pa died. You know I've honestly tried to take his place here."

Tafra waved her cane contemptuously. When she was angry sentiment only made her angrier.

"Charlotte is only eighteen."

"Oh, Mother, she's a woman—besides—"

"Besides she is not a woman. She is much less mature than she looks. You have probably frightened her half to death." Tafra's blue eyes flashed cold fire. Her fury mounted as she talked—the more so since she knew in her secret heart that she herself was not guiltless in this thing. "No Gaillard has ever mixed his blood with a Negro's yet, and you won't be the one to start."

"Haven't you spent the past six years telling me

not to think of Charlotte as a Negro? Well—I've obeyed you. I don't."

His knees had stopped shaking. He got up and walked over to the window. Looking out, he saw Leon Cavallo crossing the lawn with his gracefully erect stride.

"I suppose you still think as you said yesterday that a pure African like Cuffee would suit her—now that you're done with shaping her mind and heart into a white mold."

Tafra stiffened. "He'd be better to her than you would."

Inigo buried his face in his hands. How could his mother say such things? He remembered the rich sweetness of Charlotte as she pressed herself willingly against him—he felt again on his mouth the pointed flame of her full red lips.

"Cuffee is a much gentler, tenderer man than you are," Tafra went on cruelly. "Have you ever seen more sensitive hands on any living person?"

Inigo remembered a day when he was about twelve. He had set a squirrel trap in the woods and when he went to see if there was anything in it, he heard someone crying and hid behind a bush to see who it was.

Cuffee was kneeling on the ground springing the crude trap. And he oh, so softly took out the trembling creature and cradled it against his shirt crooning to it through his sobs in his funny Bantu way. *Whiskers,* Inigo had thought, *crying over a squirrel! A*nd he had been fascinated to see Cuffee put the tiny blood-soaked leg in his mouth and suck it to soothe the pain.

Why wouldn't his mother hush?

"To him she would be like some captured wild white bird. What would she be to you? A slave—the mother of the Negro children you would endow Normandy with."

Tafra had hit the bull's-eye. Inigo lifted his face and looked bitterly out at the oaks that had been planted to do honor to the Gaillard name. He clenched his fist and brought it down so hard on a small mahogany table that a crystal epergne of peaches crashed

98

to the floor and spilled the juicy fruit all over the rug.

Tafra pressed her advantage.

"Your duty is to make Emily be a proper wife to you. Suppose something should happen to Robert and Nick—who would inherit Normandy? If you died Emily would inherit it and then she would marry Horst Adams, and how he would love to be the master here! You are a tremendously rich man, Inigo. You need more sons than Robert and Nick to carry on at Normandy."

To Inigo the mention of Emily's name while his heart still rejoiced in the reality of Charlotte was a sacrilege. He laughed sourly.

"Emily hates me! She'd never have me—she won't even have Horst. She's had any number of opportunities but she won't even give me the satisfaction of being jealous."

"Try her. It's been over six years for her, too. And," again the cold sparks flew between mother and son, "you are not going to have Charlotte!"

He abruptly left the room. He had heard enough. But Tafra was not done with him yet.

"Send one of the boys in to clean up these peaches you knocked over."

"Brayboy," Inigo yelled. "Damn you—come up here and clean up the mess in the drawing-room. And light all the candles in the house. It's darker than hell in this hall."

The golden sunset was gone. The gold of Charlotte had turned to brass.

The hot candlelight that began to twinkle in the sconces as Brayboy and three other young Negroes rushed about with burning pine torches, chased away any ghosts that might have lingered from the afternoon.

As Charlotte and Leon returned from the river they saw the whole house ablaze with light. *Like my heart,* Charlotte thought, as she went through the kitchen and got a glass of lemon and hot water to take upstairs for Tafra to have after her dinner.

She came in to Tafra with a strange exultant smile

lifting the corners of her mouth. *She cannot throw off the spell of Inigo's kisses,* Tafra thought; but she said kindly, "You must not take Mr. Inigo seriously, child. He is headstrong and reckless but I am sure that he meant you no harm."

Charlotte raised her fine dark brows. *My heart is beating too loud to listen to you,* she wanted to say *—this love of mine is like some glad surprise. I am no longer your child Charlotte. I am ready for love—I want it. When he kissed me I felt all the fires in the world become one fire—and it was mine, all mine. Don't talk, Miss Tafra—don't talk! I am awake now. I don't like your ivory tower.*

But Tafra intended to finish this affair up.

"Where have you been so long?"

"Talking with Doctor Cavallo about Jupiter."

"You know it can't be Mr. Inigo for you, Charlotte."

"I know he is married. And you know that I am a Catholic."

"I am sad for you tonight. You and I have lived such a sheltered life together that I have come to love you like a daughter. I want good things for you to wipe out the bad things that have happened through no fault of your own. Your life would be easier if only you were less lovely. Come—sit here on the floor close to me."

Charlotte obediently sat down on a Persian rug. But she didn't answer Tafra, she was too full of new happiness. Inigo's boot struck the bottom step of the stair with a kicking sound. She buried her head back against Tafra's skirt. *Maybe he is coming in here,* she thought—*oh! I hope so.*

"Inigo is so medieval," Tafra went on as the heavy boots ascended the long steps slowly. "He would treat you with greater cruelty in direct proportion as he found that he loved you. You are so exactly the opposite of his wife that he would come to cherish you to the point of madness because his shame at loving one of the Negro race would intensify as he discovered the woman you really are. I can't let that suffering come to you or to him. You have had advantages be-

100

yond any Negro that I know of, and when freedom comes for the slaves you must be ready for power. You must shape your life with that in view, and be ready to grasp it when it comes your way. You must be willing to join your race and like it. Today has certainly made that clear to me."

Charlotte sat up straight, angry and frightened. She had listened to Tafra with mounting horror, letting it seep into her brain and heart what Tafra was telling her, that only because she was a Negro was it wrong to love Inigo; not that it was a sin to love a married man. Oh, this was terrible! She had worshiped Tafra like one of the very Saints in the Prayer Book but now, watching the cane tapping nervously on the floor, she understood with a clarity that was part of her intense nature, that Tafra was a woman who would sacrifice anything or anybody on the altar of her relentless will. And Charlotte realized how alone in the world she was. She had no Negro friends and no white friends.

A wild laugh broke from her as she heard Inigo stop at Emily's bedroom door. She felt Tafra stiffen and reached up automatically to catch the old hand that was seeking hers, and a shred of their former intimacy came from their shared helplessness as Inigo began knocking on the locked oak door. Tafra sadly stroked the shining bronze head at her knee, knowing how much more generous Charlotte would have been to Inigo than the fair woman in the west room. She looked into the night beyond the open window to avoid the clear spiritual face that accused her in the candlelight, and each woman felt that the hammer in her chest must surely beat her life away.

But louder than the thumping of their hearts was the beating, louder now, of Inigo's fists on Emily's door.

"Let me in!" he shouted. "Let me in!"

Emily's laughter could be heard mockingly as sinew and muscle exhausted themselves in a losing battle with the heavy, paneled door.

"No," Emily answered, her mouth close to the

shaking wood, secure in the knowledge that the Gaillard doors could withstand many Inigos.

"Turn this key or I'll force the lock."

"Try! I dare you."

But oak and iron are stronger than bone and as he battered himself against the door, Emily's shrill laughter taunted him, humiliated him.

"I could kill you!" Inigo gave a last mighty kick which almost brought victory, but suddenly he came aware of the house servants gathered in a terrified knot at the foot of the stairs, of Robert's sick white face wanting, yet not daring, to attack him, of Nick bugeyed with curiosity balanced on Cuffee's shoulder, of the open door to the drawing-room, of Cuffee's tears.

He ran to the top of the stairs.

"Get!" he roared to the black faces—and his sons' faces—which vanished like dust as he grasped the rail and ran stumblingly down into the hall and out to the stables.

Pushing Quash aside, he threw a halter on old Finnie and galloped off bareback through the soughing pine forest to the dunes and into the roaring surf that broke on the beach. Finnie loved the ocean and he swam far out beyond the breakers. The warm salt water washed and cleansed the sweat from Inigo's body and the vast loneliness of the night sky was as deep as his wounded soul, the great booming of the waves muffled the thunder of his heartbeats. What in the world was going to happen to him? He had to have a woman but who—Emily by force—or Charlotte in sin?

Back at Normandy, Cuffee stood outside of Inigo's window singing low:

"John saw duh numbuh, brand een duh forehead
John saw duh numbuh, brand een duh forehead
John saw duh numbuh, brand een duh forehead
Comin' up, comin' up, comin' up.

"He feel de sinning, brand een duh forehead
He feel de sinning, brand een duh forehead
He feel de sinning, brand een duh forehead
Comin' up, comin' up, comin' up."

Chapter 16

━━━━━━━━━━━━━━━━━━━━━━━━━━━━━━━━━━━━━━

Early one morning, two weeks later, Tafra came to Charlotte's room and stood leaning on her cane in the doorway, wearing her most enigmatic expression. She was starkly white under her white lace cap and beneath her patrician manner and charm lay something sinister, as though she held in her hand, all the time, the solution to the fog of misunderstanding which lay heavy between her and Charlotte and Inigo.

Charlotte shivered unhappily in spite of the July heat.

"Will you do me a favor?" Tafra asked, noting the hollow eyes circled with bluish shadows and the pathetic droop of the full mouth.

"Of course, Miss Tafra."

"Doctor Cavallo is in the sick house to vaccinate the buck Negroes. Hercules says he is having trouble. I can't manage the stairs today. Will you go?"

"In this dress?" Charlotte had put on her thinnest white muslin against the heat and had tied a scarlet sash about her waist.

"Take off the sash. The white dress will do nicely."

Charlotte went reluctantly toward the Street. Cuffee was standing outside the house and Charlotte, uneasy at the ungodly racket rocking the building, stopped to speak to him.

"Yunnuh am still lak a blowed feather," he told her, admiring the soft clinging white stuff of her dress. "Where yunnuh been hiding dese las' two weeks?

103

Hagar and Hercules been wondering whut been wrong. De big house ain't never been so still befo'.''

Charlotte was surprised that these people were interested in her. She had hardly spoken a dozen words to Hagar in all the years she had lived here.

"It has been quiet since Miss Emily and Robert went away. What's wrong in there? Miss Tafra sent me to help.''

Cuffee chuckled. "Mass Inigo in dere. He wants to lay de bull-whup on dem mens but he promise he Pa never to even have a whup at Normandy. Hit's a riot, fuh true.''

Leaving him cackling with laughter at Inigo's plight she ran up the brick steps. He was in there! He needed her. That was all she wanted to know.

Once inside she almost fainted. The stench was acrid and nauseating from the massed bodies sweating in the summer heat and giving off additional odor from fear and hysteria.

The room was packed with milling, moaning men crouching and writhing like dervishes, paying no heed to Inigo bawling and threatening them, hearing only Hagar's high shrilling, "De arms rot off. De flesh stink.''

"Oh Jesus—dat's de truf,'' the black men wailed.

"Hol' rattlesnake fang to yo' arm—hit specify less dan dat silber needle.''

"Hell—hell—and damn!'' shouted Inigo. "Big Jake, can't you throttle that banshee?''

But Big Jake hung his head and hid in the corner thumping his flat heels in protest.

"He gwine hack off yo' arm an' de blood gwine spout sukka whale.''

Charlotte looked wildly for the doctor and she spotted Leon, his face wrinkled disgustedly, standing helplessly by a table in the center of the room holding a syringe in one hand and a towel in the other.

Tafra had sent her here to prove something. To see what she would do confronted with these wild Negroes. Charlotte didn't like this at all but she was determined not to be afraid. She was angry; she was angrier by the breath.

Suddenly her bell-like voice rang out and her light

eyes sparkled. Cuffee had laughed. These people must be harmless. She'd try Hagar's tactics.

Pushing her way through the wet, unwashed bodies, she talked and called to them, "Hagar is wrong. There is no evil in the doctor's needle. There is power in his needle."

Inigo looked at her and his eyes went sick and queer seeing her hypnotizing the slaves with her electric eyes and her ringing speech. But when she pulled up her sleeve and held up the live satin of her arm, he had had enough and rushed out.

"Watch," Charlotte told the people. "Fasten your eyes on my arm—watch!" *Run away from me,* she told Inigo silently, *leave me here with these savages who you all say are my people.*

"Charlotte! Thank God!" Leon smiled and firmly grasped her arm.

A gasp choked every throat in the room as the needle broke the shining skin and a multitudinous sigh of relief followed as she again held her arm high—still attached to her body—no blood spouting.

"See—it's nothing at all. I'll give a quarter to each and every one that lets Doctor Cavallo scratch his arm and I'll give you your tin cup full of rum, too."

Big Jake came first and after him they all came—even old Hagar, rolling up her black calico sleeve and sticking out her skinny black arm to be filled with the same power that the white nigger girl had gotten.

Tafra was waiting for Charlotte when she came back upstairs.

"They'll be the heroes of the Street," she said pleasantly, "and they'll have a Voodoo ceremony tonight and howl and caper as though they were the bravest souls in the jungle."

"I gave them some money," Charlotte said tiredly, wanting to escape the ice-blue eyes and hide herself again in her room.

"That was clever of you. Hercules watched through a window and he says you were wonderful. I had him put your desk out in the front yard so the people can look at you."

Charlotte, let down after her exhilaration, did not

ponder on Tafra's actions but went obediently and sat at the desk fixed for her near the avenue.

Soon pickaninnies and small boys began peeping at her from behind bushes; growing girls wiggled past, ducking their heads and covering their faces timidly with their hands; old women—gaunt ones and fat ones —wished her a dignified "Howdy, Miss," carrying their chopping hoes as easily as white women carried their silk and lace parasols; old men scraped their feet and pulled their forelocks humbly.

It was all very mystifying and she was glad when they went back to their tasks and left her in peace with Inigo's fertilizer account.

Leon had watched all this show with concern. Somebody was making use of Charlotte. It was bad for a high-strung girl to be placed in such a position of authority as Charlotte had been this morning. She pretended to be calm and self-controlled but he had seen the trembling of her lips, the pulsing of the artery in her throat.

He watched her write in the huge ledger in front of her. The July sunlight reflected fire in her bronze-tinged hair. *She has a lot of red in her hair,* he thought, *where the sun picks it out. How alive it looks and how gracefully she has wound the knot above the nape of her neck. What would it be like to loosen the hair and bury one's face in the glossy length of it?*

He saw the fringe of black lashes brushing her skin which glistened in the midday heat and he marveled at the pale gray eyes so out of keeping with her volatile personality.

Finally he approached her. Still she wrote in her fine spidery handwriting, though she must have noticed him.

"You were very brave back in the sick house," he told the top of her head. She looked up at him and nodded vaguely. "Just what *is* your position here in this house?"

"What were you saying to me when you vaccinated me?" she asked him, ignoring his last statement.

"I was begging you not to cry out. What were you

106

saying when you stared so hard as I scratched your arm?"

"I was telling you that the two of us could control those people if we controlled ourselves."

"It's too hot for you here in the sun. Let me pull you up and let's walk in that nice cool swamp we were in that afternoon." Leon moved forward to take her hand which she held out to him but at that moment Inigo came up and she snapped erect, dropping her hand back into her lap. Leon saw the dull dry look in her eyes disappear and a glory flash into them. *So that's the situation,* he thought wretchedly. *I might have known old Mrs. Gaillard could never have excited her so strongly that afternoon.*

He did not go away, though they were oblivious of him. He was impelled to hear them talk together.

"Did you get the fertilizer statement ready?" Inigo asked her and his voice was flat with lethargy, heavy with indifference.

"You aren't ordering enough," she answered, while her heart cried out—*I love you, Inigo. You look like an oak tree standing there. Beside you this brown-skinned man is of no more substance than a blowing reed in the marsh.*

"Did we use more last year?" *How fragile and wan you look,* Inigo thought, through the heavy ache in his breast—*did I brush all the shining gold from your wings—did I destroy the crimson roses of your mouth?*

"Yes—these records call for six tons more than you told me to write down."

"Order the additional six. I am going away and I want to leave enough to carry through till late fall."

"Going away!" She scraped her pen and grasped the big book tightly in her thin fingers. "But—the cotton crop will be heavy—" She stopped wearily, realizing that she was not reaching him.

"Cuffee and I are taking Marchioness and Edisto up to Long Island for the season; then we're going to scour the country for the finest filly in the world. At least," he spoke as though he were twisted on the rack,

107

"I can have the finest horses and win all the races."

"When will you come back?" Her face was drawn and chilly damp.

"Around Christmas." He looked at her as though all she needed to do was put her hand out and he would snatch her close and ride away with her.

She could feel Leon's hot disapproving eyes on her, his disappointment in her. Pride of race stirred for the first time in her and kept her still.

"Good-by—until then," she said.

As Inigo turned to go he noticed Leon. "You are a good doctor. You handled the people very well. I hope you will help us often. Come into the kitchen and get some dinner."

Charlotte watched Leon follow Inigo. He was near her age, one of her mixed strain. Strange that he awoke no chord in her—only a lonely pride, an empty dignity.

Nobody else would ever sound a chord in her again. Inigo had refused to notice the excitement that his very presence caused in her. Her aroused passion cried out for his guiding hand, though her self-respect forced her to accept the fact that they were doomed to walk forever on opposite sides of the river.

If he would just look at her and see her occasionally! He had been so puzzlingly quiet ever since that afternoon. If the hard shell that he had crept into could just crack enough to let in one ray of her loving warmth! If he would only wave at her sometime from his side of the river! Surely that was little enough to ask? She was not in the habit of sharing her secret thoughts with anyone, Poulette had taught her that, so although Tafra sensed her unhappiness and watched her moodiness and loss of weight with alarm, Charlotte was sure she did not suspect that the real trouble was Inigo's removal of himself from her world, leaving her suspended, a captive in a sterile, lonely void.

She tried to fasten her gaze on a cloud of hummingbirds frantically trying to suck all the cloying sweetness from the white jasmine that dropped in profusion from the balcony, but she could not keep her eyes away from Inigo, who had come out on the balcony and was looking down on her with empty eyes.

Anyway her arm was beginning to sting and the unaccustomed sunshine was making her feel faint. They were all cruel—her father had been cruel to let himself get killed; Tafra had been cruel to keep her so alone; Inigo to go away from her; and now that young doctor with those fine eyes who was free—free—free!

She jumped up, knocking over her chair, and ran to her own room and shut and locked her door. She hardly reached her bed before a storm of weeping broke loose inside of her and shook her slender shoulders like a spring torrent. The tears felt like sharp splinters as they drained from her eyes and raked her face. She knew that she was weeping for the love that had come close for one bright moment but had not flowered inside of her body. *I shall grow old and ugly and dark and I shall never know love again,* she wept.

And Leon trotted his roan cob away from Normandy, miserably aware that he had fallen in love with Charlotte and that she was in love with a white man. He would try not to seek her out again. Her eyes had betrayed her when the great Gaillard had come to bid her farewell under his broad-branched trees.

Chapter 17

What Charlotte did that year from June to December was to draw more inside herself than ever, purposely avoiding the slaves and the Street, almost blaming them for her unhappiness. For she was terribly hurt, particularly in her pride. Then, too, her illusion of security and safety had tumbled down upon her. Nick and

Tafra behaved toward her just as always, but Charlotte looked for ways to hide her wound from Tafra, to pretend that the afternoon Tafra had seen Inigo kiss her in front of the mirror in the drawing-room had been forgotten and thrown away, as an old dream is discarded when a new one comes.

Somehow Charlotte managed to appear calm and natural outwardly when she and Tafra sat alone in the gold chairs, one on each side of the fireplace, talking over plantation affairs and plans; telling each other how glad they were that Emily and Robert remained in town throughout the autumn; telling each other that Normandy was just the same as it had been and would be.

But it isn't the same, Charlotte thought; *it can't ever be the same. I can't ever be the same. Not now that she's told me so cruelly that my people are not, and never can be, her people. It is all pretense and as soon as Inigo comes back, Tafra will see that pretending can't make a thing not be, when it has been.*

Charlotte knew that she must not write to Inigo, nor even ask for news of him, and as day passed over day it was only by losing herself in the management of the plantation accounts and books that she kept reproaches against herself from arising and the insidious thought that he had not truly loved her—it was not love but lies.

It was a keen chill afternoon in December when Harry Singleton rode from Heronfields to bring Tafra direct news of Inigo. In the avenue he passed Charlotte standing in the high wind, a work sheet in her hand, checking a group of women coming in late from the fields where they had been digging up dead cotton stalks and burning the brown brittle bushes in great roaring piles of fire. Her cheeks were rose pink in the cold air and her cape of fine bright-blue broadcloth billowed back to show a gold-colored hoop skirt.

It's against the law for Negro slave women to wear hoop skirts, Harry thought, speculating, as all their crowd were doing of late, on what could possibly be the outcome of Tafra's violation of the law forbidding slaves to be educated and of the eccentric non-

110

conformist manner in which she was letting this girl practically run Normandy. His wife Mildred and her Low Country lady friends spent most of their teatimes condemning Tafra's outlandish ways and prophesying no good end to Charlotte, Tafra, or Inigo.

When Hercules showed him up to the drawing-room Harry folded his long cranelike self into a chair and fumbled with what he wanted to say. The main reason he had come this afternoon was to drop a warning word in Tafra's ear—he loved Inigo and he would do anything to stop his incontinent drinking and spending. He had just come from Norfolk where Inigo had outbid him for a filly. In fact Inigo had given the highest price for the filly that had ever been paid for a horse since the States united themselves.

But Tafra made it difficult for him. She parried his insinuations and insisted on being pleasantly formal. Thus Harry did not tell her about Inigo's arrest in New York for disabling a foreign gentleman of title at a private gambling club; nor did he mention Inigo's disappearance in Philadelphia for a week; nor did he inform her of Inigo's riding Brett Carter's heaviest hunter so hard one night in Virginia that the huge animal finally dropped dead under him; he did not go into any of the mad, wasting, gentlemanly wild oats which Inigo had been sowing up and down the Eastern coast.

"Inigo's had a rather reckless summer," was all he managed to get out. "It will be good for him to come home. He said to tell you he'd surely be here by Christmas Eve."

"Yes." Tafra's blue eyes were cold. "Normandy is very isolated. We'll start by having a party for him after the hunt on Christmas Day. He can expend his energy here."

That was just what Harry and Inigo's friends were dreading. And today he himself had seen Charlotte's wild, odd beauty, whipped by the wind. Now, he could handle her all right if she were at Heronfields. Put her in her place, where the Negroes would not envy her nor white men desire her. Too much trouble was brewing on account of those miserable Abolitionists.

111

The planters were going to have to be careful, out-numbered by the blacks as they were. Queer ones like Charlotte were always mischief-makers.

"I'd like to buy Charlotte from you," he said unexpectedly.

Tafra smiled thinly and her eyes became more wintry than ever. "I would as soon sell you Nick," she told him.

Harry and Inigo had been playmates during their childhood and she realized that Harry had been trying to tell her a tale about Inigo all afternoon. But things had smoothed out nicely this fall, Charlotte was once more tractable and calm; from now on everything would surely come around naturally to her wanting. Besides, she disliked intimate discussions with lesser minds.

It was an unsatisfactory visit and after drinking a hot glass of buttered rum Harry retrieved his beaver and bowed low over Tafra's hand.

"Promise to sell the girl to me if she ever leaves here." He was in earnest. "Nancy needs a maid-companion. Mildred dotes on Hal in the same smothering way that Emily does on Robert and my daughter has been sadly neglected."

"That won't be a hard promise to make. Yes—if I ever sell her I'll let Nancy have her." She was tired. Harry had bored her long enough.

"Is that a real promise, Miss Tafra?" Harry remembered how Tafra had always done singular things when he and Inigo were little boys. He had never quite believed in her and had always been more than a little afraid of her.

"Yes—a real promise. Would you like me to promise to sell you a piece of the moon at the same time?"

Chapter 18

∙━━━━━━━━━━━━━━━━━━━━━━━━━∙

On Christmas Eve Charlotte was so excited that she ran up and down stairs all day. She was everywhere—smiling, singing, directing, helping, oblivious of Tafra's worried expression; of Emily's criticisms of the gaudy way she was decorating the house for Christmas; of Horst Adams staring sadly at her through his glass; of Robert trying to intercept her in dark corners.

"He's coming home! He's coming home!" She sang under her breath as she flew about the garlanded rooms, winding smilax in the stairs, hanging wreaths in the windows, putting holly behind all the portraits and pictures, clamping tiny candleholders on the aromatic cedar tree standing in the center of the big hall, straightening the myriad candles in the crystal chandeliers, tying mistletoe here and there, hugging little Nick a thousand times.

Late in the afternoon it began to drizzle and Nick came crying to her in the kitchen, where she was measuring cupfuls of brandy for the pudding, to tell her that his mother had tweaked his ear again. The sore one.

"Would you like to get your pony and go to meet your father and Cuffee?" Charlotte asked the big-boned dear little boy.

"Oh yes! Bundle me up tight though. I don't want an earache for Christmas."

"Don't go beyond the avenue entrance."

"Naw—naw," Sweet slapped her batter loudly,

"booger man jest pass de winder. He waitin' smack at de entranch."

Nick laughed merrily—"Then I'll stop this side of the entrance." He was used to booger men and Platt Eyes. He knew you didn't ever really see them. Well— hardly ever anyway.

But as Nick galloped his tacky away from the house spilling safe candlelight out into the first dark, he burrowed his chin deep in the muffler wound around his head and began to pray to Jesus—the known enemy of all booger men—to look after him and to please make his cross mother eat too much Christmas pudding and die tomorrow, or else go back to the town house and stay there forever and ever.

After he'd prayed long enough he felt so much better that his ear didn't ache any more and suddenly he heard the screaky sound of wheels turning in wet sand and the clip-clop of hoofs in the twilight. He pulled the tacky deeper into the shadows. He would rush out and make Hero rear up when the horsemen came to where he was. He loved to scare his Pa.

He could just make out the two figures riding in the gloomy dark. In the distance his father looked like a giant on horseback and Cuffee, tall in the saddle but tragically short in the stirrups, seemed a part of the darkling forest that crept up to the long line of cultivated oaks, the primeval wilderness of pine and brier ever seeking to reclaim the smooth ribbon of road for its own.

Every time Nick saw Cuffee riding up the avenue he thought of the story his Gran told so often of the winter day that other Nicholas, his grandfather, had come from Charleston, whooping like a wild Indian on Timoleon, waving a queerly woven basket in which lay a thin crooked-legged Negro baby. The baby was crowing and beating the sides of the strange basket made of snake skins with a charred crab claw, as the powerful stallion leaped and plunged toward his home stable. Gran said Cuffee had always had the feel of horses and now he and Hester, the long rangy hunter he was riding, seemed one being as they moved slowly beside Hero, the big gray grandson of Timoleon.

Here they were! Nick picked up his reins to dash out when he saw the men stop as a clumsy wagon groaned into the avenue from the main road, and the shrill cry of a terrified horse stabbed through the rain sounds. Cuffee wheeled Hester, galloping quickly to the wagon, calling to the filly in the van as though she were a frightened child. Nick dug his heels into the tacky and tore out—smack into Hero, who, though weary, obligingly reared up and neighed in annoyance. Inigo brought the gray down easily and leaned over and hugged Nick gratefully.

"Were you waiting for me?" he asked. "Are you glad I've come home?"

"Course, Pa," Nick answered. "Ma has been so mean today. But Charlotte and Gran and I have missed you most awful bad and all the cotton got picked!"

The clouds gathered thicker and dull thunder worried in the sky. Hero, smelling the stable, started fretting and the tacky kicked at Hero and began to buck. Inigo reached out and pulled Nick off the pony onto the saddle in front of him. The riderless tacky kicked once more and then made a beeline back to his warm dry stall. All the horses and mules quickened their pace to follow, and through the slanting rain the cedar wreath on the front door, shining with a big red bow, gaily welcomed Inigo back home.

Cuffee came up level.

"Ki, Nick," he spoke softly to the little boy. "Cuffee gots a real hoss back in dat wagon. She name Fancy and dat gal is de headingest hoss ever been in dese parts."

"Goody!" squealed Nick, leaning against Inigo's broad chest. "Pa, you reckon you can beat Mr. Singleton and Cousin Wade Hampton with her?"

"You bet, Nick," Inigo's loud voice boomed out. "You bet! I'll beat every race horse North or South, on any track, with her when she gets a year older."

A skinny little colored boy ran out to take Inigo's horse but Inigo shook his head, handing Nick down easily with one hand.

"Run on in with Sambo, Nick. I'm going to the stables with Burnt Sam and Cuffee to unload the horse."

Burnt Sam hallooed and Marchioness and Edisto in the rear of the van neighed eagerly in answer to their stable mates who had heard them coming and had the whole stable sounding. The stables were back and at right angles to the house with the east field or meadow in between. A long row of boxes for the racers and hunters faced the south, away from the damp river wind. They were made of oversized brick with a slate roof. A corridor ran the length of the row in the rear connecting two grain and tack rooms, one at each end, and the boxes; it also provided a place to work under cover. The stalls were fifteen feet square, white-washed each year on the inside. In front of the boxes was a "street" and a gate in the center gave access to the meadow on the other side of which was the training-track and the jumping-lane. Pine straw made a fragrant bed for the horses and was brought fresh each day from the pinelands. A similar row of larger stalls, each with its own yard, ran parallel to the boxes and housed the brood mares and the young foals.

Cuffee's house was near, and beyond this a kennel for the hounds. The Normandy hounds were friendly with the horses and much of their time was spent in the stables.

Pine torches, borne high by black hands, illuminated the entrance to the stables and Inigo and Cuffee stiffly dismounted in the muddy stable court as the cumbersome wagon came to a stop by the sputtering fire stands.

"Step lively, boys," called Inigo. "We want all the hands here we can get. We've got thousands of dollars' worth of horseflesh in this wagon and if the filly gets one hair skinned off in unloading her, I'll have the bullwhip skin every last one of you!"

Big Jake laughed. He adored Inigo and loved to hear him talk biggety-like.

"Don't worry, Massa. We pick her out like she a little baby. None of we would break or crack one little bone of she."

The slaves cackled and danced in their excitement, crowding up eagerly to peep through the canvas flap of the wagon.

116

Cuffee pushed them aside.

"Stand back," he ordered. "Dis Cuffee' baby. Yunnuh scare she to death ef she so much as git a glint of dem shiny white eyeballs in yunnuh faces. Dis Cuffee' own here."

"Yes," echoed Inigo, moving back, "this is Cuffee's show. Put down the track and let's see if he can get her out by himself."

They brought the padded ramp and fastened it to the back of the wagon. The rain was coming down heavily now and the spitting torches reflected yellow flares in the glistening eyes of the black men pressed around.

Cuffee walked up the ramp and untied the flap. A sharp, vicious hoof lashed out like an adder's tongue. Cuffee jumped sideways.

"Now, sugah," Cuffee's voice took on its weird, chanting quality. "Now, sugah, hit's only Cuffee. Cuffee done fetch yunnuh to yo' home. Cuffee go' bresh out yo' silber mane and Cuffee go' comb out yo' silber tail. Sweet water Cuffee go' fetch and soft warm mash for yo' parched throat."

By now he had slipped into the wagon and putting one hand on Fancy's tail he began to run his other hand up her side. She trembled until she could hardly stand. Her first two years had been spent wildly racing about a big meadow with her mother. No master had she known, no human hands had touched her until she had been caught one day and roped and put in a cold dark stall in the hold of a ship bound for Norfolk. She had called for her mother all the long sick way down the coast and when the men tried to unload her at Norfolk she had broken away from them as they pulled her down the gangway, and, her flax mane like the broken crest of a wave shining in the sun, her head high out of the water, she had started to swim home—all the way to Pennsylvania. The strange men had caught her, though. They had come in boats with strong ropes and had pulled her—strangling her—back to shore. From there she had been taken to a place where there were many other horses and loud humans who stared at her then began wildly gesticulating at her. All but one—one strange man with a dark face and shiny eyes had spoken

117

sounds that for a moment quieted her. But not for long; because she had been dragged away from that place and reloaded on this covered horror, with that terrifying horse next to her with his cruel whistle and evil hoofs. What hand was this that made soft motions on her side? She whickered nervously. Her ears pointed into twin horns, almost touching at the tips. Red fire flashed from her eyes and her breath snorted out from dilated nostrils. She pawed the bottom of the wagon.

Cuffee was up by her head now and he had her firmly by the halter. Still crooning to her he unloosed it from the ring. She tried to rear but he held her firm and began pushing her back. One step—two—and her hind feet met the ramp.

She felt the keen rain come down on her rump and almost lost her balance, she was so startled. Cuffee took advantage of her surprise and pushed her on backward—downward.

The slaves shuffled away from her wicked-looking hind legs and it was a good thing because the moment her head was out and she saw the wavering torches she became a demon.

"The hood, Jake, the hood!" shouted Inigo. Big Jake had it in his hand and as Cuffee, swinging on with all the prodigious strength of his arms, pushed her onto the ground, Inigo grabbed the halter on the other side and he and Cuffee and Quash held her fighting head while Big Jake slipped a loose hood over her eyes.

As soon as she was hooded, though still skittish and trembling so she could hardly stand, she allowed Cuffee to lead her into a stall that had been prepared for her in an honored place.

Then as a little whirling wind madly spattered the raindrops every which-way, a hand clutched Inigo's coat sleeve and he looked down into the face that he had tried to wench, drink, gamble, fight, and race out of his heart. The licking reflection from the fire stands leaped up and down across her lucent skin like hot blood and the tendrils of hair curling like tiny flames about her temples lent her the same shimmering perfection of his red filly.

His own black eyes were glowing like fox fires and

118

Charlotte impulsively held out her arms to him. A tremor shook his whole frame as he gathered her close. He kissed her, finding peace in the kiss, but only for a moment, because his senses were blood hot and his next kiss was passionate and deep.

"Let me look at you," he finally said shakily, holding her off from him, running his forefinger down the curve of her jaw. "Ah—you are beautiful—much more beautiful and exciting than I remembered." Once more he tightened his arms demandingly and she flung herself against him, praying a little, silently beseeching him to love her completely.

"Oh," she whispered, "it's been so long!"

"There's a vacant cabin in the Street. The seventh in the second row. Meet me there in half an hour." He must have her. He would have her. And she wanted him, too. He could feel it in every nerve."

But she pushed desperately away from him. "It isn't vacant any more. A family is there now." She could barely speak in her agitation.

"Well, then come with me. There's an empty stall where I keep the brood mares."

He pulled her into the circle of his cape, and together they ran past the fire stands to the stall.

Chapter 19

The row where the brood mares were kept was quite dark but Inigo knew every turn. The one door that he pushed open led into a stall that was quiet and empty. He snatched off his cape and threw it on the straw bed-ding, falling to his knees and pulling Charlotte down with him.

For a moment they knelt together as if in prayer. *My heart is crashing like the Cathedral organ,* Charlotte thought; *oh, this is love—oh, this is what I want of love.*

"I love you, Inigo," she whispered low and vibrantly.

"God, oh God, if you just knew how many faceless ones I've slept with, trying to sleep you out of my blood," he told her, lying down on the cape, caressing her with his finger tips—his whole hand; fumbling with the crossed black velvet ribbon of her bodice; loosing the net which bound her hair; catching her hair in his hands and rubbing it across his face; plunging his hot hands into her open dress, holding her soft breasts— kissing them.

"I love you; truly, I love you," she moaned the words; this was a time for moaning—not for talking.

He snatched out the thin strips of bodice ribbon that tangled in his fingers; tearing her dress. She seemed not to notice what he did—responding quickly to his every move.

"Darling—little darling—I hope I will not hurt you—" His voice was thick and something in its tone upset her.

"But you do love me? Say it—only once; then for me everything will be all right." She pushed him back; struggling to sit up—to see his face a little in the dark.

"Your hair is like a living shawl of fire. I can even see it lick your bare shoulders in this dark stable. Oh, beautiful—oh lovely—oh, I want you so. Lie closer to me—closer—"

"But do you love me? Is this that we do with love?" She was almost crying in her agitation.

"Come—lie back down. You are like fire to me." He caught her roughly by the wrist and forced her down beside him, throwing his mighty leg across her thighs—reaching down to pull up her dess.

But suddenly a light clicked in her brain—showing her Tafra's triumphant ice-blue eyes—making her hear Tafra tell how Inigo would despise the dark children she might bear him.

"Oh, but it must be love with me—it must. Let me go. I will go." She kicked at him frantically.

He held the arch of her foot but she slipped her foot out of her soft slipper, swiftly scrambling to her feet as he said loudly, "Come back—Charlotte—come back! Where are you in this fiendish, devilish hole?"

But she was gone. He thrashed about looking for her a minute before he realized that she was no longer in the stall; only *he* panted there—alone in the dark. He stumbled to the door and flung it back against the brick wall, not noticing a softness behind it, keeping it from touching the brick.

"Where are you?" he shouted.

But a third voice answered, "Eh, Massa, yunnuh gots no business here."

"What in hell are you doing here, you black rascal? I thought you were safely in the racers' row with the filly. God damn! Do you have to follow me everywhere?"

"Eh, Massa, Massa, Cuffee had to move de filly on account of Edisto am ranting raving bound to git to she. He plunging lak a wild man in de stall. Cuffee done put Fancy here wid de brood mares, so she be safe from dat black man dis night. Now yunnuh git along back to de house, fore old Miss git suspicious in she mind, wid yunnuh an' Charlotte bofe out een de night. Go long. I fetch yo' cape inside mo' later, w'en hit's light enough to bresh de straw frum hit."

Humph, Inigo thought. *Well, Cuffee would have known anyhow. He always does. But where the devil can Charlotte have run? God knows I wouldn't have raped her for the world. If she had waited a minute I would have said I loved her—if it would have quieted her. I hope she hasn't gone to Mother with her ruined dress. Hell—hell and damn,* he blasted, sloshing through the muck and mud.

When he turned the corner of the brood mare's row of stalls, Cuffee moved the stable door and pulled

121

Charlotte from the wall where she crouched, whimpering pitifully to herself.

"Ain't yunnuh shame?" he scolded. "Ain't yuh shame?" But when she started crying he changed his tone. For Charlotte was a woman to whom crying came hard and every sob was wrenched and torn.

"Oh, leetle Charlotte; po' wild white goose feather. Now hush, now hush." He crooned to her as he had done to the frightened filly, and the filly hearing, put her cold wet nose out of the top part of the next stall. As the nose explored, it touched Charlotte's wet cheek.

"Kerchoo! Kerchoo!" Charlotte began her helpless, sudden sneezing.

"Quick, move fudder down. Fuh Gawd's sake don' start dat, wid all dis udder trouble dis bad night."

He led her away from Fancy, back into the empty stall she had escaped from a little while ago. She was not afraid of Cuffee, she went docilely into the stall, and together they sat on Inigo's cape.

"Burnt Sam been already tole 'bout seeing yunnuh an' Mass Inigo kissing back yonder whey hit been hit by de fire stands. Gawd a'mighty—yunnuh cain't lub Mass Inigo! Hit ud ruin yunnuh sho. I had de headingest time, dis whole bressed summer an' fall, keeping up wid um nohow. Hunting um in de worstest places—sobering um up. He as uncontrolled right now as Edisto. He lak a rampaging wild hoss; lak a volcano ready to disrupt."

"I know." Charlotte had stopped sneezing and crying. She was so miserable that she just sat and stared in the darkness, thinking.

She knew. Bitterly she knew. She knew that if she were all white he would never have taken her into a smelly stall, no matter how he loved or wanted her.

She felt her toes turn cold and she had an impulse to scream, loud enough for Inigo to hear her in his house. Not in a dark forgotten stable! In brightness, she wanted to cry, in light and fragrance and laughter!

She wanted to see herself reflected in the pupils of his eyes beneath a many-candled chandelier, in a room gaily hung with mirrors; she wanted to glide on his arm in a haunting pavan; not to lie prostrate in a horse stall, where the only light was a stab from a distant fire stand, the only music a bobcat howling its need on the edge of the forest.

And she knew that the words *cabin, stable, stall* were a thousand times more degrading than the word *Negro* had been to her, six years ago.

All at once she thought of Leon, with his clean brown face. He had looked on her with admiration, but she had let him leave her last June, thinking she was in love with Inigo; despising her for wasting herself in a love that would never flower. For one wild moment she considered running to Charleston in her one shoe, seeking Leon. But oh, if she ran, the patrolers would pick her up, and lead her back to Normandy tied behind a mule cart, with a hempen rope cutting her waist.

Meanwhile, Cuffee had found her hair net—he was used to nighttimes—and he gently wound her hair into a relatively smooth knot and slipped the net over it. He retrieved her shawl from under the cape and put it tight around her shoulders. She was grateful; she bent and kissed his rough, tender hand.

For a while after that they sat silently, then Cuffee reached in his pocket and took out a strange clawlike object.

"Kin yunnuh see dis?" he whispered.

She nodded—a little glow from a distant fire stand penetrated the former pitch-blackness. The slaves must have thrown on more kindling and pine straw.

"Hit come wid Cuffee all de way from Africa," he said softly. "Put in Cuffee' hand by de Corramantee king who been Cuffee' Pa."

"What in the world is it?" She looked at the dirty bit of shell seen dimly by the points of light flickering from the fire stand and she shrank away from touching it.

"Hit's muh crab claw."

"What's it for?"

"Hit's pertection against de harm white mens kin do yunnuh," he told her. "Hit's a charm to ward off white men' magic. An' atter yunnuh been lying in Mass

Inigo' arms, sugah, yunnuh am sholy gwine need somepin fuh pertect yunnuh. Mass Inigo am in no mood fuh no swageing. He ready to bust wide open effen de leetlest thing do go against um."

Charlotte, hating herself for doing it, was nevertheless impelled to take the crumbly sharp thing and ram it into her pocket.

"I guess I do need help," she sighed. But she thought, *Why did I take this superstitious savage charm? Cuffee and I are much more the unknown to each other than Inigo and I. Our blackness and whiteness could never tolerate each other. He suffocates me with his wild animal smell.*

"Now let's git," Cuffee said—all at once ill at ease with the strange Charlotte. They came out of the stall just as little Sambo slithered up with a bucket of warm mash Cuffee had ordered from the kitchen. Charlotte shrank back against the wall but Sambo saw her. Cuffee took the mash quickly, telling Sambo to run back in.

Sambo ran; but he had seen her squnched dere in de dark. Atter Cuffee. Sambo ducked his head so that she could not see him make a face at her. He'd heard his mammy and his pappy laughing about her and her highfalutin' ways— She's got a black heart and a white mind, they said. She ain't nuttin'. She ain't house dog and she ain't rabbit dog. She ain't nuttin'. She ain't nigger and she ain't white. She born tangle up—she ain't nuttin'. He'd heard them—he'd heard them late in the night talking about her. Acting like she thought she was a lady!

Cuffee moved off with the mash and Charlotte once more started for the house but three Negro men came noisily by, so again she waited, pressed against the cold brick wall.

She recognized the men. They were Inigo's hunters; slaves, whose sole job was to keep the table at Normandy supplied with whatever game was in season.

Caty, the loudest one, his eyes cat's eyes in the dark, spotted Charlotte and called to her, "Nung gal what wait in darkness wait long time, and nung man go out udder gate, enty?"

124

The other hunters laughed meaningly and Caty started singing:

> *"Oh, turkle dove 'e flewed away*
> *Hice duh winduh let duh dove come een*
> *Rain keep rainin' all aroun'*
> *Hice duh winduh let duh dove come een,"*

and the two others took up the song as they went toward old Murriah's kitchen, which was a small brick building just by the back door:

> *"Oh, Norah hice duh window, Norah,*
> *Hice duh winduh, Norah,*
> *Hice duh winduh,*
> *Hice duh winduh let duh dove come een."*

Then they too were gone and she *had* to go back into Inigo's house. As she picked her muddy way, she felt mud ooze through her white French lisle stocking. *I lost my shoe,* she thought, dismayed. *I wonder if he still has it in his hand? I wonder how I will feel tomorrow when I see him again? I wonder if I will thrill to him again? Or will I hold my head high and look away no matter what he says or does not say?*

Inigo was there in his house. Was he too thinking of these things? Was he as confused as she was? As achingly lonely and heartsick?

She tried to creep up the back stairs without being seen but as she rounded the last step into the hall a hand reached out and pinched her on her firm behind. Stifling a scream she whirled around and there was Robert. She blanched and pulling her wet shawl closer about her shoulder to be sure her torn dress was hidden, she somehow managed to stare him down, then with great dignity she walked ahead of him through the dining-room, limping a little on her wet stockinged foot.

For a minute he was dumbfounded. A nigger wench making him stand back for her to precede him into the dining-room! He blushed with shame, turning back from the dining-room so that she wouldn't have the satisfaction of thinking she could do him a trick

125

like that. He'd tell his mother. She would make Charlotte twitch all right. She could make everybody squirm —even his pa! Emily's voice came lightly from her drawing-room.

"Must you go back to town tonight?" she was asking Horst Adams.

"Yes, the dear Bishop insists on all his progeny surrounding him on feast days."

Chapter 20

Inigo took his time after he left the stables, going all the way round to the front door where Hercules stood, waiting for him, looking as much a part of Normandy as the branched silver candelabra he held high, or the Samuel F. B. Morse portrait of old Nicholas looking darkly down from the far side of the hall.

Hercules hugged Inigo with his free arm, in spite of his dripping clothes and the muddy pool he was making on the priceless Turkey carpet.

"Whey yo' cape at?"

"Cuffee has it." Inigo ached all over from frustration and impatient nervousness but he could feel the house immediately warm and soothe him.

"What a handsome Christmas tree. Did you fix it?"

"Charlotte done all dis. Did yunnuh have a good journey, Massa?"

"Good enough to be glad I'm home," Inigo said— marching defiantly to the double doors that led to the small drawing-room and, without knocking, snatching them open.

The pale green room was lighted by wax candles in silver sticks on the mantelpiece and the pink marble fireplace glowed in the harbored firelight. No forest greens insinuated their alien odors of wild places in here and no holly or mistletoe messed up the cold faceted chandelier.

Emily was languishing on a pale pink velvet settee by the fireplace and Horst Adams hovered over her with a sarcastic smirk on his ascetic countenance. Robert was pouring sherry from a Belgian crystal decanter and Inigo was suddenly conscious that his son had matured and was almost a man or rather almost a foppish fashion plate. No one but Horst Adams would have advised that lavender velvet vest and that checked velvet coat!

Standing in the doorway like a huge rough Samson in the hall at Gaza, Inigo wanted to smash and destroy this room and its inmates. Instead he walked heavily over the pastel Aubusson carpet, leaving the muddy mark of his boots with every step across the pallid flowers.

"Don't come in here covered with horrid stable mud!" Emily shrieked, holding a fine lace handkerchief over her nose. Robert giggled nervously and Horst adjusted his eyeglass and daintily cleared his throat.

"Welcome home, Inigo," he said.

Inigo glared at him. The devil take Horst welcoming him to Normandy! He leaned over Emily and raised her hand to his lips feeling how she hated him to touch her. She looked away; her fingers curled up into claws as she tried to dig her sharp nails into his flesh. But he squeezed her fingers until she gasped with pain before he dropped her hand.

"I bought a new filly," he announced loudly. Nobody commented. "Aren't you even interested, Robert? My son, Robert—my heir—my blond Gaillard?"

"Y-Y-Yes, Pa." Robert's hands shook, handing his mother the slender-stemmed wineglass. He had never gotten over the sight or the sound of Inigo trying to break down the door to his mother's room in June. If only he had courage enough to tell his father how he and his mother despised him. If he were only big enough to slam his fists one after another into that dark virile face!

"Have a glass of sherry, Inigo," put in Horst, conscious of Inigo's repressed violent unhappiness. For once trying to be kind to the man who represented everything that he might have liked to be, had the effort not been too great.

"Thank you, no, Horst." Inigo turned dismally toward the door, his lonely heart aching now as well as his frustrated body. "I'll drink upstairs. Hercules!" he shouted as he slammed the doors behind him. "Help me off with these boots and call Brayboy to fetch me up a bowl of hot rum punch and a pipe."

A head appeared at the top of the stairs. Little Nick watched his father sit down on a Chippendale bench in the hall. Hercules had put a leather apron on the back of his livery and he leaned over with great dignity in front of Inigo. Inigo placed one large foot on Hercules' rear and the other between his legs. Hercules grasped the boot between his legs in his gnarled old hands and the tug-of-war was on!

"Eh, Massa, yunnuh mus' ain' tek off dese boots since yunnuh lef' here. Dey pears to be growed to yo' foots, and dey smells lak polecats."

Inigo laughed loudly. The rain was shut out and the evil effect of Emily's French drawing-room was wearing off. The rich red of the Turkey carpet was bright and comforting. The holly-crowned portraits of past Gaillards looked with approval on him from the walls and the massive gold-leaf mirror across the hall pictured Hercules who had been his father's worthy friend and now was his. As the boot suddenly flew off and Hercules shot forward, a clear peal of childish mirth rang down from the stairs. Inigo looked up. And the awful thought thrust into his consciousness, *If I love Charlotte and she has a child, it will be Nick's little Negro sister!*

The other boot flew off. He ran up the stairs in his wet stocking feet, three steps at a time, grabbed the little fellow up like a baby, carrying him proudly into the cheery welcoming warmth of the great drawing-room where Tafra sat by the roaring fire in her most dynastical mood.

Inigo kissed her white cheek that looked like crinkled tissue paper. Then he sat down and put on the warm carpet slippers Nick fetched for him.

"Welcome home, Inigo! You stayed away much too long and I am sure you have behaved very badly." Her eyes twinkled lovingly on him. "Nick and I were afraid you wouldn't get here before Santa Claus and his little goats arrived and Nick is just champing at the bit to fly downstairs as soon as he can leave off hugging you, and string some popcorn for the tree. I'm to give a prize to him or Sambo."

"To me—to me! Sambo can't stick to anything. My string will be a hundred miles long and his will only be an inch. Make it a good prize, Gran. Something like a sack of gold pieces."

"I brought you some riding-boots, Nick, with red tassels on them, and your first silk hat. Just like mine—to wear to church Sunday."

"Oh, Pa, thank you. Can I go and tell Charlotte? She wanted me to have a silk hat."

When he had gone Inigo and Tafra sat quietly for a while enjoying being close to each other. Inigo had always loved his home. Tafra thought of the merry affectionate little boy he had been. Always crashing into things because his feet were so large, always dropping things, always ready with a kiss and a smile—always brave—always obstreperous—always so very dear.

She sipped a glass of mellow Madeira while Inigo pulled on his pipe and replenished his silver cup from the steaming china bowl.

"I can't wait for you to see Fancy. Pa would probably have been so proud of her that he would have made her walk upstairs to make your acquaintance."

"Why didn't you? I never knew you to object to a filly in the drawing-room before." Her light laughter was like a worn silver bell.

"Well, I'd have had to escort her past Emily and

129

Robert and Horst and one peep at those three and she would have kicked them all out of the house."

"Why don't *you* do it?"

"Gracious, Mother—you do sound murderous!"

"Well, you might as well face facts—you've got to get rid of Emily somehow."

"Now, Mother—let's don't start that all over."

"She's been horrid to Nick ever since she came here from the town house last week. Charlotte has tried to protect him but she can't stand up to Emily. I refuse to have his childhood spoiled. Someday he will be master here. You've got to divorce her. It can be done easier now than it could have seventeen years ago. Oh, I know it will be disagreeable and embarrassing but we can live through that more easily than the alternative."

He raised his eyebrows and cut his eyes at her. A thick flush spread up from his neck. Was she a witch? Could she see the burning heart of Charlotte's lips on his? Or—he reached up and found a wisp of straw tangled in his hair. He closed it in his hands, hoping she had not seen it.

"I'm going to bed." He rose and stretched his powerful arms. "I'm tired and sleepy. Ring and ask Hercules to bring me six boiled eggs and some fried ham and biscuits. I just want a light supper. You'd better sleep, too, so you can be beautiful to greet Fancy tomorrow. And—stop planning my life!" This last was spoken gently but Tafra sensed the explosive vehemence beneath his words.

Oh, Inigo, she wanted to cry after him. *You have circles under your eyes and there are hard gashes of lines by your mouth. But you are strangely exhilarated and far too restless— I have too much to do in far too short a time. First I must see that Charlotte marries Cuffee. That will save her from you. If you could see her as the wife of Cuffee, a pure African—as the mother of dark-skinned sons—you would stop craving her and find you a lady to take Emily's place, leaving Charlotte safe to replace me here so that Normandy will be run in the manner Nicholas and I dreamed for it.*

Tafra was so intent that she dozed without being

aware of it and so did not hear the fire tongues in the fireplace spit out at her as she nodded by their warmth. Meddling old fool! Meddling old fool! Trying to play God again! Well—just wait—just wait!

Inigo bathed in a big tin tub of hot water in his dressing-room before he ate. He lathered himself with soap and lay there letting his worries jiggle up and down in his mind.

He knew exactly what Tafra was up to. Planning to marry Charlotte off! To take her away from him! To throw her to Cuffee just to prove that she was in reality black-black-black.

He was sick of the whole blasted mess he'd made of his life. He was sick of desiring Charlotte and being repulsed by the prospect of having Negro children by her. He had been a fool to take her into the dark stable and awaken the sleeping passion for her in his blood, to put the stars back in her eyes when he wasn't going to look at them. He'd better have stayed away than to come back here and wreck her unearthly sweetness.

And tomorrow would be Christmas! A family day —a day of love. Pity for himself took hold of him. His mother with her adamant nature had pushed him and Charlotte about like pawns in a chess game. She had made Charlotte into a priceless partner for him, and yet she stood between them like a flaming sword promising destruction if they came into the garden.

And this talk about divorcing Emily and leaving Normandy to a second son, even though the second son was his heartstring, was mere fiddle-faddle. She knew he couldn't do these things. She knew that the whip-lash of gossip which would zing out the facts of his private life in a divorce scandal would cut his carefully constructed picture of himself completely to shreds.

There was no door for him leading into the garden that bordered the river. The key had been turned long ago and thrown away.

The people of the Street were going from house to house talking about the new horse. A group of them carrying pine flares in the rain outside of the stable began to move away. Inigo could hear them singing as one of the older men raised his rich baritone voice and the others joined in:

> *"I pitch my tent on dis camp ground,*
> *No man look like me,*
> *'Cause de Lawd will find me, I'll be bound,*
> *No man look like me.*
>
> > *"King, oh, King*
> > *Died fuh me,*
> > *Hebben was made fuh de fus' an' de las',*
> > *No man look like me.*
>
> *" 'E rain forty day an' 'e rain forty night,*
> *No man look like me,*
> *'E make yo' garment fit yuh right,*
> *No man look like me."*

Chapter 21

The rain ceased before the dawn and Charlotte stirred fretfully as the traditional hunting-horns began to echo from one plantation to another up and down the river in a long steady Christmas call.

She was convinced that she had not closed her eyes all night, but Nick was gone from his little bed without her knowing, so she must have been sleeping; dreaming the troublous things that kept pricking hurtfully into her mind.

But not all dreaming; the charred crab claw was still there. She could feel its splintery shards as she slipped an exploratory hand under the pillow. Sighing wearily she sat up in bed, blinking against the bright sunlight streaming through the window. Blinking, too, in surprise at the pair of kid slippers she had worn out into the rain the night before resting innocently side by side, wiped clean of mud; both dry and softly polished.

I must have slept harder than usual, she thought ruefully; *Cuffee has put the other shoe there to warn me that it is now time for me to put on my shoes and get away from Normandy, from the danger that is threatening me and Inigo.*

Then, and it was the first time she had *truly* understood or comprehended the dreadful fact, she knew that she was powerless to get away from Normandy; that she was a slave in the true meaning of the bitter restricted word; that she had been a slave for six years but had refused to accept the fact.

I can never leave here, she thought desperately; *I am a slave like that ordinary Finger Ring who waves her plump bottom at every man on the Street. I have watched her when I checked the women at their tasks, and I have scorned her and all that she implies. Yet after last night I am the same as she. A Negro slave willingly lying in a stable with a man to whom I was not married. And I would have truly belonged to him if he had once told me that he loved me, if I had not suddenly felt that I was being destroyed. I am no better than Finger Ring.*

Oh, I am so confused. I am very tired of my life. This is too far to have journeyed from the sheltered courtyard on Toulouse Street, in one short life. I can hardly bear to contemplate another useless draggy year. I am losing even my personality.

Not a bit of it, a scoffing voice from somewhere deep down inside herself replied, *you've lost a great amount of vanity and that's all. Last night was a misfortune but not a tragedy. Whatever worth-while comes to you anyway won't be through the channels you have been searching since Inigo kissed you last June.*

But, she argued with herself, *what could be more deadening than my present hopelessness? I cannot have a future, being what I am.*

133

Perhaps, the inner voice said, *you are developing. This thing has at least made you think about yourself in real terms; has made you look straight at your predicament. Maybe it will help you cast off a lot of your old fancies about some special destiny—or that you are a person singled out by fate for some grand future. You'd better do the next best thing and try and make an impression on Leon when you see him again. He's at least free and the only possibility you have that can get you away from here. Besides, when you ran to meet your "special destiny" last night, it didn't turn out very happily. You'd better collect another destiny. Yes, that's it—another destiny.*

She felt better after this little argument with herself and hummed a Noel song as she put on a new dress of holly-berry-colored wool and fastened some exquisite rose-point lace at her wrists and throat.

Outside, the slaves were coming up from the quarters in a steady stream, thronging gleefully across the fields, shouting and singing about their three-day holiday, about the big fresh beeves slaughtered for them, about the casks of rum waiting for their celebration this special night.

"Chrismus gif'," they called, capering and jigging, bowing and scraping, snapping their fingers and shuffling their feet.

Charlotte hurried, now that she had comforted herself with reason, and came out on the front piazza as Inigo began booming hearty Merry Christmases to the hundreds of slaves worshiping him in spirit and in truth in his front yard. Her heart skipped crazily at the very sight of his broad shoulders in his tight pink hunting-coat, at the long strong brown hands lifted in salute to the happy people. *The first woman,* she thought, *brought about the banishment of man from Paradise. Would my love take all this from Inigo? That is, of course,* if *he loved me?*

He turned and their eyes met.

"Happy Christmas," he said spontaneously, holding out his hand to her.

"Merry Christmas," she almost sang, forgiving him completely, meeting his questioning look fully,

134

loving him again despite her morning seance with herself.

They stood there hand in hand, quite content, quite oblivious of the people and of Nick and Robert who were watching them, until Robert coughed disagreeably and reminded Inigo, "Aren't you and Mamma supposed to give out the gifts to the slaves together?"

Inigo dropped Charlotte's hand, blushing hotly, while Nick chattered out, catching the hand that Inigo had loosed.

"Mamma isn't coming. I heard Rena tell Gran that Mamma refuses to come down so early. She threw all of her shoes and scent bottles out of the window at the slaves as they passed for waking her up. One of her scent bottles hit Finger Ring on the head but it didn't break. Finger Ring says she's going to say it broke and keep it. It was that good French perfume Mr. Adams gave Mamma."

"Hush, Nick, hush." Charlotte tried to smooth the ruffled black curls.

A harsh tightness flattened Inigo's mouth. "God damn! Can't she even keep up a semblance of good will?" he muttered.

"Gran wanted to come," little Nick put in.

Inigo choked in his vexation for he dared not speak here in front of his sons.

"Greet the people," Charlotte said calmly. "I'll go with Mister Robert and Nick and give out the presents myself."

So Inigo walked alone to the wrought-iron piazza railing, raised his hand and began to address his slaves. The busy chuckling banter hushed. The running and the pushing and milling about stilled. All hands went to forelocks—all feet scraped politely.

"My people—Big Jake is over by the East Gate with lots of presents for everybody. I want you all to have a happy day. Little Nick and Mr. Robert will give out the gifts with love from the big house to each one of you. Your mistress regrets that she is unwell and unable to distribute the gifts herself. Now to the East Gate with you." His great voice broke. "And may God bless us all."

"Oh, Charlotte, Charlotte," he whispered. But Charlotte had already started with the two boys over to Big Jake and she didn't hear him. Robert was strangely quiet.

"Is Mamma really sick?" he asked Charlotte. Charlotte shook her head. She would have liked to tell this boy about his mother, but after his pinching her last night she didn't care how many worries his mother gave him.

"Your Mamma didn't want to come out so early this morning. You and little Nick must take her place."

"But," Nick danced by her side, "other Mammas always give out the Christmas to the slaves."

Robert reached over and pinched his cheek— too hard to be in fun.

"Our Mamma is not like other Mammas," he said.

"Ouch!" Nick put a chubby hand to his reddened cheek. "Charlotte is my Mamma, anyway, aren't you, Charlotte?"

"Let's race to the East Gate!" she cried, reaching over to tousle the black wind-wrinkled hair as Nick ran away from her and Robert to be first at the gate.

After all they were three young creatures and the morning was the most exciting of the whole year. Even Robert whooped with delight as they raced through the frosty morning sunlight over to the East Gate where big tables were piled high with packages containing beads, blankets, wool hats, lengths of bright dress goods, wool pants and jackets, pocket knives, and shiny yellow shoes for those who had picked the most cotton!

At breakfast everybody was dangerously keyed up. Inigo's voice grew louder and louder. Emily, palely pretty in a green velvet peignoir, presided languidly at the silver coffee urn. Tafra, looking old and shrunken, sat in her chair hugging the fire warmth as though this morning she felt the chill of the grave in her poor back.

The long table was shining with sprigs of holly scattered over the snowy white damask cloth. Garlands of smilax were draped from the crystal chandelier and a huge bunch of mistletoe stood upright in the center of the table, its pale gleaming berries cold and pure.

Hercules, assisted by three Negro boys who had

just come back from an extensive "butler education" under Lee in Charleston, brought in the breakfast. A cold wild turkey was placed in front of Inigo to carve while Emily poured coffee. Bowls of hot buttered hominy were passed—platters of sausages and shrimp and fried oysters and cold ham were followed by mounds of scrambled eggs, fried sweet potatoes, beaten biscuits, waffles, and corn bread. The woodsy fragrance of the greenery hung about the walls mingled with the aroma of the freshly roasted coffee.

Charlotte waited quietly at Inigo's side as he served a warm plate for his mother, then took it to a small damask-covered table in front of Tafra. She went back and stood by Emily while Emily poured coffee from the urn into a gold-banded china cup. Emily handed Charlotte the cup tilting it slightly so that the scalding liquid splashed on Charlotte's wrist.

"How clumsy you are," Emily said acidly.

"I'm sorry," Charlotte murmured, almost crying, as she took the cup to Tafra.

"You must learn to handle the urn more deftly, Emily." Tafra's voice was thin with annoyance.

"Please, Miss Tafra," Charlotte whispered, "it didn't burn—really it didn't and Mr. Inigo minds things like this so—here, let me get you some sugar."

Inigo looked miserably at Charlotte. She tried to smile at him and when he looked back at Emily, smug and secure as mistress of his table, the juicy turkey turned to string in his mouth and the hot peppery sausage was no more than sawdust. However, he tried to make talk for the boys' sake, and inanities flowed sluggishly between him and Emily.

Charlotte pulled down the delicate lace sleeve ruffle over the blister on her wrist. Emily saw the gesture and said petulantly, "Mrs. Gaillard, isn't that lace on Charlotte's dress the lace I asked you to give me?"

"Why, I believe so, Emily dear," Tafra replied softly. Why wouldn't the shrew stop needling Inigo? "I got that in Venice once. It's the finest rose point that can be made. I gave it to Charlotte for her Christmas present. Isn't it nice on that scarlet cloth?"

Emily quickly changed the subject. "Charlotte, go

137

and get the Eau de Cologne off my bureau. I can't bear the odor of that horrid liniment you rub Mrs. Gaillard with."

Charlotte squeezed Tafra's shoulder and slipped out. As the door closed on the red dress all warmth seemed to leave the room.

Inigo looked at the fire to see if it was still burning. He looked at Emily—sharp and green—he looked at fair Robert mouthing breast meat of turkey and then at gay dark little Nick, his face all smeared with sirup; his chest tightened and he gripped the handle of the carving knife as if he would like to annihilate them all.

Charlotte returned and handed Emily the bottle of scent which she opened and poured on her arms and touched to her forehead. And Inigo felt the fire leap up and the room take on an ascending glow from Charlotte's holly-berry dress which was made with a tight band encircling her tiny waist. His fingers laxed on the stag-horn handle; *I could almost reach around her waist with one hand,* he thought, *and her breasts are mere handfuls but firm and sweet. I wish I had not been so hasty last night. If I hadn't, perhaps—* He looked at her throat rising from the froth of creamy rose-point lace and her skin seemed alive with such a pure sheen that it was as though a candle were gleaming through the flesh.

To take his mind off her, Inigo started to extol the virtues of Fancy for the dozenth time to his mother, when the Negro huntsmen began tuning up their hunting-horns in the yard, and in response to the faint mellow blasts the joyous tongues of the staghounds sounded like a carillon of Christmas bells. At the first note of the horn Inigo threw down his napkin and turned to Robert. Inigo was dressed in formal hunting pink and when he saw Robert in his ordinary, everyday coat he said, "Aren't you coming to the hunt with me? All the boys and girls are going to be there. I'd planned to have one of the quarter horses brought along for you, as usual, to race along the road when we meet up with Harry and Hal Singleton." Robert fidgeted in his chair and looked to his mother. Emily was tensely quiet.

Her small gaiety was all gone and the pinched look about her mouth took away her shallow prettiness.

Tafra spoke, "Yes, he's going." She'd had enough of Emily. Her cane tapped warningly.

"I thought he'd stay here and help me get ready for the dinner party tonight. I feel utterly wretched, Mr. Gaillard," Emily whined, heeding the striking of the cane on the marble hearth.

Inigo quizzically raised a thick black eyebrow. The horns were really tuning up now and the hounds were calling frantically.

"Nancy will be there, Robert. Better come— I'll give you Jack to ride and I know you'll win the race."

"Oh, Mamma, please!" said Robert.

"Let him, Mamma," added Nick, his black eyes sparkling. That settled it for Emily. She didn't even look at the excited little fellow.

"I think I'll go back to bed. You'll probably find me quite ill when you return, Robert." She wandered weakly out of the room. Robert made a move to follow her but Tafra called him to her side.

"This is my last Christmas, Robert," she whispered to him. "Ride Jack for the Gaillards today and whip the devil out of that Hal." Her shaking voice had a quality of its old dominance. If she were just younger she could eventually defeat Emily. But she was so tired —and if the Gaillards did lose this boy, he was a poor sort, anyway.

Inigo fumed and banged the door as he went out. Only home one night, and God what a bad humor he was in already!

"All right, Grandma, I'll go. Tell Mamma I'll come home as soon as I ride Jack down the stretch. Tell her I won't go on the deer drive."

Inigo ran lightly, for all his tremendous bulk, down the front steps. The Negro hunters were coming around the side of the house, leading horses and followed by the pack of full-blooded deerhounds which for generations Normandy had bred true and hardily. Old Flora, grand mistress of the pack, was straining and giving the world the sound of her purpose and pleasure, her deep-chested music ringing through the early Christmas morning.

Quash came up with Hero. Hero had strong, short, dense cannon bones. His chest was deep and his ribs well sprung. His back was close coupled and his hindquarters were sloping and pear-shaped. His hocks were flat, thick, and strong and he carried his hind legs well under him. He and Inigo were great stayers—men of great heart, and the hunt was ever a thing of wonder and surprise to the two of them.

"Where's Cuffee?" Inigo asked as he mounted the gray, glad to be quitting the house.

"Um in de stall talking to dat new hoss yunnuh brung last night. Us think um sorter crazy. Won't tek time to eat, neither sleep. I think, Massa, de sooner he brek she and he kin start wid she on de outside track hit be better."

"Tell him to come on and ride Hester with me today—you can watch over Fancy. It wouldn't be Christmas for me to ride without Cuffee to the hunt. We'll try to break the filly when we come home this afternoon. Tell the people—it will be the most exciting Christmas sport they ever watched."

"Yassuh," said Quash and hurried off.

Robert, in his hunting-clothes, sullenly came up to his father. Inigo knew that Tafra had been talking to him.

"Where's Jack?" Robert asked. Inigo pointed with his whip over to a group of horses by the garden hedge. Robert walked over and snatched the bridle reins out of Sambo's hands without a word, mounted, and though Jack fretted and pranced he held him with a heavy hand and started slowly off down the avenue.

Inigo didn't have time to worry about this, for Cuffee came bucking up on Hester, his eyes shining.

"Unnuh go' brek she dis day for true, Mass Inigo?" he asked, enjoying Hester's frolicking.

"For true, indeed, Cuffee. Now I'll race you down the avenue."

They were off. The hounds were unleashed—the Negro huntsmen mounted quickly and followed as the two great horsemen pounded down the avenue with its canopied roof of live-oak branches draped in gray moss streaking them with the winter sun.

At the crossroads that led to Charleston and Georgetown and Beaufort was a small inn owned and run by a free couple of color, Boney and Sarah Gregg. This was the meeting-place of the hunt and as Inigo and his group rode up, the yard of the inn was like a village fair, so colorful were the hunt clothes and so full of spirit the planters and their sons and daughters and wives. Hounds snapped and snarled at each other and the Negro hunters and drivers were put to it to keep any sort of order while their masters and mistresses drank many stirrup cups and wished each other a happy Christmas. We are come together in exciting fellowship, they drank. What a fine life we have, they toasted.

It was customary before the hunt officially started to have a race of the young bloods to cool some of the heat off the horses and the boys. There was a straight stretch where the road turned off to Beaufort, a road that in pre-Revolutionary days the planters had hacked out of the wilderness for a quarter of a mile of track to race their horses on. In those days few blooded horses had been imported from England and they had developed a speedy small horse that could run a quarter of a mile in a flash, but which possessed poor staying power for the longer races.

Frank Huger blew a loud blast on his polished horn and called all the young men who had brought a racer with them to line up for the event. About ten young boys lined their rather heavy small horses onto the wide road. Robert avoided the younger ones because he saw Nancy with Hal, and after promising his mother not to go on the deer drive he didn't know how to tell Nancy that he wouldn't ride as her partner as he had always done since they were children. Another blast of the horn and the boys were off like the wind down the road. Harry Singleton stood at the finish line and as Robert on Jack, and Hal on a bright-coated chestnut mare streaked across the line first, he called, "A tie—and may luck be to the best one!"

The laughing group rode back up to the inn and changed horses, giving the quarter horses to the grooms and mounting the hunters that were being held for them.

Robert did not go up to the inn but, still mounted on Jack, turned at the crossroad for Normandy. Without looking back he cantered off. Suddenly he heard hoofbeats behind him. He turned and saw Nancy, stunningly handsome in a black velvet habit, on her long low hunter, Ariadne.

"Please, Robert," she said. "Your father said he'd brought another horse for you, hoping you'd change your mind. We can have such fun. Your mother doesn't really want you to stay at home on Christmas. If you do I'll have to ride alone. Hal has a date with Flossie Huger."

Emily's unhappy white face forced itself between Robert and the darkly wholesome, windwhipped face of Nancy.

"I'll come to apologize tonight after dinner, Nancy." He cut his spurs into Jack's side and left the bewildered girl staring after him as he galloped home.

The horns called the hunt to begin. Stands had been allocated to those too old or timid to ride with the hunters. A toast was hastily drunk to St. Hubert, who was converted to Christianity through the vision of a milk-white stag bearing a flaming cross on his antlers, the patron saint of hunting. Although the horns could produce but one note, the Negro huntsmen were so proficient in the art that with this one note they could communicate much information to their hounds and to the field. This they did by distinctive rhythms and tonal variations.

Cuffee on Hester and Inigo on Hero were among the first to get away. The horn gave long languid notes and the hounds started out looking for a deer track in the sandy road. They found one and to the one note blown at intervals to tell them that the hunters were with them and to keep trying, they raced across fields and pinelands. They started a stag in the Oak Drive of the Blind Preacher and raced for miles through the pine forests. They neared the swamp, and the growth of broomgrass and briers and myrtles became taller and

142

thicker. As the leaders of the party came abreast of the first bushes there was a tremendous flutter in the thick "ocean," a panicky outcry, and a beautiful doe with her two yearlings broke cover and made for the river, clearing the bushes in long bounds, their white flags flying and the frenzied pack in full pursuit. The white tails vanished through the trees. The hunters pulled up their horses. The deer reached the river and crossed.

Several long doleful notes now came from the horns and the hounds came back and started to try somewhere else. They didn't have far to look. A stag came out from the thicket as soon as time enough had passed for the doe and her young to cross the river.

"Oh, look, Mass Inigo," breathed Cuffee, "ain' nobody see um yet but we—I feels bad about dat stag—I —" he didn't get to finish for the hounds had spotted the stag, too. A great snow-white albino monarch stood there in the dappled sunlight that filtered through the soughing pine trees—twelve points he had and eyes that were battle-lit and fiery. Little sets of short quick notes leaped from the horn accompanied by two shrill screams and halloas to put the hounds in full cry onto him. For a moment at bay, he turned and then like a white dream bounded off into the heavy growth of the swamp.

Inigo and the riders who had come to this point rode together with wonder on their faces. They had all heard of the white stag but none had ever seen him before. They had thought that for the old ones who muttered about him in their cups he was a symbol of their lost shining youth—but he was real. The horses were so excited that they could not be held in and after one moment of fellowship the hunters were off again following the hounds and the staccato horn notes that warned the hunters not to try to pick out the line for themselves.

Off they went. But not all of them. Cuffee held Hester back and dropped away from the group. That stag had caught his eye and had tried to challenge him. That was a king stag and he had recognized when he turned his glistening eyes on Cuffee that here, too, was a king—one of royal blood who had been hunted and

143

captured. There had been contempt in the challenge that the stag had thrown at him. The contempt that one who has resisted his hunters and outwitted them feels for the weak who have been defeated. He, the stag, was a white one, an unconquerable one, and he had dared Cuffee to follow him. Generations of Corromantee warriors stirred in Cuffee's breast—the black ones with their rippling muscles and high heads beat a tom-tom in his veins, his eyes glowed like brush fires, and clenching his fists he swore to whatever old gods his kind had worshiped, to kill that white one. The one that the white hunters had told of seeking for many years, he, Cuffee, would meet. He would bring to his fireside the twelve points of the white antlers and prove that the black hunter was more powerful than the white hunter.

The others had raced down the broad road to cut the stag off from the river, but Cuffee thought he would double back and head northward for the sparkleberry thickets. He galloped around and as he reached a thick hummock the stag rushed out and almost jumped clear over Hester and Cuffee. Away he sailed, his stiffly erect snowy tail flashing high above the bay bushes. Cuffee and Hester kept after him and the stag looked around and kicked up his back legs with the appearance of complete enjoyment in the race; then suddenly he turned and charged straight into Hester. His cruel antlers pierced right through her heart and she fell heavily. Cuffee rolled sideways and escaped being crushed but as he looked up the stag was straddling him with stiffened legs and lowered antlers, his hot breath blowing acridly in Cuffee's face, his eyes like black flame. Suddenly to Cuffee's horror the face was not a stag's face— it was Inigo's face murderous in its large whiteness.

Jesus Gawd, he prayed, *dis a vision for true! Somepin evil fixing to happen.*

He fought against the hypnotic spell of the cruel venomous eyes, and reached in his pocket to close his hand around his crab claw—to ward off this white magic relentlessly pinning him down on the earth.

Then terror took Cuffee. Primitive terror. For the first time in his life he was without his heritage—without his protective crab claw. And for the first time he was being injured by a white being. Was it a man or was it a deer? The overpowering resemblance to Inigo rendered him powerless without his crab claw—destroyed any desire even to try and save himself.

Perhaps he fainted. Or maybe he fell into a trance. There is a fine line between the two for black people. Whichever it was, he missed seeing Inigo and three other hunters, closely followed by the hounds, crash out of the myrtle thicket and strike after the stag which gave one last vicious jab at Cuffee's face with a sharp hoof before he disappeared into the mysterious depths of the "ocean."

Chapter 22

"Charlotte, take some boiling water and some clean rags over to Hagar. Cuffee been hurt on de deer drive." Hercules was fussing about the kitchen like a querulous old hen complaining that the cream was sour and the crab meat had splinters left in it.

"Where is Mr. Inigo?" Charlotte put down the tea tray she had prepared for Tafra. He was home! He was back!

"Don't ast me for Mass Inigo. Yunnuh do what I tells yuh. Go on where I tole yuh. Brayboy kin carry Miss Tafra' tea."

Charlotte took a pot from the fireside, gathered up some clean pieces of homespun from Sweet's pile of dish towels, and went out. At the sick house she helped Hagar wash Cuffee's swollen face with the water into which Hagar had thrown some dried herbs. He was not seriously hurt but he sat unmoving and made no sound though she knew that the cuts were painful and sore. Hagar leaned over and moved her hands back and forth in front of his fixed eyes, but the piercing glittering stare did not waver; so she mixed a potion in a gourd and tried to make him drink it.

He raised his fist and without looking at the gourd struck it squarely in the middle and knocked it to the floor. Then he stretched out his long muscular arms and began to clench and unclench his sensitive fingers as though they were breaking bones in them.

"Whey my crab claw at?" he demanded hostilely of Charlotte. "Hit's yo own fault dis comed to Cuffee. Git hit. Whey hit at?"

Charlotte flew back to the house. She had been ashamed this morning for even touching such a foolish childish charm. A moldy old crab claw! She had an impulse to dash it to the floor and splinter it under her feet but she was arrested by Inigo's loud excited laughter coming from the drawing-room where the hunt party was going on.

It cannot be that he has forgotten me after we came so close for that moment on the piazza this morning. Why should he forget me? Why, dear God? Say why. He knows where I am yet he would never leave his friends and come in here to tell me that he is back—that he is safe from his hunting—to ask after my blistered wrist.

She listened to the gay talking, absorbed in a vague sense of sorrow, the crab claw forgotten. After a while Hagar came and knocked on her door.

"Um hum." She surveyed Charlotte's flushed cheeks critically. "Yunnuh sho fuhgits quick."

Charlotte held out the unharmed claw and Hagar reverently folded it in a piece of homespun and put it in her apron pocket.

"I'm sorry, I didn't sleep much last night. I guess I'm tired."

"Dem voices frum de party is too loud in hyar," Hagar told her. "Come back wid me. Yunnuh ain't never been to pay a visit wid Hagar. Come to de Street wid me. Hit's time, Charlotte, honey, hit's time and past time."

But Charlotte shook her head and unmindful of the pitying look Hagar gave her, she left her door cracked, the better to hear Inigo, and flung herself down on her wide-canopied bed. The yellow silk draperies cast a bright shadow on her hair and picked out the soft tinge of gold that was dusted over her face and throat.

She pillowed her head on her arm and tried to rest, but a nagging ugly idea kept pricking at the back of her brain. *I will never be invited to a party in his drawing-room. I will only be invited to the Street with Hagar. And I can't go to the Street feeling like I do; I can't, I can't!*

Negro laughter floated up from under her window—mingling its rich fruity resonance with the other laughter. The afternoon was growing late and the slaves were on their way to the field to watch Cuffee break the filly. Suddenly she decided to go to the field ahead of Inigo. To secrete herself in a place where she could watch him but he could not see her. *I have got to decide something,* she thought, *and all my good resolutions that I made this morning have blown away in the afternoon wind.*

She ran from her room and joined the throng of people without even throwing her shawl over her shoulders. Her cheeks were burning like the color of her dress and her breath came jerkily through her tight bodice. Nobody seemed to notice her. *They never do,* she thought bitterly. *Either here or in the drawing-room. I am a part of the background wherever I find myself. It is time for me to step out and take up my part in the play.*

She found a place close to the gate and leaned against the rail. Her head ached and her hands plucked nervously at her skirt. A tense muscle caused the corners of her mouth to twitch but she rested against the rail and as far as she was concerned the hundreds of Negroes might have been wisps of Spanish moss blowing about the field.

Back at the house the party was still in full swing in the great drawing-room. The hunters had all come back to Normandy to watch Cuffee break the famous filly. Tafra asked Hercules where Charlotte had got to but he was too busy to give her a clear answer. Tafra was trying so hard to keep Inigo a happy host in spite of Emily's pointedly disparaging remarks about horsy people, that she was using every ounce of her physical and mental resources and though for a moment she worried over Charlotte not being with her, she managed to dominate the party as Nicholas would have wished her to.

The men were drinking cups of hot punch made of lemons, sugar, hot water, and Irish whisky and the ladies were sipping sherry and Madeira. Clay pipes were being passed and Hercules was importantly supervising the making of the creamy crab stew, rich with old sherry and floating with thin slices of lemon, in the deep silver chafing-dishes, while other servingmen passed silver waiters of hot fried shrimp and crisp buttered waffles.

The men, thrilled and excited over their hunting, drank cup after cup of punch, toasting their horses, their women, and their friends, until more than one of them blinked muzzily and sat down gratefully on a soft sofa or small hard chair. Inigo talked louder and louder and went about slapping the men on the back and being rude to the ladies.

"Isn't it time for you all to go to the field?" Tafra finally got his attention, her heart sick at the wild intoxication in his eyes, the thickness in his speech.

"Let's go and break the filly," he shouted and since everybody had had more than enough to eat and drink they all bowed low to her and Emily, and even the ladies hurried away.

It wasn't cold outside. A west wind blew in from the river and rattled the marsh grass, but late roses and early camellias bloomed in the garden. They made their way across the lawn to the east field where the Negroes were gathered. Among the slaves were Negro jockeys from other plantations who had gotten permits to spend Christmas afternoon at Normandy. Yellow Pompey, Harry Singleton's prize jockey, was on the front row and all the slaves were in great spirits and making much conversation about Cuffee.

"Um wasser dan old Balimn. Um go' say, git up, mule, and beat mule wid stick, and mule go' turn round and say—whuffo you duh beat me fuh, niggah? An' she go' kick up dem big raid heels and Cuffee go' be down in de dirt on he flat nose," laughed Yellow Pompey who was Cuffee's greatest rival on the race track.

"Hush yo' mout'," said Big Jake. "Yunnuh mus' ain't nebber see Cuffee ride um, enty? How 'bout yunnuh riding she in he place?" A pleased laugh followed this and Inigo bellowed, "Everybody shut up!" A sudden silence.

"Everybody stay shut up or I'll have Big Jake after you—and stay out of Cuffee's way. Here he comes now. Don't one of you come across this fence!"

"Amen, Massa," "Yassuh, Massa," "Das right, Massa, you tellum."

Little Nick came up to Charlotte and took her hand. She tried to smile at him, but the idea of the mixed river of her blood was whirling in her brain and in her troubled, uneasy frame of mind she had become a stranger to herself. Nick sensed her unhappiness and pressed himself warmly against his side, instinctively trying to share himself with her and make her happy.

The Negroes started cheering and waving as Cuffee came from the stables leading Fancy. She fretted and pranced but he tried to keep her head turned so she could not see the people. Quash followed alongside with a polished saddle.

The gentlemen and ladies in their formal riding-clothes, seeing the world as a fine place to live in, sighed enviously as the filly neared them. Seventeen hands high she stood, the beauty and grace of the Arab marking every elegant step. Her mane and tail were pure silver and her coat rippled and shone like red satin. She had a white star on her forehead and one white hind foot. She had all the points of a brilliant race horse, being a descendant of Sir Archy and Diomed and Childers and Blaze and Bay Bloody Buttocks and Cripple.

What a pity, they thought, that she hadn't been

foaled here at Normandy. What a pity that such a one had to go through the process of being broken. For she was too radiant to run the risk of anything shattering her thrilling perfection.

Robert interrupted the silent worship with a giggle. He had been making things right with Nancy. He had a way of pleasing women, learned through his life with Emily. "It would be a big joke if Cuffee couldn't ride her," he said foolishly.

The worshipful silence changed to an ominously dead silence. Low Country folk never made jokes about superior horseflesh. A slave or a son could be replaced, but a divine filly—never!

Inigo started after Robert but Harry Singleton caught his arm and told him that Cuffee was signaling to him.

So Inigo with difficulty controlled himself and went over to Cuffee and Fancy. Between them they got her through the gate and Big Jake put up the bar.

"Hand Cuffee the saddle, Quash." Inigo held Fancy by the bridle and stroked her nose. The effect of too much punch plus the sight of Fancy exhilarated him and lifted him up onto a bigger planet where men and horses lived happily without women. He talked to Fancy lovingly, maudlin words, and she blew uneasily in his face. Cuffee gently placed the saddle on her back and Fancy threw up her head and jumped sideways. Inigo didn't stop talking to her and held her firm. Cuffee looked at Inigo and Inigo nodded. Before anyone could see what he was doing, Cuffee was in the saddle, his feet were home in the stirrups and Fancy was pawing the air with her front feet. Inigo ran over to the fence and the battle was on!

Fancy wheeled—she ran—she bucked and bucked and bucked—she reared and nearly fell over backward. She reared and Cuffee pushed her down onto her four feet—she reared and spun like a top on her slender hind legs—she jumped and she backed and she whirled—but still the man on her back clung and pulled at her tender mouth.

She was smart—she became crafty—she began to walk almost quietly. Cuffee was smart, too. He loosed the reins—a leap and his high laughter rang out across the field. Fancy tore like a whirlwind through the soft sandy soil and almost cut a backward somersault when she came to the fence. The fascinated audience could hear Cuffee singing to her in his strong, chanting voice—

"Ain't dis de hand what duh feed yunnuh? An' ain't dis de voice what duh sing in de nighttime? Ain't dis de hand what duh stroke yo' neck and make yo' mane to shine lak silber? An' ain't dese de laigs what duh run and fetch yo' water in de rainy time, and duh make yo' baid smooth and sweet?"

Fancy was lathered in sweat and flecks of foam flew from her mouth as she tossed her head like a proud woman sure of her power and thundered with long galloping strides around the field. Inigo looked glorious. He stood with his great legs apart and his huge hands on his hips. Ah! the horsemanship of Cuffee! Ah! the unbelievable speed and bottom of the filly! Fancy never stumbled—her balance was precision in motion—her whirls and leaps consummate grace.

Charlotte watched Inigo and her tormented heart saw a want of symmetry in him—saw in his attitude too much adoration, directed not at her but at the mad creature running like a streak of fire before her eyes. *How I hate that filly,* she thought, trembling with temper and with a summation of many lonely years. *How I hate the sight of her.*

The Negroes, getting restless, began to mutter and drift away. Sport without blood was but a white man's idea of play. They were too old a race to worship chivalry. They noted the setting sun signifying the waiting cask of rum, and their lips took up the songs they were going to sing at their party tonight in the church. Tonight they could sit up as late as they pleased. Big Jake had promised not to blow the horn even if they stayed away from their cabins shouting till day-come.

Cuffee was enjoying himself and showing off to the crowd. But Inigo, looking down from his planet, sensed the inattention of his people and called out, "You've done it, Cuffee; quit your foolishness and bring her in."

"Yassuh, Massa," Cuffee sang back. "Me and my little gal is on us way dis berry minute." He turned

Fancy toward the gate from which Big Jake had taken the bar. Fancy was galloping easily and not fighting the bit much—disdainfully bearing on her back the human whose legs felt kind and swift against her side.

As they started through the gate where Charlotte stood, a fit of sneezing shook and tore through her. And as she sneezed her whole heart filled up with furious bitter passion.

This is the end, she thought. *This is worse than the time Edisto killed Fifi. Everybody is staring at me. Cuffee is shouting at me to get away or I will frighten the filly. Now they are laughing at me and my red nose and eyes.* Kerchoo! Kerchoo!

"Get away from that filly!" Inigo roared angrily at her as Fancy began to rear and wheel.

Charlotte sneezed and sneezed; again Inigo yelled at her to get away. His voice was rough and arrogantly wrathful. Charlotte suddenly lost all control of herself and, squatting down, picked up a clod of hard dirt and threw it right into Fancy's eyes.

"You witch horse!" she screamed wildly.

Fancy jumped as though she had been shot, plunging into the crowd of Negroes. Shrieks and warnings burst out; children cried in panic and a wild scramble pressed part of the people against the fence and the rest stumbled and fell away from the murderous hoofs that beat the earth about them.

Inigo seemed to have disappeared, but suddenly he jumped up from the ground where the crowd was thickest and grabbed the terrified filly's bridle. Cuffee was still, in a trancelike manner, singing to Fancy, and Inigo was dragged a long way before he succeeded by sheer animal muscle in pulling Fancy to a stop.

Cuffee dismounted quickly and without a word or a backward glance led Fancy to her stall, away from the man who now resembled the vengeful stag—away from the girl who had no crab claw.

Inigo snatched up his crop from where he had dropped it and looked around for Charlotte. She was standing defiantly alone, her sneezing done, her cheeks hot and flaming. *Come on,* she wanted to cry. *Come on with your whip and your barbaric anger. You are a*

*savage, too. Beat me! What am I but a slave who has
no right—no voice, a dumb animal that spins out my
days running to do your bidding? I am glad that you
are married to a woman with no heart. I am glad that I
never let you into the circle of my rich warmth.*

The fragile lace shivered with the pulse beats in
her throat. She clenched her hands behind her and
waited for him.

The Negroes drew away from the fierce emotion
that sparked from her strange light eyes. The white
planters came closer, tensely watching to see what Inigo
was going to do.

His temper was remembered from his reckless
boyhood, and his face now was twisted with an awful
rage. For together with the anger Inigo felt at Charlotte
for having transformed Fancy from a gorgeous filly
into a killing devil, was the burning, thwarted passion
for her that constantly gnawed into him; the animosity
that he held for Emily, his wife; his galling resentment
of his mother, who refused to let him have Charlotte.
His rage told of all the heart-searing acts he had
committed in his effort to forget her; of the past
night, spent in an agony of unfulfilled desire for her.

Seeing Charlotte through the feverish haze of these
emotions, she seemed to lick upward like a tongue of
saffron flame. She was Woman and he was Man. She
had caused him to sin and suffer, and now there was no
garden anywhere. *I told you I would not hurt you,* his
dark eyes blazed—*but I will! I'll tear you up as you
have torn my heart.*

Charlotte did not move as he came up and caught
her roughly by the arm. She bowed her shining head so
that she could not see his face as he lashed her back
with his riding-whip; she only cringed when she heard
little Nick screaming at his father to stop! stop! This
seemed to add to Inigo's excitement, and the thick muscles of his neck swelled with the brute intensity of the
blows that he gave her.

Finally the gentlemen could stand it no longer, and
they closed in on Inigo, pulling him roughly away.
Charlotte crumpled on the ground at Inigo's feet and
they led him, raving and cursing, back into his house.

Little Nick bent over Charlotte. "Your beautiful lace collar is all torn and dirty," he sobbed as he tried to lift her from where she lay on the ground, her lips pressed in the dirt, making no sound, saying no word.

The people went quickly away from the sad, sad scene. Shoulda had a crab claw, they moaned—nigger needa crab claw, caze he cain't never answer back—not a word—not a word.

The farther away, the louder they moaned.

> "See how they done my Lord,
> An' He never said a mumblin' word.
>> Not a word
>> Not a word
>> Not a word.

> "They led Him from hall to hall
> An' He never said a mumblin' word.
>> Not a word
>> Not a word
>> Not a word.

> "They whipped Him all night long
> An' He never said a mumblin' word.
>> Not a word
>> Not a word
>> Not a word.

> "Wasn't that an awful shame!
> An' He never said a mumblin' word.
>> Not a word
>> Not a word
>> Not a word."

Chapter 23

Oh, Eve, where is Adam?
Oh, Eve!
Adam in de garden
Pinnin' on leave'.

Ad–u–u–m?
Pinnin' on leave'.
Where't thou?
Pinnin' on leave'.
Adam naked,
Pinnin' on leave'.
Ain't you 'shame'?
Pinnin' on leave'.
Lord, I'm 'shame',
Pinnin' on leave'.

Cuffee sat on the steps of his house, smoking a clay pipe. He had heard Inigo galloping hard away on Hero, and he knew that something must be bad wrong for the master to take Hero out—tired as he was after all that hunting. He'd better sit here and wait for him to come back. Big as Inigo was, he always needed somebody to look after him when things went wrong and he got into one of his mad spells and then ran away to the woods, being shamed.

Suddenly the vision of the white stag floated before Cuffee. The stag had definitely challenged him with lowered antlers and flaming eyes. Like Inigo, the stag had stood in his large whiteness—flaunting his whiteness! The blackness in Cuffee had stirred and accepted that challenge and one day his blackness would come to grips with that whiteness and then—in a fair fight the stronger would win! It had been an omen. As the white stag had hurt him, later Inigo had hurt little Charlotte. And it had been all his fault for not letting her keep the crab claw. His black fingers closed over the charred claw in his pocket. He must never let it out of his keeping, but in some way, somehow, he would keep white magic from injuring her again.

He heard a giggle at the steps. He put down his pipe. Finger Ring was there black and juicy.

"Come to de chu'ch," she invited him in her low husky voice.

"Uh-unh." He put out his foot and shoved her away.

"Pompey dere; I ain' want yunnuh nohow." She flounced off—flicking her high bottom at him as he laughed derisively at her.

No time to be fooling with trash such as Finger Ring. Her kind of rolling did not appeal to him tonight. It was there any time he wanted it. He was too grieved over Charlotte's crying in the sick house—like the squirrel he'd once found in Inigo's trap. He'd eased the squirrel—he hoped he could ease Charlotte. She was so lovely—like his own dreams she was. Charlotte and Fancy! Both the very essence of dreaming. He leaned back against the post of his small piazza, patting his foot in time to the shouting from the church, livened by the cask of rum. He could hear the sonorous voice of Parson Weble singing the call of God, and Field Hand Mattie in her high-pitched quick soprano answer Eve's part. The shouters would be stamping and swaying as they stooped to the ground to pick up the leaves and went through the round sexual motions of pinning them on.

> "My Lord call you
> Pinnin' on leave'.
> My Lord call you
> Pinnin' on leave'.
>
> "Oh, Eve, where is Adam?
> Oh, Eve!
> My Lord call you
> Pinnin' on leave'."

Charlotte stirred painfully on the hard bed in the sick house.

"Poulette," she murmured pleadingly. "Please, Poulette, come and get me. Poulette—" The slender hands plucked feverishly at the gray, scratchy blanket. "Everything is so dark—even the stars have gone out and I have lost Charlotte. Please, Poulette, find Charlotte for me." Suddenly she sat up in the bed and threw back the cover. Hagar gently tried to push her down but Charlotte wildly clutched Hagar by the shoulders and buried her face against the shriveled dry breasts. "I won't be whipped," she screamed. "I won't be whipped! Potee! Potee!"

Hagar loosened the frantic fingers and going over to the fire, she dipped a gourd of water from a bucket, them fumbled in her apron and, taking out a sack, opened it with her teeth and poured some fine white powder into the water. She went back to the bed and for a moment looked down into the delirious suffering face. She leaned over and pushed the tangled hair away from the fine pale brow and tenderly gathered Charlotte in her wiry arms, putting the gourd to her lips. Charlotte gulped the stuff down as Hagar smoothed the coarse sheet under the poor bruised and welted back.

"Why don't yunnuh marry wid dat doctor and quit yo' strugglin' to stay white?" Hagar's mouth was pitying and hard at the same time and her low voice had a soothing hypnotic effect on Charlotte. She closed her wild glazed eyes as the drug began its relaxing power.

Hagar talked on. She talked of the Congo where she had run and played as a child. She told of seeing a songbird once, paralyzed by a snake—its bright eyes dulled, willing its own destruction. She told of fire dances at dusk and of strange rites performed at dark and full of moon.

Charlotte appeared to be sleeping, though every now and then hot tears welled up and trickled down her burning face.

Hagar told of the day she and Big Bush had been captured and marched to Rio Ponga. They had been married a few months before, and she was twelve years old, proudly bearing Bush's son under her heart.

157

The baby was born and died in the filth of a slave ship. As Charlotte was suffering now so had she writhed amidst offal and rotten food, while her tiny bones ground the life out of the little one hopelessly caught in her loins. Bush had finally himself pulled the boy out and thrown him into the sea.

That had been a long time ago. And she had been here at Normandy since she landed at Charleston. Old Francis, Nicholas's father, had bought them and they had come here to work in indigo. Yes—she had been here longer than Tafra or Hercules even. When Nicholas had handed the baby Cuffee to her in his prince's basket, she knew that he was her and Bush's son risen from the waves of the ocean. And she had wronged him by bringing him up a pure African. Now she wanted him to be an American. She had watched the black ones sift into this white world. She had seen how hard it was for them to fit themselves into this strange, code-bound order. Charlotte was one of the few who had found the secret. One of the few who could be a leader because she knew where white weakness lay. It was going to be up to Charlotte to help the Cuffees and the Finger Rings when freedom came.

All these things she told Charlotte in a low voice, soothing her to sleep. Then, as she heard the singing in the church she began to talk louder.

"Dis am what come from living white when one of yo' gran'-mammy's been a nigger from dat same Congo. Whup! Dat's what hit's got yunnuh. Whup! But yunnuh ain't gots to stay whup! Member dat, nigger chile! Marry wid de doctor and git way from roun' here. White man ain't for yunnuh, po' li'l Charlotte—po' creetur. Black man lak Cuffee ain't, neither, but de nigger doctor laked yunnuh. How 'bout him, huh? How 'bout him?"

She held her hands down on the tea-matted eyelashes, fanning Charlotte with a palmetto frond to cool the fever. Charlotte pushed against the skinny hand holding her eyes and began a hurtful threshing about on the uncomfortable bed. Unwillingly she started keeping time with the primitive singing coming from the church as it grew louder and faster and filled the close room.

158

Hagar watched Charlotte's stomach start to twitch and heave. And Hagar's eyes began to flicker like an animal's in the firelight.

"Hag duh ride," she muttered, reaching down by her foot and getting an empty bottle that a short while earlier had held a pint of precious rum. "Hag duh ride she fuh fair! Hecklus allus said dat Charlotte been hag-rid ever since she seen Mass Inigo de fust night she come here. Now I gwine ketch dat hag and bring peace back here to Normandy. I gwine put an end to all dis black-white business."

Hagar pulled the cover down, baring Charlotte's stomach. Uncorking the bottle, she placed it over the flawless pearl of the little navel with the mouth turned down, while her left hand fumbled in her dress for a needle.

There was no time to lose. You had to move swiftly if you expected to catch a hag. If you were heavy-boned you need not try. Only skinny ones were deft enough to be hag-catchers.

Now—she'd found the needle and she was ready for the hag. Closing her eyes like an old reptile, she deliberately counted to thirty-three, the magic number, and lifted the bottle off Charlotte's stomach. Then she threw the needle in the bottle quick, and corked it up before the hag could recollect herself.

"Got um," Hagar chanted. "Got um now. Jedus Christ, I done got um. Dat hag ain't gwine cause no mo' worry between dis un and Mass Inigo, less I fool 'nough fuh give vittle 'way. Done fuh now. Hag clean gone."

Hagar swayed her thin frame and beat the palmetto fan rhythmically on the now rigidly quiet stomach.

"Oh, Eve," she sang with the distant singers, "where is Adam?"

> *"Oh, Eve,*
> *Adam don' answer,*
> *Pinnin' on leave'."*

It was nearly dawn when Inigo slipped into the room at the sick house where Charlotte lay. Bits of red still winked in the fireplace ashes and Inigo found a thin pine splinter in the wood box and touched it to the live coals.

A sharp thread of light caught the tiny torch, showing him the rough pine bed. Kneeling down and holding the light over her face, he guiltily touched her eyelids with his finger tips, and slowly the heavy tangled black lashes struggled to part from the drugged sleep that held them prisoner.

She tried to speak but her mouth was so dry she could only croak, "Oh—Oh—"

Inigo stared at the chimera of Charlotte, lying on coarse gray sheets under a rough blanket and never had she looked more beautiful to him. Never more completely desirable. He bent and kissed her burning lips and she kissed him back even though she could not force a word or a thought coherently from either her brain or her heart.

Hagar got up from her chair in a dark corner, and Inigo whispered quickly in Charlotte's ear, "I'm going to take you West with me the day after New Year's. Get strong and love me, Charlotte. Please love me."

Charlotte tried to nod her heavy head but she could not find the will to make it work.

"What yunnuh wants, Mass Inigo? Charlotte am so full of cocaine dat she easy now. Yunnuh git on back to de big house where yunnuh belongs and quit 'sturbing dis po' chile."

Inigo did not care to brave Hagar's wrath. He knew that she was definitely in league with the devil and could cast the most potent spells in the parish. So he fixed his fingers in the shape of horns to prevent her putting Platt Eye on him as he went quickly away wondering just when he had made up his mind to take Charlotte West? To tell her that he loved her? When had he decided? He knew! He had decided the very day she arrived at Normandy and laughed up at him, her wonderful eyes filled with admiration of him.

160

Chapter 24

❖❖❖❖❖❖❖❖❖❖❖❖❖❖❖❖❖❖❖❖❖❖❖❖❖❖❖❖❖

Noon burned through the glazed windows of the dreary sick house; still Charlotte did not rouse, and she breathed irregularly and loudly. Her head lolled back limply when Hagar raised her and tried to force some cool water through the dry cracked lips, so, after reporting to Tafra, Hagar sent Cuffee to the city for Dr. Cavallo.

Leon came reluctantly. He had closed the door to the corner of his heart which clamored for the strange girl and it was painful for him to be forced to attend her after such a degrading occurrence. Cuffee had minimized the details so he was unprepared for the pinched yellowish face and the ravaged back which Hagar bared to him. Seeing the ivory flesh bruised and broken in places, his whole soul faltered.

"God damn him! God damn him!"

"Hush! Hush!" Hagar laid a cold claw finger on his lips.

But as his hands explored the lovely body for injury, as he cupped each gold-tipped breast in his trembling hands, every fiber warned him that he should go quickly from here lest he weep and let her know that he loved her; lest, loving her, he fall into the same dreadful pit of love where she now lay so shamefully.

"Why?" he asked Hagar— "Why?"

"Is yunnuh ever seen she and Mass Inigo lookin' 'pon one another?"

He nodded. Yes—last June he'd seen and it had

161

haunted him ever since. Wondering if she had ever—
ever—

"Is she his mistress?" he finally choked the ugly
words out.

"Gawd no!" Hagar cackled. "Her wouldn't be lyin'
dere all tore up effen Mass Inigo ain't had too much hot
fire pressed back een he own self."

Ah, now he could help her. Now he could make
her open her eyes.

"Wake up, Charlotte." He shook her roughly and
she didn't even whimper though he knew her shoulders
were raw and sore.

"What in the world did you give her to put her in
this deep sleep?"

"Jest a leetle cocaine mix wid a leetle herrin."

"Cocaine—heroin? Where did you get that stuff?"

Hagar lowered her eyes and began to suck her
teeth loudly.

So—she wouldn't tell. He learned something new
every day of his practice. How did slaves get expensive
narcotics? Where, and what did they use for money?
Hagar shook her head and sucked louder with each
question so he made a mental note to find out for himself. This Low Country was assuredly not the genial,
sheltered way of life he had thought as he grew up on
Beaufain Street.

"Dis gal oughter be got away frum here." Hagar
changed to a safer subject. "Whyn't yunnuh marry wid
her and git her safe? She too heading a gal tuh be wase
hyar. She de kind kin take Denmark Vesey place w'en
freedom come effen her don' loss herself befo'han'."

Leon had to laugh. "You're an old fix-it," he said.

"Not as good un as Miss Tafra. She gwine outfix
de debbil some day." Hagar was having a fine time and
she did not notice Charlotte open her eyes and look
coldly at Leon.

"Go away," she whispered. "I don't want you to
see me like this."

"Well, sit up and drink some water."

"No."

He lifted her up and held the gourd to her lips,

162

and when she refused to open them he poured the water down her chin.

"Go to the house and get some soup," he ordered Hagar crisply, stimulated by the very flickering of her lashes. "She's got to eat."

But Hagar had one more thing to tell Leon. "She a strange mixtry," Hagar said softly. "Her got some kind of power in dem light eyes what her don' even know her gots. Even Cuffee am witched by Charlotte. Lowin' he am juty-boun' fuh pertect her."

When Hagar had gone to the kitchen Charlotte murmured painfully, "You are free. Free to go—to run."

So I am free, he thought, spreading an unguent gently on her shoulders, soothing her once more into shadowed sleeping. *But freedom weighs too much around my heart. Too much to take you into my keeping. You have been punished for daring to love unwisely. I will not be.*

He closed the jar of salve and snapped his bag shut —snapping the spell of Charlotte's body on his senses; snapping himself free from the fine, fierce joy of knowing she existed. And he tiptoed away, willing her not to wake until he was gone, until he was safely away from her presence. Forcing her memory to fade as music fades, forbidding the dream of her to tremble on his heart.

But as he trotted his little roan down the somber corridor of Gaillard oaks, pain and sorrow merged into an aching, longing desire to turn and ride back to the sick house and gather the forlorn crumpled figure into his arms.

No. If this beating had driven the great Gaillard out of her eyes, then—then he could let himself show her that he loved her. He would know when next they came together. She hadn't wanted to look at him back there in the sick house. He knew she had been conscious the whole time, that she dared not face the pity that he felt for her. For pity would be the final blow that would cause more hurt to her proud heart than the infuriated whip had done.

163

Chapter 25

Tafra endured five ugly, strained days during which Inigo never once came near her drawing-room and Emily's shrill, gleeful singing sowed discord among the boys, the servants, and even the hounds who were in the habit of dropping in and out of the house at will.

Then, in desperation, she sent for Cuffee, to discuss Charlotte and her future with him. Cuffee refused to come near the big house. He informed the various messengers she sent that he was down with a misery in his back.

So Tafra had Hagar in but Hagar grimly shook her scrawny black neck, which supported her proud head crowned with a turban, peaked as importantly as a bishop's miter.

"Cuffee ain't 'bout to come and 'spute wid yunnuh, Miss Tafra. He scairt yunnuh go try and mek he marry wid Charlotte and he ain't gwinter, caze Mass Inigo been to de spring fust and muddy de water."

"Don't be silly, Hagar. You know nothing has happened between Mr. Inigo and Charlotte."

Hagar nodded and sucked her teeth to indicate that the interview was over.

"I'll try once more, anyhow," Tafra stubbornly told the other tight-lipped old woman.

She called little Sambo, bidding him tell Cuffee that for Mass Nicholas's sake he must come and talk to her about Charlotte.

Little Sambo darted away on his spindly legs to the stables. Cuffee was laughing and talking to Quash as they sorted out saddles that needed cleaning.

"Cuffee," little Sambo said breathlessly, "Ole Miss a-settin' in she big chair in she big room wid all de candles burnin', lookin' lak a jedgment angel, an' a-knockin' dat quarled black stick 'pon de floor lak hit wuz yo' haid she wuz a-knockin' and she say, 'Tell dat good-fuh-nuttin' black scoundrel to fetch hisself hyar.'"

Cuffee grinned at Quash and scratched his head. Sambo's eyes were big with pride over his original message—eager to see Cuffee properly impressed. His sly little face fell in disappointment when Cuffee just stood there and chuckled like something funny had happened.

"Tell Old Miss, Cuffee got de rheumitiz in he arms," replied Cuffee, rubbing oil briskly into a big saddle.

"But, Cuffee, yunnuh ain't got no rheumitiz in yo' arms," Sambo said, looking critically at the rippling muscles that worked up and down with the massaging of the leather.

"Den tell she Cuffee got a misery in he haid and a hurt in he heart. Don't yunnuh know dat when white folks send and yunnuh don't want fuh go and yet don't want fuh hurt a old woman's feelings yunnuh gots to send a charitable message?" Cuffee stretched his muscular arms and jigged a measure on his bowed legs. "But Cuffee free. Cuffee don't go when finger crooks. Cuffee go when Cuffee ready. Cuffee marry when Cuffee ready, and not to suit nobody but Cuffee." Quash nodded his head admiringly as though if he were free he would speak with just those words. "And mind yunnuh tek whut unnuh told yunnuh to Miss Tafra. Don't twitch up Cuffee' words to she lak yunnuh done wid de words yunnuh brung from she to Cuffee. Cuffee might break yo' kinky haid wid a quarled black stick effen yunnuh do!"

The skinny legs fled.

Back in Tafra's room Sambo excitedly delivered his message.

"Cuffee done fell out a tree and bus' he heart wide open. He lying dere on de groun' a-groanin' an' a-moanin' an' he say he come when he git ready."

"All right, Sambo, run find Nick and you boys get Mingo to take you duckshooting on the Little Marsh. Nick is down at the sick house with Charlotte. Hurry!"

Everybody hurried Sambo to see the sticklike legs fly. Tafra and Jenny laughed at the hasty tattoo beating down the stairs as Sambo sped to find Nick. As the front door slammed Tafra's laugh changed to a sigh. She might have known it would be impossible to mate Charlotte and Cuffee. She would have to put Charlotte's fate in Colonel Hampton's hands. She had blundered too much already.

Turning to Jenny, she asked for a writing-board and a quill and ink. Her thoughts came out easier in writing and where Charlotte was concerned ideas contradicted each other in ridiculous disorder.

Jenny, a bright-skinned girl, Sweet's daughter, had just spent six months in Charleston being trained for a house or body servant and she was very proud to wait on the mistress in Charlotte's place. Tafra was glad to have the pleasant chatty girl around to see to Nick and keep him clean and happy.

"Miss Tafra," said Jenny, bringing her the board, "I ain't never seen such goings on as is going on downstairs. Dis oyster roast what Mass Inigo is giving must be a monstrous big party."

"Yes, Jenny, a big party. It's the main social event we have at Normandy. Old Mr. Nicholas's father started the custom and I believe that the great oaks which he planted down the avenue would weep real tears if the long table was absent on New Year's Day and the friends of Normandy not present to start the New Year off together."

Horses were heard galloping up the avenue and Tafra put down the lap board and went as fast as her pain would permit over to the window to look out and see who the guests could be. Inigo had gone to shoot geese for the party, and Emily and Horst were downstairs working out the seating arrangements for the

166

guests at the long table on New Year's Day. Two tremendous men, on fine blooded hunters, were stopping at the green lawn in front of the house and Hercules was running out to meet them.

"It's the Hamptons!" Tafra cried, her voice trembling with pleasure. "Hercules wouldn't demean himself to run down those steps for anybody in the world but the Colonel." She had hardly finished speaking before the yard rang with her name.

"Tafra-a-a-a-a!"

Jenny pushed up the window.

"Come on up, you old turtle," called Tafra. The Colonel laughed. Hercules said something to the younger man and he handed over his reins to Quash who had come up to meet them. They spoke a few words and Quash ran off, the two chestnut hunters trotting with long easy strides behind him. Hercules and the large distinguished-looking men stood talking a few minutes, then Quash returned with Rooster and a Purdey twelve-gauge muzzle-loading shotgun. The younger man swung up, got a good grip on Rooster with his knees, and reached for the gun. Quash handed it to him and with a leap forward Rooster bolted down the avenue, up which the darkly handsome, bearded man had just ridden.

Hercules and the elderly Colonel, arm in arm, came up the steps while Brayboy carried in the saddlebags.

Tafra had straightened her lace cap and hobbled back to her chair by the fire when the door was flung open and Colonel Hampton came in and gave her a smack on her cheek and a bear hug. Then he stepped back and in a more courtly manner lifted her hand to his lips.

"As beautiful as ever, my dear Tafra," said the Colonel in a suspiciously husky voice. How old his friend was looking! How transparent and skeletal she had become since he had last seen her! Her fine lined skin stretched thinly over her skull. But even her skull was beautiful!

The Colonel was beloved by everyone. He had served a bit of military service in the War of 1812 to please his father, the General, but the military life had

167

not been to his taste. Inheriting three thousand slaves and thousands of acres in Richland County and Mississippi, he preferred to let his heart, which was as large as his means, and his generosity, which was as broad as his acres, dictate his days. He and Nicholas Gaillard had been boys together and as they grew older had both become, as their fathers had been before them, breeders of famous race horses and advocates of social justice for all Carolinians, black or white.

At Millwood, the Hampton home, five miles from Columbia, he had a private race track where his horses were exercised and trained and where he and young Wade organized races for his guests' pleasure. Millwood was a center of charm and culture, and Tafra and Nicholas had spent many happy days there in company with sportsmen and planters and statesmen. George Bancroft was often a visitor there with them as was Joel Poinsett, Henry Clay, Doctor Howe, and others who labored to keep the Stars and Stripes flying over the Southland.

After the Colonel greeted Tafra he looked appreciatively around her drawing-room, picking up the miniature of Queen Elizabeth, done in the year 1574, which lay on a polished piecrust table by the mantel.

"I remember the day in London that Nicholas bought this for you, Tafra. The rest of us were so taken up with the horses we were buying to bring home that we didn't spend money on things like this. Nicholas never forgot you. You were with him everywhere he ever went."

Tafra bent her head and pulled at the corner of her cambric handkerchief. She didn't want Wade to see the tears that came so easily to her now that she was daily growing weaker.

The Colonel sat down on one of the pair of gold cabriole sofas and said, "I'm glad you haven't changed this room. I was afraid the young people would have everything here changed to fringe and tufts and new walnut like the girls have done at Millwood."

"Emily doesn't care enough to try and change this room. It's a good thing, too, because I'm sure I would

168

attack her with my cane if she mentioned it. Where did young Wade go so hastily?"

"Hercules told him that Inigo was shooting geese on the Tippicaw Marsh and he never can bear to miss any sport, so he went to join him. By the way, are things better for Inigo now?"

Tafra was glad that Nicholas's old friend had brought up the subject. In her frank outspoken way she told him of Inigo's whipping of Charlotte and how, excessively remorseful, he was now holding it fiercely within himself, as though each blow had been dealt against his own honor.

"You gentlemen," she said bitterly, "let yourself be pleasantly suspended in three nets: Honor, State, Position. But the largest, softest net is Honor; spelled with a capital H—as God is spelled with a capital G. You ride roughshod over personal feelings—over human life, even, for any real or fancied slight to your code of behavior. In the early schooldays of a boy, his honor is held up as far more important than his studies or his capabilities by his schoolmaster, and his father praises him for fighting more than for achievement in mathematics. When he is grown, to save his name, he will shoot down his best friend for some joking remark about his wife's or his sister's bathing-costume.

"I remember, when I was a child, my father fighting a duel on the beach at Edingsville for some reason so unimportant that I have forgotten it. Many planters stood by; each second jockeyed as to the position of his principal. Everything was taken into consideration— the elevation or the depression of the smooth beach, the effect of the roar of the waves, the background against which each figure would be silhouetted, the lights and shadows and, above all, the position of the sun. My father was wounded in that duel because of a shadow that he declared his second neglected to observe. As soon as he was strong enough to pull a trigger again, he exchanged cards with his second, Raoul Swinton, his dearest friend, and in the same spot—shot and killed him to avenge his honor! I began to hate the very sound of the word then, because Sendeniah Swinton, Raoul's daughter, was my playmate and I felt that my father was a murderer every time I looked on her little tear-swollen freckled face."

The Colonel was too much of a frontiersman, as Nicholas had been, to subscribe to such hotheaded Low Country ways. He went about his life in South Carolina and Mississippi in accordance with his own law of values. His children were well educated and young Wade, his favorite, was a tireless sportsman and planter. His fat, well-fed slaves laughed and sang in the twilight; his horses ran with great heart in races all over the East; statesmen listened with respect to his words.

He agreed with Tafra, knowing that the Code Duello would before many years be dissipated on a fratricidal battlefield, but he weighed his words carefully, for he sensed that Tafra was more deeply troubled than she had told him and he guessed that Emily, silly fool, was at the bottom of it. She had ruined that nice boy.

"I've tried to persuade Inigo to divorce Emily. Now that Mr. Butler has succeeded in ridding himself of that obnoxious Fanny Kemble it shows that divorce *can* happen in the best families. There are plenty of nice girls in the Low Country who would love to take Emily's place. Inigo's friends would forgive him a divorce quicker than taking Charlotte for his Negro mistress."

The Colonel sighed. "Will Inigo consider a divorce?"

"No. He's afraid Emily might tell on him as Fanny did on Mr. Butler. Inigo is not as insensitive to public opinion as Mr. Butler. He's too much a child of the Old Testament. He doesn't want Emily to take an eye for an eye."

He smiled at her. All of their circle had loved her stubborn, headstrong will—but even now he would hate to come up against it too suddenly.

"Would you be willing to get rid of the girl? You'd have to sell her. The new laws have clamped down on traveling about with slaves, so sending her away for a time isn't possible any more. You can't free her. You can't even let her go and live among the free Negroes in Charleston unless you sell her to one of them."

170

"I've thought of all those things. It distresses me that she is only one-eighth Negro, yet she is legally black. If she had just one more drop of white blood she could be freed and legally marry Inigo here in this parish, and their children would be white citizens, however dubiously they might be honored."

"Yes, Tafra—but even then—you know that Inigo, for all his hot blood, would never throw his cap over the windmill. He'd never consider marrying her. He and Wade are both much more stringent sticklers for morality and opinions than we were in our youth. Is she as pretty as she used to be?"

"Wade—she is ravishing. Her beauty has a strange, wild quality quite at variance with her intelligent trained mind. I haven't seen her since Inigo beat her. The whole affair has sickened me, and I know Charlotte is crushed beyond bearing. Hagar is going to let her come back into Nick's room tomorrow."

"Back into his house, eh? Of course, you realize that any man who lays hands in violence on a beautiful woman he loves is lost forever if she forgives him and lets him back into her arms. The rest of his life is not long enough to make up for it. She and Inigo *must* be separated."

Tafra's cane tapped nervously on the floor. The Colonel reached over and held her hand until the worried sound ceased and she said, "I told Harry Singleton, a few weeks ago, that if I ever let Charlotte go, he could have her for Nancy. But I never dreamed that such a tragic set of circumstances would arise in so short a time."

"No, don't do that. I'll buy her and take her to Mississippi when we go next week."

Again Tafra had meddled too soon! She had *promised* Harry that if she ever sold Charlotte it would be to him! Harry had known that something explosive would happen when Inigo returned. He had tried to warn her and she had refused to listen. But she was an honorable woman; she would no more renege on her word than Inigo would.

"Thank you, Wade." Her voice was cold. "I promised on my damnable honor to let her go to Heronfields if she ever left Normandy."

171

The Colonel was incredulous.

"You can't do that after the way you've brought her up! Harry has a coarse white overseer handling his slaves. There've been all sorts of ugly tales circulating about him."

"I'll make a bargain that I reserve the right to buy her back in six months. Six months ought to clear Inigo's head of *anyone*. I can watch over her this close to Heronfields."

"You'll have to let Harry have her immediately before they have a chance to come together again. It may be too late as it is. But *do* warn Harry to look after the child."

Tafra laughed bitterly. "She takes care of me, she runs the household, she does the accounts, she mothers little Nick. As Vignie told Nicholas, Harry will be getting a rare bargain in the trade."

"But you will be saving Inigo, you think."

"That's what Nicholas thought when he brought her here."

The Colonel lifted the worn thin hand from the cane and kissed it tenderly. Here was more heartache than he had known.

"Tafra," he said, "I have solved my personal problems, and they have been numerous, by substituting new problems in the place of the insoluble ones. Has Inigo shown any such interest in politics as Nicholas used to feel?"

"No," Tafra answered. "So far the only interest in anything he has shown has been a fanatical love for the plantation and his horses, and as I said before, this exaggerated adherence to the publicly accepted 'code of honor.' I'm afraid the shock of the circumstances of his marriage has arrested a well-rounded growth of personality in Inigo. He seems to have a blind spot to anything not vitally concerned with him or his physical interests."

"I was worried about him last summer in Philadelphia. He was drinking too much, and at the race course he spent his time teasing that big black stallion."

"Edisto?"

"Yes—the one that won the Stake. Inigo would

172

wave a handkerchief in the horse's face or blow cigar smoke at him every time he passed the stall, and Edisto would almost kick the door down trying to get to him. Inigo knows better than that."

"That horse has fascinated Inigo since he was a colt. Edisto has always been ugly. We all tried to persuade Inigo to geld him but he wouldn't. He resents any interference from anybody about anything. He'll never forgive me for selling Charlotte. But I must save them from each other. I must."

"Let me talk to young Wade about this. Maybe we can persuade Inigo to go to Mississippi with us. If he does, I'll try to rub off some of his gentlemanly armor and rub in enough of the frontier to make him willing to divorce Emily. There are some pretty girls in our West. Even young Wade steps around out there, and being about the same age as Inigo he can get close to him easier than I can. At present he's trying to work out a system of gradually freeing his slaves to present to the legislature in Columbia when we come back next year. He might be able to get Inigo to work with him and help get a reprieve for us planters from the mess that Calhoun has got us into," said the Colonel.

"But Calhoun is so old, and now that Buchanan has replaced him as Secretary of State aren't his fires burning low?" Tafra asked.

"Lower," said the Colonel, "but if Hammond gets in power he will carry on where Calhoun leaves off, and the real damage was done years ago when Calhoun refused to compromise with Clay on the railroad to the West. However, Calhoun is the man of the hour and his influence and eloquence still bear great weight with Polk and the Senate. You see, Tafra, the people in our state are sharply divided into Co-operationalists and Separate State Actionists. The city of Charleston and the Up Country are united against the Low Country parishes which represent most of the great slaveholders and planters of the state. Wade and I are representative of both groups and he feels very strongly that he has a mission in bringing these two groups to see eye to eye the problem of the slaves facing our state."

"Nicholas was a Union man," Tafra spoke quietly.

173

"Do you remember how he and Joel Poinsett and Dan Huger and Hugh Legare sat up all one night at your house pleading with some of the big planters who were also your guests not to push Nullification so hard that they rang their own death knell by so doing?"

The Colonel nodded. "Times have changed since then. You know our little group of cottages at White Sulphur that we used to call Union Row? Remember how Henry Clay and Daniel Webster and Franklin Pierce and Martin Van Buren, whose son Abram courted Harry's cousin Angelica, used to sit on our piazza and how we would talk and joke and plan the future of our country during the pleasant summer evenings after tea?"

"Nicholas and I did love that so, Wade. Is it changed, too?"

"Changed is a mild way of putting it. This summer the Northern guests and the Southern guests barely exchanged pleasantries, though some of us have been meeting there since 1820. Even the children playing around the grounds waiting for the cake man were conscious of the Mason-Dixon Line.

"Here in this peaceful paradise you don't feel the fever of sectional feeling that is burning high in our country. But if Wade can inject some of it into Inigo maybe it will soothe his inner struggle. Take a fever to fight a fever, old Maum Hannah used to say."

"Suppose it doesn't work?"

"In any event, get Harry over here and arrange with him to take Charlotte to Heronfields at once. Make your bargain with him that he will let you buy her back in six months. I'll break the news to Inigo. He'll take it better from me than he will from you."

"All right. It's high time I stopped listening to my heart, anyway." She didn't try to hide the tears this time. "Jenny! Jenny! Light the candles; then take the Colonel to the green room and tell Hercules to bring him up a bottle of Madeira. That's still your drink, Wade?"

The Colonel beamed. A man liked to settle problems properly. "You never forget anything, do you, girl?"

Tafra made a pathetic effort to smile as the Colonel followed Jenny through the double doors.

Yes—she must stop listening to her heart. Yet by her most impulsive action had come her greatest happiness. It happened in Vienna—the summer she was twenty. She was at a ball given by the archduke and in the rococo ballroom she noticed a giant of a dark young man who followed her from waltz to waltz with pleading eyes. At last she went up to him—she was used to going her own way about things—and tapping him on his broad shoulder with her delicate jeweled fan, asked him in German, "Why don't you dance? Are you a stranger in Vienna? Who invited you here if you do not know anyone?"

He shook his curly head and spread his enormous hands apart.

"I can't speak your language. I am here to study horsemanship," he apologized in his Low Country speech.

"Oh yes, you can!" she answered in her most Charleston manner, though she had not been there in ten years.

"Huzza!" he shouted, and while her father and the dowagers and the dukes and the tiaraed heads frowned disapprovingly, the dynamic stranger from the South grasped the tiny waist of the ambassador's daughter in his bearlike arms and whirled her around and around to happiness. She remembered the sound of his boots humming on the polished dance floor—the drumbeats of his heart.

Little Charlotte had kissed such a man in the golden sunset one afternoon, and she had worn the same look of radiance on her face that the young Tafra had seen reflected in the mirrored walls of a palace twirling to an old waltz tune.

She could not work her present problem out by the correct procedure. Euclid had determined such a cold perfection. She would like to argue with him the fact that slightly unbalanced equations might possibly give the same answer. When she got to heaven she would hunt him up. That would be a good conversation. Nicholas would enjoy it, too.

The Colonel went to his room and was warming his rear in front of the fire when Hercules entered, reverently bearing the pride of the cellar on a silver tray. He carefully uncorked the dusty bottle and poured the precious amber liquid into a tall crystal wineglass. The Colonel with his finest manner sniffed, then tasted, and permitted a wide grin of approval to settle on his face.

Brayboy had unpacked his bag and he changed from riding-clothes to a tight-fitting broadcloth coat and ruffled linen shirt. The house was quiet; Inigo and Wade, those rowdy Nimrods, had not returned; shooting must be good. He looked out of the window and saw a full, red winter's moon rising over the river. His talk with Tafra had affected him deeply. He loved his state—but he loved it as a part of the United States. He remembered a speech that Joel Poinsett once made before a group of turbulent mountaineers in Greenville saying The Star-Spangled Banner should be his shroud, pure and spotless he hoped; but if stained with blood still—his shroud. Good men like Inigo must be awakened from the exciting dream of their life. He'd talk to him like a father in the morning, explaining why his mother was going to sell Charlotte to Heronfields for a little while. He'd tell Inigo that Charlotte was doomed to be wasted if now, while she was young, she didn't try to find happiness with her own people. Inigo would listen; men did, to each other— The night was falling and the quicksilver flash of moonshine on the marsh was too lovely to miss. He threw a heavy cape over his shoulders and went out into the refreshing salt air.

He walked down to the large artificial fish pond on the shore of the river; he estimated that it would require a bullet fired from a high-powered pistol to travel its length. It was in the shape of a parallelogram, its shore side bricked up with an immense grove of live oaks overshadowing it. The other three sides were dikes reclaiming it from the river, planted with saltwater cedars to beautify the walks and protect it from erosion. The water was renewed twice daily by the ocean, three miles away, and the pond was deep enough to keep fish alive at all stages of the tide.

The moon shone brightly on Venetian bridges and small scattered islands about fifteen feet square on each side of which was a diminutive Chinese tea garden, reached by a little skiff. Built out from the far side of the pond, into and over the river, was a small house of palmetto logs connected with the shore by a bridge, from the piazzas of which one might fish in the river with a hand line or pole. In the floor was a trap door, in case of rain, through which one might catch a sizable mess of sheephead for dinner.

Inigo kept everything in perfect condition. More meticulous than his father, he had with unlimited time and labor added greater beauty to all that Nicholas and Tafra had dreamed for Normandy.

The Colonel wondered if Primus and Toney still spent their entire time keeping the pond stocked with fish. Evidently they did, for in the still night he could hear the splash of the channel bass and see its phosphorescent pathway gleam as it darted beneath the surface for its prey. He could hear the "boom! boom!" of a drum fish, the sharp angry snap of a trout as it took a shrimp into its mouth; he could see the clear, silvery leap of a mullet as it rose from the water in sheer delight of motion.

The old man, tall and erect, stood very still as an otter stole by on the bank in search of supper. In the moonlight, directly beneath where he stood, a little black spot rose; inadvertently he coughed and the reptilian head of the diamond back terrapin oozed back down into the water. He heard the scratch of the fiddler crab busily burrowing into the banks, letting the water seep through, weakening the structure of the dam. So—like this—he must make his old friend's son hear the voices that were weakening the structure of the civilization upon which he had builded his life and the faraway but unmistakable ruffle of drums that was rolling down on the north wind.

The high tune of a fiddler and the plaintive lament of some lonesome woman carried true on the clear, frosty night—

> "W'en I'm uh gone, gone, gone,
> W'en I'm uh gone tuh come no mo'
> You'se uh gwine tuh miss me, miss me, miss me,
> W'en I'm uh gone, gone, gone."

The moon was red no longer, but cold and snow-like. The yellow flames of fat lightwood and pine straw shot up from the fire stands and sparks rained in golden showers against the sky. Enough of this reverie! He must hurry and be on hand to see how many geese Wade and Inigo had brought.

The Colonel walked back up the terraces to the candlelit house, thinking of the "shrimp bush" that Sweet always fixed for him to eat with his hot toddy before supper. He loved the tiny river shrimp massed in a pink ball with green tips of asparagus and tender leaves of turnips, making a rosebush more fragrant than the Duchess de Brabant that flowered in his Piedmont garden. Hercules had told him of the crab pie baked in his honor and of oyster fritters so crisp they would fairly tickle his tongue. He had been born here in this low salt country. It was good to return for a little while, but not long enough to get the habit of it. He lifted up his strong voice and joined in the woman's song—

> *"You'se uh gwine tuh miss me, miss me, miss me,*
> *W'en I'm uh gone, gone, gone!"*

Chapter 26

The following night Tafra lay in her high bed trying to read by the wavering candlelight, but the sound of Charlotte singing "Sur le Pont d'Avignon" to Nick in the next bedroom destroyed the printed page. And more than that marred the treatise on the rights of man that she was attempting to digest, for she was experiencing that revolting traitorous guilt that comes to an enlightened mind when it exchanges its inmost convictions for security. She was more guilty than the Bessy Grays and the Talullahs and the Sendeniahs would have been, because she knew better. Her hands felt sticky and she wiped the perspiration off on the quilt as the pain in her back dug away at her consciousness; annihilating freedoms, making thought a useless vessel.

Suddenly her door opened. Nobody had knocked but she struggled to attend whoever had entered. She felt a pressure on each side of her pillows and when she finally got her eyes open, looked up into Inigo's face. He was leaning over her, resting on his hands. She was imprisoned by the huge black broadcloth arms— and she turned from the hot breath that exuded rum and brandy, from the hot eyes that were reddened and wild.

"What do you want?" she asked, drawing on some hidden reserve of strength.

"Will you treat me as a human being?"

"Certainly—how you do go on!"

"Will you give up this mad scheme of selling Charlotte?"

"No—it's the only way to save her from you. You act like you are possessed by some evil spirit."

"Then I shall take steps to make you give it up. Does she know about it?"

"No. Nick was so happy to have her with him and she looked so frail that I decided to wait until tomorrow."

"I'm sick of your meddling ways. I shall force you to tell Harry that you have changed your mind."

"Do!" He stared, amazed at the vehemence of her answer. Her lips were compressed in a thin line; her hair lay in straight white plaits on the linen nightgown, in strange dead contrast to her icy blue eyes—those eyes alive with the emotions of fear, love, contempt, and odd haunting triumph.

"Now will you please leave my room. And don't upset Nick by going in there. He is very peaceful tonight."

Unable to meet those terrible eyes any longer, he

lurched out, knocking over a cane chair by the door and banging her door hard.

He knew that Charlotte must be warned, but he couldn't face her until he had managed to prevent this stupidity. His mother and Harry would conclude the formalities after the party. He had plenty of time to thresh it out with Harry before then, even if he had to tell Harry the truth. Harry was lazy but he was a gentleman; it wouldn't be hard to ask this favor of him. What he needed now was some more brandy. Anything to make him sleep—to keep him from thinking or remembering.

Nick lay in Charlotte's lap and she rocked him back and forth and when she finished "Sur le Pont" took up "Savez-Vous Plantez les Choux?" Nick had his arms tightly around her body and his head lay heavy on her shoulder.

"Are you well for good?" he asked when the song was ended.

She caught her fingers in the crisp curls at the back of his neck; they grew in the way she loved a man's hair to grow.

"Yes, Nick. I'm well for good and you are my own sweet boy."

"I'm going to kill Pa if he ever whips you again."

She pressed her lips against his temple. "He'll never do it again."

No, he would never lay hands on her in anger any more. She saw that their affirmations and denials had brought their poor bewildered selves to this point, that it was life itself they had struck out against. And now she knew that, stable or mansion, only to give ease to his troubled soul, to satisfy his love and need for her would more than compensate for whatever shame or sorrow came her way. She didn't need to belong to any race or any people. She needed only Inigo.

"Sing some more," Nick demanded sleepily.

Her throaty low voice sang a love song to him and her heart sang, *As soon as New Year's Day is over, as soon as the Hamptons go.*

Chapter 27

At six o'clock the next morning, the whole world was sharply black and silver. Sparkling frosty rime covered the earth. The moon, pale and lusterless, was sinking through a cluster of tall pines. On a low myrtle branch a kingly eagle, jet against the marsh, fiercely eyed the man creature disturbing his morning meditation. A snowy heron standing in a pool disdainfully spread her wings into a fan and, trailing her stalky legs limply, mingled her feathers with a cloud.

Inigo stood thoughtfully on the edge of the silent swamp by the river, watching the mist settle across the savanna and trace ghost trails over the sweet gum and cypress. A fox streaked past unnoticed, and a 'possum on a cypress limb idiotically grinned down at the man playing his own game of "dead" beneath him.

Inigo was in truth dead to everything but the vision of Charlotte, seen by the shaded spark of his candle when he went into Nick's room a half-hour earlier, to wake him so he wouldn't miss the expedition to the beach to get oysters for the roast.

She had been sleeping like a child, one thin arm flung out of the cover, bronze hair flowing over her soft ruffled nightgown, thick black lashes matted together. Nick had been awake, so he refrained from bending over her and kissing her soft lips—or touching a strand of her gorgeous hair with a hungry finger.

When this day was ended he would be free for a while. This party must be gone through smoothly; then

181

he could tell his mother that if she ever meddled in his affairs again he would move her straightway into the town house with Emily. After all, he, not she, was the master of Normandy. He would never brook her interference in the future.

All at once eastern streaks of red raked across the gray sky and a thrush poured out a song of pure praise. Big Jake blew the horn and New Year's Day came officially, in a rush and bustle of activity.

Toney and Primus with a band of Negro fishermen plus little Nick had already gone in a big wagon to the place where the "whitefoot" oysters could be got. It would take hours to get enough and bring them to the salt-water pen where they would stay till the last minute to preserve their peculiar flavor and tang of the sea.

Butcher and two hundred field hands went to smooth the most minute rough places out of the avenue; Festus, the patroon, one of the three big bosses of the plantation, started his oarsmen and a large crew polishing up the boats and sailing craft; Penda, the head carpenter, superintended the setting up of a rustic table a quarter-mile long down the center of the avenue; Seneca, the blue-black Gullah assistant driver, sang a sad little minor dirge as he shouted directions to the hands who were dressing four hundred palmetto hearts, the taking of which had brought death to four hundred trees; Sanch, the head gardener, quarreled at his underlings digging the pits, placing the ovens, and piling up cords of oak, hickory, and cedar wood ten feet long, to be ready to light at high noon.

Big Jake in his blue coat and hat, straight as an arrow on Prince, rode from job to job overseeing everybody and everything.

Murriah, in the game kitchen which adjoined the house, had, with an army of trained helpers, turned the one-room brick house into a factory of culinary mysteries. No one, not even Tafra, knew what went into her venison patties. And if any black face came snooping too near as she pounded herbs and spoke special words over the mountain of minced deer flesh, she would snatch up an iron skillet and let it fly right on the prying nose. She was mixing the seasoning and later would mold the venison into hundreds of small cakes. Wild ducks were being dressed and run through the big ovens; wild turkeys were browning; goose feathers blew lazily about, and partridges fattened, stuffed with rice and herbs; red snappers were being scaled, and shrimp ground into a paste to be mixed with sweet butter and spread on the crusty bread that Juno, the pastry cook, was baking in the big kitchen. Crabs were being picked and the white meat piled high in wooden bowls until Murriah could devil them and stuff them back in their shells; and while the cooks and helpers picked and scaled and stuffed and roasted, the diamondback terrapins sighed dolefully in their buckets of salt water—knowing in their reptilian way that the stew pot would receive them before long and that they would end their existence in a succulent liquid, adding their small contribution to Normandy's fame.

By ten o'clock wagons creaked up, bringing supplies to the place where the table was to be set and the oysters cooked.

Hercules, like a commanding general, ordered every move that the house wenches made as they arranged the long table. At each place was laid an individual plate mat of coarse linen, an oyster cloth on the left, an oyster knife, with protective guards on the right, an arm rest clamped to the table, and a tumbler to receive the hot punch that was served with the oysters.

When the tables were prepared, Hercules had the under servingmen and the girls bring out in baskets the best ancestral napery, china, silverware, and linen which Normandy possessed, and place these aside to be ready, when the oysters had been eaten, to adorn the table for the feast proper.

Sanch rolled wheelbarrows laden with crimson and white and pink and variegated camellias to strew down the center of the table when the damask cloths should be put on. Silver bowls massed with narcissi and hyacinths were arranged and placed on the side tables. Odors from the house and the game kitchen floated to the front and the people of the Street wandered about and looked at things and helped when they were needed. The little pickaninnies dressed in their calico best danced and played about like colored moths. The gray moss blew lazily in spirals from the trees, remembering other tribal ceremonies under hoary oaks when Indian maidens had danced for their chieftain, their tawny hips skirted with streamers of the moss itself, through which their undulating thighs gleamed like writhing serpents.

Charlotte, sitting by Tafra's side on the upper balcony, watched all this excitement worriedly. Tafra had looked at her all morning in such an odd manner—several times she had turned and surprised the frosty light eyes staring so hard that it felt like not having any clothes on.

"Is anything troubling you, Miss Tafra?" Charlotte asked after one very long discomforting look.

"No; the wind blowing from the sea always makes me restless and chilly. It bends the oak branches almost down to the long table."

Charlotte heard the gentle southwest breeze from the river rattling the dead marsh grass. *Like chains, it sounds,* she thought, *but it is not cold; the wind is not coming from the sea.*

"I think I'll go inside for a while," Charlotte said, not wanting to talk.

"No, I want to talk to you about yourself."

Oh dear, Charlotte thought, watching the girls down in the avenue fetch bowls of hyacinths and narcissi and secretly bury their bright faces in the massed fragrance. *Miss Tafra wants to talk about Christmas afternoon and I mustn't ever talk to her about me and Inigo; not ever—ever.*

But Tafra surprised her by saying, "It is very beautiful in the Low Country. You would be happy at any plantation close by this river."

What is on your mind, Charlotte wondered; *you have got some scheme up your sleeve, and I know that it has to do with my having been whipped.*

"I have never been to any plantation but this one," Charlotte said politely.

"You don't have many friends do you, Charlotte?"

"No." *And it's because you have kept me with*

you all the time. Why are you talking today about "other plantations"?

"I think the time has come for you to make some friends with the younger Negroes."

"Cuffee is my friend."

"He is different. He is everybody's friend."

"I am not at ease with the Negro girls my age who come from the Street into the house to work."

"Well, the time has come for you to understand that you are a definite member of the Negro race. They need people like you; when freedom comes you can be anything in the world that you want to be."

"I can't feel a thing that I have never fully believed, Miss Tafra." *How can I forget Poulette saying to me, "My little white Missy—my little alabaster doll." And how I hate being what I am now supposed to be. How I hate it and you and me and Normandy and all.*

"I know it is hard, Charlotte child, and I suppose I have wronged you by enjoying you so much. Colonel Hampton has advised me to work out something different for you—a plan to throw you more with your people."

Charlotte tried to smile but the corners of her mouth were too heavy. Yes, Tafra was up to something; her eyes had that crafty expression.

"Let's go back in the drawing-room, Miss Tafra. We're both tired."

"Not until I see the match touch the fire. If the fire goes straight up it means a good year for Normandy; if it smolders the cotton will fail; but if the wind blows it sidewise—it means death will come here before the next roast."

"I didn't know you were superstitious."

"I'm not superstitious—that's an ancient Indian myth. This house is built on the site of an old worshiping-place. Sacrifices were made on the very spot where the fire is laid today to roast the oysters. We have progressed in our civilization. We roast oysters where they used to roast a human victim."

Keeping me a slave is as bad as roasting me, Charlotte thought; *I don't think people have progressed much.*

She looked down on the long table, watching the shifting pattern of Negroes. The salt air softened the hairs around Charlotte's sad face and blew them into her mouth. *My hair tastes salty—as if there were tears in it,* she thought, *but after today Inigo will make things come right. I know it; I feel it. He thought I was asleep this morning but I saw how kind his eyes were in the candlelight; how he looked so tenderly at me.*

What am I really, she wondered, *that things should all at once come right for me? Miss Tafra says that now I should never forget that I am a Negro, while for the past six years I have been trying to forget my Negro blood and to help run this plantation in the way that she ran it when she was able. Who are my people? Certainly I have more white than Negro blood. Must the few drops outweigh the stream? Maybe I am just an odd number—like Leon Cavallo. Hagar says I am the kind of woman who would never have known how a man was made unless one came along with the right ear of corn—but once he did there would be a mighty blaze in the corn crib if I wasn't careful. How drolly she express-es things, but it must be true, for I would have loved Inigo if he had been one of those Indians who roasted human flesh, shrieking with delight at the charred odor.*

Yet I don't belong with his people who will fill that table that stretches so proudly down the avenue. They would rise in horror if I went and sat among them. They would speak of an odor that seeped from the very pores of my skin. I know because I have heard them speak of Negroes in that way. Only Inigo feels the same to me as he did when he thought I was a little white girl, or almost the same. No, I don't belong with his people. But still less do I belong with Cuffee's people who live their hopeless lives on the Street.

It was high noon.

"Here they are!" Tafra whispered, breathing too fast.

Inigo and young Wade Hampton and Nick came out and walked over to the pits. Inigo was pale and haggard. *Oh, dear one,* Charlotte cried inside of herself, *how weary you look. But even so, you are full of magic for me. Wade Hampton is as large as you and quite as*

186

handsome, but you are full of magic. Full of me, and thoughts of me.

Nick gave the word to Big Jake to light the fire. Jake touched the burning torch to the pile of cedarwood and a western puff of wind caught the first flame, blowing it wildly sidewise. Tafra laughed shakily and hit her cane hard on the floor.

"Any fool with my sickness should be glad to see his release signal," she said.

Charlotte didn't hear Tafra. She was looking at Emily standing on the steps between the Colonel and Horst Adams. His wife! Oh, if it could only be she. If it only could. If only she had fine silky corn-colored hair; if only she were wearing a rose velvet dress with a black sealskin capelet over her shoulders; if only she had a white camellia with a gold heart pinned over her own quickened heart!

Cuffee and Quash and dozens of black boys began to call and yell. The company was coming, like an army with banners—all at once—eager and ready for the feast.

"Let's go in now." Tafra caught Charlotte's arm demandingly. "I've got to dress for a visit from Lawyer Ball during the intermission. I have the future of Normandy to solve in one short, small hour."

Chapter 28

The three hundred guests arrived at practically the same time and the yard and the house were suddenly filled with friendly voices wishing each other a happy

New Year. Children gaily explored everywhere to be sure that all was the same as last year; girls flirtatiously twitted the young beaux; young matrons compared the size of their hoop skirts and the gloss of curls; planters boomed out the results of hunts and the price of rice and cotton; old ones were quietly glad to have been spared to enjoy one more oyster roast at Normandy.

Promptly at one o'clock, Inigo blew a hunter's horn from the front steps. This was the signal for the hands to pour oysters by the barrelful on the live coals. The guests seated themselves swiftly, led by Inigo who took the head and Emily who sat at the far end of the table, escorted there by Horst Adams. Everybody was in a party humor and cheers greeted the procession of servingmen bearing silver pitchers of steaming punch, Hercules, as proud as a pope, in the lead with the most massive pitcher of all. This punch was to welcome the oysters to the jubilee! It was made out of lemons and hot water and sugar and double proof Irish whisky.

Inigo, when everybody had been served a tumblerful, stood up, grand and lordly. He lifted his glass, saying simply, "To our kinsfolk and guests—welcome and Happy New Year!"

They all drank. Instantly a regiment of the brightly dressed little pickaninnies ran from the fires carrying wooden bowls of sputtering oysters straight from the glowing coals. There followed a clatter of knives. To every two guests was one small Negro, whose job was to see that everyone's wooden bowl was always full and to fetch more melted butter and hot tomato sauce, shakers of salt and freshly ground red pepper. Hercules kept the tumblers wet, and the spirits and the conversation rose higher and higher.

For an hour the company ate and drank and made jolly table talk; then Billy Myers gave the signal (it would have been impolite for Inigo to have done so) for the men to withdraw, which they did by stepping back over the benches. Everybody laughed as the women tried to extricate themselves with all their flounces and hoops and ruffles and shawls. Emily stood up easily from her vantage point at the foot of the table. Nancy Singleton laughed so hard that she choked and Robert had to slap her on the back. Many of the women shamelessly pulled up their hoops, showing their white French lisle hose, stepping back as if the benches had been low stones in their path. The ladies wandered into the house with Emily, and the men, as men do, wherever they pleased.

No sooner had the last guest risen than Hercules and his staff with many of the more agile field hands set to work clearing and wiping off the tables. Then the heavy snowy damask tablecloths were spread out and the table set as for a formal banquet in the diningroom. Silver, china, and crystal gleamed and sparkled in the sunshine. Tall champagne glasses sent off rainbows from their fluted stems. The silver bowls of narcissi were placed at regular intervals and the camellias scattered down the center of the whole quarter mile of table.

Inigo set out to find Harry Singleton so that he could settle the nonsense about Charlotte going to Heronfields once and for all. God—he had been in a trance all day. It was a good thing he had played host to this affair for so many years that he could do it in his sleep—for asleep he had been as far as anybody else was concerned. He searched the groups of men, looking for Harry.

He hunted first in an excited gathering in the library, ranting over politics, but Harry wasn't there! He walked into the garden where the flower lovers were admiring his topiary artistry and the impeccable condition of his walks, calling Inigo Gaillard a most honorable gentleman who understood how things should be kept up for the generations. But Harry was not in the garden. He hurried down to the fish pond where the sportsmen were casting; catching a few fish to pass the interval, and discussing their precious state. None of them had seen Harry. He ran to the kennels where men and hounds were talking about hunting and admiring each other. No Harry.

Time was flying and he dashed out to the stables. The gentlemen had just left, Old Ben said—but betwitched effen he remembered whe'r Mist' Harry been wid um or no! As Inigo ran down the ramp Edisto's

189

head came out of his stall and he caught Inigo's shoulder in his teeth. Inigo jerked away just in time to keep from being badly bitten. Turning, he smashed his fist against the side of Edisto's head and tore breathlessly on his way, Edisto's enraged screams shrilling after him.

The ladies had scattered over the entire house, with the exception of the great drawing-room whose dark double doors were most forbiddingly closed and bolted.

"What's wrong with Miss Tafra?" asked Mildred Singleton. "I never knew her not to at least sit out on the piazza and watch the fun before."

"Oh, she is worrying over a slave girl who did something outrageous on Christmas. She has old Ball and some others in her room, selling the creature, I think," answered Emily.

"Harry is buying her for Nancy," Mildred Singleton told the curious ladies.

"You mean *the* girl?" There was a twittering as though a clump of sparrows had been startled in a sparkleberry bush.

"*The* girl?" Emily pulled at her gold and white camellia and the bruised petals fell wearily on her lap.

"Yes, dear." Old Mrs. Legare was of a former generation which had matured pleasantly, unfrightened by the booger of emancipation. "We mean the one who wears hoop skirts and sits at Inigo's desk."

"That queer red-headed Negro girl," Emily agreed.

"We'll soon get the hoops out of her skirt at Heronfields *and* she won't sit at *Harry's* desk, I assure you!" Mildred was positive and proud.

The ladies rustled their fans and snuggled their furs. No—they bet she'd not sit at Harry's desk. They knew how demanding of Harry in the bed Mildred was. Their husbands whispered it to them in the dark under the covers. Those Watson women, you know! There'd be no danger of the light-skinned girl in *Mildred's* hands.

Old Mrs. Swinton leaned forward and brushed the untreasured camellia petals from Emily's skirt.

"And dear, I'm going to give *you* a word of warning— If I had a gorgeous young husband like Inigo I would bow and scrape before his mother or anybody else who could help me keep him."

"What do you mean?" Emily's face had grown white and unpleasant-looking.

"Oh, nothing, my dear," airily answered the old dowager. "But not many men would put up with the way you spend most of your time in Charleston being beaued about by that wicked Horst Adams."

"Oh, Mrs. Swinton." Mildred Singleton laughed. "There's no harm in him. He's always been a watery soul with a dash of red pepper. We all know his stupid story too well to take him seriously."

"Well, I wouldn't put up with him sniffing around my son's wife," Mrs. Swinton declared as Emily rose and walked with stilted, infuriated steps out of the room and joined some of the younger girls who were giggling and telling secrets in the bedroom downstairs. She could impress these younger ones with her elegant clothes and her handsome husband *and* a gentleman friend. Those old planters' wives were so frumpy and dull—what did she care for them, anyway? Nannie Myers even looked like a horse and always smelled of leather. Next week she and Robert would return to the city for the winter season. She started vivaciously and naughtily telling the younger ones about the new gown with which she would startle Charleston at the coming St. Cecilia Ball—cut down to *here,* my dears! The horn interrupted her and she led the way back to the table. She passed Inigo standing on the steps, the horn dangling from his fingers. *He's drunk,* she thought. She hoped he would make a display of himself!

Know all men by these presents that I, Tafra Gordon Gaillard, of the State of South Carolina, Charleston County, have this first day of January, 1849, sold, bargained, and delivered and by these presents do bargain, sell, and deliver to Harry Dessassure Singleton, Sr., of the district aforesaid a certain Negro woman named Charlotte, aged eighteen years, which Negro I do hereby warrant and forever defend unto the said Harry Dessas-

191

sure Singleton his heirs, executors, and administrators free from the lawful claim of any person or persons whatsoever. And further I do warrant the before mentioned Negro to be sound and healthy, free from sickness and infirmities. And it is hereby acknowledged that I have this day received the sum of five thousand dollars in full payment for said Negro, being an educated woman, the receipt and payment whereof is hereby fully acknowledged to be paid and received.

In witness whereof I have hereunto set my hand and Seal day and date first above written.

In the presence of:

William Myers
Wade Hampton, Jr.
            Ptolemy Philadelphius Ball: Attorney.

The dry legal droning ceased. The drawing-room became still as death. Charlotte turned wildly from one face to another. They were all staring at her. Waiting to jump on her bodily if she made a single motion to escape. What were the words she had just heard?

For Sale! For Sale! Free from the lawful claim of any person or persons—

No—no— Surely—surely the kind ghost of Auguste Le Jeune could not let this degrading thing happen to his little one! This was worse than being displayed in a slave market, dangling a placard from cold fingers, reading—*For Sale—For Sale.* That would at least have been impersonal. This was tearing her very pride out by the roots. This sitting here while those white people stared and stared.

Where was Inigo? How could he have let this happen to her when just this morning—this morning—

All at once she remembered Leon's cool firm hand gently rubbing unguent onto her beaten back. He would never have deserted her. He would have honored her. But she, poor fool, had ignored him to feast her eyes on the forbidden Inigo. *Keep your head up,* some voice whispered in her ear, her own inner voice—*don't let them see how you are suffering. Keep your head up. Hold it as proudly as you used to do when Poulette would say, "Your grandmother, your father's mother, carried the most arrogant head in all Louisiana."*

So she lifted her bronze head high and managed to look far out of the window—far above the oak-tree tops to the flying clouds.

"And now, Harry—you have promised to sell Charlotte back to me at the end of six months and to keep your overseer away from her," Tafra said.

"On my word of honor, Miss Tafra," Harry answered solemnly—this thing had gotten a bit too complicated for him, he'd better have left it alone. Why the devil wasn't Inigo here, anyway? Plantation affairs should be settled master to master. He wouldn't anger his friend for anything.

Charlotte twisted her hands, thinking Tafra wasn't going to give her a chance to renounce Inigo. Even if she had meant to, she wasn't going to be allowed that small privilege. And Inigo—where was he? Surely the master should be present.

"Inigo would be here but he thought that I was going to wait until after the party to dispense with these formalities." Triumphant malice twinkled in Tafra's eyes. Since when could her son get the best of her in a scheme? He'd have to move a lot faster than he was moving before he could outwit her when once she had determined on a course!

Harry approached Charlotte. She gazed full in the face of her new master—trying to evaluate him. She saw a tall, almost emaciatedly thin, dark man, with a beak of a nose and black, black eyes. He looked like a brown crane as he balanced himself first on one long leg and then on the other. As he noticed the grief in her eyes, a kindly smile lit up his rather weak face.

It was a good thing he could not read her mind. She was seeking excuses for Inigo. She wanted to tell Harry that this was all a crazy mistake. That Tafra had lost her wits. That surely in a minute the door would open and Inigo would come and correct this nightmare of error—this monstrous misunderstanding.

However, the door remained closed, and as Harry Singleton and Tafra bent to sign the paper, Wade Hampton came over to her.

"Believe me, Charlotte, this is the easiest way for you and Mr. Inigo." She turned on him the full intensity of her comfortless gray eyes. He sighed deeply as he gazed into the fullness of her sorrow. "I wish you had come to us. We could have taken you to Mississippi and let you start up a school on our plantation there."

Mississippi! That was the West! That was where Inigo—or was it a drugged dream lover?—had whispered that he was going to take her!

"All right now," Tafra broke in harshly, "you men have done what I asked you to do. Get on back to your feasting; anyway—" the blast of the horn was heard—"Inigo is waiting for you. Don't for heaven's sake tell him that I deceived him. At least let the party progress in order. Do go on!"

"I'll call you when I'm ready, Charlotte." Harry Singleton followed the men out, Lawyer Ball leading, crackling stiffly at the joints like a piece of his own parchment.

Left alone with Tafra, Charlotte said nothing. She walked over to the window and saw Inigo moving unsteadily from the steps toward the table. *He looks like he has been drinking,* she thought, pressing her hot forehead against the cool pane. She watched Wade Hampton come out and take his arm, steering him to his place.

Tafra peeped uneasily at Charlotte's slight, erect back. The excitement of outwitting Inigo and the letdown that had come when she had looked up and seen the stark, bitter horror on Charlotte's face were still all through her. In her, too, was surprise at being capable of doing this thing. Now it was over she was lonely and unrejoicing and, listening to the laughter of the feasters outside, she felt that she despised them all. But looking out at the Gaillard oaks she remembered Nicholas and Normandy, so she bit her lips, saying firmly, "Forgive me and don't lose faith in me, Charlotte. It is only for a short six months. I wouldn't do this if it were not for your own salvation as well as Mr. Inigo's."

Charlotte did not turn from the window. If Inigo had only come in, Charlotte thought. And then, not suddenly, but slowly and with every faculty, she began to accept what had happened. Inigo hadn't come in. Not Inigo. So now she was going away, as she'd known she should when she saw the little lost shoe back in her room on Christmas morning. She was going to the Street. Where she would be safe from Inigo forever.

"You've gotten your way," she finally said dully, still looking out of the window. "I will have to become a Negro now. It will be difficult for me to accept living in a cabin. I may not be able to stand it. But I am leaving here and I am going to the Street as you have arranged. I will go now and change to a warmer dress."

She refused even to look at Tafra as she left the room. *I feel very little any more,* she thought. *If the door had opened and* he *had come in—I don't know then how I would have felt. As it is—I'll at least be on my way. And I won't say a word. Not a word—not a word—not a word!*

Three o'clock! The folk watched Wade Hampton propel Inigo to the head of the table and they all trouped back to their places. Inigo appeared to be terribly exhausted. Wade had at first thought that he was drunk but more than whisky had splashed that color on his face, and his breath was quickened as though he had been climbing a mountain. However his speech was clear and as soon as he was at table he seemed to steady down and become the perfect host once more.

These are my friends, Inigo told himself, looking down the almost endless table, *these are the people who live as I do, who breathe as I do, who believe as I do. And there is Harry Singleton quite calm-looking. So I will still have a chance to talk to him before he sees Mother. But I am shaking from too much running. The guests will notice my excitement. I must take a stiff drink to quiet my nerves.*

"Hercules!" he called. Hercules importantly leaned

195

down for the imperial message. "Fill my glass with Irish whisky. Never mind the lemons or water. I need a libation to whet my appetite." Hercules frowned in disapproval but he whispered to Brayboy and in a minute a large crystal tumbler of dark Irish whisky was at Inigo's hand and he downed it in a gulp.

"Now you may serve the dinner." His courage was returning and catching Brayboy's eye again he lifted his empty tumbler for a refill as the food arrived. Everything was trundled up from the kitchens in large panikins to keep the food hot. Murriah and Sweet and Juno stood beaming, close to Inigo, to receive the praise when the company saw the terrapin stew, the guinea pilau, the pudding of palmetto hearts, the candied sweet potatoes, the platters of wild duck and turkey and partridges, the thin slices of rosy brown ham, the shrimp and eggs in aspic, the deviled crabs, the baked red snappers. And when the venison patties arrived, the champagne corks popped like firecrackers, and the Colonel stood up and proposed a toast to the three cooks, their cups ran over and tears flowed down their smiling faces.

Inigo kept trying to swallow the lump that was lodged in his chest. He poured whisky on it and chased it with champagne but it would not go away. He looked anxiously at his guests but they were unaware of the clammy hands that he kept rubbing dry on his fawn broadcloth trousers. He made himself act the perfect host and nobody heard his heart break— champagne corks popped with far too gay a rataplan for anybody to notice a pitiful sound like that.

Cudeye and Big Tooth played gay tunes on their fiddles, Cymba picked his guitar, and Monday and Doodle strummed their banjos. Lucullus had an orchestra from the polished city of Naples to entertain his guests, but the Low Country folk preferred the rollicking music of their own Negro musicians to keep time to their lively flow of wit and the satisfied patting of their elegant feet.

The little pickaninnies started to jig and cut the pigeon wing, and some of the older people who were not church members began to "jine in." The Negro coachmen, outriders, maids, and footmen were eating oysters that had been left and as each course was taken away from the big tables it was turned over to them for their own feasting. By five o'clock, when Juno's frothy desserts had been eaten, Hercules and his retinue came with old brandy in cut-glass decanters and filled the tiny glasses that alone remained unused.

Inigo had by now consumed four tumblerfuls of whisky and innumerable glasses of champagne and it was with difficulty that he managed to hold onto the table in front of him and keep it steady. He leaned over and whispered to Nannie Myers, "Your scent fascinates me, madame." He took her large capable hand that could pull in any hunter however tough his mouth, and stroked the rough palms. "Thish is the way women's hands should feel—not shoft an' warm an'—"

Nannie winked at Billy and Billy whispered a word to Wade. Wade looked questioningly at Inigo and one glance told the whole story. He started a lively conversation to take up attention, and for a while the brandy kept mellow conversation drifting around the table as long tales were told and retold. Inigo's head sank on his breast and for a few moments he snored deeply but Billy Myers who was between the Colonel and Inigo called loudly, "Which is the better horseman, Colonel, you or Wade?"

"Oh, Wade any day! Why that brute has such a knee grip that I've seen him mount a bad horse and when he gripped it with his knees I've heard the poor animal groan in pure pain."

"Put 'im on Edishto! Wade! Wade! Where you Wade?" Inigo woke with a start and shaking his head to clear the fog which persisted in gathering, muttered angrily, "Gotta shee ole Harry. Dam' bashard tryin' to take my—"

Wade nodded at Billy, who rose from his seat and slipped down to Harry, telling him the state Inigo was in. Harry disengaged himself unobtrusively from the table and went into the house.

Billy and Nannie Myers had been propitiating Inigo and agreeing with his opinion of Harry to pacify

197

him. So far nobody had heard more than a series of unintelligible growls from the master of Normandy. Most of them were not far behind him and Billy shouted, "Colonel Hampton, tell us about your famous ride!"

"You mean when I brought the good news?" Colonel Hampton called back to him though they were only a few seats apart.

"Yes, that's the one!" Everyone took up the cry—hurrah—hurrah! Wasn't this a grand party? A time for shouting and singing—for noise and celebration—for oratory and platitudes.

The old man stood up, his white hair shining in the sunset glow, and told the tale of his seven-hundred-and-fifty-mile ride in ten and a half days when he brought the news of Andrew Jackson's victory at the Battle of New Orleans to the President in Washington.

More cheering and handclapping acclaimed the old hero and he bowed low as Cudeye struck up "Bile Dem Cabbage Down" on his fiddle. Farewell toasts and last-minute resolutions were being drunk when Harry reappeared, driving his buggy himself, with Charlotte sitting on the seat beside him. He waved his hand in Inigo's direction. Good-by—good-by—it was a lovely party! Suddenly a small, dark, ungainly figure darted down the avenue after the fast-moving buggy.

"Charlotte, Charlotte," screamed little Nick, his big knees pounding up and down as he tried vainly to catch onto the buggy. Charlotte looked back and started sneezing uncontrollably when she saw the child running along after the horse and buggy—and little Sambo flying up on his skinny legs. She pressed her hands against her mouth and leaned over the side of the buggy away from the horse, sneezing—sneezing.

"Charlotte—Charlotte!" Nick called, then as Sambo caught him by the shirt, he fell on his face in the avenue, beating his head on the ground, flailing his arms and legs wildly in the dirt.

Inigo lurched up as Cuffee stepped from behind a tree.

"Git way from here, Mass Inigo." Cuffee reached down for the little fellow. "Unnuh know how he feels

—Cuffee take de care of he now." And, carrying the weeping child cradled in his strong arms like a baby, he walked away from the slightly curious guests, crooning in his husky deep voice:

> *"An' e wonduh wey Mosey,*
> *An' e mus' be dead,*
> *An' e wonduh wey Mosey,*
> *An' e mus' be dead,*
> *An' e wonduh wey Mosey,*
> *An' e mus' be dead.*
> *Oh, duh chillen ob duh wilduhness*
> *Moan fuh bread."*

Inigo stood alone under his deep oaks hearing Charlotte's sneezing as the horse pulled her away from him to Heronfields. He took a step forward to follow, but was so unsteady that he staggered over and leaned against the rough trunk of a tree and beat his head against the bark. So this was the way one's world ended! In a drunken stupor, unable to fight, petrified as old wood, static as the dark branches of the oaks that could only bend low to the ground and then lift again in the evening wind. But not free with the wind— just moving up and down—up and down in the same place always until some thunderstorm or hurricane took mercy and flung them for one riotous whirl through the sky before they crashed to their death.

The guests still lingered contentedly at the table. No one paid any attention to Inigo's empty chair—no one was aware of the tragedy that had played itself out within easy hearing distance. Much more noticeable was Emily's shallow laugh and Horst Adams's witticisms which had become funnier and quite wicked after Harry flashed away with that girl in his buggy. Wade and the Colonel and Billy Myers gave the signal to rise, closing together so that Inigo, the host, would not be missed. The party was over; the sun had slipped through the long arms of the oaks; winter dusk was falling fast.

The slaves were gathering up the remnants of the feast to take down to the Street for a celebration of their own. Hagar would teach them and lead them in some of their old half-forgotten customs, before the Church had forbidden them to cross their feet.

Butcher and Seneca had caught two tremendous snakes some days past, a king snake and a rattlesnake, and had them in separate cages waiting for tonight. Tonight the snakes would be placed together in one cage and, hungry as they were, would fight until one devoured the other. There would be drums. There would be "shouting" by the Church members and dancing by the others. Hagar would lead the snake dance. Finger Ring would assist. Cymba was even now putting away his fiddle and going after his drum. Soon—when big dark came—Africa would awake and throb in their veins and the people of the Street would herald in the New Year in their own tribal ways.

The coaches and gigs and carriages full of wined and dined planters and city folk rolled away down the avenue.

The people in masses left their houses and cabins on the Street—to meet Hagar, their queen, and convene by her fire that already spat high on the edge of the big swamp. Their song died away on the night.

> *"An' e wonduh wey Massa,*
> *An' e mus'-be dead.*
> *An' e wonduh wey Massa,*
> *An' e mus' be dead.*
> *An' e wonduh wey Massa,*
> *An' e mus' be dead.*
> *Oh, duh chillun ob duh wilduhness*
> *Moan fuh bread.*
> *Will dese dry bones*
> *Rise again?*
> *Will dese dry bones*
> *Rise again?*
> *Oh, duh chillun ob duh wilduhness*
> *Moan fuh bread."*

BOOK THREE

The Slave
1849

Chapter 29

The brackish odor of dormant rice fields was heavy in Charlotte's inflamed nostrils as Harry Singleton pulled the horse to a stop near a fire stand at the Heronfields entrance burning brightly with pine straw and kindling. A tall thin yellow man walked loosely up in answer to his loud "Halloo! This is a new slave girl. Put her in the house with Chloe. I'll come down and talk to Chloe later. And have out the grooms. Miss Mildred is not far behind and there's no use to have her calling and getting into a temper if we can help it."

Disentangling his long legs from the buggy he walked stiffly up the back steps of his colonial-piazzaed plantation seat without having said a single word to Charlotte all the five miles they had driven side-by-side.

Pompey nimbly took his place in the buggy, slapped the reins on the horse's back and with a jerk they trotted back to the stables. Pompey kept cutting his popeyes at Charlotte, missing no element of her unusual desirability. He remembered her from Christmas afternoon. Jedus Christ! but Mist' Inigo had really laid it on her good wid dat thick crop! Word traveled fast from plantation to plantation. He knew all about dis white nigger.

"Why dey sell yunnuh down de river?" he asked, unable to hold his tongue any longer.

She avoided looking at him but she saw him well enough. The protruding eyes with the shining eyeballs,

203

the brows drawn together in appraisal of her, the thick reddish-brown lips.

"For five thousand dollars—not that it is your affair."

Pompey hopped out as they reached the stables and threw the reins to a ragged black boy by the carriage-house door. He came around to help Charlotte down. Her full dark-green challis skirt hampered her feet and she leaned forward to accept his assistance. Pompey lifted her out of the buggy with ease. She could feel his stringy arms wiry with hard muscle. He hadn't looked to be that strong. Heavens, what was he doing? She pushed against him with her fists.

"Put me down this instant."

But he wouldn't put her down. He brought her body tight against his lean palpitating stomach.

"Oh," she moaned, beating him on the face and kicking him with her laced slippers. "Oh no—let me go —please let me go!"

"Who gal yunnuh?" he asked hoarsely, catching her arms and pinning them to her sides. Her feet were now on the ground and she strained and writhed in his arms.

"I'm going to scream for Mr. Singleton." She opened her mouth and he immediately clapped his hand over her lips, mashing them against her teeth, cutting her teeth into them.

"Don' be no fool! Yunnuh git us both whup effen dere's trouble. Ain' yunnuh know 'bout de overseer here?" She shook her head. "Be quiet an' Pompey won' bodder yunnuh no mo' tonight." She nodded her head and he took his hand away from her mouth.

"Please take me to Chloe's house. And don't ever touch me again. It horrifies me."

His moment of desire for her had passed. "Aw— Pompey jest been fooling," he said. "Any time yunnuh git ready tuh be hug—lemme know an' I'll come right over."

"Take me home—please—please."

He noticed how distraught she was—how droopy, how very small and lonely-looking. He wasn't really a bad boy.

"All right den, hit's de secont house on de Street. Chloe is de head of de chillun house. She nuseter be de big house chillun nuss. Yunnuh will lak she fine." He had recovered his equanimity and, walking ahead, led the way through the cold moonlit night from the stable to the Street.

The Street stretched like a long black snake as far as Charlotte could see. What a strange wild silence, Charlotte thought as she followed Pompey; so strange that it seemed unreal. She herself felt unreal; as if she might, at an owl's cry, lose her hold on life, plummet out from civilization and dissolve in this barbarism—this savage pattern of black figures against a black background, noiselessly stealing from unlit cabins, massing themselves, against her or to embrace her, she could not tell. Only black could ever be in harmony here. White people would never come to this place where she was sure her world had ended.

Suddenly a door opened and showed Chloe, standing in the doorway of the second house, silhouetted against the orange glow of a fat pine fire. She was smoking a pipe and her deep voice rumbled up from her middle.

"Is dis de new gal?"

"Dis she. Pompey hopes yunnuh gits along. She's good for de eyes but powerful quiet on de years. Charlotte, dis is Chloe. Chloe will tell yunnuh where yunnuh is to sleep."

Charlotte hesitantly left the darkness and advanced into the temporary circle of light. Chloe took the pipe from between her teeth and squinted up her small, shrewd eyes to look carefully at this strange newcomer with the white voice.

"Yunnuh gots sky eyes, gal; kin yunnuh read de future?" Chloe asked. Charlotte shook her head.

"No, Miss Chloe, not even the past. May I come in? I am very tired."

"Sho, gal, step right ober de door." Chloe moved back slowly on her wide shovel-shaped feet. Charlotte followed her, and Pompey, unable to resist his curiosity as to how Charlotte was going to behave, came in also.

The walls of the cabin were dark and bits of news-

205

paper and odd scraps of old valentines and Christmas paper were pasted at random in an effort to beautify the boards. The floor was so scrubbed with lye that it was gray. A pine table was in the center of the room with two old split-bottom chairs pulled up to it. A low rough pine bed was shoved against one wall, covered with a pieced worsted quilt. Charlotte thought of the gay gold silk and the snow-white coverlet of her poster bed at Normandy. Chloe was watching her closely. *Somepin bad wrong here,* she thought. *Somepin wusser dan jest "git sold."*

"Yunnuh gwine to sleep in de udder room. Dat's my bed. Hit gits too cold fuh my old bones to sleep way from de fire. Here is yo' room." She reached down for a pine knot—touched it to the fire and, when it caught, held it high and went first through a creaking door into a chilly, damp room. The flare cast immense shadows on the wall. Chloe's shadow looked like a fat Nubian giantess and Pompey's shadow was a wavering black spear reaching out to the smaller shadow that dipped and swayed in the uncertain light. Charlotte saw that they were going to swallow her up. She moved quickly forward and her shadow moved with her away from theirs. *That's a good omen,* she thought—*at least my shadow is still my own.*

There was a narrow pine bed in a corner. Two gray blankets of dubious age were folded on the shuck mattress that was covered in dingy ticking. A rickety table held a tin pitcher and on the floor a tin bucket that was probably a slop jar leaned crazily on its side rocking in the draft that blew up through the wide open spaces between the flimsy floor boards.

Charlotte had never been into any of the houses of the Street at Normandy, but she was sure that there was nothing, not even in the lower Street where the field hands lived, that was this bad. And Chloe was an honored one at Heronfields! Tafra couldn't have known —she couldn't have!

Wise old Chloe sensed Charlotte's dismay. Pompey was grinning like a jackass and the woman reached out her arms and pulled Charlotte back into the front room where the fire at least gave out a semblance of cheer and warmth.

"Don' feel too bad, honey, things looks better when hit's day. Git on wid you, Pompey, you long yaller snake!" She picked up the charred pine knot. Pompey ducked and started for the door.

A man blocked his exit, a white man, the German overseer of Heronfields. Pompey stepped back, scraped his foot and bowed exaggeratedly low, catching hold of a tuft of his front hair as he did so in a mock gesture of humbleness.

"Evening, sah, come right in, sah," he said.

The man pushed past him. He was grossly fat. Red hair was plastered close to his ears and hung low on the back of his black coat. His lips were thick and loose, but his eyes were sharp and hard. He carried a crop in his hand and a pistol bulged on his hip.

"Is this the new slave?" he asked Chloe.

"Yassuh," nodded Chloe who had resumed her smoking and was now sitting comfortably by the fire. "Come in, Mr. Lustbader, and git warm. Hit's airish outside."

"What's your name?" Lustbader ignored Chloe's greeting.

"Charlotte Le Jeune, sir." Charlotte stood nervously too erect.

"Huh," he snorted, "two names and such speech! You needn't try any of your airs here. We won't take them. Inigo Gaillard thinks he doesn't need a white overseer at Normandy, but he'll wake up one morning with his throat cut and his wife gone."

Charlotte smiled to herself at the unhappy prospect of Emily's departure as it would affect Inigo who would wake up with a cut throat.

"What are you grinning at?" asked Lustbader.

"Nothing, sir." She realized that the less she did to attract this man's attention, the better things would be for her.

"And I hear you can read and write," the man went on.

"Yes, sir," answered Charlotte.

207

"Well, if I catch you teaching any of these niggers here to read or write I'll have you whipped. And it won't be the first time for you, I understand!"

Charlotte's teeth chattered so loudly that Pompey moved nearer to her. She looked as though she would fall on the floor if this dreadful moment did not soon come to an end. The door behind Lustbader opened and Harry Singleton stood there. Chloe jumped up from her chair and Pompey's eyes sparkled. Lustbader was so worked up that he didn't hear the door open.

"Maybe I'd better question you further," Lustbader was speaking loudly, his eyes roaming over the slight figure. "You don't suit me with those light eyes and that blanched face. You can come down to my house now—right now." He wheeled about and was face to face with the master of Heronfields.

"I think I'd better question you further, Lustbader," Harry spoke with a terrible quietness. "Maybe you don't suit me so well, either. Suppose you come up to my house now—right now!"

Chapter 30

Cuffee moved restlessly in his sleep. The scent of Charlotte which lingered in her poster bed penetrated into his dreams. He lay on his stomach and pressed himself deeper into the soft mattress. His arms embraced the pillow where last night her head had rested.

He was in a deep forest. Green-eyed owls, unquiet spirits of wicked men, hooted at him from the limbs of great trees from which old wistaria vines dangled like hangmen's nooses; wildcats snarled in the thick myrtle and on ancient tree stumps were plain hoofmarks of the devil, showing the places where he had danced the last dark of the moon. Hoarfrost covered the ground and white mist crawled up from the damp earth. Brambles reached out tearing his flesh and hindering his steps.

Suddenly, shimmering against the dark trees he saw the white stag, and Charlotte standing, white as a lily, by his flanks. The two candescent ones seemed to float toward him on the rolling mist. Thorny vines coiled out of their way as though pushed back by an unseen hand to let them through. Trees bowed before them and white flowers blossomed about their feet.

Cuffee tried to run to Charlotte but his feet were caught in a ropelike vine; he tried to call out but no sound came. She embraced the white stag whose dark flaming eyes had the look of Inigo, and he leaned over and rubbed his forehead against her breast encircling her with his widespread antlers.

A clump of silvery sycamores gleamed at the top of a hill and Charlotte and the stag started up to them. Charlotte was now a little ahead of the stag and she was singing a gay tune. Suddenly the stag lowered his head and began to paw the ground. Flame blew out from his dilated nostrils. Cuffee tried again to call to Charlotte to run, tried to throw her his charmed crab claw, but the ground beneath his feet changed into quicksand and he started sinking down—down—down.

He saw the stag rear up and strike Charlotte with his sharp pointed front feet. She fell and he stiffened his legs and jumped up and down on her, cruelly wounding her with his murderous hoofs.

Cuffee found his voice, and as he screamed a bright white light enveloped and swallowed the stag and Charlotte.

Cuffee opened his eyes to see little Nick standing in his cambric nightshirt by the bed with a lighted candle in his hand.

"You were crying. Do you hurt, Cuffee? Were you having a bad dream? Let me get in bed with you

209

like Charlotte used to let me do. I won't bother you."

Cuffee grunted and moved over for the child to crawl in. He was glad of the warm little body against him. His own was cold with remembered fear and he knew that the dream from which he had been awakened was an evil omen. He swore to himself that he would begin the hunt for the white stag tomorrow. Until that one had fixed him with his evil eye his life had gone smoothly enough. In a short week tragedy had come. From the day he had encountered the white stag a wicked spell had been on Charlotte and Inigo. That stag must be destroyed. Hagar and Hercules had taught him from babyhood the old laws of his people. He understood what he had seen. He must atone for the wrong that he had allowed to be done to Charlotte, taking the crab claw from her. He felt that she was not safe at Heronfields. Something cruel menaced her—surrounded her. The hair rose and prickled on the back of his sinewy neck.

He lay shaking with horror from his dream, holding little Nick tight in his arms. Sleep had fled and repellent gruesome visions enveloped him with their ugliness. The stag had Inigo's eyes! But that he must forget. He *must* forget.

Hercules, putting away the last of the carefully counted silver in the mahogany sideboard, sang a poignant old song to himself, softly so as not to disturb the folks sleeping upstairs.

> *"A tremblin' woman an' a tremblin' man,*
> *God gwine hol' you wid a tremblin' han'."*

Chapter 31

Inigo walked out through the garden, crossed the terraces above the river, turned around and walked back through the garden without having realized that he had moved. He must go into his office where his head slaves were assembled, in just a few minutes. God—what a head he had! Drunk at his own oyster roast! It had taken four men to get him into the house and to bed after Charlotte had disappeared into the night. Gingerly he reached up his hand and felt the scraped bruises that had come from his trying to butt an oak tree down in his drunken frustration.

His mother had won. Or, at least, she thought she had. She had successfully kept Charlotte a virgin. What she had turned her soul into was another thing. The verity of physical purity—that she had accomplished, he would admit, at least for the time being, for even loving her as he did he couldn't lower himself to seek her on the Street at Heronfields under the eyes of the Singletons and that beastly German overseer.

Yes—Tafra had fixed things perfectly! But he was leaving, too. She hadn't counted on that! Her pet monkey was not going to remain at Normandy and dance merrily while she pulled his little string. He'd had enough of Normandy and of her for a while.

He had neared the house without being aware of it. The sound of the men talking in his office came to him, but Inigo still stood intent and planned how he was going to avenge himself on Tafra and Emily. How he was going to plan some means of getting Charlotte from Harry Singleton, in spite of Harry's promise to Tafra. His mother was not to know he was going West. The Hamptons had promised not to tell, though he suspected that the Colonel had already discussed it in detail with her. But he was not going to say good-by so it didn't really matter. He'd put his big foot carefully through her clever plans. She'd never do him a trick like that again. Nobody would.

Bitterness and heartache were all through him as he walked down to the river. His beautiful river. He looked back up the terraces at his home shining rosy-toned in the cool clear morning light. His black eyes apprehended the rare quality of the outlines of the house and he sent a promise up to it that he would return someday and that there would be no more unhappiness there when he came back from wherever it was he was going. For Mississippi seemed as far away as China and the idea of starting up a new plantation in a frontier way of life beckoned to him like a black fast-running creek in a swamp in midsummer.

He turned and went into his office where his people were waiting for him. They were all very serious and in respect to them he adopted his most formal way of speaking and acting. Sitting at his massive desk he wrote noisily with a quill pen on a large piece of paper. He signed his name with a flourish, put the pen back in the jar, folded the paper, and handed it to Old Ben.

"Take this to town to Mr. Jessop at his office. It will explain everything to him and he will come out to-morrow to check on things as I have stated them."

Ben scraped his foot and pulled his forelock.

"Yassuh, Massa, but I shore hates to see one ob dem factors asetting in dat seat yunnuh am covering even fuh one day a week."

"Don't worry, Ben," said Inigo. "I'll be back by cotton-chopping time and the bears aren't going to eat me in Mississippi."

"Ben ain' worry 'bout no bears, Mass Inigo, it's dem raid Injuns whut duh cut off yo' ha'r dat Old Ben astudying 'bout. Wid yunnuh kilt who gwine rule we here?"

212

"Why, I could scalp ten Indians as quick as a flash," boasted Inigo, "and young Mr. Wade is the only man in the world who can kill a bear with a knife, then lift him onto a wagon and bring him home alone. The very sight of us three oversized brutes will scare the wits out of all the Indians in the West."

Ben looked at the dark circles under Inigo's eyes and the flat tense mouth that should have been full and smiling. But he took the paper, mournfully shook his head, and went out muttering dire prophecies and portents.

Inigo leaned back in his chair and fixed the remaining men with his keen eyes.

"You first, Cuffee," he said and motioned for Cuffee to step forward. Cuffee looked very gloomy and thwarted. He stepped up to the desk. "To you," went on Inigo, "I entrust my loved ones. Little Nicholas, my mother, my horses; guard them with your life if necessary—with your love and interest at all times." His voice trembled. "You realize, of course, that in the event of the death of my mother, the law can prosecute me for not having a white overseer on the place—what with Nick being so young. In such event try to persuade Mr. Robert to come here and stay until I can be fetched." Cuffee bowed his head. He said no word though Inigo questioned him with a long look. His dream still troubled him—repeating the queer resemblance between Inigo and the white stag!

"Hercules!" The old man came up, disapproval marking every wrinkle in his face. "You are to watch over the house and to uphold Cuffee in every way—in particular with the care of Nick."

"Yunnuh should of kept Charlotte here, Mass Inigo," Hercules said. "Yunnuh have no right to tek she from dat leely boy. Who gwine teach Nick he lessons? None of we kin read or write."

Hercules knew who had sold Charlotte. His years at cracked doors had taught him more about the Gaillards than even Tafra knew. He probably knew why Tafra had sold her, too. However, this was not the time to placate Hercules or to ponder over him. Next he called up Big Jake.

213

"Jake I have here the papers making a bargain with you as my overseer. Mr. Jessop will get Lawyer Ball to stamp it legally tomorrow. He will come once a week to do your figuring—the cotton seed is all in the storehouse, as is the fertilizer and a supply of tools. Mr. Jessop will get you anything that you ask for. Report to Miss Tafra each evening. Seneca will become head driver. I have great faith in you two to keep order with no undue harshness toward my people of your race."

Seneca showed his blue gums in a proud grin but Big Jake looked worried.

"Massa," he asked, "can't yunnuh in no way git back Charlotte? Her kin read and write and figure and unnuh could ask her things unnuh might not would bodder factor or Miss Tafra wid."

Inigo gripped his chair arms. Why in hell did everybody want Charlotte here? Would his past never let him rest? It seemed she was worth the whole plantation; to the Negroes, too. He looked up. Cuffee was staring accusingly at him. Cuffee who loved him—and Cuffee had not answered when he had put the trust to him.

"Cuffee," he spoke anxiously, "you will look after Mother and Nick and the horses?" The word *horses* did the trick.

"Sho, Mass Inigo." Cuffee met his eyes squarely this time. After all this was one of his gods and he loved him. Even gods made mistakes. "Cuffee tek de care. Cuffee jest was worrit 'bout ketching up wid dat white stag whut stob him Christmas. Unnuh planned to leave here fuh hunt him tomorrow but unnuh wait a few days—unnuh ketch um—unnuh have tuh ketch um."

"Oh," Inigo relaxed, "sure you'll catch him, and give him a shot for me when you do."

Cuffee shook his head.

"Um Cuffee enemy—not yourn," he said.

The master of Normandy stood up. "You, Festus —keep the boats shiny and in order. Take any of the family wherever they wish to go. Meet any guests. Keep your rowers healthy and strong." He faced the waiting black men.

214

"I am leaving my honor in your hands," he said. "It is now yours. By my faith in you, you must keep faith with me. I have been much criticized in the easy way I handle my people—do not let the faith I have in your race be unfounded. I can be put in jail if any of you make trouble in public. I am responsible for your behavior away out in Mississippi."

There was much scraping of feet and hands went to forelocks, but Inigo shook each man by the hand and walked out of his office without even locking a drawer to his desk.

For a few minutes they stood there in an awkward silence; then Big Jake asserted his authority.

"Git a move on," he ordered. "Effen yunnuh gots no work tuh do—set here all day. Unnuh got business in de fiel'. Come on, Seneca." In mannerly fashion they stood back to let Hercules leave first, he being the oldest. He straightened his bent shoulders and as though he were a great patriarch led the group out into the large servants' hall.

Chapter 32

Charlotte, too, walked in the cool of the morning, of the one day allotted a new slave as his own, but her thoughts were different from Inigo's bitter determinations. At every hour of the past night she had thought of him; and like the clouds of the air her thoughts disappeared and collected again, always different and always the same. She had left Normandy thinking that the next hour would surely bring him thundering up to

215

the mean cabin. But the night had been spent in sleepless silence disturbed only by the winter wind in the palmettos and the stertorous snoring of Chloe in the other room. What could have happened to him? What could have defeated him?

And as six years ago she had accepted Tafra and the regime of the grand drawing-room, now she accepted Chloe and the dingy cabin; but only as she would have accepted a frozen moment in her life which would shatter at the proper time, leaving her still lovely—still eager—still beloved.

She walked down to the river, absorbing the strange wild sad landscape with its monotonous outline and color, the low shore of sand and mud and rattling reeds, the aching throbbing of the steam rice mills, the stench of the deep ditch which was dug for a latrine behind the long rows of flimsy cabins and through which a merciful tide washed in and out twice a day.

Along the riverbank there was little attempt at ornamental cultivation; no terraces or tea houses reached by gay Venetian bridges enlivened the gloomy dike-banded river. Instead, thin ditches and canals spread out like claws to flood the rice fields when necessary. Patches of swamp were dotted here and there and luxuriant trees of magnolia, cypress, and live oak roped with winter-dead vines and mourning with moss shadowed the raised margin of the canal along which she made her lonely discouraged voyage, acutely aware of reptilian eyes glittering from the wet alluvial soil and ragged Negroes straying about like hungry birds. She wondered if she should be afraid of them, but as they gradually became bold enough to run up and finger the stuff of her dress and fondle her arms and kiss her hands yelping with delight that "W'ite Missy walk 'mongst we!" she felt no fear of them.

"I'm not white," she tried to tell them but they pointed at her hoop skirt and chuckled and cackled discordantly. Finally to escape them she found courage enough to knock on a cabin door which teetered near the water's edge. There was no answer, but the tattered band by now pressed suffocatingly around her, rolling their eyes and wallowing in the dirt in their excitement, so she pushed against the door and stepped quickly inside.

Inside all was dark and she leaned her shoulders on the door holding it shut until the sandy shuffle of departing feet reassured her. Then she realized that the cabin was occupied. Hoarse sounds of breathing and grunting were loud in the cold room. Cracking the door she let in a shaft of weak sunlight and discovered a confusion of children and chickens and ducks, scattered bits of kindling and tangles of gray moss. The ducks and chickens picked their way among the children who crouched on the drafty floor close to the hearth although the fire was almost out. They were staring with terror at her, their eyeballs rolling, their teeth shining, and as they began to whimper with awe and fear of the whitest woman who had ever stood on their horizon Charlotte spoke encouragingly to the oldest child, a half-naked boy, but he answered her with unintelligible bestial sounds while the others giggled and cried. Then she tried pantomime but this was the final torment. The boy screeched, dropping the baby he was holding on the floor to hide himself under a pile of moss in the corner away from this woman who was casting evil spells on him.

Charlotte ran and picked up the wailing infant and as she did so a leggy teen-aged girl slipped through the door and began soothing the children with strange words. She put some kindling on the fire which blazed up as she brushed the hearth with a twig and shooed out the indignant chickens and ducks.

This calm acceptance of the evil one quieted the children and the big boy burst into laughter, peeping out from his protective disguise of gray moss. Charlotte counted four other children besides the vile-smelling baby whom she laid on the rickety bed after arranging its rags as best she could. The child was wrapped in a dirty strip of red flannel, probably the one in which it had been wrapped at birth.

"Can't any of you talk?" she desperately asked the girl, who seemed oblivious of her presence.

217

"Yassum," the black girl said. "I kin caze I sews to de big house. But dese uns cain't hardly. Who is yunnuh in us house? Weuns ain't done nuttin'."

"Don't you have any mother to look after you? Why aren't these children at the children's house with the other small ones?"

"Weuns is een punishment," the girl said evenly, though tears ran down her cheeks onto her scrawny neck.

"Lula—Lula!" the four children cried, "Lula—Lula!" It sounded as though they were keening an old lament out of the liquid name. Lula signaled for them to be quiet and defiantly answered the query in Charlotte's face.

"We Pa been brought here fuh patroon. He de bestest boatman on de whole ribber but now he banish to Hell Hole swamp fuh cut palmetto logs. An' de snakes whut duh lib dere is thick and long. He been banish fuh tekking boat fuh cotch fish and he seen thing he ain't supposed fuh see."

"And your mother?" Charlotte could hardly bear the odor of the unwashed young, but she was too curious to go away.

"Her wukking in de rice mill and tonight her gwine walk slam to Hell Hole and back fuh tek we Pa some wittles. Now Lula ain't neber seen yunnuh to de house. Is yunnuh one ob dese abolitionies come to stir up we slabes? Miss Mildred sho run yunnuh off effen yunnuh is."

Charlotte said, "No," as she took the frayed woolen cap from the baby's wretched head. But she could not continue what she had started to say for all the children cried out and the boy flew from under the pile of moss, snatched baby and cap, jamming the cap back on the lolling kinky crown, grunting and muttering and casting outraged looks at her.

Did the cap hold the key to the tiny mortal's soul? How had she offended so deeply? Sighing, she felt that she had been spirited quite away from reality. How could this netherworld of abysmal ignorance be so near Normandy? She was as alien here on this miserable Street as if she had been sold to a group of screaming

218

savages in deepest Africa. But trying to redeem herself in Lula's accusing eyes, she said, "I am a slave—not an abolitionist."

This brought further cries from the barbaric children.

"Not yunnuh," Lula voiced their protest. "Not yunnuh. I heerd 'bout a new slabe last night and I heerd bad things Mr. Lustbader said atter yunnuh comed. Git from here! Run, Missy! Run wid we Ma to Hell Hole. Rattlesnake ain't hurt yunnuh lak de obersee' gwine do. Lula done learnt 'bout dem underground railroads, too. Yunnuh hatter run. Yunnuh cain't stay at Heronfield."

Charlotte started out of the door. She had upset this desolate household enough. There was no use in trying to explain to this hopeless child that only five miles distant her love dwelt. That this grim Street was not the world. That six months would soon pass and she would be gone from this ugliness forever. That the master was protecting her with his honor from the overseer.

"Kin Lula come and see yunnuh sometime?" the girl asked pitifully as Charlotte walked out onto the raised canal margin again.

"Of course. How about showing me the way to the wharf now while I'm so near the river?"

Lula shook the twig positively at each of the dirty pickaninnies in turn and gave a disgusted grunt at her brother who was guarding the youngest with fierce affection, before she skipped out on her bare feet, wearing no cloak though the air was chill and damp.

Charlotte almost had to run to keep up with the flying black legs and when she came to the wharf she wondered why she had made the effort. The whole panorama was featureless with miles and miles of reedy shores; forests of dead canes rattling in the wind, sedges whispering to the tidal salt water that twisted and looped in sinuous curves of inlet and creek as far as sight could wander. The water bore the smell but not the sight of the sea; for the sea was shut out by the eerie yellow of mud flats, swamps, and innumerable islands. Islands that lay brooding under the sky, half drowned in

219

the river, sea monsters composed of mud and sand and water, uncertain of their fate, ever changing, sliding down, dissolving, merging with the river, desiring the sea.

As they reached the wharf a steersman from a boat nearing the shore raised a conch shell to his lips and blew a mighty blast. At once the wharf became black with hurrying figures. Lula stopped quickly and catching Charlotte's hand pulled her over into a clump of withered canes, where they stood ankle-deep in icy water watching the Negroes mill nervously around as the boat drew near. When it touched the wharf several slaves seized the prow and helped the huge, sloppy Lustbader to alight. Charlotte started to speak but realizing that the whole scene was being played by silent performers she squeezed Lula's chilly fingers and made her come into the warm circle of her shawl.

Lustbader motioned for the bucks to line up and unload the boat. One by one they plunged waist-deep into the river and received bales and bundles of stuff onto their heads, struggling to stay upright in the strong ebb tide.

One gaunt Negro lost his footing just as he was about to step ashore and wildly clutching at the bundle on his head he ripped a great hole in the croker sack; Charlotte and Lula gasped as silver teapots, cups, and spoons rolled into the turgid yellow river and were sucked under. Lustbader, yelling and cursing, uncoiled the bullwhip hanging at his belt and struck the man violently across the eyes. Blood spurted from the very eye sockets and howling with pain and terror the slave fell back into the river and his body sank as surely as the silver teapot had done. But he was not to be relieved of life that easily. Lustbader lashed right and left with his whip and the men splashed into the water and dragged the inert black man out. They laid him on the wet splintery wharf boards where the whistle and zing of the bullwhip scorching and maiming his human flesh made them scream and writhe and tear their garments though the victim only twitched convulsively once or twice and then lay still.

"Run," Lula whispered, and Charlotte rushed through the swamp back onto the safety of the Street.

And with her ran the knowledge that she was not the same person who had pushed irritably into Lula's cabin—could never be the same person, for it was the first time that she had seen with her own eyes the inhumanity of slavery, what it did to black men; what it did to white men. It was like seeing death for the first time. She would never forget it.

Lula had disappeared somewhere along the way, and as Charlotte hastened back to Chloe's house the people who had been working in the rice mill were lining up in front of rows of huge iron caldrons. It was the first meal of the day and as Cook Cina or one of her wenches filled their rude cedar tubs with rice and bits of boiled salt bacon, they plunged their fingers or a piece of smooth wood into the hot gluey mess and ate ravenously as they trudged to their own doorsteps or slumped on the ground under a tree.

They paid no attention to Charlotte and her dipping hoop skirt but a group of children waiting their turn with their little tubs noticed her and came like a pack of black wolves shrieking, "Missy, gib unnuh piece ob meat! Missy, gib meat!"

She began to run from them. Chloe's house seemed very far away but at last she was in, the door slammed shut. She dropped into Chloe's old chair half laughing, half crying; of all the days and moments she had ever encountered this was the most incomprehensible! Chuckling laughter, animal noises issuing from human throats, the distant wailing from the wharf where the beaten man lay sounded from outside; under every crack in the floor she could glimpse rolling eyes, and she knew with deadly sureness that this day was only a foretaste of the alien cruel barbarism she would experience in this isolated rice plantation.

The next morning at hornblow she went to the big house to become Nancy's maid. For a little while she stood outside the sprawling colonial dwelling and compared it with Normandy. Here the grounds were not landscaped; hodgepodge flower beds struggled under the shade of immense virgin trees that darkened wide verandahs winding around all four sides of the clapboard structure. Chickens darted about and a loose horse whinnied and stamped his feet as slaves tiptoed on and off the porches, peeping through the windows to see how white folks lived, how they loved, how they ate meat.

There will be no solitude in this remote place, Charlotte thought, hearing the rice mill humming and the darkies chattering, scolding, and complaining as they made their way to their allotted tasks. She had stopped by the sick house to speak to Chloe who had sat up all night with the man Lustbader had flogged beyond further usefulness, but Chloe had been reluctant to talk to her and explain what she was supposed to do, so her feet dragged as she entered the house and passed into the dining-room.

Mildred Singleton and her beloved son Hal, lazying over breakfast, raised their eyebrows in astonishment as Charlotte came swaying gracefully through the door in an emerald-green serge hoop skirt banded with black velvet and laced with tiny silk frogs at her slender waist.

"Well!" The large dowager expelled the word like pellets of hail. "I never!"

Hal chewed his ham and biscuit loudly and drank his hot tea with a sucking sound, refusing to be ruffled.

"Good morning," Charlotte said, tightly formal in her nervousness.

"La! what fine feathers for a blackbird and what a raucous song! Don't you know that you are breaking the law, girl?" Mildred was not afraid of this girl—she was too nearly white. Besides, she had promised the ladies to put her in her place.

Charlotte curtsied. "Yes, ma'am," and started swiftly for the hall but Mildred's voice stopped her before she passed the fireplace which still wore the brittle brown remains of Christmas garlands. "Drop your hoop this instant. Negro slaves are not permitted to wear hoops in their skirts."

"Yes, Mrs. Singleton. I'll run right back to Chloe's house and take it off immediately."

"Drop it here—now—this instant!" Mildred told the erect back.

Charlotte turned her head and stared in disbelief at the large woman in the pink worsted wrapper.

"Not in front of Mr. Hal," she choked.

"Mr. Hal doesn't see you any more than he sees the sideboard over there. Are you out of your mind? Certainly drop it here. I forbid you to take another step in that hoop."

Charlotte glanced at Hal and saw that indeed he had taken no notice of her but was busily spooning fig preserves onto his plate. She defiantly pulled up her skirt and deliberately fumbled with the tape that held the hoop.

"Drop it—drop it!" Mildred shouted as Hal spilled a spoonful of figs on the tablecloth and stared at the shapely ankles covered in white lisle.

The offending article finally lay stiffly on the floor and Charlotte's face was burning with shame and dislike of her mistress.

But Mildred had already forgotten her displeasure and when she saw the hoop she exclaimed, "Why that's one of those fine French ones. I've had an order in for mine for months. Take it upstairs and give it to Sukey to put it my wardrobe."

Numbly Charlotte gathered the cumbersome hoop and marched out. But she found to her dismay that while she might have made a dignified and scornful ascent wearing her hoop skirt, carrying it was another matter. Trying not to break it and cause a further scene she struggled up, but on hearing Hal laughing at her she banged it angrily against the rails.

She was breathing rapidly when she came into Nancy's disordered room.

"Get up," she said crossly. But as Nancy meekly obeyed her, Charlotte had an urge to hug the overlarge girl wandering sleepily around the room in a voluminous Canton flannel nightgown. The room was a bewildering clutter of dark ugly mahogany furniture and the poor girl bumped into two tables and a stool before she fell into a chair in front of her dresser.

Charlotte washed Nancy's face and pulled off the gown as she would have done for little Nick. Then after she had tied the cambric drawers in place, she

223

slipped a red worsted-net kimono over Nancy's thick shoulders before beginning to brush the long heavy hair.

Nancy came awake at last and suddenly looking critically at her face and Charlotte's in the mirror, said spontaneously, "Why, you are lighter-skinned than I am! I have always been sorry about the day Robert and Hal chased you when you were little. I do hope that you will like me. Papa does but Mamma doesn't and she makes him stay with her all the time and I get awfully unhappy and lonesome when we live here in the country."

"Why does your mother make your papa stay with her all the time?" Charlotte was depending on Harry Singleton's pledge. This sounded like bad news for her.

"Mamma is scared to death of Negroes. When she was a little girl her nurse used to go and leave her at night and threaten her that lots of Negro men would come and eat her up if she cried out and let the family know that she was alone. She's especially scared of them here at Heronfields."

And well she might be. Charlotte thought grimly of the black faces pressed against the windowpanes in the early morning. "Are you afraid of them?"

"No," Nancy frowned. "But don't tell Mamma. She wants me to be afraid of them. She has always tried to frighten me so that I won't even go to see Chloe on the Street, and Chloe was my best friend when I was little."

"I'd never lived on a Street before yesterday myself," Charlotte confessed.

"Will you tell me what it is like?"

"Yes, if you want to know."

"I do want to know. I have such queer nightmares about going there and I'd like to know how wrong they are."

"They aren't wrong," Charlotte said, thinking of Lula and her little brothers and sisters.

"Did you like Mr. Robert at Normandy?" Nancy's mind couldn't keep to any one subject too long.

Charlotte twisted the stubborn black hair into a

smooth knot. She tried it one way and then another before she answered.

"Are you going to marry him?"

"Yes, if he ever asks me," pouted Nancy. "Every time he comes to the point his mother gets sick and he says we must wait till she is well. She looks mighty healthy to me to be sick so much. I have set my heart on being mistress of Normandy and so has Papa."

Charlotte went over to the untidy mahogany wardrobe and took out a scarlet and white flannel dress. Everything was in disorder. This one was only less rumpled and soiled than the others.

"This is pretty—would you like to wear this?" she asked.

Nancy shook her head.

"No, find my green velvet riding-habit and the plumed hat to go with it. I'd better ride over to Normandy and try to see Mr. Robert before he goes back to Charleston with his mother today, and get him to invite me to the ball. Papa is going to insist on our staying at Heronfields until the first of February and there's no telling who might snare him if I don't get him to ask me first."

Charlotte patiently helped Nancy dress. Nancy was round and strong. She would develop into a big woman like her mother. She had missed the Singleton long thin legs. If it weren't for the fact that Nick *must* inherit Normandy she would have been pleased that Robert had been lucky enough to have this nice healthy girl fall in love with him.

"Do you love Mr. Robert, Miss Nancy?" she asked.

"Love him?" asked Nancy in a surprised way. "Why, I hadn't thought about that. I suppose I will when I marry him. Women do, don't they?" An anxious look came on her young face. Charlotte hastened to reassure her.

"Of course you'll love him then. Women have to learn things like that."

But not she. She had not had to learn it. Such feeling as she had for Inigo was not learned—it happened. Like a brush fire—it blazed up, nobody knew

225

why, and burned with a terrible consuming power brighter and brighter. It was still burning. It had kept her wretched on her miserable bed all through the past two nights.

A child's voice was heard calling and the girls went to the window and looked out. Nick Gaillard was galloping up on his little tacky with Sambo bumping along on another one behind him.

"Go on, Charlotte," said Nancy, giving her a push. "He's missed you."

Charlotte ran out of the room and down the steep stairs. She reached the hall as the front door was flung open and little Nick catapulted into her arms. "Oh, Charlotte," he cried happily, hugging and kissing her, "guess what?"

"Kiss me too, Miss Charlotte." Sambo tried to nudge in between but Nick knocked him back. She must be all his very own— Oh, it was good to smell her sweetness and to feel her safe arms holding him warm and near again!

"What, Nick?" she asked between kisses, willing him to speak Inigo's name.

"Pa's gone to Mississippi with the Colonel and Uncle Wade!" He stood back to watch the effect of his news. She turned away.

"No!" she cried aloud. Then she clenched her teeth. *I mustn't—mustn't give anything away to little Nick. Inigo can't have gone and left me here—he can't have. We must not be parted like this—with no word, no signal, no understanding.*

The two small boys were nodding their heads solemnly as though they alone had planned and executed the trip.

"They rode away at sunup this morning. Pa didn't even tell Gran good-by and it made her very sad. Hero got so excited that he reared up and broke his bridle twice."

"Yas'm," broke in Sambo, "an' Sweet's still fussin' 'bout all dat stirring befo' daylight. Said her didn't hardly git laid out good las' night when Mist' Hecklus started pokin' um up again."

Charlotte pulled Inigo's son close and hid her

226

face in his hair. "Have you missed me?" Her voice shook but there were no tears in it. She had done with weeping more than a week ago. Like a baby goat Nick butted his curly head playfully against her breasts.

"Course, Charlotte!" *Unlike Inigo,* she thought, *he is unashamed in his love for me.* "Course! I cried and cried but Cuffee slept in your bed and he moaned and hollered all night till I got in with him. Gran said he must of had the stomach-ache from some old ducks we had for supper and she made him take a big dose of calomel. But he cried last night again as soon as he got good asleep."

"An'," Sambo was not to be left out in all these big tales, "hit tuk Big Jake and fo' udder mens to git Mass Inigo upstairs atter dat roas'in' party. Dey fair drug him all de way up, an' him acussin' an' ahollerin' lak de ol debbil heself."

Talk, Charlotte. Stop these childish talebearers. He's gone! All was in ferment within her. But it would do no good to show it.

"Your hair hasn't been combed since I left," was all she could find to say.

"No—I won't let them. I kicked Jenny when she tried and Gran told her to leave me alone, that you would be home soon and we could cut the snarls out."

And who will look out for Lula and those horrid children? she thought as Pompey came slouching up, buckling at the knees, every step just too much trouble for a man to endure.

"Who dese?" he asked, pointing at the boys.

"Nicholas Gaillard and Sambo, his personal servant. My two favorite gentlemen," answered Charlotte loudly and falsely gay. When an end came to love, tears only watered it and kept it alive. Let it wither and die.

"Fine fellows," he agreed, "but say, sugah, how 'bout going to de prayer meeting wid me tomorrow night? Hit's time fuh yunnuh to meet de people here at Heronfields. Dey's a preacher fum Charleston coming out whut kin really lay dem flat in de aisles. Dey say he kin out-shout old Grimble and he must be somepin!"

227

Charlotte studied the tan face, the shiny popeyes. She thought of how Inigo and Tafra had been repulsed at the idea of children from her body; how Leon and Lula and the ragged wretches had admired her. She *must* be proud of herself—she *must* know her race. She had never in her life been to a meeting at a Negro church. Spiritually she lifted her foot and placed a toe on the color line.

"Yes, I'll go, Pompey," she said. "Come by Chloe's for me."

"Ki, Miss Charlotte," said Sambo, "I gwine tell Cuffee on yunnah."

"You ain't either," ordered Nick.

"I is too, and he gwine beat Charlotte good."

Nick slapped him and Sambo grabbed Nick by the shoulders to throw him down.

"What's all this commotion?" Nancy asked, coming down the stairs in her green riding-habit. "If you boys are going back to Normandy, I'll ride along with you. Pompey, send out Ariadne for me."

"That's Robert's girl," Nick whispered in Sambo's ear. Sambo slanted his big eyes in Nancy's direction and giggled.

"She big enough to handle him," he whispered back, "but Miss Emily kin whup two de size ob she by jest afluttering her little handkercher'."

Charlotte, with an arm around each boy, walked outside. The tackys were happily eating pansies. Sambo darted over and snatched up their heads.

A groom led Ariadne to the block. She was a bright sherry bay hunter with a sweet head, and though her bones were not large her legs were sound and clean.

Nancy mounted and settled herself into her polished side-saddle. Here she was at home; her clumsy indecisive manner disappeared and an air of completion and grace came on her. She touched Ariadne with her whip and the mare swept away, going close to the ground with great elegance and power.

Sambo and Nick dug their heels into the tackys and galloped behind.

"I'll be back soon. Good-by." Nick waved at her.

"Mind you bring a comb," Charlotte called after him.

She watched them flying away and when they were gone she felt more alone than ever before; she was almost overwhelmed by her isolation. Everyone's hand was against her—everyone's.

She knelt and picked some pansies to put in her cabin room. Purple, yellow, white, crimson, and funny little mingled ones—white and purple, bronze and yellow, brown and crimson, white and copper. All blooming in one bed. All harmonious.

She had determined not to let her mind dwell on Inigo but looking at the mixed colors of the flowers, suddenly his face came before her as clearly as though he himself were there in all his vivid vigor.

She stood up and shading her eyes with her hand stared at the cloud of dust rising from the heels of the horses far down the road. Then she ran from the big house to the dingy comfort of old Chloe's cabin. *Oh, Inigo,* she thought—*Oh, Inigo!*

Chapter 33

The weather changed and the next night was windlessly warm and lowering. Heavy clouds banked warningly in the west but the slaves streamed restlessly in their tattered garments up and down the Street impatient for their monthly meeting.

Chloe stood in the fenced-in yard of the combination children's house and hospital talking to a dirty mother balancing a crying infant on her hip. Chloe puffed angrily on her pipe, frowning as the woman kicked open the fence gate and pushed her way into the center of a noisy group of men, although the baby cried piteously as elbows jostled and bumped its bobbing, wool-covered head.

But after Chloe with great lumbering and groaning forced her ponderous thighs to bear her weight across to her own house, her face crinkled into a broad smile as the door was thrown open and rays of light from the fat pine fire stabbed the dusk cheerily.

"Hello!" Charlotte said. "I thought you were never coming. I've got your supper all hot for you."

Chloe grunted and struggled down into the chair close to the fire.

"Dem fool niggers," she fussed, "ain't gots nuttin' in dey haids but singin' and shoutin'. I done worriet and fretted ober a po' leely sick baby all dis blessed day and now de mammy done took away de critter and won't think ob um agin twell time to fetch um to me tomorrow. Laughin' lak a skinny jackass in a mess ob men, jest fixing to get mo' baby, an' her a common field hand and nuttin' else. My—hit's good to be home and find yunnuh wid yo' bright face awaitin'."

Charlotte knelt down and heaped some hominy and a pork chop onto a tin plate.

"The cook from the house sent you this chop. She said she bet you were so mad over having me with you she'd pleasure you a little for old times' sake." Charlotte smiled at the memory of Craney's unpleasant sense of humor.

"Humph," snorted Chloe. "Dat old fool can't specify her head from her tail. Every time she crack her teet' she strews 'struction. Hit's a wonder she ain't sen' roccoon meat stead ob pork, knowing how de grease riles my stomach." She set down her pipe, greedily stirred the thick gravy into her hominy, and began to eat the precious rare treat.

"What yunnuh gwine eat?" she asked, belching loudly and sucking on the chop bone.

"I ate in the kitchen," Charlotte answered. "They had pigeons and crayfish smothered together in brown sauce with Madeira wine poured over them—so I feel more cheerful than last night, even though that kitchen is the filthiest place I've ever been in. I asked Craney if Mrs. Singleton had seen it lately and she was outraged. She said no lady ever walked through a kitchen, much less looked at one. Heronfields is certainly different from Normandy. Neither the house slaves nor the field slaves here do half as much work as the ones at Normandy, yet they never smile and they are all filthy."

"Lustbader don' want dem to wuk too hard caze he hatter reward dem effen dey do mo' dan jest enough; an' how in de worl' kin nigger wash in winter w'en hit too cold to jump in de ribber?"

"Lustbader almost spoke to me today, but I ran into Mr. Harry's study and he went away. What will I do if he bothers me while I am here? I'm utterly terrified of him."

"Ki, chile, yunnuh needn't fear Lus'bader yet —not twell de six mont' is past. Pompey come by de chillun house yestiddy morning chucklin' ober de way Mass Harry tuk de wind out ob he sails. 'Dis de onliest warnin' I'm giving yunnuh, Lus'bader,' he says, 'an' effen I hears one peep concernin' any interest yunnuh might be showing in a certain light-faced maid ob my daughter, yunnuh gwine lan' right back in de jail I got yunnuh out ob.' Pompey say de man turn right gray in de face and bunch up he fis' but he scrape he foots same like a nigger and say, 'Yassah, Mr. Singleton, I scairt yunnuh hab misunderstand my intenshuns, I gots no taste fuh wenches—dere ain't a yaller face on de plantation ceptin' dat favority jockey ob yourn. So don' dat prove de kind ob a man I is? I is yo' right hand and I does what you says.'

"Pompey say Mass Harry jest said, 'Well dat's all —yunnuh said enough—so what about dat new seed I fotched from Charleston? De factor's sheet an' yours don' seem to tally!' "

Charlotte was sitting on the floor. Her hair shone with a thousand highlights from the yellow flames of the pine fire. Chloe wiped her fat greasy hands on her soiled apron and touched the copper tresses.

"Dis been a awful day fuh me and po' beat Gabel," Chloe said weaving strands of the glittering hair across her brown fingers.

"Did you tell Mr. Singleton about Mr. Lustbader whipping him? I started to when I went in his study but after he refused to write me a pass to go over to Normandy Sunday I was too upset to say anything. Why didn't you tell him? You aren't afraid of anybody."

The purple-turbaned head shook sadly and the brown neck began to ooze drops of sweat in the fire heat as Chloe meditated on the clever way Lustbader had bound her tongue.

"Lus'bader yent gib me no chanst. He done told Mass Harry dat Gabel fell in de rice t'resher. Den he come to de sick house and dangle a big sack ob cocaine in front of unnuh eyes effen unnuh promus not to crack unnuh teet'. So Chloe hatter keep shet mout' so Gabel kin hab de dust and not care whedder bofe he eyeballs is bust open or not."

"Oh, oh!" Charlotte jumped up and hid her face in her hands, pacing up and down the creaking floor. "Can't we do *anything?*"

"Now—now—quit dat gwine on!" Chloe said sharply. "Dere's plenty to be doing. Fust weuns—yunnuh and unnuh—gots to git rid ob Lus'bader. He not only ruining dese people body, he mekking dere souls not fitten fuh freedom w'en hit finally duh git here."

"What makes you think freedom will ever get here?" Charlotte asked fretfully.

"Dere's a leely yaller nigger riding a leely gray mule pass up and down de road lately. Up and down de road. Fust yunnuh duh hear twig crackling den come a houn' dog wid he nose to de groun' trailing, and he duh howl w'en he come to plantashum whey dey is lots ob niggers. And atter a while here come a leely man wid he long hair on he shoulder, yaller, riding a gray mule. And he ride up and down de whole Street and de niggers come out on de side and he pass up and down saying, 'Freedom duh come soon. Wuk and wait. Wuk and wait.' And he pass on, and de moon look brighter, and de tree shadder look darker, and de frost on de bushes look lak snow. Sometime he come w'en de hot nights ob summer is sweet wid blooming flowers; or w'en de leaves is falling; or w'en de cold night ob winter 'stress de niggers. And de leely yaller nigger gwine keep on trabelin' up and down—up and down twell slabery days is ober. Hagar say he sperrit; mebbe so. But he been coming mo' and mo' regular lately so Chloe think freedom ain't far behime um.

"Dat's why Chloe got to git rid ob Lus'bader. He keep de people from wukkin' and dey ain't gwine be fitten to move on w'en de yaller nigger gib de word."

Charlotte was unbelieving but spellbound as Chloe told of Joe Valiant, Lula's father. Joe swore that the little yellow Negro stopped at his house by the river one night in the late fall and called his name and when Joe came out of his house into the moonlight the yellow Negro told him to take a boat the next day and fish over near Beech Island.

Joe, the smartest Negro on the whole plantation, smart like Big Jake at Normandy, took a boat, a little flat-bottomed one, and rowed out to Beech Island to fish the next day. He trolled for sheephead and he cast for trout but not a single fish took his bait so in disgust he pulled up onto the island and went ashore. And he found a rude hut erected in a clump of saw palmettos since he had been there the past summer. But before he could look inside he heard a conch blowing and saw Lustbader with the eight-man canoe land by his boat. There was no hope of hiding, and Lustbader, daring not to flog him since he was Harry's prize patroon, made him hold the big canoe while the eight men loaded it with stuff from the hut: linen, silver, sacks of cotton seed and tobacco seed, china and shawls and dolmans.

Lustbader had offered a share of this to Joe for his silence, but when Joe refused to commit himself, Lustbader had banished him to the rattlesnake pit of Hell Hole Swamp from whence few slaves ever returned alive, telling Mr. Singleton that Joe was impudent and that he had to punish him for two months.

However, Joe had managed to convey his discovery to her and, by asking here and there, she'd found

233

out that Lustbader operated a market in stolen goods. Giving to slaves from this and other plantations a bit of money, a little whisky, a piece of meat or—prize of prizes—a sack of happy dust in exchange for any household treasures they might filch from their masters and deliver to his hidden island.

Charlotte had seen the next step. Each week the boat went to the island empty and returned to Heronfields' wharf loaded with sacks which in turn were piled onto wagons, covered with straw and sold at a thieves' market in Charleston in the safety of midnight.

"Joe be home nex' week," Chloe finished. "Yunnuh hatter go long wid um one night and see fuh yo'self so w'en de folks tek yunnuh to Cha'sum in Febbywerry yunnuh kin put de word out on Lus'bader and git um cotch."

By now Charlotte was shaking with misery and horror at the endless maze that the Street had led her into. At Normandy she had suspected nothing of this dreadful side of slavery and even if she had she could not have formed any idea of the state of things in which she was finding herself almost hourly deeper plunged with those pitiful people whose well-being was becoming as vital as her own.

"You understand Negroes so well, were you born in Africa?" Charlotte asked, stroking the fat wrist gratefully. Chloe reminded her a little of Poulette and how she had talked to her on cold nights before she put her into her narrow little bed. With Tafra, she had always tried so hard to prove something that she had gotten out of the habit of relaxation.

"Um-hum." The pipe smoke drifted bluely upward.

"Not in slavery?"

"Uh-uh!"

"Do you remember much about it?"

Remember? The stars so bright that a little black hand could almost reach out and pick them from the skies, the night music of birds and the day chatter of monkeys, the deep throb of drums and the cool air fanned on a fevered little brow by a mother who smelled of earth and love and kindness. Remember? Of course she remembered.

"Um-hum."

"How old were you when they—"

"Dey cotch me in a tiger trap. I been so high." Her fat hands vaguely measured four or five or three feet.

"How old are you now?"

"Older 'n Hagar. Since Mass Harry' grandfather time. Since befo' cotton or rice. Since indigo. Jedus! But Mass Dewey Singleton wuz some mean man. He eben whup his own slaves his own self. Tored um to ribbons fuh eating a frizzle chicken. Chain um to a stob in de ground an' put he foots on dey neck and rip de pure flesh offen dere bones!"

Charlotte put her hands over her ears. Chloe shook her head sadly. "De Gaillards nebber done things lak dat. None ob Mass Inigo' people been bad. Dey treat nigger same lak he a human pusson—niggers dey raise and wild niggers."

"Miss Tafra didn't treat me like a human person," Charlotte said bitterly.

"Yas, chile, Miss Tafra did treat yunnuh human. She treat yunnuh same lak Chloe would hab treat her own nigger gal chile what pined atter a white man. Yunnuh is a crittur of moonlight, an' clouds kin mighty easy hide all yo' light.

"I been watchin' yunnuh. Dere ain't a buck from de Street so much as turn he haid to look in us window after yunnuh an' yunnuh de prettiest slabe ever been on dis plantashum. Yunnuh ain't built lak most gals. Yunnuh ain' got de twitch here an' de twitch dere whut fetches mens pantin' up to yo' skirts. But Gawd Jedus—effen yunnuh did decide to twitch, Chloe bet yunnuh could out-roll de headingest bitch on de whole blessed place!"

The coarse words did not upset Charlotte. She understood what Chloe was trying to say. Hagar had said it already. Tafra knew it. She—oh God—she knew it, too, and it was a white man that she was made to love. Whom she would never love.

235

"Find a man from yo' own kind," Chloe was saying. "Dere's allus one mo' kin light a candle fuh a gal. Eben a leely sad-eyed gal lak yunnuh. Now tek life —hit plain scare yunnuh, don't hit?"

Charlotte did not speak.

"Not to be scairt ob dis worl'," Chloe went on slowly, choosing her words with care, "yunnuh mus' belongs to hit."

"Oh, but how?" Charlotte whispered. "How?" She had tried to belong to her father's world but she had been cast out. Now she was desperately trying to belong to her mother's world.

"Belong to hit and to yo'self at de same time. Make pertend to people. Lak in nightmare w'en yunnuh gots to git from a yowling wildcat yunnuh kin howl and screech louder dan hit kin. Outholler de ole Tom heself."

"I'll try that tonight when I go to the church. Are you coming to the meeting?"

"Gawd no, chile. My feets hurts and Gabel mought start hollering. Besides hit's confusing to worship too many gods in dis life. Jedus ain't none ob my saviour. I been baptize six time an hit ain't specify nuttin fuh Chloe yit.

"I ain't so sot on yunnuh going to dat chu'ch neither. Yunnuh ain't nebber gwine to be de kind ob nigger to carry on all dat foolishness nohow."

"But you just told me to try and be like the other Negroes."

"Wal, now I'm ontelling yuh. Miss Tafra didn't mean no kind of turning into dat sort ob nigger."

Chloe worried with her pipe and for the first time she noticed the gay yellow challis dress Charlotte was wearing.

"No call to go 'mongst all dem trash dres' same lak a white gal."

Charlotte spun around the ugly room in the firelight and the dress made a circle of gold about her. "I've never been to a Negro church and it's time I learned some of the ways of my people if I'm to be like my people."

236

"Humph," Chloe grunted disapprovingly. "Dat pumpkin-face Pompey ain't none ob yo' people."

"No, but you are and Leon Cavallo is. I think I might even marry Leon someday. He's free. He can take me anywhere I want to go!" Charlotte was nervously overexcited. The past days had brought too much change. Her usually soft voice was very loud, almost shrill.

Fingers rattled against the door and Pompey strutted in like a barnyard rooster, smelling of bay rum and polished until he shone like a mirror.

"Well, Sis Charlotte," he crowed, "is you ready to be escorted to de meeting wid me?"

Charlotte picked up her scarlet merino shawl and threw it about her shoulders.

"Good night, Miss Chloe."

The old woman didn't turn her head, but her displeased muttering followed Charlotte out into the night.

Chapter 34

Charlotte and Pompey sedately walked down the Street toward the little Negro church which stood at the edge of the big woods. The Street was thick with people walking alone and in groups on their way to salvation. They were serious, and the sharp barking of a squirrel cut loudly across the quiet as they made their way.

Charlotte and Pompey arrived in time to get good seats. Extra benches of fresh-cut pine had been hastily set up outside to take care of the congregation which had been swelled by visiting slaves holding passes from their masters. Charlotte was tense with interest as the pine flares lighted up the faces eagerly awaiting the message.

The Reverend Grimble, the "locus pasture," sat solemnly on a slat-bottom chair and the visitor, Reverend Thomas, tall and hatchet-faced, stood stone-still behind the pulpit and moved his lips, talking with an unseen presence as he fixed with his over-bright eyes each sinner as he entered. The mourners' bench, the front row, decorated with a black calico bow, was starkly empty, awaiting the first penitents to heed the call.

Two strong young men pushed their way down the center aisle, carrying strange drums. They stepped up onto the platform and took up positions back of the pastors. A ripple of uneasiness passed through the waiting audience and Charlotte shivered and pulled her shawl closer about her shoulders.

The people sharpened their eyes on her and opened their mouths in indecision about her. She was delivered to the savage in them and she felt that at any signal they would break her in two; take her by the neck and shake her to pieces. They surrounded her utterly, hemming her in. Even the pastor fixed his gaze on her and pointed his long finger at her pulsing throat. Chloe had been right: she had no business here.

Tears came into her eyes and she tried to comfort herself; *In a little while I will be gone from here. I must control myself. In a little while I will go to some place where I belong and I will not return here ever. Not to these people who are incapable of any understanding. Why have I tried to exalt Negroes merely because I learned that I was one of them? Oh, the candle of my faith in myself is guttering low. I almost wish it would go out and leave me like these people—content in their ambitionless, miserable state. Then I could cease to struggle for a perfection that I'll surely never have. Even love has deserted me, even Inigo.*

Pompey was muttering in her ear, but she pretended not to hear him and he finally hushed his words.

She was afraid. Afraid of the fiery eyes, the black

238

faces, the bodies which were already giving off a definite odor of intoxication of the senses; afraid of the
threatening drums, and above all afraid of seeing too
much, learning too much. She listened for the familiar
soothing words:

Introibo ad altare Dei. Ad Deum qui laetifi-
cat juventutem meam.

Instead, a crash of both drums jerked the people
erect and shattered the stillness that had held them.
Boom—Boom—Boom—Boom—Boom—Boom! The
people began to sway from side to side with the
throb of the drum skins. Reverend Thomas stood tall
and dominant and raised his arms to heaven. His lips
moved with the drumbeats and unintelligible sounds
issued forth. The intoxication of rhythm and worship in-
vaded the senses. An overpowering lassitude filled
Charlotte and she sat closer to Pompey and waited.

The Reverend Thomas suddenly stamped his feet
on the floor boards; stopped dead in a listening pose,
motionless as a statue. Then, conscious to his very
toes of his importance and his role, he strutted
solemnly up and down the stage—a rampant cock of
the roost. All at once his movements became supple and
supplicating, completely female, like a lover in rap-
turous surrender. He minced back and forth a few
times and then his long body snapped erect, fiercely
responding to the crescendo of the drums.

"Git in de stagecoach," he shouted. "De stagecoach am pulling out. Whosoever wants to be saved,
git in de coach!" He began to shuffle his feet back and
forth in a *shoo-shoo-shoo-shoo* imitative of wheels moving slowly away. "Git aboard de Gospel coach," he
begged, again the suppliant. "I is yo' leader and I knows
de way. Satan been walking to and fro, to and fro, on
dis plantashum too much lately and I is come to vanish
him back wheresomever he come from. I is come to
hold compersation wid um—to pray you'uns loose
from 'struction and sin. De clouds hover dark on de
horizon—de t'under and de lightning is waiting fuh me
to tell dem to strike down on yunnuh and de ones

239

which is not in dis coach, neither on de bench of salvation, is going to be structed wid de lightning and knockted wid de t'under. Come on, Brudders and Titters—beat dem drums, boys—lift de people to deir foots— Let's start wid you on de second row, Titter Brown—"

The Reverend Grimble, who had been patting his feet and swaying with his flock, now stood up and took a part:

"Hise de chune, Brudder Drayton—let's give um a ring shout!"

Reverend Thomas, his eyes shut, his sinewy body furiously working up speed, had got the people chanting and clapping their hands.

Jeff Drayton lifted his high tenor voice and Sister Brown, her hips beginning to swing like ripe pears, stepped out into the aisle.

She led the way and the big drums took up the beat, thudding in an unchanging monotone—never higher, never lower, always the same—pulsating through the church and beyond to the ones crowded outside. There was no resisting their fiendish power. The sound pushed mercilessly through the fetid air like a burning fever, heightening energy and sapping self-control.

Sister Brown's goose eyes were fixed in a rigid, sightless stare as the hypnotic voice of the Reverend Thomas directed her movements—in and out between the rows, up and down the aisle, drawing followers who drifted trancelike into the snake-chain of humans.

She approached Charlotte. Sweat was pouring down her body staining her red calico dress. Saliva trickled down from her mouth—her arms were held stiffly out and her fingers wove aphrodisiac gestures. Her writhing body seemed scarcely connected with her legs. She shook her head and a violent fit of trembling possessed her. She reached out to Charlotte. An awful sickness gripped the frightened girl and she felt as if she were staring into the very depths of evil. The thunder of the drums grew to an avalanche of deafening reverberations. The Reverend Thomas stared through the whole congregation of moving people straight into the gray eyes that drew back in horror from the zombie stare of Sister Brown. Charlotte suddenly felt a violent urge to throw herself forward—the mass suggestion was having the desired effect. All eyes followed Sister Brown and came to a focus on the pale face of the new girl. The heavy air made breathing difficult—a cloudy haze swept across Charlotte's senses. The waters of unreason gathered foaming force and rolled toward her. Pompey pressed his thigh hotly against her gold dress and his quickened breathing sounded loud in her ears. She shook her head, like a swimmer emerging after being overlong under water. Understanding came back into her eyes and she reached out and roughly pushed Sister Brown away. The wave broke and spilled its power. An ugly expression twisted the Reverend Thomas's face. But he controlled himself and again controlled the situation.

"Jine in," he shouted. "Jine in."

Sister Brown moved on. The drums rose, the song swelled out. The deep voice of Reverend Thomas rolled above the rest—he was not yet ready for the great orgiastic finale of emotion, his sermon was not delivered, the mourners' bench not filled, the offering not taken up.

Toes were insistently tapping on the floor, making an undercurrent of sound that mingled with the drum rhythm—the moaning of the people was taking on an elemental quality.

The line, shuffling and dipping down the aisle, reached the platform. The Reverend Thomas, assisted by the Reverend Grimble, had formed the participants into a big circle when suddenly Sister Brown uttered a high shriek, stiffened out, and fell to the floor in deathlike trance. The droning of the audience rose, but the Reverend Thomas kept the singing going and somebody pushed Sister Brown over into a corner, where she lay like a corpse.

The ring was moving around and around and in the center the Reverend Grimble knelt and, with his head touching the floor, rotated with the group. The shouters, as they passed, pushed his woolly head "down into the mire." The many arms reaching out to push made a huge, spiderlike pattern. After the "locus

241

pasture" had set the example, he began to call the various ones out by name. The Reverend Thomas stood by, his arms folded, resting a little. He kept looking at the row where Charlotte, pale and taut, clutched Pompey's arm.

"Sister Emma!" called the Reverend Grimble. A fat woman who must have weighed over two hundred pounds dropped gratefully to her knees, bowed her head to the floor, and began to rotate her huge flabby hips with the moving circle.

> *"Sister Emma, Oh, you mus' come down to de mire.*
> *Sister Emma, Oh, you mus' come down to de mire.*
> > *Jesus been down*
> > > *to de mire*
> > *Jesus been down*
> > > *to de mire*
> > *You mus' bow low*
> > > *to de mire*
> > *Honor Jesus*
> > > *to de mire*
> > *Honor Jesus*
> > > *to de mire*
> > *Lower lower*
> > > *to de mire*
> > *Lower lower*
> > > *to de mire*
> > *Jesus been down*
> > > *to de mire.*
> *Brudder Handy, Oh, you mus' come down to de mire!"*

Brother Handy was fully eighty years old and the moaning and tapping of feet grew louder as he crept down and touched his white hair to the floor. Sister Emma remained low and Brother Handy leaned against her for support as he slowly began to pivot his old, weary body.

After Brother Handy came Sister Viney and Brother Scipio and then Sister Josie, the one Chloe had scolded earlier about the sick baby, knelt and as she knocked her thin temples against the splintery pine floor she wailed like a banshee.

Pompey put his arm around Charlotte's waist and felt for her breast. Nausea smothered her and she

242

slapped his hand away roughly. He was so carried away by the scene being enacted on the platform that he paid no attention and reached for the woman who sat enraptured on the other side of him. This sturdy field worker responded gladly to the strong fingers that squeezed her nipples, and pressed her thighs close to him, grateful for the familiar feeling that went from his fingers through her body.

Charlotte looked to the window. This night was so unreal and so raw that what was fact and what was emotion was hidden from her usually clear vision. Outside a wind had risen and the rush of air through the pines made a soughing that blended in with the old sorrow of the people sunk in the mire.

Finally the ring came to an end and the platform was covered with prostrate figures. The Reverend Thomas stepped to the center and raising his big voice shouted, "Higher—Higher—Higher!" and the drums savagely crashed louder and louder. With a wild waving of arms the inert mass rose and with the single cry of "Saved!" rushed back to their seats.

For a time there was scuffling and scraping as they found their places. The drummers rested and the two preachers talked together. Now came the offering. Again Brother Drayton lifted his thin tenor voice in hoisting the tune and the people joined in:

> *"In the City of Jerusalem*
> > *Hmnh*
> *An' Penticos' Day*
> > *Hmnh*
> *When de people got de Holy Ghost.*
> > *Aye Lawd.*
> *Time is drawin' nigh.*
>
> *Loose horse in de valley,*
> > *Hmnh*
> *Who gwine ter ride um?*
> > *Hmnh*
> *None but de righteous*
> > *Aye Lawd.*
> *Time's a-drawin' nigh.*
>
> *Judgment's a comin',*
> > *Hmnh*

How yunnuh know hit?
          Hmnh
By de buddin' ob de fig tree,
          Aye Lawd.
Time is drawin' nigh.

Don' yunnuh hear God talkin'?
          Hmnh
Um talkin' through de thunder
          Hmnh
When people ona wonder,
          Aye Lawd.
Time's a-drawin' nigh."

The members came forward individually with their
pitiful little offerings which still amounted to much
more than a tithe. A hen, a can of oil, a scrap of blue
cloth, a can of meal, a bit of bacon, a nickel taken from
the corner of a grimy nose rag, an old shoe, a sack of
feathers, two rabbits, a biddy, a clutch of eggs, one egg;
a penny hoarded for months, a piece of cake, a baby's
rattle, a half-used bottle of sarsaparilla, and other scarce
possessions were laid at the feet of the one who was
going to bring a blessed kingdom of which they would
all be partakers.

By now the crowd had sobered up and the Reverend Thomas began to warm up for the final act, the
bringing of the sinful to the mourners' bench!

Outside the sky had become more overcast and
every now and then a low rumble could be heard by
those not completely given up to the spell. Charlotte
leaned over and whispered to Pompey, "Can't we slip
out and go home, Pompey? I don't feel so good and I
think it's going to storm."

Pompey turned his glazed, uncomprehending eyes
on her and she was shocked at the witless glare that he
gave her. The man in front of her had heard also and
he looked as though he could tear her to pieces. "Unnuh weeked!" he hissed through his broken teeth.

Charlotte suddenly thought of Leon and wished he
were here to explain to her how to understand these
people. As the offerings went up and were scorned or
praised by the Reverends she tried to dissociate herself
from her surroundings and visualize a golden gate

opening into a city of opportunity, a haven of unprejudiced, intelligent people who called to her to join them in their daily life of joy and sorrow; to dance with them, to sing with them, pray with them.

"An' now," Reverend Thomas spoke with thick ponderousness, "draw nigh and listen to me fuh I is about to reveal to yunnuh de facks of de world." Softly the drums took up the beat of his words and accompanied him as he gave forth his text: "In Hell he lifted up his eyes being in torment." A shudder of anticipation ran through the audience and a murmur of approval greeted this choice of a message.

He stood back a little from the pulpit, stooped forward and in hushed tones announced that he was going to lift off the cover of the underworld. He went through the straining motions of lifting off a heavy lid and as he leaned over and looked in, an expression of horror and anguish contorted his face and an animal cry of terror and pain wrenched from his throat. Everybody sat forward and gripped their seats while he searched into hell and in vivid language began to describe the hideousness of the fate of the damned, wriggling and frizzling before his very eyes.

The eyes of the Reverend Thomas blazed with the fires of ancient Africa; his red nostrils seemed to exhale smoke, his ears pointed up, his feet danced back and forth about the pit and his body jerked and suffered in torment. The people moaned and cried—yeah—dat's right—you tellum—*umhum—u-uhum—umhum—boola—boola!*

The voice led them into the depths of hell, to the bottom of darkness, and a murky haze seemed to sift and blow about the room. In the fire the smoke rose and the people shrieked and moaned pitifully. They were led to the mouth of damnation where stood Satan himself with his long tail curled over one arm and a smoking pitchfork clutched in his hands. His head was black and pointed horns grew through his kinky burning hair—he had screech-owl eyes with red sparks darting forth from them. His hands were claws and his forked, red-hot tail swished and coiled over his arm and around his neck, never still—ever moving, and

245

everything he touched with it he raised a blister. Satan stood at the mouth of the big hole in a red-hot rock where smoke and fire boiled out, and as lesser devils, his own children, ran up with scorching victims, he caught them on the points of his fork and threw them into the fire. Oh, how those poor sinners screamed and yelled and tried to pull away! Lord Almighty! Have mercy! Jedus save me! But no use—the minute Satan fixed his claw on them, they were gone and you could hear them fry—*sizzzzzzz!* in the fire same like fat in a frying pan.

Boom—Boom—Boom went the drums— The audience was a moving mass of hysterical emotion. The Reverend Thomas's face was distorted with the effort to bring hell to earth. Faster and faster flew his goatlike feet as he whirled about the fire. His muscles writhed and cramped as under the blows of a whip; but a whip whose lashes were caresses, exciting and maddening his animal desires.

A piercing scream broke from the frothing mouth of the woman beside Pompey. She leaped up and her upper body seemed loosened from her straining legs as she threw herself wildly back and forth, up and down, speaking to the monstrous spirit of the underworld of the dread and sorrow of living and being. Of the bending in the rice fields and the rolling in the night. Tears and fears, bliss and rejoicing, carried up on a crescendo of drumbeats which now matched the throbbing in the breasts and the hoarse breathing of everyone in the place. Pompey was sitting rigid and his foolish face snapped from side to side as though pulled by wires in his long skinny neck. A heavy anesthetic scent pressed over Charlotte, clouding her senses, and giddiness swirled in her head.

"I is gwine ter call de t'under!" shouted Reverend Thomas, his face a terrible thing to behold. "I is gwine ter summon de lightning! I is gwine ter will 'struction on dis temple!"

Hummm—hummm—hummm—moomba—boom-ba—Jedus—Jedus—intoned the people.

Beat—beat—throb—crash and beat—went the drums.

Suddenly the One God, whatever might be his name, could bear it no longer. He had heard enough. He lifted his hand and in answer the bass drums of his celestial orchestra crashed and rolled, drowning out the two puny man-stretched goatskins, proving their supreme power over the little black sisters and brothers who had heeded the riffle in their own veins, thinking it was He himself throbbing there.

And as the shuddering reverberations, like the boom of iron cannon, roared forth, many winds arose and whistled about the room with such gusto that the pine flares leaped up in obeisance for a moment, then in obedience to the divine command died down altogether and extinguished themselves in the hurricane-like blast. Darkness descended and a jagged streak of lightning tore through.

The people, falling and screaming for mercy, fought and grappled their way to the mourners' bench in maniac effort to be saved before the very One himself, loose in this house, should lay his hand or claw upon them. The blackness was of the essence of the pit and they lifted up their voices in torment, lost in the dark hell of fear and wild chaotic confusion.

Charlotte kicked and fought like a wild woman to be free from these screeching damned savages. Once Pompey clutched her shawl but she wriggled out of it and left him rending the length of red wool. He had become just another devil that Reverend Thomas had let loose when he raised the lid of the underworld.

Finally she reached the door and plunged out. The rain was as welcome as baptismal water on her hot forehead. Pulling up her gold dress, she sped past Lustbader's house where a flash of lightning showed him laughing roughly at the Negroes running like frightened chickens back to the shelter of their cabins. *I wish the little yellow man could see this debacle,* she thought, as she stumbled up the rickety steps. *Would he think they were ready to be turned loose on a hostile world?*

Her breath suddenly began to come easy at the wonderful sound of Chloe's serene snoring that greeted her as she came softly into the cabin. She unlaced her

247

wet slippers and warmed her chilled toes at the low fire before tiptoeing into her cold room to undress in the dark.

Her soft flannel nightgown still held the scent of the sweet pomander ball she had had hanging in her wardrobe at Normandy and it seemed harder than ever to crawl onto the rustly, ill-smelling mattress and pull the old blankets up against her throat.

The wind shuddered up through the floor and echoes of the inflamed hysterical shouting still quivered in her brain as she began to tell her beads and say the old soothing prayers over and over, to dull the memory of the meeting. Sleep came to the rhythm of her final little prayer— *And please, Holy Mary, help me find a middle way, a place where the two roads of me can cross and come together.*

Chapter 35

As soon as the sun rose Charlotte told Chloe all the repulsive, demonic details of the meeting but Chloe merely grunted impatiently as she wrapped yards of soiled ragged flannel around her feet and bade Charlotte walk up and down the Street before she went into the big house and take another look at the faces which had frightened her so much the night before.

Reluctantly Charlotte finished tying a little scarlet bow at the collar of her white lawn guimpe, and, remembering how she'd lost her shawl at the meeting, pulled on her bright blue wool cape before going slowly out.

248

Harmless-looking men with scythes and axes lingered in groups waiting for the work horn, women walked with babies in arms and at skirt toward the children's house, and boys and girls played hopscotch and chased each other in and out of cabins. The frenzied hysteria was completely spent and they were just plain ordinary people; dirtier and more ignorant than most but still members of the human race. Charlotte stared unbelieving at Sister Brown sitting placidly plaiting a little girl's kinky hair on the bottom step of a shackeldy cabin which leaned so far on its side that a mere shove would have sent it toppling into the latrine ditch. By her side a fat small boy of two or three years stood and wiggled his toes delightedly in the sand while he greedily sucked and pulled on her full-flowing breast.

Charlotte tried to think of the summons life had issued her by making her a Negro who could understand the white race. But, oh rueful thought, she couldn't understand the Negro race, so she was not prepared to answer the challenge in any way.

The sound of her name interrupted her reverie. "Miss Charlotte—wait fuh me. Unnuh gwine sew on Miss Nancy' petticoats dis mawning." Thin, eager-faced Lula skipped up and caught hold of her hand. And as the cold little fingers gratefully snuggled in her palm she looked down the long lonesome Street which was the world to these hundreds of Whydahs, Pow Pows, Gullahs, Eboes, and Senegalese who had been snatched from their background and transplanted into a civilization so different and so remote from their comprehension that it was in tribal song and pentacostal service only that they were articulate enough to tell of hearts troubled or merry.

I condemned them too hastily, she admitted guiltily as on her way back up the Street the men waved their axes and scythes in a friendly way and the women smiled and ducked their heads in greeting to her, walking with Joe Valiant's daughter's hand proudly clasping her own.

"Kin yunnuh teach Lula to talk same lak yunnuh?" Lula asked.

"Yes. Say 'Can you teach me to speak as you do?'"

Lula chattered it out easily and she and Charlotte both laughed.

"To read, too?" Lula's voice dropped to a whisper. "We Pa slip home las' night and I tell em 'bout yunnuh and he say axe yunnuh to gib Lula some learning."

"Shh! If you'll promise not to tell, I'll teach you to read *and* write."

"Naw'm, Lula not tell. Lula been learn dat long ago. Dat why dem leetle chillen to us house can't talk good. Pa scairt dey tell things."

"Do you like to sew?" Charlotte asked as some men passed close to them and Lula pressed her lips together.

"Jedus—yeah! Lula's fingers kin fair talk and sing wid a needle 'tween dem."

Charlotte recalled the Abbé who had taught her in New Orleans. *He would like me today,* she thought, as she stooped and with her finger traced L U L A in the hard dirt.

"That's your name."

Lula knelt down and reverently traced each letter with a sensitive finger.

"Write it yourself now. Copy it."

Lula! Magic symbols—white man's magic!

"Here comes Mr. Lustbader!" Charlotte froze. She was so frightened that she could not lift one foot to erase the forbidden letters.

"Why aren't you at the house?" he asked her.

"I'm on my way there now. Miss Nancy doesn't wake up early."

"Lula—what's that you're trampling with your feet!"

"Jest a ole lizard. 'Peared lak a scorpion."

Charlotte looked down. There were no letters on the ground. No lizard either. Only a smooth rubbed place where quick little feet had scraped.

"Let's hurry."

The two girls took each other by the hand and flew toward the house.

"Jest be mo' keerful, Miss Charlotte. Hit ud sho

be a misery effen Lula was de cause of yo' gitting whup."

All in all, as the days passed Charlotte's brooding despair lessened and in her hunger for faith she began to feed her mind with the nearest and most convenient food. Thus in self-reproach and loneliness and disillusion she came to the entrance of the maze.

She forced herself gradually to outgrow her repugnance to the Negroes and began to derive a highly specialized education from Chloe, shattering her illusions about the slaves, to be sure, but also causing her to blame them less for their vermin-ridden cabins and their unclean, fetid bodies.

She snatched every scrap of information she could pick up about Lustbader and put it in writing, hiding it carefully in Chloe's bed. She would see that he was caught up with. This gave her a bond with the people. Soon she found she could talk glibly with them about his inhumanities.

Thus on the day that Joe Valiant sought her out she was ready for him and they had an unsentimental conversation about the best means possible to them as Negroes of circulating the facts of Lustbader's thieves' market. "Only we must wait for a little while," they decided, "until we can give it into the right hands."

"Come with me and let me show you the exact island," Joe suggested. "Nobody's going to miss you, because the whole Singleton family is at a tea party at the Myers' and the overseer has gone to McClellanville."

Charlotte tried to think of excuses, for though the weeks had taught her much of these people she was wary about going out alone with a six-foot-five Senegalese whose eyes were scarred from having looked too long into hell on earth.

"Please come," Joe urged. He spoke quite well. It was to protect them that he had denied his children the clarity of speech. They saw too much, knew too much. Charlotte and Chloe alone were to be trusted with the knowledge that he was planning to run away tonight after he had given them evidence enough to

251

hang Lustbader. Any more of this life would either drive him insane or, worse, cause him to sink back into the loathsome existence he had struggled so hard to remain superior to, with disastrous results to both his family and himself, since he had come here from Barbados.

"Where is Chloe?" Charlotte asked Joe before she left the cabin with him.

"She's watching outside Lustbader's house, and if he comes back and makes any move to come near the wharf she is going to set fire to the children's house. It's always empty this late. You *must* come. We are counting on you to do this thing for us."

Charlotte wanted to ask Joe who "we" were; to tell him that the nervous strain of Heronfields had worn her too much; that she was afraid of him and of the island as well as of Lustbader; that she was not prepared to indulge in any of the slaves' illicit activities when she was assured of Harry Singleton's protection so long as her behavior was above remark. However, she kept her words and followed the long, spare figure down to the wharf.

Joe rowed easily over to the island, although the wind was high and the water rough. The sunset flamed red and orange and the choppy, white-crested river reflected it in liquid fire.

Wind and water and color worked a spell on Charlotte, and the loneliness of space soothed her and helped her to forget her troubled enduring of prejudice and misery and monotony. The strange, wild shore line of the island, bristling with saw palmettos and reeds, interested her, and when she stepped from the boat onto the muddy shore she laughed at the land crabs scuttling ludicrously away from her feet. The sides of the bank were covered with moss and lichens of green and red, making her shoes look as if they were edged with coral: it was like a happening in a fairy tale. Charlotte supposed that one secret of her being able to suffer as acutely as she did without being made ill was the childish excitability of her temperament and the ecstasy which any beautiful thing brought her.

The hut was only a rude four sides of logs

thatched with palmetto fronds, but when Joe pushed open the door she exclaimed in amazement. For there was Tafra's grapevine teapot! It had to be Tafra's because the Gaillard crest was engraved on its side. So this was where Hagar got the cocaine she had given her Christmas night! She and Joe didn't say much but she took from her pocket a piece of charcoal and a folded sheet of paper and with his help made a rough inventory as well as a distinct map of the island and the route by which they had arrived here.

Darkness had fallen when they returned and Joe clasped her hands, beseeching her to look after Lula until he should have reached freedom and made enough money to purchase his entire family from Heronfields.

There was no sign of Lustbader as they hurried back to Chloe's cabin. Chloe immediately appropriated the precious document and she and Charlotte ripped open the mattress of Chloe's bed, hiding it inside. Then Joe Valiant, having done all that he was able, stole away from them.

Charlotte ran to the Street and watched him disappear into the night through the rough trees. It all seemed like the scenery from a play and yet to have shared this adventure, shadowy and unreal, with this strange fanatical man, seemed somehow oddly familiar. Charlotte thought he seemed more real than Inigo at this moment.

The starlight twisted in and out of the vines tangled up and down the trees; the wind had died down and the cabins, looking ghostly gray, broke the long line of bare ground marking the Street. Behind lay the black edge of the woods and ahead the flowing river. Which road would Joe take toward his nebulous freedom? She hoped it would be the river, because Lustbader's bloodhounds were already slavering in anticipation as they let out their eerie mournful voices into the night.

Chapter 36

Joe escaped. He was trailed with bloodhounds and sought in the river, but no sign of him was ever found.

The Singletons didn't really worry. Harry was glad that Joe had run away. He'd liked Joe but he couldn't interfere too much with Lustbader the short time in the year that he personally lived at Heronfields. Besides, Joe was a troublemaker. Let the Yankees have him. It would serve them right, he reasoned, resigned to the five-thousand-dollar loss of his head patroon, resigned to peace at any price.

The last day of January, Cuffee appeared at the back door. Charlotte saw him from the kitchen, and never had any face been so welcome to her. She hugged him and asked him dozens of questions about Nick and Tafra and Fancy and Big Jake and whether all the rye was up and the tobacco beds prepared.

"Li'l feather—li'l white goose feather!" he kept saying over and over, right in front of the scandalized Craney, until Charlotte was calm enough to lead him into Harry's office to present the note from Tafra he had brought.

Harry, seated at his enormous cluttered desk, read the note and a frown settled on his face as he took a green quill pen from the bowl of sand and scratched a pass for Charlotte to spend the afternoon at Normandy. Then, surprisingly, he handed it to her with a smile, and she was so relieved that grateful tears banked in her eyes.

"I am doing this on Miss Tafra's request only because I must grant a lady's wishes. It is absolutely forbidden at this plantation for slaves to visit other plantations, unless they have a husband or a wife living there, except on Christmas and the Fourth of July. Even then only the drivers and special servants are allowed passes. Please tell Miss Tafra that, Charlotte. Miss Mildred has become quite fond of you and you'll get along much better here if we humor her instead of Miss Tafra," Harry told her not unkindly.

"Yes sir—yes sir!" Anything was promisable just to *see* Normandy once more.

She jumped in the buggy dressed as she was, stopping only long enough to grab up her blue cape from a wood box behind the kitchen door. On the way she laughed and cried at the same time, but Cuffee soon told her about so many of the little things he knew she had cherished at Normandy that he made it seem as though only this very morning she had waked in her snowy-linened bed and had powdered her face carefully before the gold-leaf mirror of her polished Sheraton dressing-table.

When Hercules threw open the big front door to Charlotte she stepped in half expecting to meet Inigo face to face as she had done the afternoon she first came here. But the hall was empty and strangely enough she suddenly knew that this beautiful place which she had loved, that she understood perfectly, that she had thought of as her home forever, where she had loved so hopelessly, was no longer necessary to her. She ran her hands in astonishment over her forehead, but her forehead was cool, and as she looked into the face of old Nicholas's portrait on the far wall she raised her head a fraction higher so that the great black eyes would not suspect the things she had seen and heard at Heronfields or what they had done to Charlotte Le Jeune at that ugly place.

How silent it is here, she thought; *how full of a sense of death. Is it because I know that Inigo is no longer here? That there is no chance for me to hear his laughter—to answer his smile? How cold it is—the woodwork is too white—the crystal chandelier too icy —the curtains too frozen and unmoving.*

Outside she heard Nick calling to Cuffee and asking where she was. But still the macabre coldness persisted. Even Hercules, who was gazing up the stair well after her, was like a carven statue of old stone.

She came to the double doors of the great drawing-room. Her room, almost; she had spent enough time in it—all of her young girlhood, her growing-up time, her young-lady time. In here she had dreamed of a perfect love. In here she had been sheltered from the world, from everybody. Suddenly she realized: this had been a museum and she had been one of the show pieces, one of the rarest oddities that Normandy possessed. Here love had been born to her; and here she had been degraded and sold just as an animal might have been sold. *Here, too,* a voice whispered, *love will die for you. The third round has not yet been reached.*

She pushed open the doors quietly so as not to disturb Tafra, for Cuffee had told her how very ill the mistress had been since Inigo left for the West.

Hagar, standing in the bedroom door, looked critically at Charlotte before commenting on her hoopless wrinkled skirt.

"Humph! Ain' tek long fuh yunnuh to walk same lak de rest of weuns, is hit?"

Charlotte did not answer because she wanted to ask Hagar why she had stolen Tafra's teapot, but having promised Chloe not to mention their secret about Lustbader she could not think of a proper reply to Hagar's two-edged remark.

"But yo' haid am still high." Hagar seemed not to want an answer. "Mind yunnuh be kind to Miss Tafra," she whispered as she stepped aside and let Charlotte pass into the bedroom.

Charlotte tiptoed hesitantly to the bed and bent over the inert form. Tafra's face on the white pillow was transfigured, discolored, a dull waxy yellow. She must have looked like this when she was a child on that swampy malarial plantation; her features had become strangely childlike. She had given in at last to a stronger being, her mighty will obliterated in part by the long last suffering.

She looked up at Charlotte with dim eyes and Charlotte stood by the bed not knowing what to say. Death was indeed present in this house. Why had she not seen him in the dark corners of the hall? She had felt his chill finger on the crystal, his stiff form in the motionless curtains, his dead pallor in the woodwork.

Finally she leaned toward Tafra and spoke gently in her ear. "This is Charlotte, Miss Tafra. Don't you know me?"

Hagar and Cuffee need not have warned her to be kind. A rush of pity for the one who had protected the bewildered child-Charlotte flooded her.

Then, all of a sudden, Tafra realized who was close to her and cried out, "Oh, Charlotte! Charlotte, it's you! Can you ever forgive me?" She feebly reached for Charlotte's hand and Charlotte took the thin fingers and squeezed them hard as if she could express her affection in that way. Tafra tried to answer the gesture and continued murmuring, "Oh, Charlotte, my child —my poor little Charlotte."

She made a great effort to speak but she was too weak to find all the words she wanted to say, and Charlotte began to weep seeing that affection trying so hard but unable to let itself pour forth.

She was seized with a great desire to shout out, "I love you, Miss Tafra; I understand why you sent me away." But she was afraid that if she spoke she would say too much—would call Inigo's name. Tafra named it first.

"He has run away again. This was his last chance and he has lost it. Oh! If you both could only know how sorry for you I am—how lonely without you."

But the pain—for the last stage of her disease had struck ruthlessly—had taken away, in weeks, years of life. Now it leaped on her vengefully and she lapsed into semiconsciousness to continue the fight for existence. She lay so still that Charlotte strained her ears for the quick sound of her shallow breathing. Many minutes later she opened her eyes and spoke with difficulty.

"Write a note to Doctor Hugenin and ask him to come quickly. Tell him to bring all the pills and powders

257

that he knows of. I must not die until my son returns. *She* would surely report him to the court for leaving his plantation with only the Negroes here. Hurry, Charlotte—write the doctor."

"Let me write Mr. Inigo to come. You must not be here alone like this."

Tafra wearily shook her head and though her words were barely audible her tone held all the old positiveness and determination.

"No. He would suspect that it was just a ruse to make him do my way. He plans to be back by May. Then I will only have to live on until July in order to buy you back. I'm being punished for having sold you. If I'd just known that Inigo was going to ride West I could have kept you here to look after me and little Nick."

Charlotte went slowly into the drawing-room and sat at the rosewood desk thinking, *She doesn't want me to write him because she doesn't want any joining of the link between us which she betrayed her conscience to break; no letter from me must ride West to remind him of the slave who loves him most dreadfully. She and Chloe are alike. Both of them think that anything is possible if they will it hard enough.*

After she finished the note she took it to Hagar, who was squatting on the top step gossiping with Hercules. Charlotte handed her the note and watched the agile, skinny old woman walk easily down the stairs and give the envelope to Hercules to pass on to Old Ben who in his turn would deliver it to Dr. Hugenin.

"Hit'll be tomorrow 'fore de doctor kin come. Can't yunnuh stay dis night?" Hagar asked.

Charlotte shook her head. "Mr. Singleton didn't want to let me come at all. Mrs. Singleton wants me to belong body and soul to Heronfields."

"Kin yuh?"

"Certainly not. But you know, Hagar, I've felt freer there than I ever did here. I would never have dreamed of running away from Normandy, but I lie awake at night and plan just how I'll run from Heronfields if Miss Tafra doesn't buy me back."

Hagar's eyes almost popped out at such heresy

258

from the gentle, dignified Charlotte. She sucked her teeth and shook her head disapprovingly as the girl went into Inigo's room before going back to Tafra, closing the door firmly behind her.

Inside the big chilly room Charlotte could scarcely breathe, she was so choked with conflicting emotions as she wandered about, lightly fingering the things that had belonged to him. Remembering his kisses, his eyebrow that lifted so revealingly, his arms, so strong and demanding. Finally she opened the doors to his wardrobe and let the scent of him which lingered in his clothes delude her that he too was in this cold, dreary house. And lifting the sleeve of his hunting-coat, the same one he had worn on Christmas, she folded the scarlet cloth around her neck and let the sleeves hang limply over her breasts. "I love you," she whispered to the coat. "I love you."

It was hard to go back and sit quietly while Tafra tried to probe into her life at Heronfields. Yet she managed to make the account of her days seem tolerable and the affair of the hoop-dropping ridiculous.

"You'll be going into Charleston in a few days, won't you?" Tafra asked, her mind diverted from the real truth entirely.

"Yes, the day after tomorrow."

"Be sure and get one of your good dresses out of your wardrobe to take with you. Mrs. Singleton has promised to let you go to church there and you'll meet some of my Free Negro friends."

Charlotte murmured assent, then, noticing the length of the afternoon shadows cast by the huge oaks outside of the windows, she leaned over and kissed the damp brow, answering Tafra's weak smile with some semblance of cheer before going into her old room. There she picked out her prettiest outfit, although she had little hope that she would ever get a chance to wear it anywhere exciting enough to merit taking it away from Normandy.

Hagar stopped her before she went downstairs.

"Weuns heerd dat dey got yunnuh out to de meeting to Heronfields," she said slyly. "Did Chloe go 'long?"

259

"No." Charlotte squeezed the rustly taffeta dress she had folded up, making an effort to keep her temper. Hagar had been very strange all afternoon. Surely she didn't have sixth sense enough to suspect that Charlotte knew about the teapot? "Chloe is too much like Miss Tafra to be very religious."

"Is too!" Hagar cackled delightedly for the first time that afternoon. "Dey sho is two heading womens. Ain' Chloe told yunnuh dat she de head Voodoo Priestess in dis whole section? I is jest de secont head."

Charlotte was amazed. She couldn't imagine Chloe shrieking in a savage role, any more than Chloe genuflecting before a white lady with a halo.

"Hagar, I think I'll come to the next Voodoo. When will it be?"

But Hagar shook her head. "Not yunnuh. Voodoo ain't specify any mo' for yunnuh dan shouting and hollering is. As I hears hit didn't. S'pose yunnuh did come to Voodoo; either hit would disgus' yuh and den yunnuh would turn away from yo' Negro people, or else hit would set a wheel turning in yo' heart an' yunnuh would turn slam-bam away from yo' white people. All two of dem things is wrong for yuh. Yunnuh ain't lucky lak Chloe an' me an' Miss Tafra wid one people worth dying fuh and breaking up folks' hearts fuh. Yunnuh got two meanings to yo' life and yunnuh got to accept dat fack. Yunnuh gotter to be a link 'tween de black an' de white. Befo' long de slaves is gwine to be free. De yaller nigger on de gray mule did ride up and down dis very Street las' night." A holy look, a look into the beyond, shone in the dark face.

From the big bedroom they heard Tafra coughing weakly and Hagar glided silently back into the drawing-room, with no further word to Charlotte except a softly spoken "Tek care!"

Charlotte stood for an instant on the top step drawing her hand back and forth slowly and indecisively on the polished rail. She had lived here for six whole years and Hagar had never paid her any mind at all until she had tended her after Inigo had whipped her. Why did Hagar suddenly expect her to become the same sort of person that Chloe had made up her

260

mind she was to be? A hybrid thing—a bloodless symbol. Was it simply because of her light color—or was it something else of which she herself was still ignorant?

Nick came into the lower hall, calling her, and the mood faded.

She ran down the stairs to meet him, noticing the Waterford chandelier which hung like a giant stalactite sparkling with rosy fire from the sunset which was pouring through the fanlight. *It's not icy and lifeless any more,* she thought wonderingly, *and even though I am sad and grieved over Tafra, even though I know that Inigo is far away, that I will never feel the same in this house, my heart is strangely light and I have a sense of adventure awaiting me soon somewhere. Hagar must have put one of her famous spells on me! I don't even condemn her any longer for stealing the teapot now that I see how devotedly she is looking after Tafra.*

"Cuffee says I can ride back in the buggy with you. Aren't you glad?" Nick cried, grabbing her around the waist. She pulled the tangled curls at the back of his neck and they joined hands and skipped to the avenue where Cuffee was waiting for them, his eyes shining with pleasure.

Field Hand Mattie, leading a group of the bigger women home from the rye patch, stood aside as the horses trotted smartly past. She waved her hoe at Charlotte and all the other women lifted theirs too, calling her name, wishing her good day and good luck, beginning to sing as the buggy whizzed away:

> *"Dere's uh leetle wheel uh turnin' een muh heart*
> *Oh, uh leetle wheel uh turnin' een muh heart,*
> *Een muh heart, een muh heart,*
> *Oh, uh leetle wheel uh turnin' een muh heart.*
>
> *"En uh ain' got no weeked een muh heart,*
> *En uh ain' got no weeked een muh heart,*
> *Een muh heart, een muh heart,*
> *En uh ain' got no weeked een muh heart.*
>
> *"En uh cin' got no hypokrick een muh heart,*
> *En uh ain' got no hypokrick een muh heart,*
> *Een muh heart, een muh heart,*
> *En uh ain' got no hypokrick een muh heart.*

"Een muh heart, een muh heart
   Dere's a leetle wheel uh turnin' een muh heart."

Chapter 37

On the first of February, as usual, the Singletons shook the sand of the plantation from their pointed shoes and established residence in their town house for the winter social season which would last gaily until the middle of March. The town house was substantial and well planned, with wide piazzas and a delightful walled garden. It was much more tastefully furnished than Heronfields, having been left in the lovely eighteenth-century style of Harry Singleton's grandfather's time. The rooms were harmoniously appointed and the symmetrical high-ceilinged parlors spoke of gracious living and a genial way of life quite at variance with the dark silences and undercurrents of fear which permeated Heronfields.

Here even the slave quarters were comfortable and nice. Mildred Singleton was not afraid of city Negroes. The dread black men who "suck Missy' blood and crack Missy' bone' " were purely country boogers, vanishing in the safety and brightness of Charleston.

Charlotte's room which she shared with Lula was airy and cheerful with soft curtains at the glazed windows, facing on an alley, to be sure, but framing in the distance the pointed spire of St. Michael's.

Charlotte found the city highly picturesque. Every house seemed to be built to the owner's particular taste and pleasure. Some wore the dignified air of old England, some were gay and French, while others held the rich beauty and promised grandeur of Italy. And the bells of the churches and the street criers, the calls of the flower girls and the vendors, were sweet music bringing back fragments of her childhood. For being in the city, walking on brick and cobbles, conjured up Poulette and the parents neither of whom she had ever really known, but who had left their seal forever upon her heart, each pulling her a different way—clamoring for her identity.

The Street with its awful demands and implications faded for the time, and it was a good thing, for Charlotte could not endure too much ugliness and this little lull in the city gave her the happy feeling of possible pleasant adventure.

She had persuaded Nancy that Lula's clever fingers were indispensable to her wardrobe, and Lula had more than justified the request. And though the city servants laughed at her for trying so hard to "ack white," the sharp tongue facilely answered them taunt for taunt, not carrying for any of them so long as her idol continued to teach her the magic of words and the art of books and pencils at night when they were alone together.

The first Sunday, Mildred Singleton came to Nancy's room and announced to Charlotte that she had promised Tafra to allow her the privilege of attending church on Sunday nights.

"Do you have the proper clothes?"

"Yes, Mrs. Singleton." Charlotte's pulse raced and she almost fainted from excitement, but she tried with all her might to conceal it.

"Mind you don't get into trouble."

"Oh, no, Mrs. Singleton!"

"If you get drunk you will be punished. It's my duty to warn you that we aren't as lenient with our slaves as the Gaillards." Charlotte bowed her shining head meekly and Mildred Singleton for some reason felt *de trop—gauche*—all the French things that a governess she had had as a child used to describe her as being. Besides, she'd never felt quite right about

263

taking Charlotte's French hoop, even though *all* of her friends admired it enviously.

"Enjoy yourself," she said brusquely.

The middle-aged butler, Jenkins, a free Negro whose wife belonged to the Singletons, invited her to go along with him to the free church. Lula adorned her as carefully as she would have a princess. The bronze taffeta dress was woven at random with threads of fine gold silk, and at her wrists and throat were bands of sheer black lace that Tafra had given her. Having no hoop in the skirt, the stiff silk rustled like fans as it followed the lines of her graceful hips. A black velvet bonnet, with two yellow ostrich plumes nodding bravely on the brim to give her courage, perched on the back of her head.

"Jesus!" Jenkins clucked loud in approval. "Ain't never step out 'pon top de street wid nuttin' lak yunnuh befo'. Hit's a good thing Maria is lying in dis mont' or she'd sho bust bofe us heads open. Take my arm, Sis Charlotte. Jenkins am gwine to step high down dat aisle tonight!"

Charlotte clutched her hands together tight in her muff. She was so feverish with excitement that she shivered in her ocher velvet cape as they walked down the lamplit streets. Jenkins pointed out the White Point Gardens on the Battery where in the summer there was bathing in the day and music at night. He showed her the Salt Water Bathing House with its separate pools for men and women and its ice-cream and pastry saloon served by a New York caterer.

"Hit's nice here in de summer," he told her, "driving 'long de Battery and looking out on de sails and hearing de loud bands and horns."

But this winter night the gay places were closed and shuttered and as they made their way over toward Beaufain Street a thin mist rolled in from the harbor and they quickened their steps and soon were at the Church of the Brown Fellowship.

The members were having a social hour before the service and the easy conversation and pleasant manners of these people made Charlotte feel their welcome before Jenkins started introducing her.

264

She had just started to shake hands with fat, well-dressed Kezia Bethune when she saw Leon. She had opened her mouth to answer Mrs. Bethune's query about Tafra but instead of speaking she let her mouth break up into the most luscious smile. And in the pomegranate richness of her lips was a strange provocation. She seemed to have lost her aloofness and a reckless abandon livened her voice as she went up to him boldly in front of everybody.

"Doctor Cavallo!"

"Charlotte!" was all he could find to say while his heart said, *She hasn't changed except she's become more of a woman and less of an elusive child. The stars are still in her eyes. Not so bright—but they are there and they can burn up higher. And he isn't there in them!*

"Shake hands with Mrs. Bethune." He tried to be calm, to disguise the emotion in his voice.

Kezia was watching these two keenly. Tafra Gaillard had written her that the girl had had a tragic life. Well, it didn't show. She looked sure enough of herself. Charlotte gave Kezia her hand.

"Please forgive me, Mrs. Bethune. I was so surprised to see someone I knew here."

"Where did you know Leon?" Kezia was not unaware of the current that was flowing between these two people; she was no fool. But it was stronger on Leon's side. She had heard rumors of this girl and the great Inigo Gaillard. Rumors, she had found, were generally true. This girl must not be allowed to upset Leon. He was only now getting settled and he was going to have a hard road to travel, with so many doors closed on him as a black man of science. He had been more than kind to Jonas in Scotland during the long months there in which Jonas coughed away his poor lungs. Nobody should hurt Leon. She would have to make an effort to see more of this queer, beautiful girl so that she could find out whether she was good or bad.

The color heightened in Charlotte's face under Kezia's scrutiny. She had been too forward calling to Leon like that; she could sense Kezia's disapproval of her. But to see him standing there, so handsome and intelligent-looking, so kind and so responsive to the very sight of her, had been like a flung banner which read, *Here is your middle way, here is your adventure!*

"You have such a nice church," she said softly and her luminous eyes looked full into Kezia's shrewd black ones. *Perhaps she is all right,* Kezia decided. *She has good eyes—soul's eyes. She probably feels strange among us.* Her mother heart began to warm to Charlotte. She took the girl by the arm and motioned for Leon to pull her up out of her chair. She was so fat that she waddled in layers and holding Charlotte on one side and Leon on the other she made them go with her and speak to everyone in the church before the service began.

"Will you sit with me and let me escort you home?" were the only words that Leon managed to get in.

"Yes," she told him, "thank you—if Jenkins won't mind." The tremulous expression on Charlotte's face, prepared either for despair or rapture, suddenly brightened into a grateful childlike smile.

On the stage the fiddles began tuning up to accompany the hymns and J. H. Holloway looked down uncertainly at his grandson and the pale-faced young slave whose whole story he knew and pitied. *They could be the saving of each other,* he thought, *if she were free. But I must never allow him to be touched by slavery.* Since the Reverend Castle could not be present this night he was to lead the Negroes in their worship.

Leon placed two chairs very close to each other and he and Charlotte sat side-by-side. He kept examining Charlotte—her figure, her gold-shot dress, the black lace caressing her throat, the hair heavy in its mesh. She was leaning back in the chair, her shoulders poised against the top rung; her body, flexibly straight and unsupported from the hips, swayed a little as she leaned toward him, listening to him—giving of herself to him. Her lips were smiling and her eyes half closed and he felt himself revived and regenerated as he sat breathing deeply, watching her rapt expression. He could not guess that she was saying little Catholic

266

prayers to her Mother Mary. Little prayers in which she admitted that Chloe was right—that there was always one other who could set your candle burning.

They were conscious of each other all during the rather long, dull sermon. When their shoulders touched, which Leon contrived to make happen often, a message of oneness flowed between them.

This is different from the killing, pounding surge of passion that devoured me when I was in Inigo's arms, she thought, *but it is good—good.*

And Leon thought, *She is my dream of womankind. She must be mine, all mine. I will make her have a good life. I will shield her from the behemoth of our blood. We can be everything to each other.*

As they walked home through the misty night, close, so close, a kind of intoxication took hold of him. He bore himself with the diffidence and reserve in which he had long schooled himself but it was not in his power to hide his passion and he repeatedly lifted her hand to his trembling lips. Charlotte, utterly lacking in coquetry, was glad of his affection and bent her face over so that it rested against his arm.

After a while—it may have been a recognition of danger in the very charm of her attitude, or wonder at the change in her—a sudden doubt fell upon him. The image of Inigo suddenly loomed through the misty night. He wished he knew what had happened since the whipping, but he couldn't bring himself to break the spell.

They walked silently past Mr. Heyward's house at the corner of East Bay and Society Street and Leon made her stop a moment to look out over the harbor before he took her home.

"When will I see you again?" he asked her.

"Again?" Was the night ended? Charlotte spoke hoarsely, as though she had been awakened from a pleasant dream. "Why, I don't know—I don't know—I—I—"

Leon was puzzled. She had seemed to like him to touch her—to be near her. Fear brushed across his brain. Something was strange here. Now, what did she mean, hesitating like that?

"Surely Mrs. Gaillard will be glad for you and me to be friends. Grandfather says she is more than kind and gracious."

She could not think how to tell him she had been sold away from Inigo. And Leon looked off from her over the shrouded harbor; he did not want to believe that she had been playing with him—it meant too much.

"I'll try to explain," Charlotte said lamely.

"Explain!" Leon caught her arms and forced her to face him. "Explain! Are you still in love with that—"

"Hush!" she cried bitterly. "You shan't call his name! I was trying to tell you that I don't even belong to the Gaillards any more. I thought you knew. You saw me with Jenkins. You know he belongs to the Singletons."

"The Singletons! Not the ones from Heronfields?" She nodded, trying to keep her chin from shaking— trying to wink back the hot tears as he almost shouted at her, "You must have done something terrible indeed for Mrs. Gaillard to sell you to that plantation." His suspicious gaze bored into her, cut like a scalpel straight to her heart. Charlotte pulled away from him and ran down the street. But he was after her in a minute and seizing her shoulders he bent her head back and kissed her hard on her lips.

"Don't tell me why—not if it has anything to do with—him!" He kept kissing her, heedless of her unresponsiveness, thinking only that at last she was in his arms.

"I will tell you why." Wrenching herself free she wiped her lips with the back of her hand. "I will tell you, but it's not what you think. I haven't seen him since I left the sick house at Normandy on New Year's Eve."

Leon tried to embrace her again but now he was conscious of the rigidity that had taken possession of her body beneath the silk and lace and velvet clothing and he was frightened by the effect he had produced, sickened by the tragic wildness of her face—the lost magic of her eyes.

For Charlotte felt shame. She felt the ugly drab

cabin which she shared with Chloe. She felt the Street; the whip on Gabel's face; the verminous children; all the mournful, half-savage songs that were a part of the night. Then she tried to let anger beat down the shame so that something would not die inside of herself. Why should it matter to him *where* she lived? None of her life was her own choice. Why would he not dare anything to see her, to have her? She wanted to hurt him —to injure him—to tear his free heart out.

"I will say it—I am a Heronfields slave—on a filthy, savage Street! But does that make me any blacker than I was in June when you looked at me with your calf eyes under the oaks at Normandy? Look at me now—look at me!"

She was standing under a lit street lamp. The mist swirled about her pale face, her chin trembled pitifully, and suddenly far off over the black salt water came a cry like the voice of some wandering soul cast forever out of paradise and crying for its lost glory. Again it cried—again! Night held them both like a great evil bat and covered them with her foul wings.

"You won't look at me." She was oddly triumphant. What had she been thinking of? This man light her candle? Never! If Inigo didn't return for her she could at least follow Joe Valiant's example and run somewhere. She had been hurt too much already.

"Oh, Charlotte! Charlotte!" Leon tried to take her hands but she jerked them away from him. "I'll go back to Edinburgh." His breathing was quickened by danger and desire. "I daren't seek you at Heronfields. It would destroy us both."

"Go!" Never had she felt so coldly cruel. "Go!— there is no place for you here. You with your long, trained hands. Leave us to rot in our hell of slavery."

"Come on."

He had stood enough. Until tonight the fact that she was a slave hadn't loomed as an obstacle. But to have a wife at the mercy of a brutal, coarse overseer was an impossibility for him, because he knew that he would kill master or overseer if they touched her. He could hardly breathe. The mist had filled his lungs and he was choking to death. He was ready to die. He had dreamed of her so long. But a Street slave! No! He had read in one of Jonas Bethune's law books: *The children who are born of a free man and a slave woman are themselves slaves, as they follow the condition of the mother.*

His wife and children must walk where no dark clouds gathered; in open spaces where no bats flew. The first Cavallos must be free.

When they reached the Singletons' gate they had done with words but he reached over and compassionately touched the little ostrich plumes of her bonnet which now drooped and draggled in the damp misty night.

"Good night," he whispered. But she did not answer as she slipped away from him, back through the heavy iron-barred gate. It clanged shut as he let it go and watched her running down the stiffly bordered paths of the garden.

Chapter 38

The morning of the St. Cecilia Ball which came the next week—Race Week—brought a letter from Robert Gaillard to Nancy Singleton. Jenkins answered a loud knock at the front door and returned with a thin white envelope on his silver salver.

"Fuh yunnuh, Miss Nancy." He bowed low.

Nancy read the letter and her face became congested and purple and she opened her mouth and began to howl.

Charlotte picked up the letter which Nancy had

thrown on the floor, read it and handed it to Mrs. Singleton, who came running from her room to find out what calamity had befallen her house.

Nancy screeched louder at the sight of her mother, richly plumed for the races, and rushed heavily up the circular stairs. Charlotte followed and tried to reason with Nancy, but the storm gathered force as Nancy threw herself down on her bed and kicked her feet in the air. Charlotte tugged off the brown velvet pelisse and the fur bonnet and put a pillow under Nancy's head. After a few minutes she pulled in the blinds, shutting out the sunlight and brought linen cloths soaked in camphor water for the swollen eyelids.

"He's not worth your tears, Miss Nancy." She folded the cool wetness and laid it on Nancy's eyes.

Nancy gave a frantic shriek and more tears flowed vigorously down her round cheeks.

"Please behave yourself. Try to get mad enough to stop crying. You are going to look a fright at the ball if you don't give your eyes a chance to dry."

"Oh, that note—that horrible note!" Nancy croaked, her voice rasping with tears and temper. "And he didn't even send me any gloves or sugarplums when he knows that Race Week is the only time I can accept presents."

"Yes, you've said that a hundred times." Charlotte was stern. The time for sympathy was past. The crushed young thing needed bracing now, not coddling. Charlotte raged as she recalled the rude lines:

Battery House
Feb. 6th, 1849

Dear Nancy,

I must ask you to release me from the engagement which I have with you for this evening. I am sure you will understand and forgive me when I tell you that due to my stupidity in taking it for granted that my mother was planning to attend the ball escorted by Mr. Adams, my father being in Mississippi, and neglecting to inform her that I had invited you to accompany me to Hibernian Hall, I have brought great sorrow to her and caused a painful headache to attack her

271

which has prostrated her in bed and she will be
unable, in her weakened condition, to attend the
ball unless I escort her, being her son and understanding her frail health. Mr. Adams is in Philadelphia.

Ever your servant,
Robert Allston Gaillard

"I'll be the laughingstock of Charleston," Nancy
started screaming again.

The door opened and Mrs. Singleton and Hal
came in. "Hush this instant! You silly girl—you'll never
hold any man." Mrs. Singleton slapped Nancy a ringing
pop on her face.

"She's going to be all right now, Mrs. Singleton."
Charlotte winced noticeably. "See, she's stopped crying
and I'm going to try her ball dress on her."

The untidy, bosomy girl sat up and glared at her
mother and brother.

"Get out! You've just come to make fun of me and
beat me."

"You do look a sight," Hal agreed, "but I guess I
can manage to get your card filled out."

Nancy's mouth dropped open. "Am I going with
you?" she asked incredulously. "Do you want me to go
with you?"

"Not with those red eyes. But if Charlotte can
pretty you up I think I will enjoy showing Robert Gaillard a thing or two. Who does he think he is, anyway?"

"Now, Hal," Mrs. Singleton broke in, "Papa said
—forget it. It's not Robert's fault and if Nancy loves
him—"

"But Mamma, I don't," protested Nancy.

"Normandy is a big house, dear," Mildred Singleton spoke soothingly. "There's plenty of room there
for you and Robert's mother. Big fortunes don't come
seeking such healthy specimens as you twice in a lifetime."

"She'll never marry Robert if I can help it." Hal
was very angry. He liked his sister. And though he
loved his mother dearly it was obvious that Nancy was a
great disappointment to her since she had grown so tall

and buxom. Personally he thought Nancy was very handsome and on a horse she was stunning.

"Now, dear, you're young and when you bring a bride to Heronfields, think how nice it will be to have Nancy so near at Normandy."

Charlotte wrung out fresh camphor cloths and pitied Nancy. Her daughter would never be bargained about like that. Why, Nancy was no better off in the final analysis than she. She had no choice in where her life was to lie; she was a slave to custom and tradition. There were so many different kinds of slavery. Nancy's and Inigo's and hers—each different—each a prison.

"Charlotte, show Mr. Hal Miss Nancy's dress."

Charlotte opened the enormous wardrobe and took out the crimson velvet dress made with a tight waist, gigantic puff sleeves, and the widest hoop skirt that could be imported from Paris. Why had Mrs. Singleton chosen such a heavy dress? It would make Nancy look every more large and vivid, particularly with the head-dress of scarlet honeysuckle she insisted on wearing with it.

"That's beautiful!" Hal said. "I *will* be proud to show you off. Come on, Ma, we're going to be late for the first race if we don't hurry."

After Hal and his mother left, Nancy lay back on her pile of pillows and dropped into a thick sleep, like a tired child finished with its sorrow.

Charlotte pushed open one of the blinds and pulled a rocking chair over by the window so that she could be near Nancy and still see the street and get a bit of fresh air.

Fat maumas pushed fancy lace-trimmed baby carriages of delicate wicker, and flower girls passed with flat trays of camellias, jasmine, and jonquils balanced on their heads. A cart rattled by laden with juicy, salty oysters and in the distance she heard the rowing song of some crew bringing a planter's family up to town for the ball.

A street vendor passed beneath the window. Fully six feet tall the black woman carried the huge split basket on her red-turbaned head as proudly as though it were a crown. She set her wide feet purposefully and squarely down on the brick sidewalk, yet her straight body glided swiftly along with an animal grace. Surely, Charlotte thought admiringly, anybody who can carry her burden with such harmonious dignity must have innate pride and balance. She started to call to the woman but already the shrill minor crying was fading up the street:

> "Yeh crab
> She-crab!
> Yeh swimps!
> Yeh oshta!
> Byer swimps!
> Teker oshta!
> Yeh crab
> She-crab!"

The memory of the past Sunday night still galled her very soul. She rocked and brooded and told herself that she hated Leon Cavallo. Hated him! She gazed through a chink in the shutters and followed the bits of clouds that were framed in the narrow slit. And there with her face pointed and pouting and her eyes hard, she thought of ways to make the young doctor suffer if she ever saw him again.

Fingers rattled lightly on the door panel. Charlotte opened the door softly so as not to wake Nancy.

"Come here a minute." Jenkins's voice was shaking. Charlotte closed the door and stepped into the hall.

"What's wrong? You look as if you had seen a ghost."

"I is seen a ghos'—I done heard one, too."

"What are you talking about, Jenkins?"

"De baby boy of Kezia Bethune been here just now. He say dey been to de trial."

"What trial?" Charlotte was impatient and started to go back into the room but Jenkins caught her arm.

"Hit's one of Kezia' best sons, Jonas. De one just been to college in Europe wid Leon Cavallo and got de tuberculars. Now axe me what de law gwine do wid um —axe me."

"Why I'd rather ask you what he did."

"He ain't do nuttin—dat's what."

274

"Well then, they can't sentence him if he didn't do anything."

"Dey done sentence um. Times is changing and free niggers is treated wuss dan slaves dese days since dem Abolitionies been here a-marching an' a-singing 'bout John Brown' body!"

"But what sort of jury would sentence a free man that didn't do anything?" Charlotte wrinkled her forehead and shook her head; Jenkins was the kind of Negro that was just too emotional.

"White folks been on de jury; and po' buckra been on de jury; and crackers been on de jury and dey sentence um to ten years on de work gang."

"Oh no—they couldn't have! Not with tuberculosis! He was going to open another school for the free Negro children. They couldn't have done that to him."

"Somebody had hit in for um—dey falsify against um—dat's what. O Jesus, lemme live jest twell freedom and Jenkins gwine kill and kill and kill."

"Hush, Jenkins—somebody might hear you and then you'd be whipped. Tell me about his mother. Is she terribly upset?"

"Naw—Bethel say she ain't grieve much. She know dey ain't no use to grieve. She raise dem chillen right and fill deir haids wid knowledge and she ain't grieve. She got sense. She know what gwine to come, gwine to come. And den she got six mo' sons. Bethel say she gwine keep a-sending dem and one day one of dem is gwine git dere."

Charlotte stood close to Jenkins as if by their very nearness they could bring safety to each other. Someday she might stand in Mrs. Bethune's shoes, because her sons would be educated, too—and they would be Negroes. What would she do then? How would she feel?

Nancy turned over heavily and Charlotte and Jenkins looked desolately at each other before they went their separate ways. Charlotte slipped into the bedroom and bent over the pillows. But Nancy slept on.

Shocked by Jenkins's news, Charlotte tried to gain control of herself by saying, *Tonight I will hear an orchestra play "Oh, 'Tis Sweet to Remember," and the*

Elzinore Waltz and the Hyacinth Do and the Galop Russe, but my feet will be correctly folded under my hard chair and I will sit with other slave girls who like me will hold richly bordered merino shawls and Angola shawls and figured silk gauze shawls. I will watch the ladies arrive in their hoop skirts of white and black and scarlet and green velvet, or gold and white and crimson brocade. They will look at me but not see me because in their world I do not exist. They will look through me.

I will adorn their hair with dawn feathers and egrets and sarsenet ribbons. I will help the older ladies adjust their wigs and frisettes.

I, Charlotte, who can dance a pavan with more pride than a peacock, I who can whirl in the waltz with all the abandon of a blown feather from a white goose's breast. An egret bloom in my hair would reflect the live ivory of my cheeks; a scarlet brocade dress would match my lips.

But I will be chained to a hard wood chair by a flung silver scarf, watching the ball from the back room because of the very ivory of my face.

What a long evening it will be. I will try not to think of the keen black face of Kezia's son; of the bleak acceptance of his punishment; of Leon's face when he learned that I had been sold to Heronfields. I will think only of my own loneliness and on the long drive home after the ball I will listen patiently to Nancy's eulogy of Robert Gaillard, whom she will already have forgiven.

As though she sensed her presence in Charlotte's thoughts, Nancy stirred and woke. She looked over at Charlotte. Her dark eyes were clear and shining from sleep.

"Is it almost time to dress?" she asked eagerly.

Before Charlotte could answer, Lula burst in and grabbed the skirt of Charlotte's soft white challis dress and started pulling her toward the door.

"Do Gawd, Miss Charlotte—dere's a man at de back do'. Fust he been at de front do'."

"Lula," Charlotte spoke sharply, "try to talk more plainly. What in the world are you saying?"

"There's a man at the back door. First he came to

276

the front door but Jenkins sent him to the back door. And he looks lak he plum' sho crazy een de haid. Unnuh means—he is all 'stressed up and 'bleeged to see you quick. You better go. He ack like a wild man."

Could it be Inigo? Her very heart turned over. No —Jenkins would never send him to the back door even if he were in his cups. Who could it be? What was wrong?

"Will you let Lula help you dress, Miss Nancy? She's much cleverer than I am. She can make you look like a queen."

Nancy stretched her healthy rested body on the featherbed. "Oh, I suppose so—if you'll promise to tell me all about this strange man when you are through talking to him."

Jenkins was waiting in the hall.

"Hurry, Charlotte, hurry. I put um in yo' room. I scairt fuh any of de Singletons to see um. Even any of de house servants. Hit's de doctor and he's in a bad way."

The hall of the slave house was dark. The late afternoon sun did not reach into its secrets and strange people came and went unknown to the master or the mistress who thought that their bondwomen were not possessed of needs and desires and lonelinesses, like themselves. A coach clattered into the court and Charlotte heard Mildred Singleton giving the footman a piece of her tongue because he had stumbled against her as she alighted.

Charlotte's room was at the far end and she walked softly, telling herself that she must never let Leon suspect the hurt he had given her, that she must be distant and polite and keep her temper closely and quietly in check. *I'm getting to be too impetuous,* she told herself. *I must be more careful.*

Out in the court the mistress was now laughing with her son. The palmetto trees whispered faintly in the late afternoon breeze, and Charlotte wondered how many pairs of eyes had seen her slip away from the house, or seen him close the door to her room. As she reached the door she heard restless footsteps crossing the room toward it.

277

Charlotte's light figure, though she had warned herself to be cool, was all on fire now, and she resolved to make him desire her—even though she was through with him forever. She opened the door and came in flushed and ready to attack him.

But the sight of him was so different from what she had expected that she immediately assumed a mask of dignity to disguise her nervousness and emotion.

Leon's soft hair was in wild disorder. His tie was torn and his ruffled linen shirt was soiled and dripping with sweat, though the February day had been cold. He must have lost his coat, and the light trousers were stained where he had wiped his hands on them. His lip was bleeding where he had bitten it. The sight of Charlotte sobered him and he passed an unsteady hand over his face.

"What in the world is the matter?" Charlotte's heart pounded as she remembered the news Jenkins had brought, but she tried to keep the fear out of her face.

"Charlotte," he said in a broken voice, "I've just come from Jonas's trial."

Relief came, and a surge of interest she tried not to show.

"I see. But—why are you so frantic? I thought you were going back to Scotland, away from us Negroes here. It's not you who has been put in jail."

"Oh, you don't understand. You won't understand. Jonas is my friend. He is the gentlest, frailest person alive. Not that he'll be alive long." His voice was bitter, shaken. "They tied him to a stob in the ground to keep him from running away and he coughed until blood gushed from his mouth, and when I went to help him an Irish policeman put his filthy hands on me. Me!"

"What did you do? Did you say 'yes sir' prettily to him?"

Leon jumped up and shook her until her teeth chattered. "You vixen! Your heart is nothing but stone. You have no blood in you at all. Kezia Bethune was nice to you. Don't you even grieve for her?"

"Let me go. I don't want you ever to put your

278

hands on me again. Certainly I'm sorry for Mrs. Bethune. I will ask for a pass to go there tomorrow."

She would never have dreamed that Leon's was such an emotional nature. "What did you do when the policeman hit you?"

He paled. "I lost control and knocked him down! And then the whole pack of them were on me, howling, 'Nigger, Nigger, hit a white man'!"

He had Charlotte now. She was breathing with him—panting with him. "Then what?"

"Jonas was pulling at his leg trying to loosen it from the stob and come to help me. Then Doctor Hugenin ran up." The fire died in Leon's face. "He shouted to them to stand back. Said my white grandfather was the most influential man in the city and it would cost every one of them their jobs if they laid a finger on me. There I stood! One brown man with a heart full of hate, protected by the very thing that I was hating."

"Poor Leon!" She came to him and drew his head down to her shoulder. "What can you do? Where can you go?" *Both of us,* she thought. *Both of us!*

"Do! Go!" He raised up and looked her straight in the face. "Why, I'm going to stay here and carry on Jonas's work. I can't teach them, but I can make their bodies strong, study cholera and yellow fever—and help our people in other ways."

Then Charlotte said a strange thing. "If you can just keep from being bitter."

"Bitter? Maybe later I won't be, but right now my heart is sour as wormwood. Grandfather Holloway was in the courtroom; he sat there and shriveled up into nothing before my very eyes. He's always been treated with dignity and respect by the white people, and he's given them the same respect. When he tried to speak up for Jonas, they ordered him out of the court, and when he didn't move right away, a common ditch-digger, one of the spectators, rushed at him and kicked him. Called him a Free Issue and an Abolitionist. Said he probably was storing weapons in his attic to foster an uprising. Haiti would seem mild if the Negroes did rise up here. We outnumber the white people two to one."

279

"You're calmer now. Maybe you'd better go home. I've got to go back to Miss Nancy."

"Will you marry me?"

"Marry you? And have you despise my children as you did me a few nights ago, because I'm a slave?" Charlotte's pride had risen up. "Never. I'd do better to marry black Cuffee. He thinks I'm perfect."

"Is that what you want from a man?"

"It's more than you can offer me."

"Is there any water in that basin over there?"

"Yes. Here's a towel."

He doused his head in the cool water and scrubbed his cheeks with her towel. *She is right,* he thought. *Bitterness would eat me up. But I am staying here and I am going to make me a good life here. And one for her, too.* He turned his clean, now relatively quiet face on her.

"You have been very kind. Now if you will forgive me for Sunday night and stop letting your pride speak for your heart, I'll try to show you how deeply I feel about you."

Charlotte felt sick right down to the pit of her stomach. There was no use complicating her life any further. If she let herself marry him, her children would belong to Harry and Mildred Singleton, and every day she came to resent more and more the way they treated their slaves. To resent all the seeming endlessness of slavery—resent being in bondage in any way, even to love. Love had burned her enough already.

"There wouldn't be any use," she told him.

"Why? Is it because of—him?"

Ah—*him!* She knew every turn of his head, every intonation of his speech, every hair on his hands. In comparison—as she had seen them together last June— Leon was only a brown man with marvelous eyes that somehow did not say quite enough.

She looked out into the tiny hall. Nobody was there. She motioned to him and together they made their way down the steep, narrow stairs into the courtyard, then through a heavy wooden gate that led into an alley littered with garbage. Over the rotten food flies buzzed,

280

and through it rats' beady eyes gazed fearfully at the two unhappy humans locked in a feverish embrace, each seeking from the other something that no one else could give.

Chapter 39

Charlotte expected Leon all the next day but he did not come. On the second and the third and the fourth day it was the same.

She had no desire to go out anywhere and wandered from room to room, with Nancy or without her, idle and listless; she wept secretly at night and refused to eat with the other house servants in the late afternoon. She blushed continually and was irritable. It seemed to her that everybody knew about her impetuous embrace in the littered alley and was laughing at and pitying her. Strong as was her inward grief, this wound to her vanity intensified her misery.

Once she tried to explain to bewildered little Lula what was wrong with her, and suddenly began to cry. Her tears were those of an offended child who did not know why she was being punished for having done probably the rightest thing in all her recent calamitous months.

Lula tried to soothe Charlotte who after first listening a moment, interrupted her. "Leave off, Lula! I don't think and don't want to think about it! He just came and then went away, went away—"

Her voice shook and she almost wept again, but

recovered and went on quietly, "And I don't at all want to get married. And I am afraid of him. I have now become quite calm, quite calm."

The day after this conversation with Lula, Charlotte put on her most cheerful yellow dress and that day she returned to the old, controlled routine of life which she had abandoned since the afternoon Leon had come to her for comfort.

Having washed Nancy's hair, she left her drying her long, black mop by a hot fire and took the wet brushes out onto the upstairs piazza to dry in the sunshine. When she had arranged them to her satisfaction she leaned against the rail and stood looking with interest down on the passers-by and humming a pavan that had once particularly pleased her.

She listened joyfully, as though she had not expected it, to the charm of the notes spilling down onto the sidewalk and slowly dying away, and all at once she felt quite gay.

"What's the good of making so much of it? Things are nice here away from that horrid Street," she said to herself and began walking up and down the high piazza, listening to a flower girl crying her narcissi and camellias, as gladly as she had to her own song.

This morning she had returned to her favorite mood—contemplation and satisfaction in herself. She would be in nobody's way if only they would leave her alone. But now, however much they left her alone, she could not be at peace, and immediately she felt this.

From the bedroom the piazza door opened and Lula called softly that *he* was at her door.

Pale and agitated, Charlotte ran to her room. And as she crossed the flagged courtyard which led to the slaves' house she cried to herself, *This is awful, it is unbearable! I don't want to be tormented! What am I to do?*

Before she could answer herself, Leon met her at the door with a disturbed and serious face. As soon as he saw her his face brightened. He seized her hands and kissed each finger, then, turning them over, pressed his lips into her palms.

"I have not seen you all these days because I have been definitely deciding on my life. I completed my plans this morning." He was obviously in haste to say what he had to.

Something gripped Charlotte's throat, and regardless of the ears and eyes that were always lurking, she shut her door and clicked the latch, staring straight at Leon with wide-open eyes.

He smiled with relief at the tenderness in her face, and their kiss was complete with love and compassion in equal measure.

Is it possible that this man can so suddenly have become so necessary to me? Charlotte asked herself, and immediately answered—*Yes, it is possible. He alone is now dearer than anything else. He is my future.*

"I have loved you from the moment I first saw you in Grandfather's shop when you were a little girl. Will you marry me?"

"How can we marry? Why speak of that so long as I must remain in this hopeless situation until July, when Miss Tafra will surely buy me back, and—" She paused suddenly.

"And then?"

She drew near to him and he kissed her lips.

"Do you love me?"

"Yes, yes," Charlotte murmured, as if in vexation. She sighed, and catching her breath more and more quickly, began to sob.

"What is it? What's the matter?"

"July is so far away," she replied, smiling through her tears.

Leon held her hands. "You are so young," he said, "and I have been through so much confusion in my life. I am afraid you still don't know yourself."

Charlotte listened intently.

"Hard for me as waiting will be," Leon continued, "it will give you time to be sure of yourself. And when you *do* return to Normandy, should you find that you do not love me, or should you find that you still love—" His mouth twisted unnaturally.

"Why do you say that? You know that what has happened cannot be erased. But since the day of Jonas's trial, I have loved you," Charlotte cried, quite convinced that she spoke the truth.

"When you're back at Normandy, you'll know for certain."

"That seems so long!" Charlotte repeated, almost fearfully. "So long!"

"I cannot tell you how long it will seem to me. But these months are too precious, too important for our future, to waste. Let me explain more of my plans. I have arranged to spend six weeks or so in Philadelphia, at the Pennsylvania School of Medicine, for some special study in the treatment and prevention of cholera. Doctor Hugenin has helped by recommending me to two of his colleagues there. And he feels—wisely, I'm sure—that for other reasons, too, I should go away for a while. Not just that ugly incident the other day— being in other surroundings for a little while is the best way to prepare myself calmly to meet the situation, face the tension that's rising in Charleston—plan my future course in this whirlpool of dangerous forces."

Charlotte knew how true this was. It had been an upsetting ordeal for Leon, with his Edinburgh training, to face the embarrassments, the fettering rules which now applied in Charleston to free Negroes as well as slaves; the quarrels and intrigues; the social and racial problems which were growing like an avalanche with the agitating vision of emancipation in every mind.

"Then, too," Leon said soberly, "we need sometimes to commit ourselves, in order to get hold of ourselves."

"I shall die here in the city without you." Charlotte looked into her lover's face and saw in it a look of commiseration and perplexity. "No, no! I'll be happy! Even when I go back on the Street!" she said, not wanting to cause him any hurt.

"Does the overseer annoy you there?"

"No, he daren't for the duration of my six months."

"And then? Suppose Mrs. Gaillard *doesn't* buy you back?"

"I mustn't suppose that. It would ruin me to lose hope."

284

"Answer me, anyway."

"Old Chloe has information about Lustbader which will protect me. And I can always run away."

"What information?"

But Charlotte shook her head and Leon suddenly laughed at her.

"You're not the same at all," he said wonderingly.

"How? Am I uglier?"

"On the contrary, you have acquired a noble beauty," he whispered to her. "My princess!"

Chapter 40

Leon had not returned from Philadelphia in late March. By that time Dr. Hugenin and Bishop Adams had effected Jonas's release and the Singletons, with Charlotte silent and contemplative in their retinue, had moved back to Heronfields so that Harry and Hal could personally supervise the breeding of their blooded mares in season and be on hand to cast the first handful of rice into the spring ground as their gesture of overlordship to their slaves.

The sowing of the rice took place the day after they reached the plantation. Charlotte watched the exciting process with Nancy from the dykes and canals, thinking, *How different this is from the other time I walked here in the dead of winter brooding over Inigo and grieving at my degradation in being sold to this place. Today even the landscape is changed. The slaves are busy and bright and in a festival mood. Can my new love for Leon explain my changed feelings? Or is*

*it just that the winter has passed and spring is here, with
all it symbolizes? That I know Leon will come back
with April?*

Gone were the dead, brown, rattling reeds and in
their place waved the green and gold strips of the
marshes, bowing and whispering, shining like ripe
wheat in the sunlight; starry wild lilies and blue iris
perfumed the damp places; creamy honeysuckle and
scarlet woodbine ran rampant over the latrine ditch,
masking it and covering it with fragrance; pink and
white Cherokee roses spilled from the trees, as well as
Spanish moss, and out in the drained, dry fields the
women, their heads bound in multicolored turbans, followed the dug trenches holding their aprons filled with
seed rice proudly in front of them, sowing it with a
flowing forward movement of their brown arms as
rhythmically and perfectly as trained dancers in a
chorus. And a chorus indeed accompanied them. The
Negro men bearing muskets kept up a steady round of
noisy firing to frighten away the ricebirds hovering in
clouds, eager to settle and devour the tempting seeds
before the water should be allowed to flow back in the
dry field. Children rushed about clapping shingles.
Clackety clack—clackety clack! Jigging and cutting
cartwheels and shouting gaily up at the twittering hungry little birds cheated of their sustenance.

Can this be Heronfields? Charlotte gazed wonderingly at Harry and Hal walking along the dikes
laughing with Lustbader, who even stopped every now
and then and, looking covertly at his employer to be
sure of his attention, patted a little darky on the head
or complimented one who clattered his shingles above
the others.

After reaching the cabin that night Charlotte was
restless and troubled. She was tormented by the insoluble question whether she loved Inigo or Leon. She
loved Inigo. But she also loved Leon; of that there was
no doubt. Her love for him had caused her very attitude
to everything to change and sweeten, just as the honeysuckle sweetened the ditch behind the cabins. It meant
that his kindness, his loving, affectionate self had made
it impossible for her not to love him. But what would

she do if, when Inigo came again, she found that she loved him too much? She asked herself this over and over, but she was unable to find an answer to the terrible question.

The next morning when she went out the fields were flooded. The lovely green and gold marsh grass was hidden under sheets of blank unmoving water, and the people moved, as she had remembered them, lazily about their dull tasks. Harry and Hal Singleton, having done their duty in walking along the dikes for the sowing, were now free of their slaves for another year. Charlotte kept looking uneasily at everybody, as if trying to fathom each and everybody's real nature.

"Dey jest de same as allus," Chloe tried to tell her. "One day ain't gwine change eternity."

So it was not her new-found love for Leon which had made her see this place differently. Neither she nor it had changed! It was just a day, out of a year of days, that shone a little. Was her love for Leon that kind of love, just a day clutched out of her need for sympathy and affection? Should she break off with him and again give in to her hopeless hunger for Inigo? She recalled her sudden love for Leon in all its strength and at the same time knew that she could never forget Inigo. She vividly pictured herself as Leon's wife, and the prospect of a busy, happy, useful life with him unfolded in glowing scenes in her imagination. Only so could she be completely happy, but must she forever abandon the dream of Inigo in which she had lived so long?

That same night she found Chloe sitting on the front steps smoking her pipe to ward off the swarming mosquitoes and sand flies, the only things except the centipedes and snakes that prospered in this warm, damp atmosphere.

"Why are you waiting for me?" Charlotte's nerves had been on edge all day. "Are you afraid I'm going to run away like Joe Valiant?"

"Unh—unh!" Chloe said in a low voice, shaking her head. "Look 'cross de Street."

Charlotte peeped in the direction indicated by the smoking pipe. There by the door of the cabin opposite stood the bulky figure of Lustbader, glaring angrily at her in the dark. So—he knew about her trip with Joe Valiant! Some slave, currying favor or desiring yellow shoes or maybe even a bottle of whisky, must have found out and told him. Fear choked her, and Chloe fastened a fat hand tightly on her arm to warn her against screaming in terror.

After that Chloe neglected her duties in the children's house to wait for Charlotte whenever it was time for her to go back and forth from the Street to the big house. She kept a fire burning in the little cabin all through the hot nights, with a pot of water boiling lustily just in case the round, red face dared to come to her window. That round face would make an easy target for a pot of scalding water. Sooner or later, if her plan to turn him in to the law failed, she had to kill him, anyway. That she was sure of, and to scald him to death would be as accidental and easy as strangling him in his bed. It didn't worry her at all to contemplate this thing. Her hands had done justice before. She had too many plans for Charlotte. If Lustbader touched her beauty she would not hesitate to kill him.

Chapter 41

While Lustbader bided his time and kept up his unpleasant scheme for frightening Charlotte into silence, waiting for the proper time to pounce upon her and render her harmful knowledge of him useless, Cuffee Gaillard, warned by another dream in which the white stag attacked Charlotte, took up the hunt for the wild male creature. In his uneasy, superstitious heart dwelt a suspicion that Inigo had not gone West at all, but had changed into the beast, as he had surely done on Christmas and practically before Cuffee's very eyes. It did not occur to Cuffee that his dreams stemmed from the tales drummed from Heronfields about the overseer's interest in Charlotte, his spying on her every move.

But the white stag had disappeared from the sight of man, and though Cuffee with all his cunning, and with the assistance of all who knew about the search, looked in the piny woods and in the thickets and in the swamp and on the lonely beaches at full of moon when the deer played and sported in the surf—still there was no trace of him and none could tell of seeing his whiteness flash by as they fished or hunted or roamed in the secret forest places.

Tom turkeys high up in the tops of the tallest pines knew where he was, but not by one iridescent bronze feather did they betray the king stag. Eagles wheeled and screamed in derision above Cuffee and little Nick as they cantered across cleared spaces, but the eagle respected and cherished the snowy flag as it waved through the myrtle bushes. Blue and white herons rose lazily from the marshes and pointed their spearlike heads away from the sanctuary, trailing their long legs limply behind them. Egrets in stately splendor sat in cool, ferny places and stared insolently at the little boy and the dark man who dared penetrate their court. Swamp canaries and mockingbirds sang gaily as insects chewed greedily on the hunters' necks. Snakes slithered across their path. Tomtits and hummingbirds played hide and seek in the scarlet trumpet vines that flung themselves riotously heavenward. Wood doves called for rain to cover any hoofmarks that might be seen. Gulls flapped foolishly up and down as the hot sand screeked between the bare toes of him who sought to kill a monarch at his bathing-place. Turtles peeped from slimy logs, slyly hooding their eyes, wondering where they had left their eggs. Bullfrogs and toads croaked— Not here! Not here! Over there! Over there!

It was a weary time.

Holy Mary had forgotten Charlotte; Jehovah seemed oblivious to Tafra in her pain; the Voodoo gods turned closed ears to Cuffee's pleas and promises; and Inigo—by the waters of the Mississippi—seemed to have forgotten them all.

Tafra was only the shadow of a substance in her huge bed. Her great eyes had become wells of sorrowful acceptance, but the determination to live until Inigo should return once more to Normandy still burned brightly in their light-blue depths. Emily wouldn't get a chance to make trouble for him—she'd see to that.

Dr. Hugenin came once a week from Charleston in his new steam launch. The slaves rushed down to the landing at the sound of the chuff-chuff of the strange engine and the churning of the wheel. The smoke which bellied from the stack entranced them. They were sure that Old Satan, complete with tail, horns, and fork, came thus each week and demanded that their mistress go with him, and when they saw the boat turn laboriously and chuff away they chuckled and sang merry songs in praise of Old Miss, who was still stronger than the Devil himself and would go when she got ready.

Late in April a letter came for Tafra, but that was one of the days when she lay mercifully asleep under an opiate, and there was not one soul on the whole plantation who could read the letter for her. So Cuffee, desperate in his frustration, and determined to see for himself that Charlotte was still safe, rode over to Heronfields in broad daylight, though the overseer had sent word to all of the Normandy Negroes that he would whip any one of them who dared set foot on his Street. Fortunately Charlotte was in Chloe's cabin, having been sent there earlier in the day by Mildred Singleton, who had found her huddled in a chair in Nancy's room, shivering with fever.

The letter told of Inigo's intentions to arrive at Normandy on the first of June. Cuffee was bewildered at the easy tears the letter brought to Charlotte and when she read it to him he asked incredulously, "Ain't yunnuh glad?"

Charlotte tried to speak, but her teeth chattered in the malarial chill that gripped her. Cuffee stroked her arm with the sensitive soothing tips of his fingers.

"What bin wrong? Don't be sad—hit hurts Cuffee to see yunnuh lak dis."

"I hate it so here. What difference can his coming make to me, anyway?" She was vehement and jerked her arm away from Cuffee. Feeling hurt, he walked stiffly out of the cabin and yelled at the huge black horse he'd tied to a near-by tree. Following Cuffee, sorry she'd spoken crossly to him, Charlotte fell into an even more chilling fit of cold trembling. The horse reared and bared his teeth, shaking his head furiously.

"Oh, don't get hurt!" She ran toward Cuffee, sneezing as well as trembling.

"Git back," he yelled. "Dis a killer hoss. Unnuh kin manage." And in a minute he was safely up. Though Edisto threw back his head and plunged up and down, Cuffee made him stand a minute.

"Jedus," he breathed, "yunnuh is a funny li'l gal. Scairt to death yet yunnuh come to help Cuffee! Even sneezing yunnuh did come—even sneezing."

"He's a horrid horse. I hate him!"

"Po' Edisto. He too mean to lib, but Cuffee ain't got de heart to git rid of um. Anybody else ud sho kill um quick."

As he rode away Charlotte felt a pain in her breast—a tingling at the nipples. *Edisto looks like black fear—like Death. He just suits this whole nightmare,* she thought.

That same afternoon Mildred Singleton and Nancy were paying their weekly neighborly visit to Normandy, bearing calves'-foot jelly and a great bunch of sweet peas. As they sat in Emily's parlor waiting for Hercules to take them upstairs, Dr. Hugenin came in and perched precariously on the arm of Emily's little pink satin French love seat. Picking up a tiny turkey-feather fan from a marble-topped table, he plied it vigorously back and forth in front of his face.

"Don't go up today, Mildred," he said.

"Is she worse? Can't you make Emily come? Nancy says Robert confided to her when he came out for the little party at the Myers' last week that he wanted to come himself, but that Emily kept putting him off from day to day. Can't you make her see?"

"No." Dr. Hugenin laid the trifling fan down in disgust at its poor performance. "Emily knows how people are talking, but it seems to please her. So I guess you'll just have to do your Christian duty and send Charlotte back here to help Hagar nurse Miss Tafra."

Nancy held her tongue like a good girl but Mildred opened her mouth to refuse and then compromised. "Charlotte has malaria, Doctor Hugenin. I made her lie down this morning because I could tell she was feverish."

"All the more reason." He put on his most fatherly manner. "The girl isn't accustomed to the dampness of Heronfields. She'll cure up in a few days back here in this dry heat. Tafra must have at least one person she loves by her at the last."

Mildred bit her lips in vexation but she didn't dare deny a request of Dr. Hugenin. No Low Country lady would dare; he knew too much about every one of them. So she nodded, and Nancy sighed audibly with relief at her mother's doing the proper thing.

"All right!" Mildred said, and immediately felt Christianlike and generous, so generous that she added, "Charlotte will be a comfort to Miss Tafra. She is certainly an original, strange girl, but she has a good heart. I'll send her tomorrow. It's time *somebody* takes Emily's place here."

Chapter 42

━━━━━━━━━━━━━━━━━━━━━━━━━━━━━━

Free! Free from Heronfields, *I mean. Free for a while,
anyhow, from Lustbader. And if Tafra lives until July
and* they *let me stay, perhaps I will never have to go
back.*

For her first few days at Normandy this was all
that Charlotte could think of. Neither Leon nor Inigo
entered into her utter delight in the pure creature
comforts she had so missed in the cabin. Then gradually the same feeling that this house was no longer
necessary to her, which she had experienced the day
she visited Tafra in late January, stole back. And after a few nights reveling in linen sheets and blankets
sweet with dried lavender her dreams were as troubled
as they had been on Chloe's dirty bed.

Outwardly she was calm and seemingly fitted into
her former niche, though she was not really happy. She
never laughed now without the sound of tears in her
laughter. She could not sing to Nick in the twilight for
thinking of all the miserable little ones she had encountered on the Heronfields Street. As soon as she began to
laugh at uninhibited Sambo, or to sing a love song to
Nick, tears choked her. Tears of chagrin, tears at the
recollection of Inigo, tears of vexation that she was a
slave and that if she married Leon their children would
be slaves like her and denied freedom of mind as well
as of body.

At all times something now stood on guard within
her and forbade her every joy she had formerly known

here. She realized that she had lost all the old feeling of being a vital part of this Normandy. The long-ago days in New Orleans when life had offered her the liberty to dream were now what she recalled oftenest and most painfully. What would she not give to be back in that time! Where the possibility of ever being at the mercy of a man like Lustbader could not have existed. That time was gone forever. Yet it was necessary for her to live on.

It was small comfort to her to reflect that she was worse off than anybody else in the world. And she continually asked herself, *What next?* But there was nothing to come unless Tafra managed to live until July.

She kept away from Hagar and Hercules and Cuffee and felt at ease only with little Nick. She loved him so dearly, and when alone with him she sometimes laughed.

She hardly left the house except in the late afternoons to walk up and down the Street, comparing it with the one at Heronfields. She was ashamed that in all her years spent at Normandy she had held herself aloof from these people. They were good people. They were clean and orderly and only wanted a little guidance to make something of themselves. And at day's end the Normandy Negroes watched and waited for the light-skinned woman who was running their plantation like a white woman, yet who was one of them. They nodded and waved to her as she passed their orderly, comfortable cabins, a slim, pale, ghostlike figure in the twilight with her gold gauze shawl flung back from her shoulders, reflecting the moon quality of her slender neck. *We might be like her someday,* they began to think, *or our children might. Mr. Inigo tells us that freedom will come in our lifetime and that we must be ready for it. She can show us the way now that she has come from her cocoon and walks among us as one of us.*

Just to see her walking in the evening, self-sufficient, alone, gave them a peculiar pride in themselves. An awareness of horizons that they had but dimly dreamed of before. She sensed this and she thought, *Leon and I together could do so much. How sad that*

*we are separated by the law that keeps me a slave, as
surely as Inigo and I are separated by blood.*

One hot night she walked in the dusk without her
shawl. Her pale-green muslin dress was caught around
the waist with a sash of yellow satin. Overhead the sky
had a hot greenish glow where the sun had set through
the tall cypress trees that hugged the pond. Tafra had
been very low all day, and Charlotte felt an urge to
talk to someone who might clear the heaviness out of
her heart for a little while.

"Finger Ring," she called to the round shapely
girl who was making haste across the Street to a cabin
which was dark and closed tight. Finger Ring halted
and rolled her wide, almond-shaped eyes. With an undulating lilt to her hips, she moved on, pretending she
had not heard, but Charlotte called to her again and
Finger Ring stopped.

"Finger Ring, would you like me to teach you to
read?" Charlotte's low, husky voice was like a part of
the night itself.

Finger Ring beamed and strutted a step closer to
examine the pale green stuff of the soft dress that clung
like mist about Charlotte's slender thigh. Lawd Gawd
a mighty, she'd been scairt that the pale woman wuz
fixin' to mek her specify where she wuz going. She
shifted her hot eyes in the direction of Pettigru's cabin.
She could feel him waiting for her in the thick, airless
darkness. Her sinuous body strained forward to min-
gle with his, but she was a "most" Voodoo priestess, so
she remembered her manners.

"Sho, Miss Charlotte. All un us wants to learn to
read. I kin talk mo' better dan de ole uns already. But
kin I wait twell tomorrow? I is in a bodacious hurry."

"All right, Finger Ring. Good night."

Finger Ring disappeared in the shadows before
Charlotte finished speaking. Charlotte sighed. *That is
the way it might have been with me and Inigo,* she told
herself; *slipping and hiding in the dark. We couldn't
have borne it.*

She had smelled the shut-up cabins on the Street
at Heronfields. She had been in cabins that she knew
were harbors of stolen emotion. Somewhere in the night

295

a wildcat shrieked. Charlotte shivered as though one of her own garments had been torn from her. She clasped her arms across her breasts; the muslin was soft and cool. She stood shadowed under a tree, back from the glow of the recently lighted fire stands, and watched the big house that belonged to him whom she would have given the world to see for a single minute—he who was now the forbidden web of her dreams, the scent of the bay blossoms, the farthest star in her whole sky, but —oh God!—still the brightest.

Slowly, slowly May moved on. Hagar sat with Tafra in the nights and Charlotte watched over her through the long hot days. The odor of illness had now become so overpowering that Hagar kept a smoldering fire of roots and herbs in the fireplace to make it possible for her and Charlotte to remain in the room, and that made the heat worse.

Most of the time Tafra dozed or, when consciousness was forced on her by the pain, she would ask through pinched gray lips, "What day is this?"

It was the hottest May on record in South Carolina and the grain lay skimpy and brown in the fields, while Big Jake and Seneca and Field Hand Mattie urged and ordered and goaded the sweating laborers to get in the crop. Vegetable patches were withered and fruitless, and the small revenue which would have been derived from the sale of peas, beans, lettuce, and cabbages was a heartbreaking loss to the slaves. Evil had come to Normandy when Inigo had ridden away. Only the cotton and the weeds flourished greedily in the dry sickening heat. Children cried in the night with the running off of the bowels, and blisters made from splintery hoe handles refused to heal. Frizzled chickens appeared in too many yards and the need for their own satisfying Voodoo worship became apparent to all the people.

On the night of May thirty-first, Hagar did not come to relieve Charlotte at dusk. Instead Sweet came with a cup that Hagar had mixed for Tafra, and said, "Yunnuh hatter stay on here tonight. Hagar say de people am gitting restless and her and Big Jake think dey gots to hold a service for de good ob eberyt'ing

296

here on de plantation. Finger Ring down in de swamp."

"Will you sit here a minute then, Sweet, and let me run outside for a breath of fresh air? I feel so sleepy from the fumes of the fire."

"Sho, gal, Sweet try and make Miss Tafra drink dis cup whilst yunnuh am gone. Don' hurry back—git yo' supper. Yunnuh looks lak a ghos' in dis dim light and hit's hotter'n hit was at daycome eben though de sun riz hot."

Charlotte called to Nick. He was sitting on the carpet in the dining-room by the door. His thick black curly hair was plastered wetly on his forehead, his face dirty and his blouse torn.

"What's the matter, honey?" Charlotte asked, smoothing back his curls, twining her fingers in the hair that grew on the back of his neck.

"Sambo tried to make me come down out of the mulberry tree."

"But you know, Nick, that that tree is rotten and your Gran told Sambo to keep you out of it." Charlotte tried to be severe but her lips were smiling at the hot, sullen little face.

"We found that out." Nick had to smile back. "Sambo fussed and threatened me with all sorts of things, from chigger bites to piles, if I didn't come down, so I climbed higher and he had to come up after me. He got ahold of my blouse and started pulling me down and the limb he was on broke and we both fell plumb to the ground."

"Oh, Nick, did it hurt you?"

"No, not me," Nick boasted, "but it sure busted Sambo's head open."

"Sho did!" spoke a voice from under the table and Sambo crawled out, his head swathed in heavy cloth.

"Let me see it," Charlotte said, unwinding the piece of homespun sheeting. After yards had been unraveled a scratch about an inch long was brought to light.

Even Sambo laughed and he began to jig up and down on his flat lively feet.

"Us waiting for Mass Inigo," he announced, quick

to change the subject now that his ruse was unveiled.

"Well, come in the kitchen with me and let's get some supper," Charlotte said. "Then you run home, Sambo, and I'll bathe Nick and put him to bed."

"Ma tell me to stay on a pallet in Nick's room tonight," Sambo said. "Dem gwine wid Hagar to de woods."

Charlotte looked out of the window and saw a bright flame spit up into the darkening night. The throb of a drum, low but insistent, beat like a wild heart. She fed the boys and quickly ate some cold chicken and biscuits; then as soon as the two were washed and in bed she went back to Tafra's room.

Sweet was waving a palmetto fan gently back and forth and singing a weird slow song. Tafra appeared more peaceful than usual and Sweet got quietly to her feet and put her arms around Charlotte's shoulders.

"I hates to leave yunnuh tonight," she said. "Dere's a presence in dis room besides weuns."

Charlotte felt a thin breeze blow for a moment and the low fire flickered up and died down again. She shuddered and looked at Sweet. Sweet met her eyes and nodded.

"Tomorrow's de fust," she said. "Dat's de day her been waitin' for, enty?"

"Yes," Charlotte said. "Are you going, too?"

"Ki, chile, Sweet need Voodoo same lak de rest."

"Tell Cuffee to come here when he finishes," Charlotte asked.

"Good night," said Sweet.

"Good night, Sweet," said Charlotte.

"Good night," murmured Tafra tranquilly.

As Sweet left the room Tafra motioned for Charlotte to come over and sit close to her. Charlotte put her hand on Tafra's forehead and felt the heat of the fever that had started that day burn her fingers. The air in the room was fetid and foul. There was no freshness or fragrance even though Charlotte had filled vases with full-blown roses and put a bowl of ripe, sweet May peaches on the mantel.

"I'm very cold, my dear," Tafra said faintly but

298

firmly. The cup which she had drunk seemed to have eased the pain but left her mind unusually alert.

Charlotte pulled up a worsted quilt and gently chafed the skeleton wrists.

"Talk to me, Charlotte. Tell me in detail all about your days. Old Dewey Singleton was a devil but Mr. Harry was always a nice boy. Miss Mildred hasn't got any sense, of course, but—"

Whatever it was in the cup had overstimulated Tafra. Charlotte looked at the glittering pinpoint pupils of the ice-blue eyes.

"Let's don't talk about Heronfields, Miss Tafra."

"Are you so very unhappy, little Charlotte?"

What must she say? This was the end for Tafra. They both knew it—their hands clung together and love for each other spoke through their pulse beats what they could never say in words, since there was so much that must never be said between them—ever.

"Would you like me to tell you what happened to me in Charleston?"

Tafra whispered a weak "Yes." They both loved Inigo—they both wanted his happiness. Soon Tafra would find out whether she had been wise. And another thing she must attend to when she got there. She must speak quite sharply to the angel who was in charge of putting the color on the faces that the potter turned out. There must be no more strange ivory pigment brushed on beauty which God had planned to be adored and cherished by a sweetheart, on beauty born to walk in honor under great oaks that were the very essence of a home place.

But what were these words that little Charlotte was saying? Leon Cavallo? That nice man who had once come and stood for a moment under Inigo's oaks? J. H. Holloway's grandson—and the Most Honored So-and-So's grandson? Why, this was a perfect tale that Charlotte was telling her tonight. She wouldn't have to reprimand an angel as soon as she got to heaven—everything was going to come out right. Now she could find Nicholas first and tell him all about everything.

"Tell me when midnight strikes, Charlotte. If I

know that the first of June is here I can sleep easily. Did you see Cuffee today?"

"Didn't you hear him whistling for Nick before sunup this morning?" Charlotte asked.

"I heard a robin singing," Tafra whispered.

"I thought it was a robin singing, too, but Nick knew it was Cuffee. We went to the window and there was Cuffee, as proud as a chieftain, on that red filly he loves so. He looked up at us and his face was completely happy. He was smiling and stroking her neck. He waved and Nick threw him a kiss; then he touched Fancy and the sun came up as they flashed across the field to the training-track. The filly looked like a red streak of lightning with a thundercloud on her back!"

Good—good, Tafra thought. *The black baby prince will be happy, too—his filly will bring him the acclaim due to the king he believes himself to be.*

"I wonder what Hagar put in that cup. I feel ever so much stronger." Charlotte felt the pulse. It was fainter than ever, and Tafra's breath came from her throat instead of her chest.

The night throbbed on with the insistent drumbeats. Shadows reached in for them from the tattered clouds that scudded back and forth across the moon, blown by sudden gusts of hot, damp wind that for a moment alleviated the heat and flickered the candlelight.

Toward midnight Tafra slept. Charlotte kept her finger on the faint surging of the lifeblood through the body. Suddenly Tafra spoke—lying rigid as a statue. "Charlotte, you love me?" she said in a soft trustful whisper. "Charlotte, you will not deceive me? You'll tell me the truth?"

Charlotte looked at Tafra with eyes full of tears. "My dear Miss Tafra!" she repeated over and over, straining all the power of her love to find some way to help.

And again in this last futile struggle Tafra, refusing to believe that it was now her time to die, with her beloved son not by her bedside, escaped from reality into a world of delirium and spoke in a strong unnatural tone.

" 'And Delilah said to Samson, Tell me, I pray thee, wherein thy great strength lieth, and wherewith thou mightest be bound to afflict thee.' "

Charlotte listened, feeling death all around. The harsh speaking broke off and Tafra mumbled incoherently for a while, then again the voice, as of another who had come into the shell which had been Tafra, spoke.

" 'But the Philistines took him, and put out his eyes, and brought him down to Gaza, and bound him with fetters of brass; and he did grind in the prison house. Howbeit the hair of his head began to grow again after he was shaven.' " A long tottering sigh followed this pronouncement and Tafra shriveled down into the bed and her breathing became labored and from the well of the stairs midnight struck in clear hard strokes.

The dark hours passed. In the distance came the sandy sound of the people stealing back to the Street, and the cessation of the drums made the night more empty and lonely than ever.

Will Hagar never come, Charlotte wondered. *Suppose I fall asleep. Suppose I die here alone with Tafra who is already a memory.*

The moon went away and the big bedroom was filled with the humid grayness of a June dawn.

Charlotte, exhausted and hollow-eyed from her long vigil, was bending over Tafra as the door slowly opened. Looking up she saw Hagar, sharply triumphant and full of a thin piercing vitality, come into the room. Hoofbeats thudded up the avenue and Tafra opened her eyes.

"Is it the first of June?" she asked.

"Yes, Miss Tafra," Charlotte answered.

"Is that Inigo coming up the drive?" Tafra's voice was a worn thread of sound.

Charlotte went to the window and Hagar felt the bony wrist.

Charlotte stared out of the window a moment, then, as she started to the bed Hagar questioned her with her eyes. Charlotte shook her head and started to speak but Hagar spoke first.

301

"Yes, Miss Tafra, hit's Mass Inigo. He's putting up his horse. Jest yunnuh rest yo' self twell he gits here."

"Ah, that's good—good—"

The thread wore through and the mistress of Normandy, confident that she had done her full duty, stepped over into another world with the same control and dignity with which she had walked in this.

Chapter 43

All that morning Charlotte sat at Tafra's desk and mechanically attended to the details. Penda, use the oldest oak for a coffin—carve the cross on the lid yourself. Seneca, take the coach and fetch Mr. Robert and Miss Emily from the city. Big Jake, attend the people. Hagar—you and Sweet tie bands around the chin and ankles when you have finished washing the body. Cuffee, please keep Nick in the stables.

All the while, through her head crashed the knowledge that now she would forever belong to the Singletons. Tafra had not even tried to live on beyond the day appointed for Inigo to return. She had forgotten her evil bargain. There was now no hope at all. No human power was as strong as the signed document. Lustbader would conquer her as he had done all the other Heronfields Negroes. This situation had been brewing since the day Tafra informed her of her Negro blood. The sound of the big plantation bell, tolling and tolling to the people revitalized by their night with Hagar, tolling up the wide clean Street and over the

302

fields, interrupted this thinking and kept her too busy to give way to her despair for a long time.

The mirror in the drawing-room that had once held her sparkling, love-eager face gave her back a pale forlorn image, but no tears dimmed her eyes and her voice was crisp with authority as she sent Old Ben, dressed in his smartest livery, to hitch the two fastest and fanciest hackneys to Tafra's gilded coach—it had been her wedding present from Nicholas—giving him a large black crepe bow to hang on the door of the empty coach and a basket of notes to deliver to all the plantations within each reach by road. She gave a black bow and a basket of notes to Festus also, and he and his crew set off in the big boat for the river seats and the resort of Edingsville, where Tafra's city and planter friends had gone to escape the summer's malarial fevers. Quash and the jockeys she directed to more distant plantations. Finally she put Cuffee's freedom papers and his guardianship documents in a big envelope and sent them out to the stable with Hercules, bidding him have Cuffee saddle a fast horse and ride West for Inigo.

Then, sighing, her shoulders drooping with discouragement, she rose and took a candle out of the largest sconce, lighted it, and went into the bedroom where Tafra lay in state on her great bed. Charlotte held the candle high and let the beams of light flicker across the lips, giving a semblance of breath and life to the snowy face.

"You failed me. You failed both of us," Charlotte told Tafra with great bitterness in her heart and in her voice. Then she blew out the candle and with firm steps walked out of that room and into her own, which was no longer her own and would never be again.

Chapter 44

Robert met Seneca at the kitchen door of the town house, and from his strained white face Seneca knew that he would not be returning to Normandy with him. However, Seneca sat grimly, his blue gums hidden under his thick lips, and listened to the argument going on in the dining-room.

"But, Mother, Seneca has a coach and two easy horses. Please come with me. People will criticize us if we don't go on out and take charge of things."

"Now, Robert," the cultivated, honeyed tones of Horst Adams broke in, "your mother is quite pale today. Suppose she contracts malaria from going to the plantation? You know how frail she is. I hardly think she could survive a bout of fever."

Seneca clenched his rough, horny fists and beat his knees. Just so did a blacksnake hiss after stinging you good. Nasty snakes; he respected a rattler that at least gave you warning before it struck, or a copperhead that let you pass if you did not molest its privacy, more than the kind that didn't even have venom enough in its fangs to barely irritate you, and that would go out of its way to coil and spring from a dark vine.

"And you, Sonnie, suppose you contracted malaria?" put in a quavering voice that Seneca recognized as Emily's. "That horrid graveyard of the Gaillards is under all those old oaks and the moss is alive with mosquitoes."

"Oh, but Mother, I have to go," Robert said. "Why, Pa could be summoned to court and fined tremendously—"

"Fined?" queried Horst. "For what?"

"Oh, you know that silly law, Horst, that makes it obligatory for a planter to have a white overseer on the place at all times when no adult member of a family is in residence."

"No!" Horst figuratively licked his chops. Seneca groaned. He and Jake and Ben and Festus and Hercules and Cuffee and Mattie and Hagar had tried so hard to run the plantation to Mass Inigo's liking and to show him that they were worthy of his trust in them. Robert must not let these white ones ruin it all for them. Not when the Negroes had done their very best and had one of the biggest stands of young cotton growing green in the fields to welcome their master when he came back to them.

The voices continued.

"Emily, I think you're right about the danger to Robert in going to Normandy in this heat. He looks almost ill now." What a good joke this was on Inigo, Horst was thinking. And Tafra would approve. He'd always enjoyed the old matriarch. This would set Inigo more against Emily than ever!

"Oh, Robert, darling—are you ill?" Emily asked. "Horst, please send Clinch for Doctor Hope—tell him my pulse is far too rapid and that Robert has a fever."

"I must go, Mother." Robert was desperate—a small animal futilely striking at two hungry beasts. "Gran was good to me and Pa will beat me if I do him like this. Besides, Nancy and the Singletons will think we both should be there. Who will attend to things if we don't go?"

"There, there, Robert," Emily said. "Put your head in my lap and let me rub the fever away. What a sweet boy you are! Your Grandmother would be the last person in the world to want you to come to that malarial plantation as ill as you are. Nancy will forgive you. That meddling Charlotte has probably already arranged for the service, and we'll go out there as soon as you feel better. Run tell Seneca to go to Atlantic Street and pick up Cousin Lalla and Cousin Leslie—they love funerals and they'll adore taking charge."

Seneca didn't even rise when Robert, shaken and distraught, pushed wearily into the kitchen. The house servants were lined about the wall, bug-eyed with the awe with which their race met death in any guise.

Robert repeated the directions to the cousins' house. Seneca lifted his round close-cropped head and shot a contemptuous look at the puny young man as he went out into the courtyard.

Back at Normandy the people wandered aimlessly about in the yard and up and down the Street. Nobody seemed to know what to do. Little Nick snuffled and every now and then cried some more as he sprawled over Charlotte's lap and waited the coming of distant relatives and friends who would take charge and arrange the manner of Tafra's funeral.

The hot silence was broken presently as Field Hand Mattie, gaunt and rangy but immaculate in her green calico Sunday dress, started a group of women to singing in tribute to the departed spirit.

Keep uh runnin', keep uh runnin',
Fiah gwine tuh obuhtek you,
Keep uh runnin', keep uh runnin',
Deat' gwine tuh obuhtek you,
Keep uh runnin', keep uh runnin',
Yeddy ole Egyp' duh yowlin'
Way down yonduh een dat lonesome grabeyaa'd.

"Ahooooo, ahooooo, yeddy ole Egyp' duh yowlin',
Ahooooo, ahooooo, yeddy ole Egyp' duh yowlin',
Ahooooo, ahooooo, yeddy ole Egyp' duh yowlin',
Way down yonduh een dat lonesome grabeyaa'd.

"Mmmmmm, mmmmmm, yeddy ole Egyp' duh yowlin',
Mmmmmm, mmmmmm, yeddy ole Egyp' duh yowlin',
Mmmmmm, mmmmmm, yeddy ole Egyp' duh yowlin',
Way down yonduh een dat lonesome grabeyaa'd."

Chapter 45

Jake and Seneca and Old Ben and Festus carried the coffin. The Reverend Phillips of the parish church, sweltering in his full vestments, led the way on foot from the house to the family burying-ground beyond the avenue, where Nicholas lay, on a hummock crowned with oaks, alive this late June afternoon with bird songs and insects and squirrels chattering to each other in excitement over the activity that had been going on all day.

Little Nick walked behind the casket, his legs and arms too long and his feet too big, awkward in the tight-fitting black broadcloth suit that Charlotte and Jenny had made him. Hercules walked a step behind the child. He wore a high silk hat and his black frock coat would have done honor to an ambassador. Next came the relatives, whispering loudly about the absense of Robert and the way Emily had imposed on them. Each family brought flowers from their own gardens arranged lovingly by the mistress and kept in water as long as possible, to try to keep them alive in the desperate heat and dust: white roses, larkspur, baby's breath, seven sister roses, oleanders, ferns, lilies of every color and shape, cape jasmine, altheas, and poppies.

The line of planters and their families was long; the hoop skirts swayed slowly and the bonnets bobbed with the tongues that criticized a mother who would send a seven-year-old child to walk alone as head of one of their oldest families. After the planters came the slaves, hundreds of them, dressed in their best and bearing their offerings of honeysuckle and cockscomb, cosmos, zinnias, and magnolias. Charlotte walked with Mattie and she carried an armful of swamp bay blossoms that looked cool and satiny despite the lingering heat of the day. The people shuffled their feet and swayed their bodies and in low tones—like the humming of many bees—sang to themselves, their lips almost closed:

> "*U-m-h, u-m-h, I hear a mighty moanin',*
> *U-m-h, u-m-h, I hear a mighty moanin',*
> *U-m-h, u-m-h, I hear a mighty moanin',*
> *In some lonesome graveyard.*

> "*Mother, Mother, don't let your daughter condemn yuh,*
> *Mother, Mother, don't let your daughter condemn yuh,*
> *Mother, Mother, don't let your daughter condemn yuh,*
> *In some lonesome graveyard.*

> "*U-m-h, u-m-h, I hear a mighty moanin',*
> *U-m-h, u-m-h, I hear a mighty moanin',*
> *U-m-h, u-m-h, I hear a mighty moanin',*
> *In some lonesome graveyard.*"

When the long perspiring line reached the grilled fence that encircled the remains of past Gaillards, the minister stopped just inside the gate and read the Episcopal burial service. Then gently, gently, the four pairs of strong black arms lowered Tafra down beside her husband.

Hercules pushed Nick forward. He had heretofore carried himself with dignity and dazed quiet but now he drew back.

"No, Hercules, no," he whispered.

"Come on, Nicholas," the minister urged. "You're the head of the family here today."

Charlotte stepped forward to the frantic child who was staring with horror into the great black space at the bottom of which lay his grandmother.

"Come, Nick," Charlotte said calmly as a buzz of disapproval moved over the disgruntled congregation. The minister smiled at her and handed her the shovel. She put it in the child's hands.

"Now," she said. "Just look at me."

And Nicholas Gaillard pushed the shovel into the great pile of waiting earth, filled it, and cast the first dirt into the grave. It echoed thuddily on the coffin and the child burst into wild sobs and clutched Charlotte tightly about the waist.

She pulled him back and then one by one in order of their nearness and right of blood everybody stepped up, took the shovel, and did his part in saying good-by to Tafra. The planters first, then the slaves one by one, moaning and sobbing and screaming, cast their shovelfuls; black and white alike in the same way casting the same earth on Tafra that would one day cover them.

Afterward Harry and Mildred Singleton came over to Charlotte. Mildred was almost literally drenched with perspiration, her blue voile dress stained and rivulets of water pouring down her cheeks. Harry, thin and spare in his broadcloth coat, looked not one whit hotter than he had at the oyster roast in January.

"Pompey is waiting for you in the cart," he said.

"Oh, please let me stay with Nick tonight." She reached out and caught Mildred's arm. "He's all alone and he's so little and frightened."

Harry stared, expecting Mildred to slap the Negro girl's hand roughly away, but Mildred was looking down into the tear-stained face of Nick who could not keep his eyes off Charlotte. He was only seven. She remembered how sweet Hal had been at seven, how she'd adored him.

"Where is your mother, Nick?" she asked very gently.

"I want Charlotte," he began to cry and Mildred knelt down and with her cambric handkerchief dabbed at her own eyes before she kissed the child.

"Of course Charlotte can stay the night," she told him and Nick returned her hot hug very graciously indeed.

"Won't you need her to pack Nancy for White Sulphur?" Harry was incredulous. Besides letting a Negro actually touch her, she was saying pleasantly to Charlotte, "Lula can pack Nancy's things and you can

309

stay here until tomorrow afternoon. We aren't going until Saturday, are we, Mr. Singleton?"

"Thank you, Mrs. Singleton." Charlotte put her arms protectively around Nick and pulled him close to her. Harry Singleton blushed and walked away. Damn it, she was more of a lady than Emily Allston—and he did think it, he did. But she'd have to change now that she belonged irrevocably to Heronfields and he couldn't protect her from Lustbader any more, not and have him keep the other slaves under control.

The Negroes slipped away down the darkling paths. Their voices were uplifted in a hymn and the high wailing notes sent chills through the nerves of the planter folk hurrying to their carriages. The carriage lamps twinkled like fireflies as they passed quickly down the avenue, leaving one small white child with a thousand souls of whom they spoke as "savages"— singing—singing—

> "Moonlight—Starlight,
> O-o-o-o Moonlight,
> Believer, what's de matter?
> John lay de body down!

> "Moonlight—Starlight,
> O-o-o-o Moonlight.

> "John lay de body tuh duh tomb,
> O-o-o-o let me go.
> John lay de body tuh duh tomb,
> John lay de body down!

> "Moonlight—Starlight,
> O-o-o-o Moonlight!"

Chapter 46

After supper Charlotte and Nick walked up and down the avenue under the oaks. The moon came up and hung like a burning paper lantern over the river. At the far wood's edge a pine reached skyward and scraped the polestar with its sharp needles. The Dipper rode high and Libra was low, near the horizon. Tree frogs called ceaselessly, trying to drown out the cheerfully chittering crickets. The evening was full of sound and starlight.

"Sing to me, Charlotte." Nick clung fiercely to her arm.

Low and sweet, she sang, and he cried a little, knowing that tomorrow she would go away from him again and this time for always.

A dark form stole silently into a shadow and stood as motionless as some old pagan god until she had finished her song, then crept out into the moonshine, his queer eyes gleaming like a cat's.

"Miss, unnuh gwine flounder-stickin' ober to de beach. Hit's a fair gran' night. Lemme tek de nung massa 'long."

"I'm afraid he's too tired, Caty."

"Oh, Charlotte, please! I've always wanted to go and Caty never would let me before. Please!"

"Hit mought would ease um, Missy."

"How are you going?"

"Got two mules right here." How had he brought them without her hearing? She would never fathom these people.

After they clumped off she stood and drank in the perfume and peace of Normandy. It was good of Caty to think of helping the funeral night pass quickly. Nick was going to have dull days ahead until Inigo came home.

She started into the house but suddenly stopped dead still. It is always a shock when a verity appears where a dream was planted; to know that what one has accepted as the ultimate unattainable is, for an instant, in one's very lap. She smoothed a stray curl of hair and gracefully lifted a corner of her soft green muslin skirt.

Her light eyes tilted to the balcony, silently saluting a little spirit girl in a stiff gray silk dress who was hurt and utterly bewildered. Just at this moment the woman Charlotte was nervously aware, her weariness forgotten. For this night she was mistress of Normandy! For this one night! But so lonely a mistress, so very lonely!

Her muslin skirt whispered as elegantly as a satin train; her head was poised for a tiara. The front door swung wide as her feet touched the piazza and the shaft of light from the hall spilled out like a golden carpet for her to walk on. Hercules, bearing high a silver-branched candelabra, stepped back and bowed low to her as she came into Inigo's house.

Up the stairs she went, playing her royal role to perfection. With a mere tip of her fingers she pushed into the great drawing-room. Only one candle was burning and the moon, watching through the sheer curtains that billowed in and out with the light breeze, moved a trifle farther in its orbit, casting shadows from the various pieces of furniture. Other selves of themselves brought to life by moonlight, starlight, so that they swayed and dipped like courtiers, welcoming the slender figure now of the same substance as they—shadow!

But Charlotte did not want to be a part of the darkness. She touched a long twisted bit of paper to the one candle and went through the room bringing light and sparkle; annihilating the grotesquerie of self which existed in the semi-light.

She looked with pleasure on the mellow pictures, the gold and blue furniture covers, the polished old tables, the colorful rug. *Tonight they are all mine,* she thought. Then, going over to the music box, she pulled the tiny lever and the tinkling tones of an old waltz brought ghosts into the room. She felt the delicate presence of a young, vivacious Tafra and heard the deep, low laughter of the giant Nicholas. *Ah, they are dancing,* Charlotte thought. But the scrape of imagined feet flying in a mad dance about the room was interrupted by a precise knock on the door.

She pushed back the lever. Her breath came more quickly as she tried to guess who might be standing on the other side of those heavy double doors, ready to order her away from this room, back to the Street where she belonged.

"Come in!"

It was Leon Cavallo!

"Why did you shut off the music?" he asked, advancing and taking one of her icy hands into his strong warm ones before crushing her in an embrace.

"Leon! How did you get here?" For the first time since Tafra's death tears began to rain down her cheeks. Why did he affect her like this? Always making her do the natural thing—the impulsive thing.

"Doctor Hugenin sent me. I only got home yesterday. I'm afraid there's a case of cholera on the Street. I've been trying to make Hagar lay down the law and isolate the old man so it won't spread, but she only sucks her teeth and waves branches in his face."

"You came too late for the funeral?"

"Yes; but I have been watching you in your role as mistress. You play it well. It's a pity that Mr. Inigo is not here to see what a grand lady you can be."

The tears stopped. She shook her head imperiously. Now—he had made her angry. She sat down on one of the sofas and motioned him to sit opposite her in a chair.

"I'm surprised that Hercules let you come up here. How did you find me?"

"I've got a way with Hercules. I had a long talk with him about you. He's very fond of you; he's worried about your going back to Heronfields. Charlotte—is it so terrible? Why didn't you answer any of my letters?"

Coldly she described her days at Heronfields to him. He should have realized that no letter would ever reach her—she had almost decided that he had forgotten her; that he had only been amusing himself with their stolen meetings, their kisses, their sharing of thought and dreams with each other.

"And now you've spoiled my one night as mistress here."

"It's dangerous for you to play-act so much. I intend to bring you back to my earth. You're too prone to walk on moonbeams."

"This room is where I spent my girlhood," she said thoughtfully, wanting him to know all about her; telling him everything, willing him to love her enough to make her forget all the things that had happened to her in this room.

He could not reply to her revelations for a moment. He came over and sat beside her twining his brown fingers in and out of her restless creamy ones; looking on her face as if he found something new, unusual and bewitchingly tender that he had not seen there before.

"Charlotte, this is a magical night, isn't it? Do I seem as far away from my everyday self to you as you do to me?"

She nodded dreamily, answering the pressure of his hands with her own as he continued. "I had wondered at your upbringing that made you so sure of yourself, so ready to assume the place as mistress of this colossal plantation, so dangerously self-controlled. Now that I see you here in this room, I continue to marvel, for your situation is so much more unusual than I had imagined. And you are different, too, from the girl I loved in Charleston."

"How?" She was through talking and now she lay cradled in his arms, limp and submissive, listening to his cultured voice.

"You're much less self-reliant than you appear. I can touch you off with a carefully aimed slight any time I try. A part of you is still remarkably childlike! How have you managed to remain so unspoiled?"

314

"I don't think I understand. I've never had a chance to be spoiled."

"Hercules and Hagar tell me that all the Negroes look on you as a deity of some kind. When you walk down the Street they say it's comparable to the evening stroll of a princess."

"They exaggerate. They are old—they belong to another world entirely."

"Don't be too sure that they don't understand 1849 better than you do."

"Ah, but they are not at Heronfields! I have come to the point there of thinking Lustbader, hating Lustbader, planning how to run away from Lustbader."

"You told me in Charleston you knew something about him that could ruin him completely. Tell me what it is."

"I meant to tell you, till Jonas's trial taught me that we don't stand a chance to accuse him in court if we can't even be sworn in."

"No—Negroes aren't allowed to testify against a white man, but Doctor Hugenin will help me any time."

"Lustbader conducts a black market of stolen goods. Slaves from various plantations bring him all sorts of things that they steal from their masters and he gives them whisky and cocaine and things they seem to crave. Oh, he's a terrible man. The Singletons have no idea how awful he is, for the slaves are afraid to tell on him. Even I'm afraid. He watches every move I make."

"Can you prove this, Charlotte? Or have you just heard about it? If you can prove it, I will bring him to trial."

"Yes—I can prove it. I have written it all down and Chloe has the paper containing the list of things I saw in the hut and the map of the island."

"*You* saw it? How did you get out to the island?"

"With Joe Valiant."

"The runaway? The one advertised for in all the big papers in the country?"

Charlotte nodded. Leon let out his breath in a whistle. What dark ugly things had happened to this girl! Yet she seemed outwardly unchanged from the little girl he had first seen with her hand so confidently in Inigo Gaillard's.

"Hercules tells me that you are going to White Sulphur for several months. When you come back I will be more settled myself and I will get you away from there somehow."

"Chloe is planning to kill him." Charlotte spoke quite matter-of-factly and Leon nodded seriously.

"Or I will. But let's not talk any more about that — This room fascinates me. I don't see how you survived going from such a gilded cage straight into the darkest pocket of a Street I know of on any plantation. I guess because you are so completely unworldly. I've lived abroad for six years but in the few months I've practiced medicine in Charleston and on the plantations, I've come to know more about Negroes and whites than you even dream of—or have tried to know."

"Lately I have tried, Leon. Really I have."

"Only in condemning the white people and being sorry for the Negroes *and* in the way you flaunt your dark flag. Why? You and I are not typical members of our race. That's one reason we are so drawn to each other."

Charlotte closed her eyes. He wondered if she were asleep but when he too became silent she raised his hand to her lips and he could feel her full mouth whisper: *Go on.* He wanted to hush his harsh words to her, to love her completely, to shield her with his body and his soul, to lock her protectively inside his heart and brain. But he must help her open her eyes; she was willing her own destruction in this escape from realities which she was going to be forced to face.

"We are not typical," he told her, putting his arm tighter around her. He stroked her hair and a thrill vibrated and passed electrically through his fingers into her blood. "You expect too much of these people. It will take generations to accomplish what you would pretend they are now. Just teaching them their A B C's can't make Bay Street out of the jungle. And there's no reason why it should. America is a big country. It just happened to be easier to transplant the culture of the

316

Thames than that of the Congo. But someday, if people like you and me will act as guideposts, we can help channel the Congo so that it will enrich this land as fruitfully as the more peaceful-flowing rivers."

"You sound like Jonas," she told him. He sighed deeply.

"I suppose I do. It was a pity that it took his tragedy to wake me up."

"I wish you could have known Miss Tafra." Charlotte suddenly sat up straight, wondering how Tafra would behave if she knew that a Negro man was sitting on her gold sofa. "Let's turn the music box back on." She ran over to the table and a pavan, her song, tinkled out. He followed her, watching an expression of wonder pass over her face.

"We are alone here!" she suddenly said in surprise.

A strange disquiet fell upon them and for a moment they stood looking at each other, each with a tightened throat.

"Some day," Charlotte tried to be light, "you will grow weary of looking at me."

"You are beautiful as in my dreams of you," he told her.

"Will you tire of waiting for me?" she asked.

"Tire of waiting? How little you know of love, Charlotte. The way I love you is always with me like blood or breath. I could never weary of recalling the smallest gesture that is yours. What lovely music! Come —dance with me!"

"Not here—not in here!" She flung herself into his arms.

"Why not?" He pushed her back and searched her eyes.

"Well—I—I—" She was shaking. "I've never danced with a man."

"Then—at least I can be first there." He circled her waist but she stiffened her arms around his neck and lifted her mouth.

"Is it this room?" he asked, thrilling to her, holding her.

"Yes—there are too many ghosts out tonight in the moonlight."

317

Chapter 47

Lustbader himself came for Charlotte the next afternoon. Many of the Normandy slaves were assembled in the front yard to watch her go away. They were very quiet as if expecting something to happen when Charlotte and the gross, red-faced man met.

As Charlotte, at Nick's side, passed through the crowd of Negroes behind Hagar, her turban mitered higher than ever, who cleared the way for them, she heard Senegalese Mattie speaking about her in too loud a whisper.

"Ain't she skinny? But she am so purty."

Charlotte heard or thought she heard the names of Leon and Inigo. But she was always imagining that. And this afternoon it seemed to her that all these slaves were thinking only of what had happened and what was happening to her. And Charlotte in her soft saffron Swiss dress trimmed with black velvet bows walked, as a woman can walk, with greater repose and stateliness the greater the shame and pain in her soul.

With a sinking heart, wretched at the sight of the leering overseer mopping his brow with a bright red bandanna, she heard little Nick begin to cry and tightened her clasp on his fingers.

Lustbader had the sense to hold the horse still while she climbed onto the hot cracked leather seat of the buggy beside him. The feeling of the massed Negroes for the pale girl penetrated even his insensitive hide and he realized that if he so much as spoke loudly

318

to Charlotte they would jump on him and beat him to death.

"Good-by!" Nick called forlornly and Hercules looked sadly at Charlotte and prayed to his God to help and protect her. Charlotte managed somehow to wave cheerily at the people but in her heart a great fear of her future hammered and caused her voice to break as she called a last "Good-by, Nick."

"I know about you and Joe Valiant going to my island," the coarse voice told her as soon as they were out of hearing of the Normandy slaves, just as he might have commented on the intense heat or on the thick clouds building up in the southwest, where storms came from.

She tried not to look at him; to pretend she had not heard. He tapped her clenched hands with the butt of the buggy whip.

"But I know how to make you keep your tongue just like I know how to make that old hag Chloe keep hers." He laughed disagreeably.

Charlotte felt herself drenched with nervous perspiration; her armpits, her legs, her neck became hot fountains. She was breathing so fast that the Swiss ruffles on her dress fluttered like snared birds. But she wouldn't talk. He could not make her answer him, question him.

He didn't seem to care at all. The obvious effect he was having on her was pleasing him enough. Leaning near her face he spat a stream of tobacco juice across her shoulders spraying her ears with the hot liquid.

She shrank farther away from him. Noticing this, he spraddled his knees apart and pressed her painfully against the metal arm of the buggy. Wincing with the hurt to her side, she had to turn back toward him and it was then that she noticed that his face was flushed purple and he was chuckling uncontrollably, a thin trickle of brown saliva running down from the corner of his thick wet lips.

She moaned a little and, hanging over the side of the buggy, she vomited into the sandy road. She almost fell out, so violent was her nausea, but Lustbader closed

319

one of his fat hands over her shoulder and jerked her safely back beside him.

"I ain't fixing to bother you, you fool," he said. "I wouldn't touch your black skin except with my bull-whip. You'll never get me in no trouble. Want me to tell you how I can make you keep quiet about me? Say —answer!"

"Yes," she finally whispered. "How?"

"By beating Joe Valiant's daughter half to death, that's how. That'll learn you and him both. That it will —it will. Then, next fall, you'll accidentally fall in the rice thresher just like poor Gabel did. Right on your face, too—just like poor Gabel!"

"Don't you touch Lula!" She forgot her terror for herself and shook his arm in horror at the idea of his touching the pathetically thin little black body which housed such eager life, scarring the quick little mind so capable of good thinking.

His thick shoulders shook with his laughing. He threw his head back and roared. A lone horseman riding by turned and stared at the spectacle of Harry Singleton's overseer making such a fuss on a public road.

"That was William Myers," Charlotte told Lust-bader.

Lustbader hushed instantly and looked back to see if she was telling the truth. Seeing that she was, and that the boy had stopped and was watching them, he sobered completely, and except for a constant spitting of tobacco juice across her he did not notice Charlotte any more until they turned in at Heronfields. But as she jumped down from the buggy he spat a last mouthful, making sure that a great part of it stained her dress.

Charlotte ran to Chloe's cabin and finding Chloe sitting on the stoop, she threw herself into the black arms, hid her head in the soft, not too clean, lap.

"Hush—hush, baby." Chloe put her dusky face a minute against the copper hair peeping from under the thin summer bonnet. "De peoples is jest been waiting to see yuh all dis blessed day. Set up and smile at dem. Set up and smile."

"Oh, I can't ever smile! I just want to run away to

320

Charleston and let Leon look after me. Oh, Chloe, I can't stay here!"

"Yunnah ain't gots to stay here but dese uns is. Yunnuh am gitting out to de Springs tomorrow and de res' of weuns is gwine stay on right under Lus'bader' nose. Now set up—here dey come!"

Charlotte reluctantly sat up and then immediately she stood up, seeing the tattered Negroes scrambling and shambling back and forth in front of Chloe's cabin. They got in each other's way, cackling, scolding, pushing, shoving. Many of them strayed in and out of the cabin like hungry hounds, some squatted on the floor. All of them were barefoot, most of them were ragged, all smelled of acrid sweat, sour food, and marsh mud. Some fondled her arms and kissed her hands, others touched her dress, but most of them did not come too near.

"Hello," she said to them as they grinned and waved at her. "I've come back," she said to all of them. And they giggled and cried in their mighty effort to understand how this beautiful woman could be one of them.

When they were all gone, Lula came bringing her little brothers and sisters, freshly washed and plaited to show Charlotte how well they were learning to talk. And Charlotte shuddered at Lustbader's threats about Lula.

After Lula left, Charlotte and Chloe sat alone under the stars. Charlotte told Chloe about the good things and the bad things that had happened to her at Normandy and on her drive back here.

"Why did the Negroes want to look at me?" she asked. "Why did they seem so pleased to see me again?"

"Yunnuh and de yaller nigger. Yunnuh and de yaller nigger. Bofe of yuh is a dream to weuns. Chloe gots to see dat yunnuh stays safe, so dat when de yaller nigger ride fuh de las' time, den yunnuh kin tek he place and help dese po' ignunt creeturs know whey to go and what to do."

"But who can help me? Leon says he can—but we both know that he can't."

"Mass Inigo be home soon. And he ain't fuhgit yunnuh, no mo' dan yunnuh has fuhgit him."

"Don't talk about him, Chloe. There's nothing he can do either."

"Anyhow—he be home soon."

Chapter 48

~~~~~~~~~~~~~~~~~~~~~~~~~~~~~~~~~

Inigo was welcomed home by the sight of the sheriff sitting comfortably on the piazza on the joggling board, a glass of cool punch in his hand, listening with great interest as Hercules recounted dramatically and at length the glory of the Gaillards.

Sheriff West was a kindly man, so he had another couple of glasses of punch in order to give Inigo a moment alone at Tafra's graveside, and time to hold little Nick close against his strong chest, before he made him ride into the city to appear in court on the day he was served. The sheriff hoped this promptness would result in a lighter fine. The judge had been prejudiced against Inigo by people who had written indignant letters about the way he had left his plantation at the mercy of hundreds of undisciplined Negroes.

Inigo rode into the city grimly, mounted on Grizzle, a son of old Monarch. He made no apologies to the judge, who lectured him severely on his duties to his class and kind and then placed a whopping fine on him as restitution to the law for the injured feelings that had led to his denunciation. Inigo only asked to see one of the letters. The judge handed him one which he said was an example of the more vitriolic objections, signed by a gentleman and a scholar—from the family of *Bishop* Adams!

Inigo sent for his factor and arranged with him to pay the sum. It was a crippling fine, and with the dry weather ruining his grain, most inopportune for him. But proudly he paid it and then left the courtroom to pay off the man who had brought this unpleasantness on him.

Cuffee had told him on the long way home of the order and system of work that had existed on the plantation. There had been no tale of troublesome ones or lazy ones or drunken ones. Inigo's stewards had served him well and if in paying the fine he had in part paid them in an intangible way, it was not money ill spent.

He laughed mirthlessly as he cantered slowly toward the Battery. Six months ago he would have been shamed beyond bearing at a court summons for negligence toward the law for the protection of his class. These months with Colonel Hampton and Wade had been full months. The nightly conversations, unmixed with any personal animosity, about affairs of state, plus a gradual awareness of the imminent disruption of the Union in which his fortune and his way of life existed, had fallen on fertile soil. Inigo had been ready to grow up and the timeliness of his sojourn away from Normandy had made it possible for him to bring into better focus the lens through which he viewed his life. Even if it only proved that he *could* live without love.

Clinch opened the door of the town house to him and gasped at sight of the travel-worn man.

"Is your mistress at home?" Inigo asked.

"Yassuh, Mass Inigo," stuttered Clinch. "She am in de parlor but—but she have guess'es and she be mighty mad if yunnuh goes in dere befo' yunnuh changes. Dey is special company, not lak weuns Gaillards."

"Thanks. Go and announce me," ordered the master.

"Mass Inigo Gaillard," Clinch announced in fearful tones, and Inigo stepped into the conglomerate Victoria and Louis Quinze salon.

"Good day, Mistress Gaillard." The eyebrow was tilted up and the cynical, rather cruel smile curled the

323

full red lips. "Good day." He bowed to the group of gay crinolined city ladies and tight-coated city gentlemen.

Their mouths were round O's of astonishment—they thought Mr. Gaillard never *never* came to the Battery house. They had heard how uncouth he was, but this man in the doorway was not even clean! They pulled their skirts away from him and one of the men guffawed loudly. Robert had stepped behind a *chinoiserie* screen, but Horst Adams sat and stared as though some dangerous oversized mongrel had pushed across his path.

"I have just come from court," Inigo said slowly.

Horst Adams's tapering fingers crushed into the pink-fringed chair arm.

"I believe," Inigo went on, deadly calm, "I have the honor of facing the person responsible for my being served with a warrant for arrest."

"Oh, do go away, Mr. Gaillard." Emily was furious and frightened, too; she had thought it a great joke to have Inigo arrested, to let him feel her claws.

"But I've just arrived, madame—in time for tea."

Clinch, thinking to avert trouble, had hurried the under butler and they almost ran in with the tea things on enormous silver trays. Inigo sat down on a slender gilt *bergère* and Emily winced at the sight of his dusty boots staining the yellow velvet. However, she pressed her thin lips in a tight line and resignedly began pouring.

The spell broke and light chatter again filled the pale room as Clinch gravely handed the Meissen cups of fragrant topaz liquid to the guests.

Cakes and biscuits and thin waffles smothered the talk for a time, but as the interlude passed when one could relax by stirring a shiny silver spoon into a fragile porcelain cup, Inigo rose to the full height of his six-foot-three and walked over to Horst Adams.

"Sir," he said, "I think I have the honor of thanking you for my arrest." He struck Horst full on the face with his worn, sweaty gauntlet and added, "I will pass down the right side of Broad Street, going east, at seven o'clock tomorrow morning. The clock in the steeple of St. Michael's Church will indicate the hour."

Clinch, with a pleased, proud smile on his face, held the door open for the master as the ladies rushed to assist Emily and hold smelling-salts under her nose.

Chapter 49

Horst Adams swore liberally as he stood in front of his dressing-stand and fastened an elegant stock about his neck. It was just like that oaf of an Inigo Gaillard to challenge him to a duel to be fought in the old manner, without seconds, on a public street. Pistols, too, instead of the rapier at which Horst, in the German tradition, was a master.

He'd underestimated Emily from the first, thinking she was only a shallow, mean little thing without a brain in her head, the perfect instrument to use as a goad against Inigo, who had everything he himself lacked, including sons he could be proud of. And not only did Inigo have his own sons, but he stood as guardian of Leon Cavallo. But now this damned Inigo was going to get even with him for the years of petty irritations he and Emily had caused him.

Yes, Emily had outsmarted him. She'd used him as *her* cat's-paw all the time he had thought *he* was using her. It was easy now to realize that all along she'd planned to humiliate Inigo publicly and *he,* the brainy one, had put his head obediently, nay, willingly, into the pretty noose she'd tied for him, *letting* him be the one to sign *his* name to the warrant!

What a mess, Horst thought, *I've made of my good life ever since that one youthful folly. I have more sense*

*than that whole pack of planters who play their silly
game with horses, who sweat under the summer sun
to bring forth fortunes out of white rice and white cotton cultivated by black muscle and bone. And yet
I've gotten exactly nowhere.*

It had been fun, though—making everybody think
he was having an affair with Emily Gaillard. It had
been like pulling the strings of a marionette to teach
her to say pretty, empty speeches and to cultivate the
wicked folk whom he had manipulated into a coterie
in the center of staid old Charleston—vulgar ones who
dared poke fun at custom and who indulged in all sorts
of vices under the very noses of the rulers of society.

He had adored spending Inigo Gaillard's money
and spoiling the Gaillard town house, as a monstrous,
crude gesture. He had satanically directed Emily in the
undermining of Robert, the scion, and making him un-
fit for the management of a huge estate. Ah, he had re-
venged himself on the dull provincial bores whom he
had been forced to make his life among, they whose
snickers and laughter had forced him to abandon the
only woman who had ever meant anything real.

He felt his chin. Custom demanded that he be
shaved at Hurley's barbershop on Broad Street at the
same time that Inigo would be getting shaved at Minor's.
Inigo would come out on the street first and saunter by
Hurley's. Then Horst must step manfully out and it
would be the first one to draw who would remain upright on the Charleston pavement.

He looked at his gold watch. It was six-thirty. He
pulled the bell rope and his scared servant poked his
head in the door.

"Yassuh?" he asked, terrified lest he have to accompany his strange master.

"Has David Oliver arrived yet, Ball?"

"Nawsuh."

The door knocker struck loudly. Ball scurried to
answer. Horst took one last look at himself in the glass.
Tall and smart, brilliant and appreciative—what a
waste to be buried in this dull hole of a town, what a
waste!

Horst stirred restlessly in the barber's comfortable

chair. Mosquitoes whined and buzzed and sand flies gnawed at his ankles. The heat had intensified and though it was early morning the temperature was the same as it had been at sundown.

"That's all, Mr. Adams," spoke the voice of doom in the person of Mr. Hurley, the barber. "A beautifully shaved cadaver you will make, sir," he almost added, but seeing the worried frown on Mr. Oliver's face, he kindly forbore the last remark.

Horst rose and reached for his broadcloth coat. His pistol bulged in his shirt front. He fixed his beaver at a rakish angle as the whisper went about the shop, "There goes Inigo Gaillard!"

The clock in St. Michael's pointed to seven. Broad Street, from Church to Bay, was as deserted as the opera house on the morning after a concert. Inigo Gaillard loomed immense on the hot brick pavement. His black hair curled tightly under his high beaver hat; his long arms hung loosely at his sides. He walked as though he had no care in all the world save to enjoy the empty street before the day began. Whispering could be heard on all sides and heads surreptitiously peeped over walls and from behind gates.

Horst hesitated in the doorway of Hurley's, then giving a shrug and smiling his usual contemptuous smile, he stepped onto the street.

Inigo was watching the door and the moment Horst stepped out he quickly drew his pistol and took aim. Horst, used to the signal which a swordsman gives, was slower than Inigo and seemed to sway uncertainly. Inigo remained with his weapon pointed at his opponent and Horst, fumbling at his shirt front, brought out the heavy pistol but instead of firing, clumsily dropped it onto the bricks.

Inigo still stood taking a dead aim, and as Horst stooped to retrieve his weapon, Inigo pulled the trigger. A shattering report crashed up and down Broad Street and a shattering scream burst from the heretofore superior mouth of Horst Adams as—coattails flying in the breezeless morning, both hands holding his bleeding rear, he fled howling toward the Bishop's house while loud shaming laughter from the doors of Hurley's and

Minor's shops, filled with delighted spectators, pursued him down the street.

Leon Cavallo turned the corner of Broad Street just as Horst tore down the alley toward the Bishop's wailing and cursing.

And they *call* us *savages,* he thought wryly, not having noticed the shape of Horst's high-bridge nose, or his intelligent, slanting eyes—not even the sensitive, shapely hands duplicated on the soft black leather bag which Leon carried proudly.

Chapter 50

Having completely settled his score with Horst Adams and partially with Emily, Inigo threw himself into the books and accounts of Normandy like a man preparing for some final conflict. There was going to be an explosion, whether he or someone else set it off.

His cotton fields were without flaw, his horses trained to clocklike precision, but at evening he wandered about his womanless house and missed the flowers on his dinner table, the pomander balls in his wardrobe, the lavender scent in his linen sheets, the fragrant potpourri of rose petals and spices in the jar on his desk.

It was hard, after Mississippi, to get the habit of the Low Country again. The sound of the Mississippi had opened his ears to new days, to a fresh vigorous way of life in which a man acted according to his own thinking rather than his father's and grandfather's. Back in his head the idea of moving West for good was beginning to take shape. He felt sure that California would soon be admitted into the Union as a free state, and though Calhoun was orating with every breath to extend the Missouri Compromise, the last golden frontier was a beckoning dream—however remote and hard to reach it might be.

And here at Normandy, where Charlotte had passed six years under the same roof with him, the tug of her enchantment made the ache of remembered sweetness grow keener every day that she was not making his house, his trees, his river alive and magical. Would he ever be able to live without her, in his sterile honor?

One sweltering, lonely June night he leaned far over the rail of the upper balcony and the heat of the night settled in his brain. Hot air, the river like lucent mercury, the soft gold gauze curtains hanging limply at the windows! God—how empty and unbearable all of it was without Charlotte. Even Tafra, for all her years and dominant personality, had not left so much of herself behind in this house or in his heart as had the little slave girl.

Why couldn't he have the courage to go and confide in Harry? They had done untellable things together on their Grand Tour as young gentlemen that had brought them great tolerance of each other. And now there was nobody in the great drawing-room standing like a sword between him and Charlotte.

If he could just be confident that he was right. That he would be happy throwing all this away. These trees that stretched in front of him, sentinels of his family; that river which proudly bore the Gaillard-crested boats to honored places; this house built for him and little Nick. Tomorrow he would go and see her. He must be sure—very sure.

But on the morrow he dillied and he dallied. He added figures and he subtracted totals. He saw where he could afford to buy the Miller property in Mississippi and he made a list of the slaves and goods he would take with him to clear and found a new home place. He did everything imaginable, remaining safely in his office while the day rode close to noon.

He was glad to see the doorknob turn but though he hated to admit it to himself, he was sorry when little Nick entered. *This will force the issue,* he thought. *I can see by his face that he is miserable.*

"Pa, can I come in?"

"Of course, Nick. Where is Sambo?"

"He's sick. Hagar says he's got worms and she gave him some awful medicine last night. He's hollering his head off in the sick house."

"Why aren't you with Cuffee?"

"He's combing Fancy's tail with your best hair comb. It's full of witch stirrups. He says the devil's wife herself rode Fancy last night and the flies are so bad from the stink she left that he made me come in the house to you."

"Did you want anything special, son, or are you just lonesome?"

A tear flickered on the black curly lashes. The babyish mouth turned down. Nick crawled into Inigo's lap.

"When will you get Charlotte for me, Pa? Gran promised me it wouldn't be long. Cuffee said you would get her as soon as he killed the white stag, but he and I have looked and looked and we can't even find anyone who has seen the stag at all. You've been home a whole week. Can't you go over to Heronfields today and see Mr. Singleton?"

"Would you like to go into town and visit your mother?" Inigo countered.

"Oh no, Pa, you know she and Robert don't want me. Did you know that Robert didn't even come to Gran's funeral?"

"Yes—I've heard that from many sources," Inigo replied. That fact had given him much to think on. What an heir he had produced for Normandy! However, through the long nights that he had spent this past solitary week at the plantation he had worked out a scheme to get around leaving Robert the land. He would amass plenty of money, leaving Robert so rich

330

that neither he nor the gentry would think it strange for the family seat to go to a younger son. Robert had played into his hands by not turning up at Tafra's funeral. The planters had thought it unforgivable for Nick to walk alone in the procession, but having appeared publicly as the master of Normandy, he had been regarded as such.

"Pa—you didn't answer me about Charlotte?"

A June bug buzzed into the room. Nick jumped down and he and Inigo rushed about after it until Nick finally imprisoned the iridescent bad-smelling insect in his grubby little fist.

"I think I've got a length of twine in my desk." Inigo opened the top drawer. The only twine was bound around a package. He paled and his hands began to shake but he clumsily untied the knot, loosened the string, and with difficulty helped Nick fasten it to the creature's leg.

"Now turn it loose, Pa. It's my slave and it can't get away."

The big bug zoomed up and hit on the ceiling.

"Take it outdoors. Run with it so that it can fly easily. Then it won't know it's a slave."

"All right— Good-by."

Inigo watched Nick through the window running up and down with his prize. Poor lonely little boy.

He sighed and went back to the open drawer. Tearing the paper off the velvet box he pressed the catch and caught his breath as the long-mended topaz necklace twinkled wickedly—hotly—before his eyes.

Quickly he closed the box and put it back. Then he took up his crop and walked out shouting for somebody to fetch Hero up in less than five minutes or they'd catch it!

As he rode in the dusty heat he felt more deeply than ever the growth that had come to him away from this old way of living. Distance had soothed his confused emotions and gradually under the great tolerance and integrity of Colonel Hampton and Wade he had come to hold a different conception of what the words "duty to class" really meant. Out there Emily had taken her rightful place in his heart—a wash drawing com-

331

pletely obliterated and faded out; Robert existed—that was all; little Nick was his beloved son, while Charlotte's face had always in his dreams shone clear and purely sweet—his heart's desire. To admit these things was so much better than the long wrestling with shadows that had taken up the best years of his maturity. Yet what a fool he was being this minute, deliberately seeking to stir up trouble for himself.

Heronfields appeared deserted. He could hear the long sad work song of the rice laborers trying to keep their bodies moving in the enervating damp heat:

> "John say yunnuh gwine reap whut yuh sow
> Reap whut yuh sow— Reap whut yuh sow.
> Effen yuh sow een de rain
> Gwine reap een de same
> Yunnuh gwinter reap whut yuh sow."

The blinds of the house were all pulled shut and a clang of the brass door knocker brought no shiny black face in answer. *This is the first test,* Inigo thought; *if she is not here I will know that I was not supposed to see her.*

He remounted and cantered slowly back to the Street, just in case. *Not that I want to juggle with the Fates,* he told himself.

The sick house baked under the two o'clock sun. Fretful babies lay in pannikin baskets pulled under a China tree, and five- and six-year-old children sleepily waved palmetto fronds over the heat-rashed faces. Chloe was sitting across on her own porch wearing nothing but a loose shapeless gray thing which might have been called a Mother Hubbard but which barely covered either her pendulous sweating breasts or her swollen thick-veined legs. Her damp cheeks glistened like eggplants and the smoke from her clay pipe circled bluely above her large round head, swathed in a bright purple turban. She recognized Inigo at once. She and Hagar and Tafra used to have great visits before she got too fat to venture beyond a few steps of her own hearth.

She struggled to her feet and called out to him. He reined Hero in and she groaned down the steps and met him at the paling fence.

"Howdy, Mister Inigo."

"Good day, Chloe. Looks like the folks have gone away and left you all by yourself."

"Is too." She cocked one of her small crafty eyes and for a moment scrutinized him carefully. Aware of her purpose Inigo squirmed and mopped his dripping face with a big handkerchief.

"Did Charlotte go with them?" Might as well get it over with. She probably knew as much about him as he did himself. He got down from his horse.

"Um-hum. Been anudder man here yestiddy astin' de same Gawd thing."

"Who—Cuffee?"

"Uh—uh."

He wanted to beat her. She was playing with him. Forcing him to tell her everything.

"Who was he?" he blurted out.

Chloe realized that his temper was rising. No use to rile white folks but just to their limit.

"A doctor man from Chasum. An' he am pyuor crazy fool in love wid Charlotte. A nice boy—gimme some salbe fuh muh veinses and—"

Inigo had to laugh. He was familiar with this kind of game.

"Is she in love with him?"

Chloe took the pipe out from her teeth. She too was finished with the preliminaries.

"Nassuh, Mister Inigo. Dat pretty haid ob hern is a smothered up wid a dream w'ich ain' gwine do nuttin' but hinder her on her way. Dat Charlotte am chasin' wull-o-de-wust lantern w'ich has already brung her on de Gawd's aidge ob 'struction fuh true. An' dere ain' nobody kin tell her nuttin' eben though dere's dis udder steady lantern lightin' de way straight up to de top fuh her."

Inigo's hands gripped the sharp fence spikes. He was conjuring up the pale spirit face before his eyes, and suddenly he could feel her soft flesh bruise under his passionate whip, her delicious body crumple desolately at his feet.

"Is yunnuh seein' a hant?" Chloe leaned forward anxiously.

"What if I am?" Inigo was nettled. He whistled to Hero but Chloe changed her tactics.

"Come closeter," she whispered and as though he were witched Inigo bent his ear close to the cracked old lips.

Chloe told him everything, about Charlotte and the overseer, ending up with a revolting account of the beating Lustbader had administered little Lula Valiant a few days ago for teaching her brother to read. Telling him that he *must* get Charlotte away when she returned in November or terrible things would happen to her.

"Chloe mought be daid den. De yaller nigger knock on my do' las' night and dat's usually a order to go 'long wid um. My heart swole up an' lak tuh bust but I kep' abreathing caze I hatter see yunnuh an' git a promise frum yunnuh to keep dat gal safe. I sont Leon Cavallo to talk wid yunnuh. Ain' he been?"

Inigo shook his head miserably. Oh God, if he'd *just* stayed at home! Here he was all mixed up in another mess already.

"Wal, he be dere."

"Is Mister Harry here? Does he know that the child was whipped?"

"Yas, sir."

"Why don't you tell him these things instead of me? I'm not your master."

Chloe narrowed her eyes and her mouth curled contemptuously.

"He too sof'. He keep shet eye and deef year. Yunnuh hard."

Inigo put his shiny boot toe in the stirrup iron. "Is that all?"

"Naw. One mo' thing. Stop shinin' yo' wull-o-de-wust lantern in dat gal face. Let de doctor hab her." She would not have dared speak thus to Harry Singleton. She would not have cared, either. But this was a good man. No use letting him ruin his life as well as Charlotte's. They were both worth saving.

As he cantered away toward the front Chloe waved her pipe at him.

"Good-by, Massa," she called in her friendliest voice.

334

He nodded curtly but before he went around the corner of the house he turned in his saddle and waved high to her where she sat uncomfortably like a fat heathen idol in a hard Christian chair.

At the front he met Harry Singleton racking up the drive on a lathered sorrel gelding which was fretting and tossing its thick mane in annoyance at the yellow flies and gnats busily intent on eating every piece of flesh off its powerful bones.

"Good afternoon." Harry tried to make his horse stand but it was a physical impossibility for the poor beast. "Come to the house. Braden is eaten up with the flies and gnats. I've just come from Pineville to see if Lustbader is up to any tricks. Mildred and Hal and Nancy are at White Sulphur until November but I'm staying with Brother Joe. That damned Lustbader whipped a girl here so badly last week that Chloe sent for a doctor and now the doctor is prosecuting Lustbader and has unearthed facts which prove that he has not only been unwontedly harsh to my Negroes but is at the bottom of the whole slave market in stolen goods."

"What kind of a market?"

"The slaves meet at a certain place in the city at midnight and turn over any silver or china or linen or jewelry they can filch from their masters. They receive a little money and dope for things that are sold for large sums. Oh yes—and cotton seed. They steal and sell bags of the best cotton seed—probably yours."

"No, not mine." Inigo was irritated and nervous. "My people don't steal and I don't beat them, either. Where's Lustbader now?"

"He's here and I'm on probation. Responsible for his lenient behavior. Let's go in. Pompey's always tucked away in the kitchen with some cool drink mixed for me which he consumes when I don't get here. We won't be welcome because I got here late yesterday and found him dead drunk in the front hall. He had consumed a whole pitcherful of punch by himself."

"I hope he's done the same today. It will break his wind and he won't be such a hard rival for Cuffee to beat in the big race in February." Inigo dismounted for the third time, fixing the reins so that Hero could not

335

step on them, and slapped the gray on the rump. "Run about and eat some of Harry's nice green lawn," he told him lovingly.

"Won't he make off?" Harry called for a stable boy and threw his reins to the dirty little urchin who came running.

"No—my whistle is sweet music to him. He loves me. He'll come."

The house was dark and cool inside. All the blinds were latched so no shaft of hot sunlight could filter through. The matting underfoot was dry and fragrant like sweet grass and the men chose hard cane chairs to sit on instead of the smothering sofas and seats.

After Pompey unsteadily shuffled in with the cool drinks, they sipped quietly for a while and wondered about each other. Inigo broke the silence. *Chloe's right,* he thought desperately, *Harry is soft and callous about his people.*

"You've got to let me have Charlotte back. Nick is like a poor little orphan without her. My house is as dead as a tomb."

Harry was in an unpleasant mood. Inigo was his best friend but he did annoy him with his ideas—thinking that Negroes could run Normandy and be trusted with his whole damned business, and never getting into messes like the one Lustbader had gotten him into.

"What about yourself?"

Inigo blushed and squirmed in his chair. He swallowed his drink in one gulp.

"I want her to raise Nick. It's for his sake that I'm here begging."

"Is it?"

"Oh, God, Harry, be human."

"I am being. I promised on my word of honor to sell her back to your mother in six months but that's off now of course. This whole damn thing was done to keep you in the straight and narrow. I think you'd better stay there."

"Oh, Harry, be a good sport. I'll pay you ten thousand for her."

"I'd pay you ten thousand to beard Mildred in her den if she should happen to disapprove. This is funny.

Yesterday I had the same offer for her from another man."

Inigo wanted at this particular moment to do nothing but die. Life was becoming more unbearable with every sentence.

"All right—who?" His eyes were wretched, his hands blocks of ice, his heart a trip hammer.

"Leon Cavallo—old Holloway's grandson. He buzzed around her the whole time we were in the city last winter. He's written her countless letters which Mildred religiously reads and then destroys. Truly, Inigo," he was serious now, "it would be the salvation of her if I did sell her to Cavallo. She is going to be in bad trouble with Lustbader when she comes back because she's the one who got the information about his stolen goods. But I can see Mildred hit the ceiling if I lowered myself to trade with a Negro. And one who was prosecuting her overseer at that."

"I'll have to stand for Cavallo in court. Will you be very angry with me? I'm his guardian, you know."

"No! I never knew that!"

"Pa admired old J. H. Holloway and he commanded me to discharge my guardianship duties faithfully. Didn't you know that the fact of my being Leon's guardian was the reason Horst hung around Normandy so much, doing his best to pester me and put me in a temper?"

"Gad! I always wondered. Nobody ever believed that he and Emily— But I'd like to get Charlotte away from Heronfields. The girl Lustbader whipped so badly is one whom Charlotte had taught to read. Lustbader found her with some books with Charlotte's name in them. I'm afraid I'll have to have her whipped just for an example when she comes back."

Inigo's arms twitched like bull ropes.

"I'd kill you!" he whispered through clenched teeth.

Harry knew that he meant it. He decided to mollify the issue. The main thing he wanted was to be out of the whole affair. Hal couldn't keep his eyes off the strange girl now that he'd turned nineteen, following her like a sheep all the day before the family left for

337

the Springs. He'd had enough of that girl, a dangerous piece of goods at best. She emanated some quality that had already influenced his slaves. He'd seen them sweeping their yards and washing their clothes twice as often as they used to before she landed in his Street.

Suddenly his thin crane's face lighted up. He slapped his knee with delight.

"I know a way I can hand her over to you—maybe. But at least Mildred won't open her mouth, being stricter in her etiquette than I am."

"Quick—tell me." Inigo gripped his glass and almost shattered it in his excitement. This was it. Harry always finally understood things.

"I'll let you wager me Festus. My patroon, Joe Valiant, ran away last winter. Mildred thinks Festus is your show piece. Wager him against Charlotte on the race between Meteor and Fancy in February and I'll take it!"

"Oh!" Inigo sank back in disappointment. Could he manage until February? Would she be safe here? He had to be with her and test his feelings before he could make up his mind what he must do. "Hell, Harry, I've got to have her sooner."

"Take it or leave it, Inigo. Mildred is in a tizzy over this Lustbader affair. She hates anything that upsets our way of life. She is furious because I'm not at the Springs to dance with her every night. Her letters are one long complaint about how I have spoiled her holiday. Come on—shake hands quick. I might change my mind—or have it changed for me—if we don't seal the bargain properly now. And you'll have to persuade Cavallo to drop his suit against Lustbader or *I* won't agree to this wager."

Inigo snatched the thin fingers and crushed them in his own.

"Agreed—on our honor as gentlemen!" they intoned solemnly in unison, bowing to each other quite as formally as though the whole Low Country were lined up observing their pledge.

"Let's have another drink on it. Pompey—more punch!" Harry handed Inigo a palmetto fan. Inigo plied it so vigorously that a bunch of peacock feathers, in a

338

vase on the marble-topped table by his elbow, flew wildly about as though on the verge of flying straight to heaven.

"I'm definitely going back to Mississippi after the races," he said loudly, but Harry was not through with his bargain.

"Oh—one other thing." Two lines worried down Harry's forehead. Inigo leaned closer. "You'll have to promise me not to come to see Charlotte until after the race. Nancy is too unstable as it is. A whisper of this kind of thing might set her off for good."

A fine daughter-in-law I'm going to have, Inigo thought. *What grandchildren, hers and Robert's! Well, I won't tell Harry but she'll never sit at the head of the Gaillard table at Normandy—or in Mississippi either for that matter. I'm going into town and change my will tomorrow.* Aloud he answered gravely, "Certainly I won't, Harry. But if anyone lays a finger on Charlotte he will have me to settle with. Will you guarantee her safety until the races?"

Harry nodded lazily. It was so damn dull and hot here. Inigo rose; he was ready to go home now. He had done what he could. And he would abide by whatever happened. He flexed his biceps. He was still whole and strong and if he changed as much in the next six months as he had done in the last, who knew what he might not be willing either to reach for or leave alone forever.

There was one more thing he must say to Harry. As they walked down the steps he got it out.

"Harry, I've never had a white overseer. Big Jake runs my plantation to perfection. There isn't a whip on the place except for the mules and horses. I pay the people for work done beyond their 'task'—I offer prizes for cleanliness and gardens and poultry and things like that and you can hear my people singing at all times of the day and night. Why don't you try that system here?"

Harry smiled and shook his head. "Mildred thinks Negroes are all savages. She locks her door every night and prays that she won't be murdered in her bed. I'd rather keep her peaceful than try to change a whole

339

social order. Besides, Lustbader is the best rice man in the whole Low Country. What do I care about his side lines of business?"

"It's coming though, Harry. I learned a lot in Mississippi. We are going to be in a bad way before ten years have passed if we aren't more careful."

"We'll be prepared. While you were away Governor Seabrook recommended the establishment of depots for military stores and instruments of war at strategic points throughout the state; each one to be commanded by a graduate of the Citadel. We can have a good time for another ten years, anyway."

"Suppose I can't persuade Cavallo to drop his charges?"

"Oh, he will if you'll promise to sell Charlotte to him."

Inigo sighed. "Forgive me for not being too pleasant today, Harry. I haven't been happy since I returned to Normandy."

"We forgive you anything, Inigo." Harry squeezed the muscular arm. "I almost hope Fancy beats Meteor in February."

Inigo patted the birdlike hand and whistled for Hero. The gray came trotting briskly.

Inigo smoothed the strong neck and playfully tugged at the blowing mane, whispering a welcome to Hero before he mounted. As he cantered away something inside of himself was leaping about for joy. He had another chance at Charlotte! Cuffee and Fancy were both super-creatures. Charlotte was as good as his right this minute.

Then a sadness came close on the heels of his joy. Festus was going to be terribly hurt. His boats were his life, he had made a profession of them. He was as skilled as any patroon on the rivers. How he would hate a rough white overseer. What a shame that for every happy thing something ugly squatted in the shade beside it.

Chapter 51

White Sulphur Springs
July the Fourth, 1849

Oh Leon,

If I could just hear from you! I know you must have written, but Miss Mildred seems determined that I shall be denied the privilege of letters from anyone. However dear Miss Nancy promises to be on the alert for the postman and having engaged Mr. Hal's assistance in exchange for our silence concerning his interest in a certain lady from the North there is a good chance that at least one of your letters may find its destination.

I try very hard to keep my spirits high and not wonder whether I will be forced to spend next winter (or a succession of winters) at Heronfields, in spite of my wild daydreams and imaginings of escape. Yet I am afraid that I will have no alternative. You will be surprised to hear that the reason for this is Lula Valiant! This is what happened: Lustbader has threatened to harm her if I make a move to expose him or to attempt to run away. He was very horrid about it. He cannot endure Negroes and, thinking of them as less than humans, will delight in torturing me through anyone that is dear to me.

Life goes on here in a most interesting way. Mrs. Singleton has been very kind and affectionate to me, even to the extent of having returned my French hoop and bidding me wear it so I will be quite as elegant as Mrs. Van

Schuyler's free maid, who is a forbidding Negress over six feet tall with a tight knob of oily black hair worn like a crown on her arrogant head.

Here, Mrs. Singleton realizes that even though I *am* a Negro, I have a life. I only hope this attitude will withstand the atmosphere of Heronfields when we return in November. She encourages my participation in various parties and gatherings given by the free Negroes who run this hotel, and through my association with these intelligent, educated people I have come to see how right you were about me.

I was not only unfamiliar with 1849—time itself has lain asleep for me these long seven years. I am dazed and bewildered at the new trends of thought and ideas. Having walked under the delusion that I was the only tragic creature who had eyes to see and deplore the yoke locked across both the minds and the hearts of the black people—going my solitary mournful way wrapped tightly in my own personal affairs, had you not come along and prodded me out of my martyr's role—I fear that my soul had grown very small indeed.

Here at the "White" the great and wealthy of the North and the South are gathered together in the name of fashion—all their requests and fancies quickly and luxuriously indulged by Proprietor Calwell, a man of genuine good will. But while on the surface the social life is full and gay, in reality the Northern visitors and the Southern visitors are lined up against each other, calling names and wearing unsheathed swords beneath their silken manners. War is indeed imminent! Emancipation, like the falling stars we watched together last winter in the city, is blazing down the sky in our direction.

Yet today all the guests, whichever side of the Mason-Dixon Line they came from, together with the free help and the slaves ranging from black to—well, me, danced and clapped and cheered the celebration of this country's freedom. Surely that must mean something. One day *can* light a road, can't it? It must.

I have thought much on the things you and Miss Tafra and Hagar and Chloe have told me and I know now that I have delayed long enough. I *must* declare myself irrevocably a Negro so that I will be able to lead the way for less fortunate Negroes when they are freed. They will listen to me because I have lived among them on their Street, because I too have been whipped; because I can still carry my head high.

Pray for our coming together. I pray constantly to our Lady of Sorrows to keep you in her holy and mighty care. I also love you.

Charlotte.

Leon read this letter for an uncounted time and let his head drop wearily for a moment on the cool worn paper. He had buried his mother yesterday. Now she would be always at peace. Perhaps even gay once more. Yellow fever was raging in Charleston and he was working from dawn to dawn healing and cleaning and giving hope to all who came crying to him here on this neat street. This little letter had borne him along when ordinarily he would have fallen senseless from lack of sleep in any gutter that presented itself.

It had sustained him when Chloe had sent secretly for him and taken him to the filthy cabin where the broken child, Lula Valiant, lay on a bit of damp gray moss on the earthen floor, her woolly head lifted from the ground by a three-pronged bit of stick. It had given him the courage to pick up the unconscious bloody frame and carry it boldly past Lustbader's house, laying it gently in his buggy to fetch it home to his Aunt Julia to ease and attempt to heal. It had sustained him today when he sought the Great Gaillard at Normandy and stood in his office pleading for help.

It had been difficult to maintain his usual calm dignity face to face with the man who had whipped Charlotte. Somehow he managed to keep his hands steady while he unwrapped the grapevine teapot and set it on the mahogany desk. Inigo, watching him with the same critical eye he would have used to inspect a blooded stallion come to serve a thoroughbred mare, gasped with amazement on recognizing the Gaillard crest blazoned in the side of the teapot.

"Where in the world did you get this, Leon?"

"Is it yours, sir?"

"My God, yes! I would have sworn that not a slave on my plantation would steal from me! Who could it have been? Sit down, man, and tell me where you came on this. I'm glad you've come—there's another matter I must talk over with you, also."

At first Leon talked. He explained how he had discovered the black market headquarters and with Charlotte's listed information he had searched for this teapot so that Inigo could have definite enough proof to stand up in court and swear his oath for him against Lustbader.

Then Inigo talked. He explained the wager he had made with Harry Singleton, bound with the promise that he would *not* stand for Leon in court against Lustbader.

"And being your guardian—" he stopped a minute and stared at Leon's clenched brown fists, "I can forbid you making your information public."

"But Charlotte has written it all down for us. I daren't let her come back to Heronfields where that monster lives," he cried desperately.

"I promised Harry Singleton *not* to prosecute," Inigo insisted stubbornly. "Besides, have you considered the fact that if we do hang Lustbader, whom Mr. Singleton seems to find indispensable, he'll never under heaven let either of us get Charlotte?"

There—it was out! They faced each other hostilely like two jealous small boys eager to start with their fists.

"I must prosecute. Lustbader is wicked and cruel to all the Negroes at Heronfields. Doctor Hugenin helped me get an injuction ordering Mr. Singleton to abide at the plantation on probation on account of the brutal way Lustbader beat Lula Valiant. But I can't go further unless you, as my guardian"—God, what bitter words to have to utter!

Inigo made an effort to appease. "Believe me, Leon, I hate Lustbader quite as vehemently as you do, but knowing that Mr. Singleton is unwilling to take upon himself the onerous job of landlordship, the friendly wager is our only chance of securing Charlotte from him."

"But Lustbader might hurt Charlotte."

"Mr. Singleton guarantees her continued safety until the race in February. He's a gentleman. He'll keep his word."

"Lustbader beat one man blind last winter and reported that he fell in the rice thresher. Accidents can't be guaranteed against."

Inigo rubbed his big thumb thoughtfully across the etched crest on the teapot.

"He won't dare move now since you've already got him before the court for cruelty. He's been in jail before."

For a few minutes they sat and each measured the other. Then Leon, with a mighty effort, swallowed his pride.

"Will you sell her to me if Cuffee wins the race?" he blurted out. "She has promised to marry me." He watched with fascination the thumbs grip the pot so hard that they went white.

"Has she?" Inigo asked softly. "Has she?"

Leon understood then that Inigo had no notion of giving Charlotte up. He started to leave without any more words but on impulse he reached out his beautiful brown hand and said, "My teapot, please, Mr. Gaillard."

"Why, it's not your teapot, Leon. Not with the Gaillard marking on it! Can't you read?"

"I have the bill of sale for it, Mr. Gaillard. Surely you can read that."

Both men paled. Leon knew that Inigo was thinking—*this comes of dealing with a man who is not a gentleman.* Let him think what he pleased. Maybe it would make him think of Charlotte as not a lady, either. It might make him not want her so much—see her in a darker light. Realize that a bill of sale was necessary for her, also.

Leon folded Charlotte's letter and opening the lid of the teapot, in front of him on his surgery table, dropped the letter inside for safekeeping. He gave way to a sigh of tenderness and joy that restored him, remembering the softened, grateful, shining look she had given him that enchanted night in the Gaillard drawing-room after Tafra's funeral.

Shall I write her about Lula? Shall I tell her that she is wagered on a horse race? That Inigo Gaillard promised Mr. Singleton that neither he nor I would come to Heronfields to see her until after the race is run in February? Leon asked himself, going over to the window and looking out over the feverish city. It was clear and hot. Above the dirty, ill-lit streets and black roofs stretched the starry sky. Only looking up at the sky did Leon cease to feel how sordid and humiliating his interview with Inigo had been this afternoon compared with the heights to which this dear letter had raised his soul.

Below, he heard the grim grinding of heavy wheels and the mournful cry that told of another death cortege, another yellow fever victim. The crier put all kinds of woes into his mournful chant. In Leon however the cry aroused no fear. On the contrary, his attention never wavered from contemplation of the stars which in their constant luminous brilliance seemed to prove the hope and promise that softened and uplifted him through his great love for Charlotte.

Yes—he would tell her everything. He wanted her to know everything about himself and about what she would be faced with when she left the Springs.

Returning to his chair in the circle of the hot lamplight he dipped his quill pen into a well of ink and wrote a letter to his love.

Chapter 52

━━━━━━━━━━━━━━━━━━━━━━━━━━━━━━━━━━━━

Neither Leon nor Inigo, Chloe nor Cuffee, Mildred Singleton, who now was *really* fond of Charlotte, nor Lula herself, could have foreseen how the news of Lula's beating would act on Charlotte. She hadn't received Leon's letter and it had fallen to Chloe to tell her about Lula and the wager and the men's promises to stay away from her until the race.

Flushed and agitated, she now went about Heronfields dry-eyed, occupied with the most trivial matters, distressing herself endlessly as if not understanding what was expected of her, taking little interest in anything, saying over and over, *It was my fault for teaching her to read. Leon and Inigo should come to see me despite their promises. Can Cuffee win me on Fancy? How humiliating to be won or lost publicly on a horse race!*

Throughout the dreary winter her unhappiness grew. She became thin and dark shadows settled about her enormous tragic eyes.

She was terribly lonely. It was unfortunate that now, when she was ready to like being a Negro, a wall had arisen between her and the slaves. They audibly blamed her for Lula's beating and she didn't dare walk up and down the Street admiring a new-swept yard, or a tuft of gold chrysanthemums, patting a baby's woolen-covered head or urging small boys to wash their scabby ears. The slaves shifted their eyes away from her, muttering about her, making images of her in clay, fighting for strands of her hair or bits of fingernail pairings.

"Sen' her down to de Swamp," they grumbled, "whey de trees is tall an' de moss hang long an' gray; whey night mek she sign an' whey hooch owls on daid limb talk 'bout de daid; whey de blunt-tail moccasin crawl through de grass an' stink de air wid he stench; whey de water is green; whey worms crawl een an' out de groun'; whey de groun' is mud and quicksand; whey de varmint an' de bugs live; sen' her into de land of pizen; whey de yaller fly sting and bring fever; whey death duh live.

"Caze she been on de wharf when Gabel been beat blind; an' she 'sponsible fuh Lula Valiant been beat cripple. An' she warn't here to see tear run down Lula' face and hear de chile axe fuh mercy. Chile mek noise

347

lak a hurted beast but it ain' do no good. No good.

"Charlotte ain' hear all dat; needer de yaller nigger."

Thus the slaves muttered—fawning on Lustbader; willing Charlotte to keep away from their door. Her and the yaller nigger both.

Chapter 53

On the opening night of Race Week in February Mildred Singleton, deciding that it was high time for seventeen-year-old Nancy to find a husband, hoping to force rich Robert Gaillard to declare his intentions, decked Heronfields in smilax and camellias, hired an eight-piece orchestra from the city, had herself fashioned a stunning watered blue silk, had Nancy fitted in a bulky mustard-yellow velvet, and entertained all the young eligibles of the Low Country at a country dance.

Nancy's room spilled over with girls chattering excitedly, eager to start flirtations that might just possibly last all week and bring them pretty presents and sweets from lots of beaux. Ah, Race Week! Tomorrow night the St. Cecilia Ball; Wednesday evening a soiree at the Ravenals' town house; Thursday evening Tobin's comedy, *The Lottery Ticket,* at the Dock Street Theatre; Friday the climax, when engagements might be announced by ducklings magically changed into swans during a whole week of glorious, marvelous attention—the Jockey Club Ball at St. Andrew's Hall!

Negro wenches, under Charlotte's quiet supervision, darted efficiently about pinning curls, adjusting hoops, laughing merrily at the fantastic whims of the visiting girls who were no younger or more intoxicated with the music than they.

From the hall came the rollicking notes of the "Doctor's Bell" and the dancers slid rapidly over the glassy floors in a fast galop. The crinoline skirts rustled down the stairs and were met by tight-trousered boys waiting to whirl them far out in the mad, fast time of the new dance.

Venice and Daphne and Kate followed the white girls and hung over the stair rail, their feet tapping up and down on the top steps, their thrusting little behinds jiggling gaily to the vagabond tune.

Charlotte was glad to be alone with the piles of clocks and shawls and dolmans, bags and baskets—mute representatives of their harum-scarum owners thrown every which way over the massive furniture. She laid a worried hand over her eyes. Everybody expected her to go calmly about her tasks just as though she were not aware of the overseer's cold agate eyes—cat eyes which stalked her purposefully in the house, out of the house; in the morning, in the evening.

She shivered as she remembered Chloe's grim words to her the day she came back from the Springs all aglow with the summer and fall.

"Yunnuh am now up on a wager, done made las' June by Mister Inigo and Mass Harry, on de races in Febbewerry. Chloe been prayin' all summer to ebery bressed Gawd she eber heerd tell un fuh dat Fancy filly to win yunnuh away fum here caze Lus'bader is got a new tongue ob honey fuh de w'ite folks an' a heart ob rock fuh ebery po' nigger in de worl', specially fuh de one done had de gall to teach a black gal to read and write and skiver he islunt. He jest waitin' fuh Mister Inigo to tek out fuh de Wes' an' den he plannin' to burn yunnuh up wid de bullwhup same lak he done po' Lula!"

Leaning against a square overlarge post of Nancy's bed Charlotte let herself be caught in the haunting strains of the "Olga" waltz which drifted sweetly upward. The orchestra blew high trills from their silvery flutes and the violins sobbed swooning notes from their mellow hearts. She could picture the scene downstairs; beneath the red damask hangings, the gilded ceilings, the crystal chandeliers, the waltzing couples would be multiplied in the surrounding mirrors as the murmur of voices rose.

In the garden a dull fiery glow fell from the red Chinese lanterns strung about the long arms of the old oaks, throwing a distant reflection of desire over dark shadows drifting in and out for a breath of air or a kiss or a sworn troth.

A vague odor of perfume lingered in the candlelit room and such a longing possessed Charlotte to become a part of the flaming oneness of love that she had to cling to the bedpost to keep from rushing to the window and calling a name—but which name?—to the winking lanterns, drowning out the haunting waltz tune and the tender laughter stealing up from the garden.

She remembered the dance she had refused to share with Leon in Tafra's drawing-room, and suddenly she reached out to him and leaning lightly on a phantom arm, turned and turned about the room, her head thrown back, her lips parted, her eyes half closed.

The three Negro girls ran in and found her thus whirling in utter abandon. Kate rushed up and shook her roughly to break the strange spell which held her.

"What is it?" Charlotte's eyes opened dazedly—and she knew clearly that something terrible had happened.

Kate looked at Venice and Daphne and they covered their mouths and shook their heads like three puppets worked by one string.

Charlotte, overwrought by her aroused feelings, slapped Kate on the arm.

"Tell me! Tell me this instant!"

"A fight been start. Dat Gaillard boy done knock Mass Hal."

Charlotte was out of the room before Kate had finished speaking. She flew down the stairs. The whole first floor was deadly silent. Dancers stood clenched together, their mouths open, their eyes huge. Butlers gripped trays of refreshments that trembled in their white-gloved hands until the champagne glasses rang together like Christmas bells.

Robert's slightly drunken voice cracked across the room.

"I said I did not like Nancy in that horrid color because it makes her look like a mulatto."

"And I say that that is an insult to my sister and I challenge you to a duel. A horse race, this instant, between whichever horses I see fit to name. Will you accept the challenge?"

"Certainly I accept the challenge. Come outside and we'll decide on the horses. William Myers—will you be my second?"

The boys turned and stamped through the front door. Mrs. Singleton came bustling in and seeing that something was wrong, not realizing that her darling Hal was involved, marched up to the amazed musicians and spoke positively to them. Whereupon the "Hyacinth Do" blared out and the dancers moved on. Manners triumphed over curiosity and the party flowed on as though nothing had happened.

Chapter 54

Charlotte pushed her way through the hall and on to the kitchen. Pompey was disappearing through the back door. She called his name and the rage on his heretofore foolish face made her draw back in alarm.

"Where are you going?"

"Going fuh do monkey business."

"Tell me—I know something has happened. I heard part of it. What is it about?"

"Well—I tell yunnuh. Pompey hate Cuffee fuh true but Pompey want to get even wid Cuffee in Pompey' way and not in no white boy' trick." Pompey was beside himself. His long thin fingers clawed ferociously about the riding-whip he carried.

"What are they going to do? Stop talking so much and tell me." Charlotte was frantic.

"Dem two fool boys—Mr. Robert Gaillard and Mr. Hal—done had an argument 'bout de color of Miss Nancy' dress, and both two been drinking too much of dat claret cup and fust you know dey is slapping one another 'side de head and gitting set to fight a jool."

"A duel! But how does that affect Cuffee?"

"Mr. Hal is challenged Mr. Robert to race dat Fancy filly 'gainst Thundercloud tonight down de old race road. Mr. Robert think Thundercloud de hoss Mass Harry running in de race on Friday but Mass Harry running Meteor against Fancy. Mr. Hal done fool Mr. Robert so Fancy won't be fitten to run in de race. Now dat ain't right, cause me and Cuffee gwine race dat race and hit ain't fair for Mr. Hal to cheat me out of beating Cuffee."

"Are all the men in Charleston?" Charlotte asked.

Pompey nodded and Hal Singleton, flushed and inflamed, stormed into the kitchen.

"Get going, Pompey," he ordered. "Baal will saddle up—come on!" Hal was stocky like his mother. Powerfully built and beautifully co-ordinated, he seemed the perfect picture of a horseman, but Pompey, with the lazy walk and long, loose skinny legs, could outride him ten to one. The two eyed each other angrily for a moment, then Pompey ducked his head and shambled out to do the white Singleton's bidding.

Going to the window to see what was happening Charlotte glimpsed the overseer's eyes shining through the frosty pane at her like peeled Malaga grapes. Lustbader's previous ill-natured cruelty had never sickened her as his new diabolically evil watching silence did.

He had been biding his time for something like

352

this to happen. Waiting to get her in his clutches, to break her like a butterfly at the whipping-post. He had never spoken a word to her in all the three months she had been back here. But wherever she was, indoors or out, he lurked and waited, his thick fingers twitching restlessly on the leathern whip he now wore coiled like a devil's tail at his belt.

If the horse race on which she was wagered was lost through tonight's folly, she would run and hide anywhere to escape the obese, red-faced man with the malevolent hog's eyes and cruel hands.

Lucius, one of the butlers, came in with an empty tray.

"Wash dese glasses," he ordered. "Ain' neber seen younguns drink so much ob claret cup since Jedgment Day."

Two women started dipping the goblets in hot soapy water and handing them to Charlotte to dry. Horrified by the face of nightmare leering in the window she automatically rubbed the warm silver into a sheen, but her eyes were bleak and her mouth trembled to cry. She was hopeless. This was the final blow, this she would never get over. Oh, she must help herself—she must.

"What ail yunnuh, gal?" asked the old butler kindly.

Charlotte told him quickly, her hands gripping the goblet until she almost bent the silver stem. Lucius reached over and gently took it from her.

"Go tell um," he whispered. "Nobody miss yunnuh dis night. Dey is all drunk or in love or mad wid each other. Hurry though, fore Lucius change he mind and tell yunnuh different. I'll inform de obersee' dat yunnuh is staying de night in Miss Nancy room."

Lustbader had followed Pompey to the stable so Charlotte darted with the swiftness of the hunted to the dim path through the woods which had been pointed out to her as a short cut to Normandy. All bird songs had ceased and she heard only the sighing of the pine boughs and the rustly whispering of the palmetto fronds as they scraped together. She tried to mark her way but realized that a tree was no sure landmark.

Suppose she arrived at Normandy and Cuffee was gone to the race track with horses? How would she find her way back to Heronfields? One forgets a tree and wanders in a circle. The forest grew lonelier and more terrifying.

The smell of a forest is different from other smells, thought Charlotte; *more mysterious than the fruity blossom scents of the garden; a smell of earth and moss is damp in the forest, a smell of green frogs and the cool cucumber smell of copperheads.*

She passed into a cleared space and the gray moonlight wanly lighted her path. The stillness kept her heart fluttering. *I am afraid of the forest,* Charlotte moaned to herself, *I am afraid.*

But fear of Lustbader was more powerful in her fast-beating heart than fear of moccasin or copperhead or pouncing cat. This race to be run in two days meant life or death to her. And if Cuffee were to be deprived of this chance as he had been of the opportunity to grapple with the white stag, there was no telling what path his mind, still pervaded by African superstition, might take. "O Mary—Mother—Holy Mary—" she prayed, "let me save us all. Let me get there in time!"

Her feet slithered on the slippery pine needles; she ran swiftly on. Her feet bogged in swampy places; she struggled forward though briers tore her legs and vines caught her hair, unloosing the neatly coiled braids. Her feet moved heavily over plowed fields and more than once she came to the edge of the big road and lay crouching in a ditch while rough boys, their tongues loosed by wine, galloped up and down, riding patrol as though it were a game of "hunt the nigger"; shooting their pistols in the air in order to frighten those who had passes written properly for them so that they too would run and could be hunted down like hares.

Once she had to cross the highroad, and bending low she scuttled across with an alien cunning. Never had she hated the sound of hoofs so much. *They will be the death of my poor heart yet,* she thought. *They have always had a knell-like sound to me.*

It seemed ages since she had left Heronfields and indeed it had taken her almost an hour to travel the short cut to Normandy, her way had been so complicated. Finally she came to the formal garden and slipped through the shrubbery border, through the maze, across the green sward and on to Cuffee's brick house at the head of the Street.

She leaned panting against the door, too spent to knock, and her weight pushed it open. Big Jake was smoking a pipe and Cuffee was kneeling on the hearth helping Nick toast a biscuit when the wild-eyed girl appeared like a spirit on the threshold. Her gray eyes held the terror of the hunted and her bronze hair was matted wildly on her shoulders. Cockleburs clung to her torn skirts and one breast was bleeding through her dress. Cuffee jumped up and caught her roughly in his arms.

"What yunnuh duh do here at dis time of night?" he asked. "Who bother wid yunnuh?" He ran his hand over her tangled hair and touched her cheek softly. Little Nick kissed her hands and pulled up a chair.

Charlotte was speechless in the bright, warm security of the room, but she patted Nick's arm and thirstily gulped the dipper of raw rum which Jake handed her. Cuffee kept smoothing her hair with his rough hands, waiting for her to talk.

The warm rum began to relax her tense, strained muscles and she told them about Robert and Hal's quarrel.

"O-o-o-o, Pa will kill him this time!" Nick said what they were all thinking. " 'Cause you're supposed to be won back to Normandy!"

"Jedus!" whispered Jake, "Mass Inigo gwine tear dat boy to pieces. What us gwine do?"

Cuffee had been standing rigid, with a dull glaze in his eyes. He shook his head in a slow, numbed way, and though he continued stroking Charlotte's hair he seemed to be in the grip of a thing that was too much for him to cope with.

Charlotte began to cry. She had counted on Inigo's being here. Little Nick, looking at the distressed faces about him, remembered that once he had really been master of Normandy and had done what was indicated even though it had been terribly hard. He thought of the things Tafra had told him about his grandfather —the other Nicholas. Years accumulated on him.

"I know what to do," he piped up in his treble voice. The other three, their faces streaked with fire-light, stared at him. "Pa is either at Lee's in Charleston or at the Dock Street Theatre. The whole club was going there tonight to see *The Rivals*."

"Oh, Gawd," Cuffee found his tongue, "why yuh duh ack so? Why yunnuh duh tek Mass Inigo to Charleston and lef' Cuffee and Jake to work wid bad-ness nigger gots no business wid?"

"Hush, Cuffee," Charlotte sat up. "Let's hear what Nick is trying to say."

"Jake, you take Lot and ride to the city. Tell Pa what has happened. It will be morning before he can get here. Cuffee and I will hide Fancy—maybe the boys are not here yet. Charlotte, you hurry back to Heronfields before they catch you out after hornblow without a pass."

"Seneca will take yunnuh back, Charlotte," said Jake. "Dis boy has specified de right way. Unnuh ride to de city and Nick and Cuffee kin take de filly to de swamp."

Cuffee came to life.

"Das right—Nick is sho' de spi'it and image of ole Mass Nicholas. Um say de right words. Unnuh stop dis thing. Come on, Nick, les git Billy fuh yunnuh and Cuffee ride Jason—ole Whalebone kin outrun any of dem boys' hosses." His short legs flew toward the door.

Charlotte and Jake and Nick ran along with him to the stables. Flinging open the door to Fancy's stall they all exclaimed in relief, for the beautiful filly was peacefully munching sweet hay.

"Take her into the swamp before Robert comes. Boy! ain't he going to be mad?" Nick was gleeful. Cuffee quickly threw a halter over the filly's head and jump-ing on her back he had her out of the stall in a minute and they disappeared silently into the trees, leaving not so much as a leaf quivering behind them to show which direction they had taken.

Charlotte felt lightheaded and giddy from the rum and was barely aware of Seneca lifting her into a buggy and Hagar throwing a carriage robe over her weary, chilled body. The approaching sound of Robert's and the Myers boys' horses was pleasantly far away. Seneca, seeing her so worn-out and frail, grimly put one of his huge arms around her and let her heavy head drop back against his shoulder, and when he stopped the horse at a safe distance from the scent range of Lustbader's hounds, he picked her up in his arms and carried her, now sound asleep, noiselessly and gently to Chloe's cabin door.

Chapter 55

It was breakfast time before Inigo and Jake galloped up the avenue of Normandy. Little Nick, sitting disconsolately on the front steps, was nursing a black eye that Robert had given him, trying to make him tell where Fancy was. Inigo sprang lightly from Hero and scooped his son up into his arms. He swore angrily at the discolored bruise on Nick's eye. *Thank God,* he comforted himself, *I've already got my will drawn so that Nick will someday be master here and the keeper of my people.*

He tried to tell Nick how proud he was of him, but at his first kindly word the tears started and Nick was suddenly a very small boy who had done a man's job and was ready to crawl back into his safe babyhood once more.

But Inigo was inadequate to give Nick the mothering that he needed to make him whole again. And unless Harry agreed to act sensibly about this pestiferous boys' quarrel Nick might never have Charlotte's mothering again.

Hercules came down the steps and joined his white men in the yard.

"Cuffee back, Massa," he said. "He' sleep in Fancy stall. Yunnuh best go out and talk wid um. Effen hit hadn't of been fuh dis nung man here, last night would of been a bad time fuh de Gaillards. Hagar say Robert threaten to kill him, but we baby ain' say nary a word, not even w'en dey knock um."

Cuffee woke up as Inigo opened Fancy's door. He was lying, his queer shape curled in a tight ball, right under Fancy's belly and Fancy was standing as carefully as though her own colt lay beneath her.

"Ki!" Cuffee stretched his short crooked legs and grinned up at Inigo sheepishly. Inigo did not answer the greeting. He leaned on the door and hid his broad face in his hands.

"Robert has messed things up good this time, Cuffee. The challenge that Hal made him is already all over Charleston. I am going to Heronfields now to try to straighten out the damned affair, but if Mr. Singleton insists—I'll have to let Robert ride Fancy in the race Thursday."

Cuffee scrambled to his feet and rocked back and forth, clutching his thick body with his arms as if it might of its own volition leap away from him and throttle this huge lump of whiteness standing against the light, breaking his dream in two. The other stag had only torn his face—this one was killing him inside. An unbidden cantation frothed from his thin lips.

"What did you say, Cuffee? Are you putting a spell on me like you did on the stag?" Inigo spoke bitterly. The lines of pain and sorrow in Cuffee's face reproached him too deeply for what he was doing to Nick and Charlotte as well as to Cuffee—his little black brother.

"No—no—Mass Inigo!" Cuffee was desolate. "Yunnuh can't not do thing lak dat. Yunnuh am ruinin' Fancy an' Charlotte an' Nick an' Cuffee jest to ease yo' own self. Charlotte can't not be left wid dat overseer at Heronfields. Hagar tell Cuffee thing whut Chloe tell she. He gwine kill dat li'l gal, 'caze he hate de very scent of her."

"I've already told Mr. Singleton that if harm comes to Charlotte they will have me to deal with."

"How dey gwine deal wid yunnuh in Mississipp'?" Cuffee buried his black face against Fancy's gleaming shoulder, and though Inigo prodded and begged he refused to say another word.

The sight of Cuffee's broad shoulders drooped beside the shining grace of the filly, the sound of the worried little whickers which Fancy gave, almost made him recant his code. He'd better get away before he did something silly and promised Cuffee that he would not let Robert ride Fancy—not for all the honor in the world.

Honor? Honor? Never had one word haunted and sickened a man as that word did him today. It meant sacrificing the little boy he had grown up with. It meant throwing away a woman's love, and his son's happy childhood.

Notwithstanding, he called for Hero and wretchedly rode over to Heronfields to set the seal on the affair.

Harry was waiting for him on the piazza, talking to Lustbader. Inigo looked furiously at the coarse brutish face. His feet twitched to kick the obese wet mouth. He glared so threateningly that Lustbader backed down the steps.

"That was my overseer," Harry told Inigo as the man slipped safely around the house.

"Yes. Where'd you get him from, anyway?"

"Out of the Georgetown jail. I guess that explains his quick hand with the whip. He's quieted down a lot since last summer and the rice crop is huge. The Street has been no trouble at all this winter. You hardly hear a sound from there any more."

Inigo cocked his eyebrow. "I like to hear noise from my Street. It's Negro nature to sing and laugh. They work better when they're happy."

"I wouldn't know about that. Evidently mine work well enough for this man. All I ask is the crop and that is what I get from him."

359

"Show me Meteor." It would be easier to ask a release from Harry in the stables, away from this house —the symbol of gentility.

Harry proudly opened the stall door. Meteor stood at ease in his box, resting his near hind foot and showing the folds of his beautiful muscular neck as he turned his forehead toward them and looked them over with his fine eyes.

"Wade Hampton is going to be badly disappointed at Fancy and Meteor and Lithgow missing their race. It was the main reason he and the Colonel came home from Mississippi this winter." Inigo laid his hand admiringly on the lustrous chestnut flank.

"I don't know what ever possessed Hal to make such a foolish demand of Robert." Harry shook his head.

"If only so many people hadn't heard them quarrel," moaned Inigo.

"Pompey is furious with me." Harry's thin face was sad.

"Everybody is furious with me. Don't you think we could agree between ourselves that our respective honor is still untarnished and give both boys a good horsewhipping?"

"I've spent the whole morning in Mildred's room promising her a diamond necklace if she'll let me do just that. But last winter while you were in Mississippi, Robert did Nancy a trick about not taking her to the St. Cecilia after he had already made the engagement with her, and though I've told Mildred that Emily was at the bottom of that, she says that this is the last time Robert will ever publicly insult one of her children; that she will insist on this race to the point of making a scene at the course if I try to do anything about it. And you know how those Watson women are when they make up their minds!" He smiled weakly. Inigo fought a wave of nausea. He had clung to this straw all the time he was telling Cuffee that nothing could be done. He had convinced himself that Harry, as great a lover of horses as himself, would never let his finest animal make any but the best race possible.

"I'll have to tell Charlotte myself. Will you arrange some way for me to see her?"

"Certainly. Come into the library. I'll send her down. But be sure to lock the door. Lustbader watches her like a cat does a mockingbird. He'll make every effort to eavesdrop."

And so would Mildred if she knew. She would skin him alive if she found out he'd let a wench meet a gentleman in her house. But damn it, a man had to live with himself, didn't he?

Inigo waited impatiently in the library for Charlotte to come to him. He had not said a word to her since she had been sold away from Normandy.

He mustn't think of that. Today he must be controlled, kind, firm. To divert himself he studied the beautiful, unread books which decorated the shelves. Then he kicked a red velvet ottoman from beside the fireplace and knelt down to rub an ancient hound's head that was practically in the ashes.

"You'll burn your brains out, old girl," he whispered.

The hound raised her head, took Inigo's hand into her toothless mouth and caressed it for a moment with her gums, then, giving a great grunt, turned over on her back, legs in the air, to have him rub her stomach.

Inigo obligingly scraped his boot up and down while she beat her tail on the floor in exquisite delight. The sound of the flames dominated the room. He was not ready when the door opened and Charlotte came in softly, but he jumped forward and instinctively caught her in his arms and kissed her over and over.

"It's been so long," he whispered, as she had done the other time. "So long."

She hid her face in his chest, letting the hard thumping of his heart drum through her cheeks. How could she have forgotten the power of his presence? Had she deliberately clouded the section of her brain in which he dwelt in all his fiery splendor?

Neither spoke after Inigo's first flung admission. This thing that was between them had nothing to do with words or principles. It was—and alas, ever would be as long as they both walked the earth.

He buried his face in her bronze hair. She reached up and smoothed the crisp curls at the back of his head.

361

What could she say to him? What can any woman ever say when the man she loves will never be her lover?

His hands explored her loveliness, as though to memorize her body for all time as a blind man might do. She pushed away from him—leaning back on his arms which were not yet convinced that they must let her go. He looked deep into her bottomless gray eyes soft with love and heavy with unshed tears.

"What are you thinking of?" he asked her. But she shook her head. How could she say that he was more beautiful than she remembered, that his black hair shone, and that the comeliness of his body made the fawn broadcloth clothes seem fitted over a god's statue?

He pressed his mouth on her hand and let her go. She gathered up her red wool skirt and moved slowly from him to stand by the fire. Here, away from the magic of his touch, she at last found her tongue.

"How is Nick?"

"Weeping for you. He's found out that Robert and not Cuffee is riding Fancy in the race that was to be your passage back to us at Normandy."

"Oh no!" Charlotte gripped her throat to hold her very pulse from leaping out. "Oh no! I got there in time to save Fancy."

"My son has accepted a challenge to a duel. He must meet it."

At these fatal words an electric shock ran through Charlotte's whole being. Anguish and fear struck like ice in her heart; she felt a dreadful pain as if something were being torn out by the roots inside her and she must surely die of hurting. But the acute agony was immediately followed by a feeling of release from the oppressive necessity of having to choose between two men who loved her.

She sank down, moaning a little, on the velvet ottoman. The red dress and the carmine stool made her sudden pallor more pronounced.

"How can you? How can you?" she whispered loud enough for him to hear, but really to herself. "There are too many tragic things that will happen if you do this to me. Don't you know how revolting my life is? Can't you see how neglected little Nick is? And

362

Cuffee—this will make him lose his sanity entirely. He's been a lost soul all his life—this was his one chance to come into the world of reality."

"We've all been frustrated." Inigo answered her low pleading harshly. "I've suffered as much as you have—more! I hear you have got yourself a lover. I have dreamed only of you."

"If you are talking about Leon Cavallo, I'm going to marry him if freedom comes. Not before. Probably never now because I shall run away if I have to return to this place after the races. There is an overseer—" her voice trailed off into space as she raised her eyes to the window. Inigo followed the direction of her gaze. The round red face was looking through the pane. Inigo strode over and whacked his crop sharply on the glass. Lustbader moved away and was gone.

"He didn't hear," Inigo assured her. "We'll just have to pray that Fancy can manage to win despite Robert."

But Charlotte was staring into the fire. *Oh Leon, Leon,* she was thinking, *forgive me! A moment ago I was ready to throw all your fine love for me into the fire.*

She stood up and turned her back to Inigo, kicking aimlessly at the burning logs with her soft kid slipper. "If that is all you have to say," she told him, "I'll go back upstairs." She should have known there was no use in seeing him. She was such a fool, always believing in him.

"Charlotte!"

She heard him come up to her, and felt his arms go around her shoulders. Her head bowed back against his chest and her hand clutched his jacket; and there they stood, their two spirits utterly spent in the struggle against their love. Leaning on each other, they rested together a moment in bewilderment. For they knew that what was passing between them was not the passage from one emotion to another but a recognition that they themselves, the instruments of emotion, had changed.

Leon would never have sacrificed me, Charlotte was thinking. And Inigo thought, *Ah, how afraid for*

363

her I am, how unhappy for her I am. Little Charlotte with her softness, tenderness, and strength; possessing too much of something ever to be entirely happy. But I have done what I could, though it was never enough. How inadequate I am, how hollow; I resound emptily, even to myself. Each felt that an old self had gone and that from now on life would be lived with a self that was different, and in this change there was something very sad and weary.

"I'll seek you out at the races." Inigo tried to make his voice light but as she moved away from him the inconsolable sorrow in her eyes made him catch his breath in misery. He impulsively reached out to take her in his arms again. Charlotte neither noticed nor saw him. She went away with rapid steps, pausing at the door for an instant as if still struggling with herself, and then ran to the stairs.

"Good-by!" she called back over her shoulder.

Inigo stood in the door and looked with compassion on the slender back, the poised and queenly head. This year had but heightened her great beauty. And with all the ugly things that had buffeted her about, she was still in essence the little white girl who had come to him out of the rain. The little girl who had told him, *And I can dance, too!* Poor bird, she had never had much opportunity for the gaiety that bubbled in her gentle nature. He had never asked her to dance a pavan —she had never worn an egret feather in her hair. But she was steel all right! Steel! She had taken his pronouncement that a Gaillard must defend his honor on Fancy's back, as a great lady might have taken a sentence to the guillotine. And—she was almost at the top of the stairs now—that back would never bend!

Turning to pick up his hat he heard a slight sound in the room behind him. That loathsome fat creature who had looked in the window was bending over the fire replenishing it with pine though it burned overhot already. Suddenly Inigo realized that his and Charlotte's renunciation of each other was not yet a final thing. He'd have to kill that man if he touched one little finger of Charlotte's hand.

Charlotte, hidden in the draperies, watched from a

364

window as Inigo mounted Hero and thundered away. Her heart was bursting with a pain that would never be stilled. She had loved him so. But resolutely she made her vow to make Leon a good wife and to keep him happy forever and forever.

Chapter 56

━━━━━━━━━━━━━━━━━━━━━━━━━━━━━━━━

Thursday, February 7, 1850, was cloudy early in the morning with a chill breeze blowing in from the sea, but as the day wore on the weather cleared, a southerly wind swept away the clouds and gaps of blue welcomed the throng that began to press into the Washington Race Course.

The road from Charleston was a compact, interminable file of vehicles, from chariots to oxcarts. Frequently several carriages drove abreast and the whole road became a maelstrom of dust and curses. Flat bush wagons and sixpenny bonesetters jammed in between four-in-hand landaus. Fast crabs in match carts, elegant stanhopes, stylish cabs, and every type of barouche scraped sorry old hacks drawn by nags that had cheated the trashman, and all were inextricably mixed up and jostled by lumbering omnibuses and thousands of fancy gocarts, wagons, and hackney coaches. The field inside the course was thick with wheels and pedestrians. Every few seconds horsemen galloped by and swarms of scared people rushed madly among the carriages. There was an ever-increasing hubbub of voices and cracking whips. A ray of golden sunlight licked across the course, lighting up the polished harnesses and the varnished coach panels and touching the ladies' dresses, while high up in the dusty radiance the Negro coachmen in all their finery stood like gods beside their great whips. The grandstand and the other buildings, designed by Reichardt, a pupil of the great Shinckle, were covered with flags and gay banners.

Charlotte, driving in with the Singletons, did not want to be here, but she had not been permitted to refuse Mrs. Singleton's kind offer to sit beside her and Nancy in their box rather than wait dully in the retiring-room with the other Negro maids. Listening to the noise of the crowd she felt very sad with a sweet lost sadness. *Oh, God, why must I be forced to witness my own sentence?* thought Charlotte. *If Leon were only with me perhaps I could find some hidden courage and rise above it all. I would not be so silly and let the very sight of Inigo clog up my heart and my eyes. I would embrace Leon—if all these other people weren't here—cling to him and make him look at me with his slanting searching eyes and then I would ease his mind of wondering about me and Inigo. What can Inigo ever matter to me again? I love Leon. I must not think of Inigo; not think of him but forget him, entirely forget him, forever. I can't bear this day!* And she turned away from Nancy, making an effort not to cry, as the chariot drew up with just the proper flourish in front of the ladies' stand.

Mildred Singleton descended pompously in her regalia of lace and fur and ostrich plumes, followed by Nancy, for once dressed suitably in a soft tan broadcloth suit trimmed with mink skins and wearing a rakish cap of the soft fur on her neatly coiled black hair.

"Mamma, wait! Charlotte is not out of the chariot yet!" Nancy called to the broad lace-trimmed back marching ceremoniously through the door held open by a liveried attendant.

Charlotte climbed slowly to the ground and lifting her rustling gold taffeta skirt trailed after them.

The ladies' stand was a handsome saloon which communicated by large windows the whole height of the building from ceiling to floor, with a wide balcony accommodating hundreds of people and commanding a view of the entire course. On either side of the saloon were retiring-rooms and refreshment rooms, and Mildred went in to rearrange her frisette. The retiring-room buzzed with animation as the Negro maids gaily compared their mistresses' snacks and smelling-salts and Eau de Cologne and bundles of extras. A magnificent Turkish carpet covered the room, which was furnished like a grand drawing-room. Massive silver bowls of camellias, narcissi, and winter jasmine added their color and perfume to the crimsons, golds, and other rainbow shades of the silk and velvet hoop skirts circling about.

Charlotte and Nancy made their way out to the box on the balcony of the grandstand. A lady sitting in the box beside theirs shot a glance of curiosity at Charlotte. A hum passed through the group of ladies. "That's the girl who is wagered on the match race between the Gaillard boy and Hal Singleton! That's the one Inigo Gaillard—buzz-buzz-buzz!"

Charlotte flushed scarlet but she pretended that she had not heard, and smoothing down her skirt scanned the brilliant tiers of seats. A sensation she had never experienced before—of hundreds of eyes looking at her shining hair, her moon-white skin—suddenly affected her both pleasantly and unpleasantly.

Today, thanks to her agitation, she was particularly pretty. She struck the curious onlooker by her gentle dignity and beauty combined with a seeming indifference to everything about her. Her gray eyes looked at the crowd without seeking anyone and her delicate ivory hands, ungloved, lay on the red and white covered rail, weaving in and out of a gossamer gauze shawl and unconsciously tearing it into shreds in her nervous excitement.

"Look, there's Miss Emily," said Nancy, "with her dull cousin, Hettie Allston. I guess she's lost without Mr. Adams. He's carried her everywhere for the past few years."

Charlotte looked at Inigo's wife. Emily was wearing a bright-green silk hoop skirt and a fitted black sealskin jacket which hugged her infinitesimal waist. A black fur bonnet perched perkily on her silken curls and she was tossing her head, snubbing two of her former *salon* companions who were laughing at her behind their handkerchiefs.

"Where is Mr. Adams?" Charlotte asked Nancy.

"Papa says Bishop Adams sent him to England to visit some distant cousins for a long time. Even the street boys and flower women began laughing at him after that funny duel with Mr. Inigo."

Mildred had now joined them. "And Emily's wicked little coterie deserted her after Mr. Adams left. She thought she was the smart one but without Horst Adams to direct her witticisms she was just mean. I tried to speak to her a few minutes ago but she cut me cold."

"She's mad about the race," Nancy told her mother. "I'm not mad, are you, Mamma?"

"Certainly not," Mildred snorted. "A duel is supposed to end a quarrel, *whatever* it might be about."

Behind the Singletons, old Mrs. Legare sat with Mrs. Swinton. They were looking at Charlotte and saying something, smiling to each other wickedly.

They are talking about me, thought Charlotte, *and no doubt having me in bed with Inigo by night. They needn't trouble themselves; if only they knew how little I am concerned with any of them.*

The balcony of the grandstand had steps down to the course so that the gentlemen could come and go at will. Nancy was tempted to run and seek Robert and make things up with him. She wished she were one of the vulgar females from the citizens' stand who could promenade and flirt and bet and even rush to the rails when excitement ran high. It was so dull to always have to be a lady! All she could do today was either sit here with Charlotte, who wouldn't talk at all, or parade around and socialize with other girls and their bossy mammas. Hearing Charlotte sigh disconsolately, she thought, *Poor Charlotte! I guess she hates being wagered on a horse race. But I wouldn't, I'd like it. I'm responsible for the duel, though. I'm important, too!*

She patted her neat hair and adjusted the velvet bow at her thick brown neck, suddenly admiring herself very much.

Inigo was in the jockeys' quarters in the basement of the grandstand talking to Mr. Rose, president of the South Carolina Jockey Club. Nick was watching the jockeys weigh in, in the new chair that had just arrived from England.

"Nick," Inigo called, "come over here and speak to Mr. Rose."

Nick importantly shook the proffered hand and made a quick bow.

"Inigo," Mr. Rose turned from the little boy, "the officials have definitely decided that since this match race is a personal challenge it will have to be four mile heats instead of three."

"But, Arthur, this is my filly's first race. It isn't fair to push a young filly that hard."

"I think this whole business is unfair. I intend to try at our next business meeting to have a ruling made against such hot-headed highhandedness on our course ever happening again."

Inigo shrugged. He was in no mood for a scolding from the club president or from the Lord God Himself today.

"Go out and tell Cuffee that the race will be four mile heats," he told Nick shortly. "They've made up their minds that this duel will indeed be to the death of somebody."

Nick looked up at his father and a lump swelled in his throat. His father looked like big Samson in the Bible that his Gran used to read about. The one who didn't have any eyes and who was brought into a big temple and mocked and teased by the wicked unfeeling heathens.

His father was the handsomest man in the world, even if his eyes did look so vacant and unseeing. Today his black hair was longer than usual and curled thickly over the lace ruffle that softened the powerful lines of his muscular neck. His heavy black brows were drawn worriedly together and his broad red mouth looked as if it might start trembling any minute. His pale-blue broadcloth coat stretched tightly across his magnificent shoulders and was caught about his waist with a buff satin sash and long fawn-colored trousers followed

369

the lines of his strong shapely legs. There wasn't another man anywhere half as big and good-looking. Not on the whole course!

Nick thought that this was the worst day he had ever lived. His father was so sad; Charlotte was going to be lost to them both; Cuffee was acting like a dead man; Robert was scared silly. Even if he did hate Robert he had to feel sorry for him just a little bit.

"Wait just a minute, Nick." Mr. Rose beckoned to him and he came back up to the two men. "Do you know that part in our Jockey Club Handbook that tells how a sportsman should behave on our course? I'd like to have you say it for your father's benefit."

"Oh, yes, sir!" Nick, oblivious of Inigo's discomfiture quoted glibly in his childish voice, "It should be borne in mind that no Carolina Turfman prepares his horses and brings them to the starting-post as a business, but only as a recreation. Horses are bred and trained in South Carolina only, by those who keep thoroughbred stock on their plantations, as a pastime and for the promotion of a good breed of horses."

"Go on and tell Cuffee," Inigo said crossly.

Nick heard Mr. Rose say as he slipped out, "Don't fret so, Inigo, maybe something will turn up to make things not so serious as you fear. Robert might go all right. The Singleton boy is in as much of a funk as he is, and Harry Singleton says he's going to horsewhip him as soon as the race is over."

Nick ran up the sandy, oval track. This track was exactly one mile around and a light rail enclosed it on both sides. He had to dodge the horses coming up for the first race as the judges from their stand at the right of the grandstand gave the warning notice that the Jockey Club Purse was about to start. Wade Hampton passed and waved at him, following his treasured Lithgow gloatingly with his eyes as he stepped onto the course. Nick hurried away as a busy movement commenced in every direction. Groups formed on all sides, horsemen rode from place to place and people swarmed about to make their bets or to get good positions. The crowd was immense. Bookies stood about where gamblers and gentlemen could find them easily—back from the hastening throng pressing up to the rail. The stewards took their places, the judges their posts and arranged their watches. The horses were led to the starting line and the card read:

> N. Green's b.h. Free Trade, 5 yrs. by Monmouth Eclipse
> Wade Hampton's b.c. Lithgow, 3 yrs. own brother to Millwood
> J. Harrison's ch. m. Rosa Lee, aged, by Boston out of imp. Emily
> R. C. Richardson's ch. c. Paragon by Bertrand Jr. out of Zoe

Two three-mile heats!

Nick reached the stables and jostled his way through black water boys and rubdown boys and feed boys to Inigo's stalls. He peeped into the first one. Cuffee was squatting on the floor rubbing Fancy's hoofs, moaning a sorrowful chant to her. Cuffee had on his jockey suit—the Gaillard colors, red silk jacket with white sleeves and a black satin cap.

"What you got those things on for?" Nick asked bluntly.

Cuffee didn't look up and replied sullenly.

"Yunnuh go fum here. Cuffee in no mood to mess wid nobody—leastways Mass Inigo. Done took Charlotte and give she to dem Singleton folks and now fixing to give Cuffee filly to um."

Nick paid him no attention and sat down on the ground outside the next box wondering where Sambo had got to.

A hard thump against the door battered his back. Cuffee stuck his head over Fancy's bottom door.

"Git 'way fum dere. Set by dis do'."

"Why?" Nick stood up and, hands in pockets, stared curiously at the shut doors. "If you'd open the top door maybe the horse wouldn't act so. Who is in there, anyway?"

"Edisto. An' he in de headingest bad humor he ever been in. T'rashing and knocking. Unnuh open de top an' he kin move de latch wid he teet'. Unnuh scairt to tek no chancet on um gitting out. He a killer hoss fuh true."

"When is his race?"

"Not today, bress Jedus. He'd kill de udder horses in dis humor."

"What's made him so mad?"

"Mister Green' mare, Glossy, smell too good to um. He tryin' to git at um. Women sho does cause all dis worl' troubles."

"You aren't mad at me any more, are you, Cuffee?"

For an instant a smile touched the sad black face.

"Ki, chile, when Cuffee ever been mad wid he li'l colt?"

Satisfied, Nick sat by Fancy's door and Cuffee resumed his heartbroken lay.

Shouts and screams finally announced the end of the first heat of the purse. Sambo ran up and squatted by Nick through the half-hour rest period and they talked about Cuffee and Robert and Fancy and Charlotte as though they were old, old men. Hercules appeared, splendid in his high silk beaver hat and voluminous frock coat, and took out the massive gold watch which hung on a thick gold chain.

"Hit's 'leven o'clock. Time fuh yunnuh to eat yo' dinner fo' de race start," he announced gravely to Nick. He kept up the standard of the family even when they sat on the ground outside of a horse stall. "Come on wid me to de coach. I gots lunch all fixed."

After lunch he took the two boys to explore booths and bazaars in the citizens' stand, where admission was free. He wanted to make Nick as happy as a child should be at a gay place like this. The littlest Gaillard had been raised too serious-like; he'd never had the proper fun he should have had.

Tents and stalls for card-playing, eating, and fortunetelling bloomed like exotic flowers on the sandy sides of the track. Black faces and white faces and tan faces peeped and peered and exclaimed in wonder at the calf with two tails and eight legs. They went into a tent where a dark man with a handlebar mustache was proclaiming a grand exhibition of a wonderful dog just arrived from Europe who could play cards, cast accounts, spell, divide, add, and multiply; who could select the handsomest lady in the room (much coarse jesting greeted this) or the gentleman most capable of attaining this lady's affections (nudgings and guffaws rippled through the audience), or answer any question proposed by the company!

Hercules soon dragged the children away from this bit of chicanery and took them to see the painting by Correggio, hung in a clean booth, representing "Mercury Instructing Cupid to Read in The Presence of a Naked Venus." Sambo sucked his thumb and went to sleep standing up, but Nick gazed at the round pink-tipped breasts of the undressed lady and sighed. He did want a mother so bad! Today was the day he was supposed to have gotten Charlotte back. He doubled up his fists. When he grew up he was going to kill Robert. He hadn't decided just how, but he was—he was! And then he was going to Mississippi. He didn't like living here any more.

They passed by the huge tent where Robinson and Eldred's Circus was playing after the races, with the great English clown, Mr. Wallet, and stylish equestrian riders and posturers—Herr Franz and his children and Master James and Mamselle Henrietta Robinson and their horse company.

Sambo begged to be allowed to peep for a moment but the wild cheering of the milling crowd announced the end of the first race and Nick ran from Sambo and Hercules back to the stables to see what had happened.

Wade Hampton's colored jockey, Fed, trotted by on Lithgow with an expression shinier than his own sweaty face. His blue jacket with its red sleeves was dusty and he'd lost his blue cap—but there was no need for Nick to ask who'd won. Lithgow danced away to the Hampton stalls, shaking her head and switching her tail as though she knew better than anyone how sweet is the taste of victory.

And now the warning drums ruffled out. To Cuffee and Inigo and Nick and Charlotte it was the sound of doom. The moment had come!

The bookies were deluged with bets on Robert and Hal. Folks who knew Inigo bet on Robert and folks who knew Robert bet on Hal. The crowd was less noisy and riotous than it had been earlier. The emotions which gripped Inigo and Cuffee and Charlotte and the fear which possessed Robert were so strong as to settle like a miasma on the holiday spirits. This was more than a race, this was a duel, a spectacle on which men through the ages had looked with awe and reverence, one man pitting his skill and force against another man's, and the stronger one the right one! Different civilizations have worshiped different gods: the body; the mind; the soul; but to a Southern gentleman of the mid-nineteenth century, his honor was the god. Personal honor was the bright star he followed, and to it everything was subordinate—family, possessions, even political beliefs. That was why this match race was permitted on a public track; it was considered more important than a planned race. But to Inigo today the star seemed dull and the super-importance of the group ideal an unhappy lane to traverse.

Inigo and Robert came out of the weighing-room as the Singletons went in. They walked slowly, not speaking to each other, back to the Gaillard stalls. Inigo opened the door of Fancy's box.

"Bring her out, Cuffee," he said in an unusually quiet voice.

There was no reply.

Robert stood slim and tall in Inigo's colors. The red silk of the jacket did not suit his pale coloring and the white of the sleeves matched his twitching face. His hands were trembling on his crop.

"Put down that damned whip," Inigo said furiously. Robert tucked the whip in his belt.

"Damn it," Inigo roared, "bring that girl on out." Edisto, in his stall, neighed and pawed angrily.

"Bring she yo' own self," was Cuffee's answer. Inigo went into the stall. He took one look at Cuffee's tear-stained face; then he picked up Fancy's reins and when

374

she leaned over and began to nuzzle his shoulder he had to swallow hard.

"Poor little girl," he whispered, smoothing her shining coat, "poor baby." *Poor little Charlotte. Poor little love!*

He led Fancy out.

As soon as she was on the outside she became a different creature. This was her first race! This was the day for which she had been foaled! She had never seen so many people or heard so much noise. Except for the Christmas Day she had first been ridden, she had known only her comfortable airy stall or the fast, sandy track at Normandy. Nobody but Cuffee had ever sat on her back.

Inigo held her firm while Robert mounted. She immediately began to back her ears and paw the ground. What strange, trembly knee was this pressed into her side? She sidestepped and kicked a water bucket which a black boy was fetching, high in the air. Inigo stroked her neck and led her, dancing and ghosting, up to the starting-post as the five-minute warning sounded.

Harry Singleton, in a brown coat and tight buff trousers that made his long thin legs look more like broomsticks than ever, walked loosely up leading his big, brown Meteor, ninth in direct tail male from the Godolphin Arabian. He was frowning up at Hal as he met Inigo and Fancy at the post.

The starting-post was included in the picket fence, so the curious thousands were shut away entirely.

Fancy and Meteor were snorting and pulling at their bits, objecting violently to their riders. Meteor backed into Fancy and Fancy lunged out at him with her quick vicious back legs. Inigo and Harry held calmly onto the reins and tipped their hats to each other. The judge stood up in his stand. Inigo and Harry loosed the reins and stepped back off the course. Old Colonel Hampton was waiting to take Inigo by the arms and he held to him tightly as they listened for the judge to give the signal to start.

Cuffee sobbed in Fancy's stall. Leon stood unnoticed by the course rail and gripped it with his hands until his knuckles shone like tan marbles. Charlotte leaned over the rail of the balcony and prayed. Emily chattered to a visiting gentleman from "off" who told lovely naughty stories. Nick and Sambo crouched in a good position by the fence. Hercules and Ben stood in their frock coats with the importance of two dignitaries speaking Voodoo words to their own gods. While Inigo's world whirled and churned as though loosed from its pole within his heart. He couldn't believe that this was happening—it must be a bad dream.

The pistol sounded in the air. Fancy reared and plunged. Meteor got off quickly and was pulled in hard by Hal. Robert jerked the crop from his belt and laid it on Fancy. Fancy leaped forward in such a burst of speed that Robert was almost thrown off. Meteor was about three lengths in the clear but Fancy came on. Robert now made free use of the whip and tried to draw over to the inside of the course. When the horses approached the commencement of the stretch the space between them was about a full length and a half. Hal was not using a whip but maintained a hard steady pull under which Meteor seemed accustomed to run. Robert couldn't collect himself from his bad start and though Fancy was lasting well he continued to lash her with his whip. He looked like a disjointed scarecrow, for his right hand was disengaged from the bridle and his arm flailed up and down in the air.

On the balcony of the grandstand Nancy turned in bewilderment to Charlotte.

"What in the world is wrong with Robert? He always had a fine seat on a horse."

"He's frightened to death, Miss Nancy. He's afraid of the horse and his father both," Charlotte answered calmly while her fingers completed demolishing the shawl brought for Nancy's hair.

"My God!" breathed Wade Hampton to Billy Myers. "Look at Robert!"

Fancy made an effort to get close to Meteor but gained only a few feet and Meteor came in two lengths in the clear. Seven minutes, thirty-seven seconds! And the odds on Meteor went up to 6–1!

The field became more animated than before.

This was going to be a pushover for Meteor. The Gaillard horse was licked from the start. The bookies were swamped and the citizens' stand resounded with catcalls and the merry quips of tipplers and rough women who throve on the hysterical ebb and flow of excitement in the crowd, as with each heat a new climax was feverishly reached.

Nick ran around to look at Fancy.

Blood trickled off her back. She was covered in sweat, and bloody foam blew from her mouth. Cuffee miserably bathed her off and dabbed medicine on the hurt places before throwing on her blanket to let her rest out the thirty minutes.

Inigo dragged Robert into the adjoining stall. He was talking to his oldest son in low tones. Nick, standing outside listening, felt chills run down his spine, the voice was so full of deadly contempt and hatred. Inigo told Robert exactly how to ride Fancy in the next heat and a grating sound was heard as he ground his big heel into the bloody whip. In the stall on the other side, Edisto whistled and kicked at the wall dividing him from the human whom he hated.

Too soon the drums ruffled the end of the rest period. Inigo led Fancy out and again she tried to get away from the cruel pull on her torn mouth. The spectators in the citizens' stand stamped and swayed, anxious to be caught up again in their orgiastic absorption. Horses were neighing in their harness, tent canvases flapped, and a crowd of pedestrians rushed to get places along the fence. As the signal to start was given, silence fell as though everyone was holding his breath.

Robert, bereft of his whip, his ears ringing with Inigo's instructions, just held on, and Fancy leaped out neck and neck with Meteor. Hal forced the race and the horses came up the quarter stretch with a speed that outstripped the blood boiling in the veins of the stimulated people.

I suppose it has to be like this, Charlotte thought. And staring at the powdered and primped faces, feeling the warm air heated by the crowd, she began to pass little by little into a state of resignation. She forgot

377

where she was and what was going on and why this race was being run. The strangest fancies disconnectedly passed through her mind. The idea occurred to her of jumping over the edge of the boxes onto the ground and running and throwing herself under Fancy's madly pounding hoofs as she rounded the curve in the track; then she wished to throw the torn shawl into Mildred Singleton's satisfied face; then just to stand where she was and scream at the top of her lungs.

The horses thundered over the track and their legs seemed to grow longer as they raced and then looked delicate as seaweed when they flashed around to the other side. Hal kept a close watch on Robert while he pushed Meteor to his utmost. Robert pressed close to Hal, trying to run Fancy up against Meteor and break his stride. Fancy was running freely and Inigo began to breathe more evenly when Wade Hampton struck his shoulder.

"See Fancy, Inigo! Look at Robert—by heaven, on the inside!" Some strain of courage was being born in Robert and he had cut Fancy over to the left side of Meteor in a desperate effort to pass. Suddenly Hal pulled Meteor sharply over and forced Fancy against one of the poles that marked the quarter. At this, so close were the two boys, Robert wildly raised his fist and struck Hal full in the face. Fancy plunged ahead as Hal reeled in the saddle and Meteor broke his gallop. Hal immediately collected Meteor and he came level with Fancy and again neck and neck, nose to nose, almost stride for stride, they flashed over the finish line together. The time—8 minutes!

The crowd was wild. Bravo, Fancy! Bravo, Meteor! There was a flood tide of applause and the women in the balcony waved their fans and their shawls.

Charlotte crumpled limply against her chair back and gave herself up to grief for Fancy. Fancy had tried so hard, had given everything she had, and yet she couldn't win. She couldn't because fate had cruelly placed an extra weight on the scales against her. *Like me,* Charlotte thought, *she can struggle until she drops defeated, all her capabilities exhausted, her light gone out.*

Staring down on the kaleidoscope of faces she suddenly picked out Leon, handsome and sturdy in his faultlessly tailored fawn broadcloth suit, looking up at her. She waved listlessly at him and he pushed his way over until he stood under the balcony.

She leaned over and he called up to her.

"I'll wait for you by the door after the race. I have something I must tell you."

She nodded her head and he hurried away before anybody could have a chance to order him off. Negroes, excepting personal servants, were not allowed near the grandstand.

Betting became more inflamed as the odds changed—4–1 in favor of Meteor. The citizens heaped abuse on both boys, who were behaving like street urchins, the while they hugely enjoyed the anger and temper which lent added zest to the race.

Robert rode to the stalls on the still struggling Fancy and dismounted as Quash caught her head. Hal rushed up from the Singletons' row and jumped on Robert the minute he hit the ground. He swung his fist and smashed it into Robert's face. Blood gushed from Robert's nose and he hung in the air a split second before he went down. He simply folded down. Slowly the upper part of his body crumpled forward until he was lying in the dirt, with sand in his mouth and nose and hair. He just wanted to stay there—where there were no horses, no Hals, no Pas. Passionately he wanted to lie there, but some drop of Gaillard blood way down in the pit of his stomach dragged him up. Futilely he hit out at Hal but again Hal's hard knuckles cracked solidly at his head. Once more he went down and once more he dragged himself up as the cry, "A fight! A fight!" emptied the citizens' stand and the gentlemen all rushed down the steps from the balcony of the grandstand.

By now Robert was beyond fear; he was so dazed that he retained no power to feel pain or shock and, in a haze that had two fists whirling around his head like pinwheels, he started to fight back. He was mad now and he wanted to kill Hal no less than Hal was trying to kill him. Hal gave ground and Robert,

lunging forward, got him hard behind the ear and Hal
went down. Robert kicked him where he lay and then
Hal got up and beat Robert some more. They came
together and embraced as closely as lovers. Hal
clenched Robert about his waist and with a twist of his
right arm threw him in the dirt.

Then Inigo thundered up. Trailing him were
Wade Hampton and Harry Singleton and Billy Myers
and Mr. Rose and other Jockey Club members with
ruffled stocks and smooth fawn trousers.

"By heaven, Inigo Gaillard, put a stop to this outrageous business," cried Mr. Rose as Robert reached up
and caught Hal by the ankle and, twisting it, pulled
him down flat on top of him. The boys rolled and grappled each other on the ground as the crowd closed in,
eyes battle-lit and ready for the kill. Suddenly a flame
of hot emotion shot through them as Inigo and Harry
came to their senses and each grabbed a son. Harry
laid his crop on Hal's shoulders and Inigo shook Robert like a limp puppy.

"Stop it, I say!" an enraged cultured voice
boomed out.

Inigo and Harry stopped and glared angrily as
Colonel Hampton, his face scarlet, pushed into the cen-
ter of the group and placed himself between Inigo and
Harry and their sons.

"Honor be damned!" he cried. "Put a proper
jockey on those two fine horses and give this crowd a
race." Yells and whistles and cheers met this bit of
rank heresy. Colonel Hampton continued, "Send these
whelps back to their nurseries and by gad, if such a
disgrace as this occurs again on this course, I'll load
up every horse at Millwood and move them to Mississippi. Now, Robert, you and Hal shake hands—this
duel's fought. You're both wounded and—the rest period is almost over."

The boys sullenly shook hands. The crowd dis-
persed to discuss what had happened and to make new
bets, amid a deafening fugue of rumor that reached
even into the ladies' stand and streamed like hope over
Charlotte's despairing heart. Another chance, the rumor said—there's still time for another chance.

Inigo stood paralyzed, his mouth open and his arms stretched stiffly out. Old Ben and Hercules, watching him, quickly made strange signs with their rheumatic fingers to ward off evil spirits.

For in Inigo's brain the whirling, disordered compass of his world suddenly found its lodestone and came to a steady, strong forward current— The heresy that had issued from the most honored gentleman in the state had caused Inigo's dark face to flush and a light to kindle in the black eyes; had caused the hard, tight look about his mouth to fall away, leaving in its place a smile that had been there nineteen years before. And Inigo knew that his strength had returned, that the hollow places had filled, that he was ready to plunge into the river.

He strained at the pillars of the temple and heard them crack.

"Honor be damned!" he yelled at the top of his giant lungs. He again grabbed Robert by the scruff of his neck and shook him. "Honor be damned!" he shouted toward the grandstand—to Emily, pale and contemptuous on the balcony. "Honor be damned!" he bellowed to the citizens' stand and to the whole milling, wind-whipped throng who instinctively moved back, away from him. Was the great Gaillard suddenly gone mad? Wade Hampton stepped up.

"Control yourself, Inigo," he said. "You're making a display of yourself."

Inigo loosed Robert, who scuttled off with Hal in search of Nancy.

"Why should I control myself, Wade? I've controlled myself for nineteen years, and for what? For a mockery that even the Colonel knows to be secondrate. Did I tell you I had only time for Normandy? Well—I recant. I will have time for every project that you and the Colonel have spoken of. I have grown six feet taller in the last five minutes. I feel powerful enough to change the whole system of Low Country manners and to free every slave. Honor be damned!" he shouted again and then he let out a shrill, high yell that carried with it so much of pent-up emotion and passion that the whole multitude took it up.

381

"Honor be damned!" he whispered, his voice breaking, and turned and ran as fast as he was able over to Fancy's stall.

Chapter 57

Nick, who had been clinging to Hercules' coattails during the excitement, let go and followed his father. Inigo rushed up to the stall and flung open the door. Poor Fancy drooped under her blanket, dripping and draggled. Quash had tended the scraped side, rubbed her down, and was bringing some water. Cuffee huddled like a hurt animal in the corner. He knew when Inigo came into the stall but he didn't look up.

"Why the hell aren't you tending to your filly, you black scoundrel?" Inigo shouted in his new exultant voice. He had found himself. Oh, but he wished that Tafra and Nicholas and Charlotte were here. There was so much he had to tell all of them! He banged on Edisto's stall. "Holler—you bastard!" Edisto reared and cracked his head against the door so hard that the top door flew open and the vicious black head snaked out, teeth bared, breath hot.

"Let Fancy rest. Yunnuh done ruint Cuffee' filly. Cuffee not gwine lif' one li'l finger to do nuttin' fuh none of yunnuh Gaillard' never no mo'." Tears poured down Cuffee's face. Inigo walked over to Cuffee and leaned down and lifted him up onto his short crooked legs.

"I tell you, Cuffee," he said, very gently, "you know it was like putting a knife in my heart to let

Robert make a fool out of himself and me and Fancy. To risk losing Charlotte forever. But it's all over now and you're riding Fancy in the next heats. And you've got to win them both, for Meteor will win the race if he wins this next heat. And it's our last chance to get Charlotte back."

He hadn't finished before Cuffee had Fancy's blanket off and was at work rubbing her with a soft cloth.

"Come clost, Nick baby," he said as Fancy blew softly and shifted herself around. "Run as fast as yun-nuh kin to de gran'stand and git Charlotte. Her ain't belongs to dem Singleton' no mo'! Her us own and dis de place fuh she. Git out de way, ole Quasha," Cuffee sang. "Lemme run Cuffee' hands down Fancy' side twell she know again whey she at. Lemme smooth out she lubly mane and rub up she wind-swif' legs." Fancy had quieted the minute Cuffee touched her.

Inigo picked Nick up and hugged him so hard he couldn't get his breath. But he put his arms around his father's neck and kissed him full on the mouth for the first time in his life.

"Oh, Pa, thank you—I do love you. I do. But put me down so I can go tell Charlotte quick."

"Listen good to me first. Get quiet so you'll remember." He put Nick down and knelt in front of him until their faces were on a level. "The minute the last heat is over, you and Charlotte hurry away ahead of the crowd. I'll see that Ben is at the exit gate for you with the coach. And when you get to Normandy don't go in the house because I'm coming home when the race is over as fast as Hero can gallop and I want you and Charlotte to be standing there on the piazza waving at me—welcoming me home."

"Goody! Goody!" Nick flew away and Inigo sent Quash to give Old Ben the directions.

When the saddle signal ruffled, Fancy stood too quietly, and when Cuffee mounted she did not move.

"What's wrong, Cuffee?" Inigo asked. "She doesn't look right to me."

"Sho—dis baby fine." Cuffee had gone into another world. Fancy walked stiffly toward the course.

Meteor was already on the course and long, yellow Pompey in his bright red-silk cap jeered happily at Cuffee as he came up to the starting post.

"What dat yunnuh on—could dat be a hoss? Or is dat ole Mr. Turtle?"

The grandstand and the citizens' stand rose as a body, clapping their hands and cheering with pleasure. As the two horses lined up a long shiver of delight ran through the crowd while a fresh peal of cheering came from all those standing on the rail. Men leaped and spun about on horses while others with shouts of nervous laughter threw their hats into the air. The noise did not cease but swelled up and reverberated on into the city, and back at Normandy, Hagar and Big Jake heard the news tapped out from drum to drum from the course to the city to the plantations.

"Now de time," Hagar said, knocking out the ashes from her pipe. "I is gwine to de woods and be where de messages come."

And at Heronfields Chloe sat by her fire and nodded as the tapped news reached her sensitive eardrums.

To Charlotte all this affair seemed grotesque and amazing. She could scarcely follow the horses or even attend the shouting. She saw only the gay flags, the tan and white and brown and black faces packed together like masses of round balls, and the gaudily dressed men and women who ran and shouted and made bets so avidly in the brilliant sunlight.

She felt agitated and tormented, wondering what Inigo had shouted in her direction, hearing the ladies gabbling excitedly, speculating on just what *had* happened to Inigo.

Oh God, she thought. *I am lost! This* must *be the end!*

Everything seemed dark, obscure, and terrible. Then suddenly little Nick was in her arms, kissing her face, crying in her ear, "Everything is all right. Everything is going to come out right."

She held him fiercely, telling him how she'd missed him.

"I like this pretty gold dress." He rubbed the stiff silk between his fingers.

"I like you," she said gently, trying to be calm, wondering how, if things should come out all right, she would face Inigo after they had so definitely renounced each other. Would they live side-by-side as strangers, or would he let her go to Leon? How stupid they had been even to dream that this race could solve their emotional problem—even if it solved the problem of her personal safety by removing her from Lustbader's power.

They're off!

"Watch hard," Nick said.

I'd better pray hard, Charlotte thought.

At the starting signal Meteor got away first but Cuffee and Fancy were not quite a length behind. Cuffee rode Fancy with a strong steady pull and though she seemed to lack her usual spirit, she kept her place well. About the middle of the second round she edged up to Meteor's shoulder, Cuffee ready to profit by any error or mishap that Pompey might fall into. As they started on the third round Pompey called back to Cuffee, "Fly away, ole Mr. Crow, dis ain' de pace fuh yunnuh to go."

Cuffee's lips moved as though he were singing and as they streaked down the track at a terrific gallop Fancy stretched her legs longer and like a slender bird flying against the wind, made a great push for the turn. The enthusiasm in the stands approached frenzy and as the horses tore down the last stretch, as if blessed with magic, Fancy's hoofs began to pound faster and faster. She was coming up, she passed Meteor's hindquarters, she was abreast, she passed his head and the thousands cheered—Fancy is up—she is going past—she leads! And they came to the finish line so fast that Cuffee and Pompey themselves hardly knew how fast they came. But Fancy won by a length! The time—7 minutes, 36 seconds!

Fancy! Fancy! Fancy! She had captured the stands. They saluted the beautiful red filly and her spirit, and as she left the course she whisked her tail at them and cavorted away.

Three heats run! One won by Meteor; one tied; one won by Fancy! The betting was even and Inigo walked exultantly, like a strong man amid the ruins of a heathen temple.

Charlotte and Nick stood up as soon as the heat was over.

"Good-by, Miss Nancy," she said. "I see Mr. Robert and Mr. Hal coming to talk to you."

Nancy playfully ruffled Nick's hair.

"I think I'll wait for Nick. How would you like to be my sweetheart, Nick?"

"Oh no," he answered, "I don't need a sweetheart. Besides, you'll take Robert back—you always do."

Nancy sighed—yes—she'd take him back. Hadn't he sent her gloves *and* sugarplums this Race Week? The ladies sitting about laughed.

Charlotte and Nick hurried away through the ladies' room. Emily was sitting on a damask-covered chair holding a piece of cake in one hand and a cup of tea in the other.

"Wait a minute," she called to them.

"Come on, Charlotte." Nick pretended not to hear but his mother followed him and caught his arm. He struggled to get away and several ladies came curiously close and formed a knot about the child and his mother.

"Why, you poor boy," Emily intoned in what she believed to be a perfect maternal voice, "however did you hurt your sweet little eye? Has that wicked Robert been mistreating you again?"

Nick stared at her in horror as though a snake had tried to possess him. Then the Gaillard fury descended on him and he doubled up his hard little fist and struck her on the chest, making the tea splatter over her green silk dress, crushing the cake against her fur jacket.

"You aren't my mother," he shrieked at her, pushing through the shocked ladies to catch Charlotte, who had walked on and was waiting at the door for him.

"You horrid nasty boy!" Emily stamped her little feet and would have run after Nick and slapped his face, but fat old Mrs. Swinton, loaded with ostrich plumes and dripping with pearls, puffed by and tapped her smartly on the shoulder with a sandalwood-and-lace fan.

"Well, you've lost Inigo!" she said loud enough for everybody to hear—said it triumphantly, waving her plump ringleted hand happily.

Buzz—buzz—buzz, went the ladies. So *that* was what he had shouted at the stand during the rest period before last! What a shame he'd waited so long. They drew aside their skirts and with their long noses high, skirted Emily on their way to the balcony to watch the finish.

Unfortunately Emily had delayed Nick and Charlotte too long for them to go back to the stalls. The rest period was over when they managed to get through the surging mass of blacks and whites inflamed and wild with excitement. However they found a hole, left by a group of men who were going to change their bets, right by the finish line, and they pressed themselves against the rail and waited. Old Colonel Hampton saw them and called to Charlotte.

"Do you know where Old Ben is?" he asked. "I want to pay him ten dollars I owe him and make a bet with him on this heat."

"Here I is," said Ben, removing his shiny beaver. "I been behind yunnuh all dis day. Yunnuh ain't gwine off and lef' Ben holding de sack dis time." They shook hands and the Colonel counted out the greenbacks and tried to make a bet with him on the coming heat, but Ben patted the wad of bills lovingly and slipped away to fetch the coach to the exit like his master had told him.

A deep clamor welcomed the horses when for the last time they pranced out onto the course. Harry Singleton patted Pompey's skinny legs as he passed into the enclosure and Inigo cocked his eyebrow at Cuffee, who winked back as Fancy's flaxen tail slashed a face that was leaning too near the gate. The horses came fairly quietly to the post. Pompey's face was set and crafty, but Cuffee had a burning, glistening light in his eyes. The din and the cries of the crowd sounded not in his ears. He sat lightly in the saddle, crouched forward, with his stirrups short, and as the intoxication and high pressure of the crowd increased, Fancy began to dance and toss her head, sidestepping up to the heavier and more powerful Meteor.

The crowd pushed and crushed—fists were clenched—every man was fighting for himself, everybody personally sped the horse he had chosen with gestures and with voice.

The signal was given.

They're off!

Meteor got away first. Long yellow Pompey this time put him to the whip and spur from the start as though he were afraid that Meteor might fade unless kept in the lead.

Fancy was a length behind but close on Meteor's heels. At the quarter Fancy was still at Meteor's heels but going strong and lasting well under Cuffee's powerful ebony hands.

"What dem hoof sounds up dere in dat black cloud?" asked Hercules in Charlotte's ear. She looked up but heard nothing. Had Hagar been there she would have seen a Coromantee warrior in full battle dress mounted on the swiftest Arabian horse that had ever run in Africa. She would have seen him reach down and guide Fancy into the rail and before Pompey could notice, push Fancy into a fresh burst of speed and make her pass Meteor on the inside rail. Away galloped the cloud hoofs and then came the death struggle as the two horses galloped together into the home stretch. It seemed either's race. Cuffee kept his eyes on Meteor, measuring his power that he might judge exactly when to make his final effort. He seemed to breathe flame and Pompey stood in his stirrups and lashed Meteor as though he would drive him over the line. Neck and neck still they hung on to each other—even within a few yards of the finish neither had the advantage, up to the last stride they kept nose to nose.

Then as the mob of spectators went frighteningly still at the final climax, Cuffee seemed to put his own heart into Fancy, and in a fit of furious strength, with tremendous skill and coolness he lifted her forward drenched in foam, with eyes of blood—and flung her first at the post by a head only! And the time was 7 minutes, 51 seconds!

A rip tide of sound rolled over the entire course. Charlotte and Nick leaned far over the rail to call to Cuffee as he galloped slowly past them back to the stalls. They shouted at him but his eyes were fixed and strange as he crouched low on her lathered neck; they heard his voice, "For you' mane duh shine lak silber and yo' hoofs duh sing lak song."

Chapter 58

The crowd still lumped together for a time after the race was over. Charlotte and Nick made their way with no difficulty to the exit where Old Ben sat in his highness on the box of the Normandy coach with Hercules beaming by his side.

"Let's git going." Old Ben cracked his long whip expertly in the air and the two hackneys pawed and reared.

Nick jumped into the coach but Charlotte, the first shock of unspeakable relief having passed, leaving her unsteady and shaken yet filled with rejoicing, hung back and looked about for Leon. He had asked her to talk to him. Many months had gone since she had written from the Springs telling him she loved him. Those alert days seemed very remote since she had returned to Heronfields. Joining the Negro people, as one of them, had ceased to matter in comparison with the desire to escape the desolation prophesied for her in Lustbader's eyes. And she had escaped! Yet the sight of the hackneys cavorting and prancing frightened her. She sneezed tiredly and felt her eyes begin to sting and water. *I can't get in the coach,* she thought. *I mustn't go near the coach or those terrible ponies. I have a feeling that they are waiting to take me to disaster. Oh, why do I have to sneeze?*

"Hurry." Nick stuck his head out of the coach and called to Charlotte as Leon came up. Leon's face looked sad and he carried himself jerkily. On seeing Charlotte beside the coach, he rushed over and seized her hands. The tickling eased in her nose and she could breathe a little better.

"Just let me look at you good. It's wonderful to be so close to you after all these lonely months. I always forget how beautiful you are—how small. Here —let me wipe your eyes. Have you been crying?"

She managed to smile at him, explaining how sometimes it was like this with her around horses. Not always—but sometimes.

"I'm on my way back to Normandy," she whispered.

"Thank God!"

"Do you mind?" She was uncomfortable with him. She looked down so she need not see the fear in his wretched eyes.

"Yes—I hate it. Don't go. Come home with me. Mr. Gaillard will let you do anything you really want to do."

Nick put his head farther out of the coach window. "Is that Leon?" he called.

Charlotte couldn't get a grip on herself. Leon was behaving stupidly. Couldn't he see the carriages beginning to wheel up impatiently behind them? But he drew her away from the coach so that Nick couldn't hear him.

"You'll be a prisoner all over again," he was saying. "Come with me—today. It's not fair to let Nick adore you so much. You will ruin his life just as you've ruined his father's."

"You talk nonsense. Help me into the coach. We're in a hurry." Why did he always have to wake her up? Make her so ill at ease with herself—so intolerant of herself.

"I didn't mean to prick your pride,"—he squared his stalwart shoulders—"but I'm going to follow you to Normandy."

From under her drooped black-lashed lids she saw the expression on his face, and that he was standing stiller than the tall posts at the finish line.

"No, Leon—please. You will be a fool to go." She didn't want him to see her standing on the piazza waving to Inigo. To see her face lit with the welcome for Inigo that she would never be able to hide. There was no use for him to be needlessly hurt. Suddenly she met his eyes coolly.

"Wait—give me a chance this time to win my own victory!" And without another word she held out her hand for him to help her into the coach. As he put her in he pressed her arm above the elbow. Agitated and excited, she turned around. He was looking at her possessively determined that this time he would not let her get away from him.

Old Ben flicked the whip and the ponies started smartly.

Oh God, how afraid I am for him and for myself and about everything, Charlotte thought. And long after Leon's image had blurred in the rising cloud of dust she sat wide-eyed and motionless gazing at the harsh sunlight through the windows of the coach.

"Listen!" Nick interrupted as they passed the last buildings on the Washington Race Track. "Listen!"

A great sound of screaming and yelling rose from the enclosure and the frenzied mob cry of "Loose horse! Loose horse!" followed them down the road.

Chapter 59

"Why doesn't Pa come?" Nick ran down the avenue a piece, straining his ears for the heavy hard sound of Hero's galloping.

Charlotte, her legs weary from standing by the wrought-iron rail so long, shook her head and pushed back a tendril of hair that kept blowing across her face in the keen wind from the sea.

It had been three o'clock when they left the course and she had expected Inigo no later than four. Now the five o'clock shadows of the February afternoon cast their long black fingers through the oaks, marking the day's end plainly on the avenue's sandy floor.

Hercules came out the front door.

"Charlotte," he called softly, "Hagar on her way up frum de woods and all de people from de Street is strung out behime her lake a debbil's tail. What yun-nuh reckon hit specify?"

Hercules' face was one big wrinkle of concern. Charlotte walked stiffly to the door and tried to pacify the old man. "Maybe it's just to welcome Mr. Inigo home and celebrate Fancy's victory."

And mine, she wanted to say. *Leon was right. I must not stay here under the shadow of these family trees. I'm glad he let me come alone, though. I will tell Inigo tonight that he must let me go away tomorrow with Leon. Please, Mary Mother, give me the will to face Inigo and tell him about Leon. Veil my eyes against his wonder!*

Suddenly they heard a tortured neighing from far down the avenue. An anguished heartbroken message that was instantly received by the horses back in the stables and by a harrowed straining from hundreds of black throats. Um—hummn——Um hummn——Um hummmn—

Nick came flying up the steps and grabbed Charlotte around the waist, utterly terrified.

"Charlotte—Charlotte—that was Hero calling and he's not galloping—he's walking. Is something wrong? What's happened?"

Now they could hear wheels and the plod-clop of many horses pulling a vehicle through the heavy sand. Charlotte and Nick clung together on the piazza. The people, humming mournfully like a gigantic swarm of bees, lined up the avenue and banked about the house. And as the huge chariot—not a Normandy one—drew heavily up to the steps the humming grew to a mighty moaning. Then Charlotte saw Hero following behind the chariot—with Inigo's scarlet cape thrown over the empty saddle. Oh, poor heart—stop now—don't endure another throb of agony—stop!

Nick pointed at Hero drooping riderless. "Look." His teeth were chattering. "Something has happened to my pa."

The door to the chariot opened and Cuffee stumbled out. He stood, his face a dead blank, and reached unseeingly out first in one direction and then in the other. Hagar disengaged herself from the mass of moaning people and went to him and taking him by the hands pulled him back into the midst of the Negroes who now were thrashing and flinging their arms about in desolation.

Charlotte hung back against the door and held Nick as tightly as she could. She must not run forward to meet this thing. Nick would need all her strength. Her face was set and dry; there were no tears. Their love would always sing on in its loneliness. The oaks could take up the song and sing it high to the heavens, raise it to the clouds, give it in all its unblemished glory and sadness to the angels themselves to sing, so that the sentences that she and Inigo had never said to each

393

other might not go unended but in some eternity have their expression.

After Cuffee, Wade Hampton and Billy Myers and Dr. Hugenin got solemnly out. Little Nick sobbed and tried to break loose and run to the steps but she held him safe against her and cradled his sorrow close to her own, while Wade Hampton's vibrant, heart-wringing words reached Inigo's people.

"Friends—your master is dead!"

Um-hum—de det' owl duh holler.

"His troubles are over and he sleeps in peace."

Po' Mass Inigo—yo' troubles is over.

"The horse Edisto found his door unclosed and opened it with his mouth. . . ."

Det' owl got een Edisto' mout'!

"Edisto ran loose just as your master came running up, shouting his joy over winning his race, his face shining with happiness."

Po' Mass Inigo—ole debbil hoss got yuh!

"The devil horse screamed and reared on his legs and towered over your master and clove his skull in two."

Oh, Gawd hab mussy. Hoss rored up and cut um in two!

"And now I beg you to be merciful and conduct yourselves as he would have wished. And know that his eye is watching you from the clouds where he now rides in glory."

On de wings ob glory! Angels fuh he hosses! Oh, po' Mass Inigo!

"Charlotte, Charlotte," Nick screamed, tightening his arms around her. "Edisto killed my pa."

Charlotte turned his face into her breast and let him cry. Hiding from him the sight of Big Jake and Seneca and Festus and four other big strong bucks who at a command from Wade Hampton began tugging and lifted their master from the chariot. None looked on Inigo's face before Dr. Hugenin snatched the scarlet cape from the spent Hero and flung it over the great body.

The powerful Negroes groaned and strained un-

394

der the dead weight of their master as they struggled up the steps and through the wide door into the hall.

A-a-a-a-ah-o-o-o-o! A-a-a-a-ah-o-o-o-o! Yeddy ole Egypt duh yowling!

The people could not restrain themselves. It was too much to ask when the light was suddenly taken from their world.

Charlotte and Nick followed the men. Hercules, tears running down his cheeks, asked Charlotte, "Whey we gwine put um?"

"Pull the big bench in front of the fireplace for the present."

So Inigo was laid under the crest of the Gaillards; a man who had ever walked honorably in the sight of all who knew him or knew of him.

On the piazza the people packed and jammed to get a glimpse of the crimson-shrouded figure lying in state before the wide, deep chimney piece. Field Hand Mattie, at a word from Big Jake, stepped into the hall and facing the people, lifted her voice. And as the high mournful notes cut through the falling dusk to the evening star, Charlotte went over and stood among her people and sang with them:

> *"Moonlight—Starlight,*
> *O-o-o-h Moonlight,*
> *Believer, what's de matter?*
> *John lay de body down!*
>
> *"Moonlight—Starlight,*
> *O-o-o-h Moonlight!"*

EPILOGUE

1865

Charlotte came slowly into her pretty little parlor on Beaufain Street. She was so tired that her legs refused to carry her up the stairs to bed. She and Leon had worked all day at the Freedmen's Bureau. The tatter-demalion horde with no money, possessions, or qualifications for anything but directed work were all clamoring and demanding the "forty acres and a flop-eared mule" which had been promised them as soon as they entered the gate of freedom and opportunity.

Dressed in whatever they had walked away from their former masters' plantations in, many had gone for months without a change of clothing. Their horny black hands, which could flex dangerously but so often lacked the know-how to grasp and hold onto anything, hung limply by their sides. They streamed in and out of the bureau chattering and gesticulating like monkeys, a natural act straight from a circus.

They were of every tint and caste, from the light octoroon to the deep black; from the genteel servingmen to the rough laborer of the rice or cotton field. They walked and shuffled in secondhand black frock coats of dubious age, snatched from their masters' closets as they left; in stovepipe hats like the gentility; in cheap yellow shoes squeaking gloriously for the admiration of the less fortunate or less rascally ones who still wore the coarse, dirty work garments they had worn in the field the day they dropped their hoes and walked quietly away from work, home, and family; in the stub jackets and slouch hats of the heavy back worker, without shirts, hiding their necks in lengths of old wool. Some, lucky enough to have thick brogans, clumped dully, torn trousers hanging mutely on their scraped, skinny legs. Few women were among them—most of them had remained at home or were huddled together in some empty house waiting for the men to get work so that once more they could eat fat back and hominy grits and lie safe at night listening to the pleasant crackle of a yellow pine fire.

These, thought Charlotte, reaching for an unopened letter and a package on a marble-topped table, *are my people. These hungry homeless ones who are finding freedom a bitter cold dish with only scraps upon it.*

They didn't depress Leon as they did her. He laughed and joked with them and soon persuaded most of them either to return to their old homes or to accept new places working for wages which, though they left the Negroes in physical comforts about where they were before, yet gave them a sense of equality and a proud knowledge that they had definitely made a step forward into the new world.

She knew that it was because of her nightmare adventure at Heronfields that she expended herself for these people—because of the humid days spent dodging Lustbader and the dark frosty nights listening for the snuffling hound of the "yaller nigger"; because of the Joe Valiants who had run away and the Chloes who had been tough enough to remain.

She slit her letter with a silver knife and her face brightened as she began to read:

Dear Charlotte,
    I can hardly wait to see you and give you a kiss and a hug for the wonderful way you have directed Big Jake and kept Normandy for me during the past bitter years. When I came to see you in Charleston the day I returned from the misery of Appomattox I was too intent on having you soothe my desolate spirits and build up my self-confidence even to ask you about the plantation. When I left you I realized that I was riding home and yet hadn't learned whether the house at Normandy still remained or whether, like Heron-

fields, it had been put to the torch by Sherman's army.

You can imagine how my heart cheered when I saw the outline of the roof straight and secure between the chimneys, for the houseless chimneys standing along the roads from Virginia down had haunted me like evil dreams and I had made up my mind that Normandy, too, did not exist, except in my memory, any more.

Thank Leon for me for letting you give so much of your time these many years to me and my home. (I always feel it is your home, too.) I'll never forget the way you looked the day after Pa's funeral, standing on the piazza in that cream-colored dress, your eyes dry and sad, waving good-by to me, your very own little boy, as I rode along with Wade Hampton, proud to be in Pa's saddle on Hero—sick at leaving you—eager to see Mississippi and the Hampton boys who took me in as their own brother. I know now that it was the best thing for both of us because if we had shut ourselves away together from the world while I grew up, I would never find the courage now to pioneer (as the next few years must be regarded) and keep Normandy what it has been in the past through the hard future.

Very few of my Negroes have gone "up the road." The wage system you devised works well and they seem content and pleased with the order of things. I am glad you sold the pictures first and then the rugs, because if the crop comes in this year we'll make enough to pay the new exorbitant taxes and have enough left over to carry us through the slack season—and thus can keep most of the furniture and silver.

I rode over to see Nancy yesterday. It is a pity she and Robert didn't have any children, for I don't believe she'll ever marry again. She and her mother live in the overseer's house and every Negro on the place has vanished except Pompey, who cooks and does for her and Miss Mildred. I don't know what they would do without him, for he seems to have settled down and is trying to run the plantation since Mr. Harry and Hal were killed in the Wilderness. And Miss Mildred, who used to hate all Negroes, lets him handle everything any way that he wants to. I have told Big Jake to give him enough seed to get his crops in this year.

Chloe and Hagar live like two old witches out in the sick house, but they look after the children and do their task quite as well as though they weren't each almost or over a hundred years old.

Hercules has become childish and fussy but he insists on waiting on me at the table just like I was Pa. I humor him for I know that Lillian will love it when I find time to ride to Richmond and fetch her to Normandy. Hercules was delighted with the teapot that you *made* me bring home. I'll tell Lillian the teapot is your wedding gift to us! She is very anxious to know you and thank you for the love and all the letters you wrote me through my childhood that kept me from being a poor little orphan. You gave me the richest, warmest mother memories that any boy ever had, Charlotte.

I'm sending you a little package that I found in the top drawer of Pa's desk. It's got your name on it so I, though it was hard, forbore even to peep at the contents.

Bring your children out and spend a day with me next week. I particularly took to the little imp with the gray eyes who insisted on barking at me as I left.

> With my dear love always,
> Nick Gaillard

P. S. No sign of Cuffee anywhere. It's been since the day Pa was killed, hasn't it? I took one of the hounds last week and tramped over all the places where we used to hunt the white stag. I wonder if there ever really was a white stag? I thought maybe Cuffee was still hunting, but nobody has seen or heard of him since that night. He just disappeared. I never quite believed you when you wrote me about it. It seemed so unlike him to leave Normandy and the horses.

P. P. S. Go by and see Mamma sometime in the town house. She wouldn't speak to me at all but just sat looking out of the window at a sea gull flapping hopelessly against the wind. Cousin Hettie says she hasn't passed through the front door since the news of Robert's death at Manassas reached her. If she's ill I want her to be cared for, but there's no use for me to go any more. The only thing she said was to Cousin Hettie as I went through the door, "How large and dark and ugly he still is!"

The box in its tightly wrapped secrecy lay on the cold marble. Her heart began to pound and all weariness disappeared as she picked up the oblong package and tentatively shook it gently. No rattle. But it had come from *him*. Over the years it had lain and waited for her. Perhaps waiting for just such a tired, drab day to give her a message. To reach across the river of life and say, "I did exist; there is magic in the world; there was a white stag."

The paper made a dry cackling sound as she tore it clumsily. When her fingers touched the soft velvet, she knew. Knew so well that there was no use to open the box and have the golden firestones blind her eyes grown used to the softness of plain moonlight—starlight.

Leon came into the house and standing on the threshold of the parlor, for a moment watched his wife —so beautiful and beloved—in the blowing candlelight, holding the velvet box in her hand. He wanted to go to her and thank her for the many years of love that she had given him. That was something which could never be stolen from him—even though the strange sparkling quality on her face tonight was the same he had once seen lit by the great Gaillard under the oak trees of Normandy.

For a moment he was even glad to see the radiance. She had appeared so sad and dispirited today as the uncouth, ignorant men clamored and hovered around her. Everybody insisted on having Miss Charlotte talk to them. They didn't like the stern hatchet-faced ones who worked at the bureau for philanthropic reasons, or the plain scrawny ones come to educate them, or the greasy smooth ones offering them unbounded credit if they would buy cigars and whisky

403

and dice and yellow shoes. No, they wanted the light-skinned woman who was a Negro like themselves—the one who, they had heard, had even been whipped by her master—had even been won on a horse race—had even been loved by a white man.

When she looked at them with her deep, clear eyes, they ceased their whining and their cringing; they tried to stand erect. They understood the things she told them. They wanted her to be proud of them. They agreed to whatever job she suggested and promised her that when she came to watch them at work the next week, they would be straining their backs, and their pockets would be bulging with the money they had earned.

Often for long snatches of time Leon would slip to the door of her office and watch her thus giving of herself, yet never realizing the effect she had on the people or how much of her spirit she poured out trying to set a dream afire in their breasts. She would sit lost, as it were, in the vision she was bringing to their dark days, where the light fell on her face and her temples, now winged with silver, her lips moving, smiling, her gray eyes promising, urging. The hand which did not hold the pen would be pressed against her breast as if trying to keep her heart from actually beating out to meet the one to whom she was talking.

Leon would withdraw to his clinic as from a vision of perfect love, convinced that at last Charlotte had found true happiness. That by her own efforts she had saved herself from slavery in any form—spiritual or actual; that she had triumphed over her indecisions; that she had forgiven fate for the cruel trick played on the little white girl from New Orleans.

He coughed lightly to give her a chance to snuff the light in her eyes—to quiet the fingers lovingly caressing the blue velvet box. But at the sound of his footsteps Charlotte jumped up and—thank God! The radiance was still there and all the glory of her was directed at him and to him!

"Leon!" She ran to meet him. He held her fiercely—hungrily. "I thought you'd never get home. This has been the queerest day. So many things have happened, and I can't wait to tell you about them all. One minute I'd feel like screaming and beating every last Negro in the bureau, and the next I'd want to love every one of them and tell them what wonderful people they were."

He laughed and kissed her with the desire of a young lover, on her throat and then on her lips, for he found her even more enchanting and dizzily intoxicating than she had been fifteen years before.

The front door banged and their children rushed noisily into the hall.

"Let me go—stop—they'll think we're old fools." Charlotte tried to escape from his arms but he could not loose her—the need for her was so strong in him.

"You'll never be old," he told her, kissing her once more before Lanny and John and Taffy burst into the parlor.

"Guess what?" Fourteen-year-old Taffy, a dark replica of her mother, her lips parted and panting from running, grabbed Charlotte and whirled her around and around the room.

"You're silly," growled brown John, bearing his twelve years seriously and solemnly, with the quiet vigor of his Grandfather Holloway.

"Silly, silly!" slant-eyed Lanny wickedly chortled, surreptitiously stealing a lozenge from a jar on a table in the corner.

"Mamma, Lanny's stealing candy." Taffy flew to her ivory-faced little brother and snatching the hard sweet from his grubby fist, popped it into her own full, red-lipped mouth.

"You bad girl—Lanny kick you."

Leon caught his baby by the middle and tossed him high in the air. A merry smile crinkled the pale fawn face and Charlotte, seeing his resemblance to Horst Adams, sighed and turned back to her hoyden of a daughter, so like and so unlike the child she herself had been.

"What were you going to tell us?" she asked, calmly sitting back on the hard chair and slipping the unopened box into her reticule.

"About a funny, wizzled old man who has been following me around all day." Taffy shook her black curls and smoothed her apron over the red merino skirt she had worn to school that day.

"A man following you?" Leon laid his fine hand on his daughter's shoulder. These were times to beware. Too much freedom that was not freedom was souring in the dark men's breasts. Too much whisky was pouring down throats unaccustomed to the fire it produced in their blood. Too many idle ones, restless in their wandering, from plantations where the marriage vow had never been taught or deemed necessary for Negroes, roamed the streets.

"Where were Lula and Lanny? Where were you?" Leon demanded sternly.

John hung his head. He had promised his father to look after his big sister and his small brother but he and crippled Lula had slipped out to peek in a window where all sorts of fancy dresses and shiny hats were on display.

"Oh, there was no harm in him." Taffy plumped down on the floor and embraced her beautiful mother's knees. Why couldn't she have been as light as Lanny? Why did she have to be the darkest of them all? Her mouth pouted. "He was really like a small animal of some kind. Not really small—but he talked so funny."

"Talked so funny? How?" Charlotte leaned down and cupped the delicate brown chin in her hands.

"Like the Song of Solomon Papa reads us. For a while he followed me, muttering, 'For her hair duh shine lak black silber and her cheeks is dark bee honey'—"

Leon and Charlotte looked at each other.

"Cuffee!" they both cried.

"Quick, tell us more. Where did he go? Did he have little crooked legs and broad shoulders and a clear-cut black face?" Charlotte felt her breath quicken. Oh, she must get to him—help him—tell him to come home; that Nick was there and Fancy, that a baby colt lay in Quash's kitchen.

Taffy was puzzled. She had thought that this time she was going to shock them good. Wouldn't she ever be able to make her mother look with awe upon her accomplishments or dangers? She turned sulky, and

406

reaching in her pocket she took out a crumbly old object and let it slip from hand to hand.

"He waited until John and Lula sneaked away to look at the fancy clothes in the store window, then he came up close to me."

"Were you frightened?" Leon asked curiously, cradling his gray-eyed son against his chest, blowing small love words into the pointed ears.

An expression of bewilderment came on Taffy's bright face. She shook her head.

"No." Her voice was throaty and soft like her mother's and when she was moved it had the same quality of emotion lying dormant. "He shuffled up and stood right in front of me. He had on a raggedy old stub jacket and he had sacks wrapped around his feet. And he sort of sung, 'Yunnuh am lubly. But yunnuh am changed into a dream.' I couldn't speak because he was staring at me so hard. He stared and stared, then he passed his big old hand very gently across my face and reached in his pocket and took out this—" She handed the crumbly object to her mother. "He told me to keep it. That it would protect me against white man's magic since an evil spirit had changed me into a Negro. That it would protect me from the hoofs of the white stag which would come seeking me because—" softer and more emotional grew the lovely voice— "because I was so beautiful!" Her smoky eyes, flecked with gold lights, dreamed far away back to some lost happy hour. Then she scrambled up and looked defiantly at her parents.

"His crab claw!" Charlotte whispered. "His most prized possession!"

"He must have thought she was you, Charlotte." Leon put down the littlest boy and they all crowded around looking at the dirty moldy old bit of charred crab claw.

Suddenly Charlotte closed her fingers tight around the claw and pushed it into her reticule, jamming it hard against the soft velvet of the blue box.

"Give it back to Taffy," Leon's words cracked across the silence that held the Cavallos strained with each other for the first time in their lives.

407

"No, Leon, no! It's pure superstition. It's symbolic of the very thing that is keeping all the people who come to me every day for help, in bondage, however free the government tells them they are."

"Give it to Taffy." Never had he spoken so harshly to her. She slowly took out the charred crab claw and put it into Taffy's outstretched demanding brown hand.

"Take out the box, too," he ordered.

With trembling fingers she drew out the velvet box.

"Open it!"

"No, Leon, no. Not with the children here."

"Yes—I want them to see what is in there. Why deprive them of beauty?"

So she opened the box and the topazes gaily winked and pointed sparkling fingers of gold light straight into her heart.

"Oh," the children cried, "how wonderful! Are they yours, Mamma?"

"Yes." Leon's mouth was smiling now at his wife. "They are hers. There's no use to hide them, Charlotte. They are just as much a part of your heritage as the crab claw is of Taffy's."

"I'd rather have the necklace," Taffy cried.

"You will some day, Taffy. But guard the crab claw carefully, too. That you must never scorn. Nor the little man who gave it to you. Look for him tomorrow and bring him home," Leon said.

Charlotte put her hand gratefully in Leon's. Now at long last there was nothing between them. Tonight all the ghosts were laid forever. Lula came limping to the door and called the children to their supper. Conscious of something beyond their understanding they trooped meekly into the dining-room to tell Lula all about it.

"Let's go upstairs until our suppertime." Leon embraced Charlotte tenderly. And smiling a strange secret smile she picked up the crab claw and the necklace and hurriedly dropped them back into her reticule together.

ABOUT THE AUTHOR

ELIZABETH BOATWRIGHT COKER was born in Darlington, South Carolina. Her marriage to James Coker in 1930 joined two of the oldest and most aristocratic families in the South. Mrs. Coker is the author of seven best-selling novels, including *Daughter of Strangers, India Allen* and *La Belle,* which are all set in the South of the Civil War. Her books were book club selections and have been translated into half a dozen foreign languages. She now lives in Hartsville, South Carolina, the seat of Coker College, established by her husband's grandfather.

RELAX!
SIT DOWN
and Catch Up On Your Reading!